Kingdom of the Hollow

The Story of the Hatfields and

McCoys

Kingdom of the Hollow

The Story of the Hatfields and McCoys

By Phillip E. Hardy

© 2006

Published by Lulu.com

ISBN: 978-1-4116-8127-9

Contents

Prologue:

This book is a work of historical fiction based on actual events that transpired during the Hatfield-McCoy Feud. For entertainment purposes, fictional characters have been mixed with real participants. This is <u>not</u> a history book; it is a retelling of a legendary American story, imparted in a way that has never been done before. This book would have not been possible without the previous work of Virgil Carrington Jones, from which some material of this book is largely based.
Phillip E. Hardy

CHAPTER ONE: THE HOG TRIAL

"I'd sure as hell rather be one of you boys, feeding my face and lying out in the sun like one lazy son-of-bitch," Floyd Hatfield proclaimed.

The filthy, fatted and musty smelling wild pigs squealed out a song of protest, as their keeper poked and prodded them into the rickety wood and barbed wire structure. As he headed for shade of a nearby tree, the dirty farmer raked the thick, brown dust from the faded, blue overalls on his large frame. His sweat soaked biceps ached with pain and his bronze skin glistened in the bright sun.

Floyd reached for the rusty handled dipper to draw a drink of cool water from his nearby well. Sitting back on the ancient oak stump in front of his hog pen, he felt the satisfaction of completing his painstaking task. His hogs carried the weight of summer months spent grazing on acorns, in the wooded hills above his farmhouse. It was far too hot for this grimy work, but he did not want to leave his livestock on the hill much longer. "Hogs got a way of disappearing, winding up in another man's pen," he thought to himself.

Randolph McCoy, who lived down the road about a mile, was Floyd's closet neighbor. He stood outside his home without any notion of doing strenuous work. Stringtown Kentucky, where he lived, was nothing more than a dirt road with a few dozen farms and cabins. The old man had walked the pebbled trail thousands of times savoring the smell of jasmine trees while enjoying the sound of small, flowing tributaries. "Maybe I'll go take a look-see at what Floyd's up to today" he mumbled, pleased that he had a mission.

As he ambled along, McCoy's lanky frame could've been mistaken for a willow tree. His long, straight nose detected the familiar scent of dirty grunting animals. During his walk Randolph scarcely broke a sweat on his milky white face and his generous salt and pepper hair claimed barely a speck of dust. This endowed him with a feeling of haughtiness when he saw how hard his neighbor was working.

In spite of hearing footsteps coming up the gravel entrance to his farm, Floyd did not look up from counting the heads of his wild pigs.

"That's a mighty fine hog you're tending too," Randolph said in a loud voice as he walked up to where his neighbor stood.

"Thank you" Floyd replied, but continued performing his head count.

"I was speaking to them which are God's creatures."

"I'm glad you finally found someone that you could talk to Ranel. Maybe the Lord's creatures want to hear what you have to say. No one else pays much attention."

Randolph continued a further attempt to get a rise out of his neighbor. "I see your trying to fatten up them scrawny critters, maybe if you'd feed them something besides what the hills have to offer."

Floyd quickly shooed in a hefty brown pig that attempted to turn in the opposite direction. "That's what I like about you McCoy, your advice is free flowing like a creek and as welcome as a plague of locust."

"All right, don't get snippy, I was just being neighborly."

"Neighborly? You wouldn't know how if the Good Samaritan taught you. Can you find the way back to the trail or did you need me to draw you a map?" Floyd sarcastically asked.

Randolph had not set out to offend his neighbor but he felt like the unwanted wallflower at a barn dance. He turned around but noticed something stopping him cold in his tracks. "That old boy's got my markings on him," He uttered excitedly.

Floyd's peaceful look gave way to one of vexation. "It's real hot outside today, especially for a man your age. Maybe the sun has baked that so-called brain of yours?"

Randolph folded his slender arms tightly. "Could be your head that ain't right Floyd?" Maybe you got overworked and trespassed on my ridge." The older man pointed towards the sun. "Then being struck by fever, thought you'd round up one of my hogs."

This unexpected interrogation put a match to Hatfield's fuse. "You best get on out of here before I commence to taking you down."

In spite of experiencing a knot in the pit of his stomach, McCoy stood his ground. "I'll be on my way, when you give me back what's mine, boy" He yelled back, glaring at the younger man.

Floyd angrily advanced three steps closer to his neighbor. "The only thing you'll get is a mess of trouble, if you're so inclined."

Feeling his courage wane, Randolph retreated spouting his last word. "We'll see about that, we'll see who's in for trouble." Nervous and livid, the older man turned and hurriedly retreated from the modest farm.

On the road towards his house, McCoy worked himself into an

agitated state. Prominent veins popped out of his temple and he began
to have tremors in his right hand. "Stealing another man's livestock was
the same as robbing him of his livelihood," he thought.

By his reckoning, Randolph was certain that he had seen his ear
markings on the animal in question. He was also sure that it was no
accident that it wound up in Floyd's pen. The old man was not afraid of
a fracas if that's what it would take to gain his property back. As a
veteran of the War Between the States, he had done his share of
fighting. However, he knew that most Hatfield men could shoot the eye
out of a possum at two hundred yards. Using a gun to tangle with his
sharp shooting neighbor would not be the sensible way to seek redress
for his grievance. Randolph had another idea on how retrieve his
property. He would visit the local authority and let him settle the
matter. He quickly walked the two and a half miles from his cabin in
Stringtown to a place called Raccoon Hollow.

McCoy arrived at the cabin of Deacon Anse Hatfield. Though
the preacher was Floyd's cousin, Randolph saw no problem asking him
to swear out a complaint against his kin. He had known McCoy for
years and was on friendly terms with him. The Deacon had even
baptized several members of his family.

It was mid afternoon on an otherwise ordinary autumn day
during the year 1878. A week's worth of fallen leaves surrounded the
shaded cabin, covering the ground with a brownish hue. Loud knocking
accompanied by an angry voice outside of the door rousted the gentle
man from his peaceful nap.

"You get on out here Anderson Hatfield, we've business that
needs tending to," McCoy bellowed.

The half-dressed preacher poked a sleep-wrinkled face out of
his front window. Shaking off his grogginess, he stretched out his short,
thick arms. "What the devil has you so stirred up today?"

Randolph walked around, standing on the deacon's front porch.
"You preach the Lord's commandments on Sunday. Thieving ranks
high on the list of ten," he said cryptically.

Deacon Anse was slightly annoyed by his rude awakening.
"Would you kindly tell me what in blazes you're talking about?"

Randolph became more diplomatic. "It's your cousin Floyd;
he's taken something that's mine."

Tucking a faded white shirt into his waist, the preacher
stretched suspenders over his wide shoulders. "Go on, I'm listening"

"He took one of my pigs. Its markings are plain as day. Your
cousin looked me right in the face and told me I was crazy. You know I

don't go accusing folks of things they ain't done."

The preacher quickly bowed in acknowledgement. "I know that."

"I know you're a fair man deacon. I want you to do something about this; and I mean now. That boy stole my pig and there just ain't no denying it."

Pondering a sensible way to address this situation, the deacon ran his stump-sized fingers through his dark beard "I'll handle this, I will. If what you say is true then I'll get to the bottom of it."

McCoy narrowed his eyes like a ferret. "Well that doesn't give a man much to go on preacher. I want to know just what you intend to do."

The deacon remained calm as he answered. "I'll hold a trial here in my cabin and settle this thing between you and Floyd."

*****

On the day of the hog trial, the Deacon's cabin buzzed with the sound of chatting spectators waiting for the proceeding to begin. Most of the men assembled were friends or kin to the Hatfield and McCoy clans and were happy to have some excitement. Both groups were anxious to see justice served and willing to let the preacher settle the matter, legally. Still, some of the men inside cautiously clutched their Winchester rifles, in the event a miscarriage transpired.

With dozens crammed into the dark wooden structure, the reverend's damp, cabin appeared smaller than usual. With a rusted bucket full of soapy water and tattered old mop in hand, the conscientious man spent his early morning hours washing a years worth of thick, black dust off the primitive floor. Short vegetable crates from the dry goods store in neighboring Pikeville had been acquired, along with seven-foot long wooden slats to provide benches for the spectators. In the front of the courtroom cabin, lay exhibit number-one—a plump, bound up hog nicknamed "Evidence."

The Deacon was dressed in his Sunday suit, in addition to his only pair of black, lace up shoes, which were polished as bright as a new silver dollar. Even though it was Saturday, the day before his usual time, he took a bath and trimmed his long beard.

Scanning the room with his deep green eyes, the preacher inserted some store bought tobacco into his hand carved pipe. As he fired up the smoke, his pale white complexion was briefly illuminated inside the dully-lit cabin. He puffed his favorite blend and stared at the men who awaited his words of legal wisdom. Hatfield realized this affair might be akin to a brown bear sticking his nose in an angry beehive. He also suspected this dispute might not only be about the rights to a hog. It could also be motivated by Randolph's jealousy over the economic superiority of the Hatfield clan; a deep down envy that had been seething for years.

Solemnly, he began to speak. "Before we get started I want to warn you about something. This is a court of law, and I don't expect any of you to wave any guns around."

"Courtroom, I thought this was your cabin Deacon," spouted Ellison Hatfield, another one of the preacher's cousins.

Deacon Anse raised his bushy eyebrow. "Sure enough was two hours ago. With God's grace and my old mop I sure fixed it proper." This elicited a slight chuckle from the spectators of the ersatz courtroom. "When we're done you suppose you could help me clean up?"

The tall man paused, feigning thought. "Sure, as long as you cook up some hominy and give me a little nip of that jug you got in your cupboard, I think we could do some business." Ellison pointed to the rickety bed in the corner of the room. What's that for your honor?"

"Oh, that's in case the defendant or the plaintiff don't feel so well after we get done with them." The men in the courtroom broke out laughing. Walking over to his cousin, the deacon abruptly yanked the shotgun from his loose grip. With weapon in hand he glanced around at several others brandishing firearms. "Now boys, I don't want any guns in here. It ain't proper. Just place all your hardware up against the side of the courtroom." Out of respect, all the men obediently complied.

The judge figured he had the perfect solution to insure a fair trial and a just verdict. I'm going to need six men from the plaintiff's party and six who side with the defendant." The spectators all nodded.

The short trial began with the testimony of a heavy set man named of Bill Staton. He had come on behalf of his friend Floyd. Recently married, he was Ellison Hatfield's brother-in-law. In spite of the fact that he was also the Randolph's nephew, he hated him. On occasion, he had his own disagreements with the man.

Years earlier, during the winter of eighteen sixty-five, Asa Harmon McCoy came back from his service in the Civil War. He was Randolph's only brother and was killed soon after he returned to his home in Peter Creek, a sleepy province located on the Kentucky-West Virginia border. Their inhabitants were largely sympathetic to the Confederate cause. However, Asa was the only man whose loyalty went to the Union. Even his own kin thought he was a traitor to the cause when he came home wearing the uniform of a blue belly. It was for this same reason Harmon was forced to hide in a cave like a crazed animal, when he heard that he was a hunted man.

Ironically, the Union man's ex-slave Pete brought biscuits and coffee to the mountain location where he was hidden. The Logan County Wildcats trailed the unsuspecting servant and discovered the location of the fugitive Yankee. These vigilantes were a collection of ex-rebels who banded together to organize an independent home guard. Upon discovery, they promptly shot Asa full of holes. On that day, Bill Staton rode along with the Wildcats. It was rumored that he possibly fired the fatal shot into Randolph's brother.

Staton sat down in the makeshift witness chair while the deacon administered the oath of the court. He motioned the witness to put his hand on the bible. "I figure you understand that you're giving sworn testimony before the Lord," he said reverently.

Deacon Anse slowly paced the floor in front of the twelve-man jury. "Mister Staton, tell these boys just exactly what you saw the day before Randolph McCoy made his claim about the hog in question."

Dripping with sweat, Staton tensely glanced around crowded cabin. "I know for a fact, Floyd didn't steal no hog from Ranel McCoy. Everyone knows that's free range up in them hills above his place. Hatfields, McCoys and Statons, been running their pigs up there as long as I can remember. I was with Floyd when he found that pig the old man is talking about. That old boy didn't have any markings on him, Hatfield or McCoy. So Floyd marked him, gathered him up with the rest and brought him home and that's all there is to it."

Old Ranel's supporters moaned loudly. Sam McCoy stood up abruptly shouting. "You're a damn liar Staton, you never saw anything."

The witness shifted uncomfortably in his chair, nervously rubbing his chubby hand through his thin, blonde hair. Deacon Anse's normally soft-spoken manners gave way to vexation. "If you open your pie hole again I'll chuck you out on your hide.

After the preacher's warning, the young man sat down scowling next to his older brother. "You know that old man could do it if he wanted to" Paris McCoy whispered.

Deacon Anse moved within three feet of Staton's pie shaped face and looked him straight in the eye. "You sure were there when Floyd found that hog?"

Staton leaned back in his chair while meeting the preacher's stare. "I ain't given to lying."

When the brief testimony ended, the Deacon excused the first witness and called Randolph McCoy to the chair. He folded his hands, resting his long chin upon the tips of his index fingers. "Ranel, you got any witnesses that'll swear that the pig in question belongs to you?"

"No, I don't but I know he's mine" Randolph insisted.

"Can you identify your mark on that old boy?"

Randolph raised his eyebrows. "No, I looked at this animal, but that don't mean Floyd didn't switch him before you got to his place. He might have ate my pig," he answered.

The cabin roared with laughter causing Randolph to turn beat red.

Deacon Anse attempted to hide his own smile, but managed to muster one more question. "You really don't have any proof to show this court that hog belongs to you."

McCoy fired back, "Look, I know what I saw. Floyd had a pig with my markings in his pen!"

After Randolph spoke his peace, the preacher addressed the courtroom spectators "I'm going to have to ask the rest of you fellers to wait outside while the jury renders its verdict." All the men slowly filed out of the stuffy cabin, enjoying a breath of fresh air, conversation and pipe smoking.

Bill Staton had a reputation of being a hot head, easily given to violence; but during his testimony, he had kept calm while stating his version of the story. Randolph only had his word against Floyd's and that wasn't enough for jury. They found Floyd not guilty of stealing the hog. The swing vote came in the form of one of McCoy Family kinsman who actually voted in favor of a Hatfield acquittal. His name was Selkirk, who claimed that he didn't have any reason to doubt Staton's story.

After losing the verdict, Randolph stood outside the courtroom cabin with his sons Tolbert and Pharmer along with his nephews Sam and Paris. "Damn Selkirk is more worried about his job at the Hatfield's mill then he is about his own kin. Well, that's that," he said wiping his hands. "I had my so-called day in court and that's as far as I got."

Big Sam McCoy chimed in. "You may be done, but that weasel Staton best watch where he goes. He and that idiot Selkirk ain't worth the powder to blow them to hell."

"Amen to that son," agreed Old Ranel."

*****

Three months after the hog incident, Bill Staton was on his way home after fishing all day. With his belly full of skirmishes with

Randolph's nephews, he was jubilant when he spotted Sam and Paris coming down the road by his cabin. After a recent fistfight and exchanging shots across the river, they were becoming a perpetual nuisance. It now appeared he had an opportunity to rid himself of these pests.

The Tug River had an array of good spots to ambush people. With densely wooded areas, steep limestone hills and miles of secluded terrain, a man didn't have to keep company with humanity. Hatfields and McCoys lived on opposite sides of the Tug Fork, which flowed into The Big Sandy River as you went south. The river divided these two clans between the neighboring states, though in reality they only lived a few miles apart. McCoys generally made their home in Pike County, on the Kentucky side of the Tug. Conversely, the Hatfields lived mostly in Logan County, on the West Virginia side. Today, Sam and Paris were treading the Hatfield side of the river.

As the two brothers talked while going down the dirt road, they were unaware they were being watched. Staton knew that big Sam was a crack shot and scrutinized his every movement. If he could get a bead on him, he was not going to let that opportunity slip through his fingers.

Sam and Paris headed home from rabbit hunting by way of the Hatfield Tunnel, on the mouth of the river. At a slow-footed pace, they shared a few nips, discussing the day's activities while walking down the tree-lined path.

Burley Sam McCoy carried a jug of corn liquor around his neck. At his side he wore a leather holster, which held a well oiled, thirty-six caliber Navy Colt. Strapped across the back of his crisp, white shirt, Sam toted his Winchester forty-four rifle in a leather scabbard.

Paris, who was Sam's older brother wasn't powerfully built like his sibling. At age twenty-three, he had a smooth baby face with prominent blue eyes and coal black hair. Strong but rail thin, he ate nearly as much as Sam and was quick enough to occasionally wrestle him to the ground. He walked along side his younger brother resting an old Peterson Shotgun on his shoulder.

"I know that Mary Lou Langford is partial to me," said Sam.

"How did you figure that out, did she send up a smoke signal like an Injun?"

Sam turned towards Paris and stopped in his tracks. "Nope, you don't need a smoke signal. A feller has ways of knowing what a gal is thinking. When a woman wants to, she will give you a doe-eyed look," he replied confidently.

Paris began to mock his brother in a friendly way. "It's a good thing I live with a man that has your experience with gals; would you give me some pointers?"

Sam's long face turned red. "Yeah, well joke if you want to, but I'm trying to be serious with you brother."

Paris wiped the smile off his face, offering a more respectful look. "Alright then, tell me what happens next?"

Sam grinned and began excitedly. "Well now, after you set a spell with a gal, you know, passing the time with some clever small talk. They'll get real quiet and there's usually a bit of an uneasy moment between you and her. That's when they get all weepy eyed and look straight into your eyes like they can see inside your soul. That's the doe-eyed look— the signal."

"What Signal?"

Sam wildly threw his arms in the air. "You know; the signal to come and get it."

"Oh, that's sort of like the dinner bell?"

"No, more like this," Sam replied, throwing his water pouch at Paris.

Though it seemed interminable, Staton cautiously watched the McCoy brothers for two minutes. He positioned himself between two thick pine trees, which stood approximately a foot from a massive crevasse covered by dense brush. Elevated by twenty feet above the main trail, he was only yards away from the Hatfield Tunnel. With little risk of being seen, Staton could get off two or three good shots in rapid succession.

As the McCoy brothers reached the clearing below his hiding place, Staton carefully aimed his Winchester at them. He took a few deep breaths to calm his trembling hands but his heart still pounded like a woodpecker. He tried to compensate for his shaky hands by gripping his rifle tight enough to leave an imprint on the stock. With a heavy sigh he squeezed of two quick shots. Paris McCoy cried out with a high-pitched scream as one well aimed bead smashed into the side of his body. Grabbing his hip, cupping a hand full of blood, he cried out to his younger brother. "Sam I'm shot, God almighty I'm shot."

A stunned but quick responding Sam McCoy drew his revolver, firing up at the bushwhacker with one remarkably accurate shot. The bullet hit Staton's left shoulder, causing him to plummet to the ground landing five feet away from Paris McCoy. Though momentarily stunned after hitting the rock hard ground, the crazed attacker lunged forward with the fury of a foam-mouthed, rabid dog. Thrusting his heavy body on Paris, he savagely sunk his teeth into the wounded man's throat. Paris again desperately squealed out in wrenching agony. "Get him off me!"

Sam momentarily stood above the two men, who were kicking up a cloud of dust, hastily firing bullet into the back of Bill's upper right shoulder. The frenzied bushwhacker rolled over, reached into his boot for a hunting knife, while still looking up into Big Sam's wrathful face. He grabbed the handle of the weapon and lunged at his opponent's hefty leg barely grazing it.

Big Sam was impervious to any pain in his limb, flying into a red rage of anger, shouting at the top of his lungs "I'm going send you to hell boy."

Staton's eyes bulged with shear terror, when he realized that he was going to die. "Don't kill me, please," he bellowed, stretching out his hands in a futile attempt to protect his face. Big Sam coldly pointed his pistol, firing a round into Bill Staton's brain.

Reeling from the loud shot, Sam stood there silently for that first surreal moment. He couldn't believe how quickly he had ended a man's life. He had shot squirrels, deer and even a bear, but had never killed a man before. He pondered whether or not he should feel some remorse. Whether after taking a human life he should experience a twinge of guilt or emotion; instead he felt a calm, satisfied feeling.

Standing over the dead man, Big Sam began to speak to him as if he thought he could still hear his words. "You shouldn't have tried to bushwhack us boy. You see what happens when you tangle with me. I told you once you best watch your step and you had to go and prove me right."

Sam walked over to Paris, pulled out his handkerchief and placed on his brother's bloodied hip. "Keep that on the wound till we get home." Lifting his brother's arm over his muscular shoulder, he pulled him up into a standing position. "Your wife is gonna kill me when she sees the way I'm bringing you home."

Paris chuckled out in pain, halting the two men for a moment. "Please don't make me laugh because it hurts my hip awful bad. He looked thoughtfully into Sam's giant face. "Thanks for saving my life" he said.

Sam gently patted his older brother on the shoulder. "Forget it." Not another word was spoken as he helped Paris hobble the four miles back to his home.

CHAPTER TWO: ROSEANNA AND JOHNSE

The Tug River region of the Appalachian Mountains was sparsely inhabited by a durable group of men and women. Their families lived for generations sometimes suffering the wrath of nature or the hardships of the difficult terrain. Yet it was a territory of lush green hills covered with endless thickets and narrow, almost hidden valleys. Between the next mountain pass one could travel for miles before seeing anything that resembled a hamlet, let alone a town.

If a man lived closer than a half mile from his neighbor, it was deemed as over population. It was a speck of humanity far removed from the Grey billowing, smokestack factories of newly booming cities in the east. Apart from a few timber mills, the valley was an unspoiled landscape that lay but a generation away from the coal-mining onslaught that would change it forever.

Cabins were a way of life, with one room for cooking, which typically centered on a stone fireplace and a second room for living quarters and sleeping. Blood, sweat, muscle and a good axe were required to chop huge logs that would become the framework for these rustic dwellings. Clapboards were laboriously hewn for the sides of the structure, with sticks, stones and mortar to fill any cracks.

To earn their living, most men hunted, fished, cut timber and made moonshine whiskey. Women generally tended to the farming, which primarily involved growing corn, the staple of their family diet. The food was cooked in cast iron kettles or pans on a large open fireplace, which doubled as a source of heat during the harsh winter months.

Friendships established were long standing. Loyalty was held in the highest regard. If you betrayed a trust, it could be dangerous. It wasn't often that a man in the hills got angry enough to take up arms against his neighbor. When an offense could not be settled with reasonable words or fists, it was settled with the cracking fire of Winchesters.

There was a dearth of social gatherings or opportunities to meet with other people. One of the few, most festive occasions was a county election. Almost everyone on either side of the river would attend their precinct. Even people that didn't vote would come from miles around, to get their fill of food, drink and the latest news.

During the warm spring of the year 1880, the local elections in Pike County were conducted. The Blackberry Precinct was located at the house of Jeremiah Hatfield. Also known as Jerry, he was related to the Kentucky side of the Hatfield clan. They were generally on more cordial terms with the McCoy family, than Hatfields living in West Virginia.

Jerry owned a run down, centrally located cabin. It was situated in the middle of a thick, wooded hollow about three and half miles from the Tug. Two smaller creeks broke off from the sizable river, providing sparkling clear water only a stone's throw from the house. His desirable land was encircled by mammoth oak trees, which supplied welcome shade for the redwood table's setup on Election Day.

This voting transpired long before congress implemented the Nineteenth Amendment to the United States Constitution. Women were not allowed to vote because they were thought to be emotional, high strung creatures, certainly not capable a making such important decisions. In spite of their lack of suffrage, the female contingent retained their fair share of influence on the male voting populace. They appealed to the intellect of their manly counterparts by bribing them with sweet breads, cherry pies and lemonade. These political flavors were used for leverage in of swaying votes for their preferred candidates.

In addition to the serious task of voting, the men tended to lie around the shade trees, discussing politics or events of the day. To assist them in rational exchange of ideas, the voters resolved to get sufficiently inebriated up by the end of the afternoon. Perspective candidates generally supplied the strong drink to woo their constituency. They too believed that a little refreshment might render the outcome they desired. However, some individuals didn't handle their refreshments well as others, which often resulted in a fistfight.

Though it was not their voting precinct, some of the West Virginia Hatfields paid a visit to Blackberry Creek on Election Day. These self-reliant men possessed their own thoughts about the candidates running in Pike. A few of them appealed to their political sensibility, but mostly they favored ones related to their substantial family.

No matter where they tread, The Hatfields usually traveled in well-armed groups. Though generally agreeable people, they displayed little concern to humanity telling them where to go or what to do.

The head of the West Virginia clan was Anderson Hatfield, who was commonly known, as Devil Anse This was an appellation he received during the War Between the States, while fighting for the Confederacy. Towards the end of 1864, he had a minor disagreement with a troop of seasoned Yankee infantry. As the legend went, he sat up on a hilltop frequently changing positions while picking off scores of Union men. A Cavalry Captain, who observed the bodies of his soldiers, was informed by his second in command that they were snuffed out by one Confederate Sharpshooter. "If that was the work of one man, then he must be the devil himself," said the officer.

Devil Anse carefully trotted his yellow mare across the shallow portion of Blackberry Creek. Sitting stoop shouldered in his well-worn saddle, he placed the balls of his boot covered feet on the stirrups of his mount, slowly traversing the small body of water. His nearly eight-inch beard flowed in an airborne state, as he pivoted his six-foot, two-inch frame back towards his two sons. "I'm bout ready to have my fill of pie and coffee when we get to Jerry's place," he said with a crooked grin.

"I'm with you Pa," responded his oldest son Johnse.

"You sure look pretty today brother; and you smell like a cathouse!" his younger brother Cap observed.

"What would you know about that youngster?"

"I heard things," Cap nervously answered.

Devil Anse scowled. "Well don't ever let your mama hear you talk like that."

In tandem, the three Hatfield's rode the last few hundred yards of the trail up to their kinsman's home. Devil Anse looked his firstborn up and down for a moment. "Cap is right son you look like you're ready for a shotgun wedding in them fancy duds. You must have peddled a substantial amount of distilled beverage to afford that catalogue suit."

Johnse lightly stroked the sleeve of his new blue suit. "This old thing, I got this coat and britches nearly two months ago."

Devil Anse glanced down at his oldest son's footwear. "I see you also got yourself some shiny new brown shoes."

"A man doesn't spruce himself up with a new suit of clothes and then put on an old pair of shoes."

In addition to his taste for store bought clothes, Johnse owned the looks that appealed to a sizable number of young women on either side of the Tug Fork. He decided to focus some attention on his brother. "Pa, you should be glad that one of us knows how to dress."

For Election Day, Cap Hatfield chose to wear a yellow shirt with cutoff sleeves and pants from an old Confederate uniform. With an unusually large head, mature face and powerfully built physique, the sixteen-year-old appeared considerably older.

Cap smiled, pausing in thought before he responded to his brother. One of his steel cold, blue eyes was dull pale. It was severely scarred from a childhood mishap, which caused his rifle to accidentally discharge backfiring into his left eye. "I haven't been as prosperous as you as of late." Cap turned towards his father. "I'm told Johnse would never peddle a bottle of whiskey that he wouldn't be happy to drink himself."

Devil Anse grinned back. "Seeing as how you don't share his fancy taste in duds, you don't need the greenbacks to afford your britches."

Cap turned his head to the side and spit a wad of chaw on the ground. "Not by a damn sight."

The three Hatfield's had arrived at Jerry's place at one o'clock in the afternoon. They wasted no time joining the festivities. As Devil Anse tied his mount to the hitching post in front of the makeshift polling place, he pointed his long index finger at his boys, "you best mind your manners and don't make me out a jackass."

"Don't worry Pa, I just want to sample some of the grub," Johnse said, turning to walk towards the food tables.

"Be sure that's all you sample," warned Devil Anse. Unsure that his last remark registered with his son, his long face had a look of concern while he observed his sons strolling off. After a short deliberation, he shrugged his shoulders and walked over to greet his cousin Deacon Anse and his friend Selkirk McCoy.

Johnse anxiously rubbed his hands together as he saw all the women hovering over tables covered with heaping quantities of cooked meats, fresh vegetables, various side dishes and baked goods. Flashing a wide grin at his brother, he motioned him towards the feast. "Don't be shy you big pork chop, let's go sample the wares."

With Cap in tow, he went around to each table, delighting at all of the food and flirtation that was being offered by the local gals. His younger brother remained quiet and polite, while Johnse did all the talking, flattering the baking talents of every girl present at Blackberry Creek.

As the Hatfield Romeo made his rounds, one particular young lady attracted his attention. She was one of Old Ranel's thirteen children and her name was Roseanna. She had ventured to Blackberry

Creek with her older brother Tolbert with the intention of helping some
of her neighbors prepare refreshments.

After cooking her yam dish, Roseanna sought the refuge of a
solitary oak tree, about thirty yards from where the tables sat. To
relieve herself from the heat, she removed a yellow ribbon exposing her
long brunette hair to the cool breeze coming from nearby Blackberry
creek.

Johnse ate a piece of fried chicken while admiring the curves of
Roseanna's long, shapely frame hidden underneath her sundress. He
imagined what she would look like without it as he proceeded to
scrutinize the fine features of her pale face. She caught the attractive
young man staring at her and calmly returned his glance.

Johnse eagerly nudged his brother's protruding stomach with
his bony elbow. "Cap, look at that sweet young thing standing there by
her lonesome."

Cap seized an opportunity to tease his brother. "Yes, pretty lil'
turned up nose, just like a trembling jackrabbit; nice lips that appear to
be as red and delicious as Mama's cherry pie; and take a gander at that
silky hair, black as coal dangling down to her hind end." He paused and
contrived a sigh. "She's a bit pale for my liking, but her eyes look like
they could melt ice cream on a cold day; and underneath that yellow
dress it appears she has a child bearing figure. I think I may go talk her
up and down."

Johnse slapped his brother's shoulder. "You do and I'll have
your hide for breakfast."   Cap clutched his hands to his chest and
swooned like a girl. "Oh my Lord, I think my brother's been struck by
cupid's love arrow."

Johnse ignored Cap, set down his plate and swaggered over to
where Roseanna was fanning herself. "Pardon me for saying so, but
you might just be the prettiest gal in the whole damn county. If you
please ma'am, my name is Johnse Hatfield," He said tipping his hat.

Roseanna smiled politely, stealthily looking into his large green
eyes. "I know who you are," she replied.

Johnse had a cocky grin. "How'd you know?"

"Some of the other girls were talking about you when you rode
up."

Johnse bubbled with delight and took a seat underneath the
shadowy oak. "I'll bet they didn't have anything good to say."

The pretty mountain girl hesitated but then took a seat next to
her young suitor. "You might be surprised at what they did say. For
instance, Jenny Hood said that you've made the rounds with a few gals.

Annie Spencer said you were no better than a snake oil salesman."

Johnse offered a look of mock indignation. "Did she?"

"Yes she did. She said that you could charm the Devil out of his red suit. In jest, Roseanna batted her eyes. "Could you do that?"

"Why don't you find out for yourself," he answered coyly.

Roseanna pursed her lips and seductively leaned in toward Johnse's face. "Why don't you go over and get me something cool to drink."

As the afternoon progressed, most of the male voters got good and inebriated, taking naps under the shade trees. The women had the thankless task of cleaning up after them. Roseanna was not among them as she slipped off into the woods chatting with Johnse for several hours. With a mutual attraction increasing with each passing minute, they wandered along a mile to Peter's Branch. On the way Johnse gathered up stones, tossing them into the creek while Rose Anna gossiped about one her cousins named Nancy.

Discovering a secluded stretch of creek, the young man laid out his saddle blanket for the furtive duo to plop down under a maple tree. When he finally ran out of small talk, Johnse was nearly bewitched, intently looking into Roseanna's pitch-dark eyes. He gently reached his hand up to touch her silky hair. "Damn, you are pretty" he whispered.

Old Ranel's daughter stretched out her arms underneath the stream of sunlight cutting through the tops of the surrounding trees. "It's so peaceful and beautiful out here. And now that you stopped talking about yourself for a minute…"

"Yes…" Johnse quickly responded.

"You think you could use that mouth to kiss me with?"

"Yes ma'am that was my intention." He leaned in, wrapped his arms around her small waist and softly kissed Roseanna's generous lips. Giggling and kissing for several hours, the smitten couple forgot about their friends, family and particularly the time.

With the onset of the dusky evening, the infatuated girl abruptly broke out of her spooning trance. "Oh my lord, what time is?"

Johnse pulled a timepiece from his pants pocket. "Quarter passed six. We best be getting back before someone thinks we're missing."

By the time the pair returned to Blackberry creek, all the food tables had been taken away and worse yet, Jerry's place was clear of the all the Election Day celebrants. Nightfall had descended and Roseanna's happy mood changed to a depressed one when she discovered that her brother Tolbert had left Blackberry Creek without her. "Oh my Daddy's gonna kill me when get back. What am I gonna do?" Her voice had a tone of desperation, as she hoped her new admirer might have a plan of action.

Johnse became nervous when he thought about the consequences of his actions but concealed those thoughts from his companion. "This calls for some serious thinking gal," he said firmly. The spring had yielded a clear, crisp, moonlit evening and he thought hard on what to do. As he stood out in the middle of Jeremiah's front yard, feelings of infatuation and responsibility surged through him. Suddenly, the solution became as clear as the evening sky. "You could come back to our Place," He said enthusiastically.

The naïve mountain girl was incredulous at his spontaneous idea. "Come back to your daddy's place? Are you touched in the head? You know my daddy ain't exactly too fond of your family right now."

"That may be, but they're gonna be madder the wet hens already. You may as well come back with me, and give your daddy the full volley."

Near the point of a breaking down, the distressed young women rocked back and forth with her arms folded tight against her breasts.

Johnse pulled one of her hands away, caressing it softly. "Come on girl, it's the only sensible thing to do and it will give me time to think of something." As the words left his lips, the young Hatfield man began to comprehend the ramifications of what he had proposed.

A steady stream of tears began to trickle out of Roseanna's eyes. Feelings of remorse for her impetuous actions were not going to change the situation. "We best be on our way," she said with resignation.

Johnse helped her climb on the back of his spotted white mare, which his father had left tied up at the front of Jerry's home. The tardy couple proceeded to ride the six miles back, to the home of Devil Anse and Levicy Hatfield.

Assisted by a full, vibrant moon, the trail home was well lit, as Johnse went by way of Peter Creek to the Poundmill run, crossing the Big Sandy River. With her arms wrapped tightly around his slender waist, he could feel his new sweetheart trembling not from the cold but from the stream of negative thoughts running through her frightened brain. By mid evening, the tired sweethearts arrived at the Hatfield cabin. In spite of her fatigue, Roseanna experienced acute feelings of apprehension.

The day had been a long one for Devil Anse as he had stayed up late wondering whereabouts of oldest boy. He and his other son left

Jerry's place at about six o'clock that afternoon. That was after Cap informed his father why his brother had wandered off from the festivities. He sat on his front porch, lit his pipe, poured a glass of bourbon and waited.

Levicy Hatfield was still awake, as she was worried about what happened to her boy. She brushed her fine stranded hair as she looked into a dull, cracked mirror that hung on the wall of her small bedroom area. She and her husband had the only room partitioned off from the rest of the cabin. Her reflection offered a face that was round, with plain features; yet she possessed a self-contained, gentle quality that pleased her husband. After putting on her nightgown, she walked outside to front porch and sat quietly with her man.

Levicy and Devil Anse talked for about on hour before Johnse arrived home with his guest. They were less than pleased when they saw who he had with him. Her son barely dismounted his horse before his mother greeted him with a frown. "Boy, you taken leave of your senses, what are folks gonna say?"

Johnse forced a smile. "I reckon they're gonna say we're friendly folk. Momma, Daddy, this is Roseanna and she needs us to put her up for a spell," he added.

Levicy stood, gaping at the young couple, for what seemed to them to be the longest twenty seconds in history. After the uncomfortable silence, she looked warmly into Roseanna's face and smiled. "Of course we'd be happy to have you stay." She grasped her hand tightly, motioning her inside the house, "come in child, I'll make up a place for you to sleep."

Johnse proceeded to follow the two women into the Hatfield home when Devil Anse spoke up. "Not you boy, you and I need to have a talk."

The nervous young man anticipated hearing some well-chosen words from his father.

Leaning up against the splintered rail of his front porch the head of the family spoke softly. "She's a mighty pretty gal."

"Yes, she surely is Pa."

Devil Anse reached for his favorite pipe and began filling it with tobacco. "She's Randolph McCoy's little girl, ain't she?" he inquired, while lighting his smoke.

"Yes Daddy, she surely is."

The older man looked upward towards the evening sky, pointing his long finger at the largest star in the sky. "Son, see that one big light up there?"

Johnse glanced up where his father pointing, squinting his eyes. "Yes, I see it. What about it?"

"That big lit globe up there in the heavens is the North Star. It gives off one pretty light don't it?" he asked rhetorically. When I went to Ohio last year I visited a museum where they had a big device they called a telescope. Just so that stargazers can get a closer look at the moon and such. They say there are millions of stars up there just as big as the North Star.

"That's nice Pa but I'm not sure I follow you."

"What I mean to say, is that you may think this McCoy girl is for you; but I'm telling you now that she ain't. There are plenty of other gals that will make you happy and give you a lot less trouble than Old Ranel's daughter."

Johnse began to protest. "Now wait a minute."

Devil Anse raised his hand to silence his son. "Now you're going to hear me out. Randolph McCoy and I, we used to be friendly but now we don't exactly see eye to eye. He thinks I robbed one of his kin of some timberland a few years back. With you taking up with his daughter, now he's going to accuse me of stealing his little girl. Don't you see that?"

"Your business with Mister McCoy ain't got nothing to do with Roseanna and me. I ain't done nothing to the McCoys."

"The past got everything to do with it. You're my blood kin and nothing's gonna change that. And you meddling with his little girl's like rubbing dung in his face.

Turning away from his father, Johnse looked down at the ground without speaking for a moment. "Daddy, I don't know what to say to that. I guess I wasn't thinking about that today. When I first saw her, I didn't care about nothing else. All I know is that she's pretty, sweet and makes me laugh. And I don't know if I give a tinker's damn about what her father wants."

Devil Anse shrugged his shoulders. "Your hankering may be get you pumped full of buckshot. I say you get her back home tomorrow before someone gets hurt.

Johnse shook his head. "Nothing doing; I'm willing to take my chances with Old Ranel."

Devil Anse stretched out his long arms and yawned. ""Nothing we can do about it tonight, we'll talk more tomorrow" he said calmly. "Goodnight son, I believe Mama gave Roseanna your bed. You can sleep in the barn tonight." The old mountain man cackled under his breath, turned around and went inside his cabin, leaving his son to ponder his words.

Roseanna's sense of apprehension diminished slightly after she entered the Hatfield home. She was impressed with the clean, organized condition maintained by Levicy. The kitchen had a separate fireplace with a broad hearth, in addition to several organized hooks and cranes. Various cooking pots, alongside two large diameter black kettles hung above the fire, with other accessories stacked neatly on a wrought iron utility shelf her husband purchased on business excursion.

In the main room, two rosewood rocking chairs sat on a colorful woven rug, which lay upon a stained puncheon floor. Roseanna smiled at the sight of a sizable golden hound dog sleeping at the foot of the chairs, with his head resting atop an old yellow blanket. On the far side of the cabin was a row of oak beds where the family members slept. She noticed several of the beds were doubled up with young children, who were already put down for the evening. Levicy put on clean bedding on her eldest son's bed for her newly arrived guest.

After the initial surprise of receiving an unexpected visitor, the Hatfield's enjoyed having the well-mannered Roseanna as their guest. Levicy thought it a blessing to talk to her during the day, as all her daughters were too young for mature discussions. For the first time she had someone to help her with the burden to tending to the children, the cooking, farming and clothes washing.

One afternoon after a full day of chores and cooking, the two women sat down at the kitchen table for a short respite. Levicy served up fresh coffee with chicory to her guest who was becoming fond of having a surrogate mother.

"My husband and I have a rule about having company. They're welcome to stay as long as they like. I love having you here for selfish reasons child, but you've been here nearly two weeks," Levicy said smiling. "You must miss being at home with your own family."

Roseanna nodded politely.

Levicy paused, "You know you'll have to face them sometime." She looked intently upon her young friend's face. She was nearly overcome with maternal feelings as she observed the ghostly demeanor of this sad beauty.

Roseanna hung her head down for a moment. When she raised it again, Mrs. Hatfield noticed a tear welling up in her eye. "I'm plum out of my head thinking about that. They must think of me as some kind of Jezebel."

"I'm sure that's the last thing they would say."

"You don't know my Daddy. I've never been away from home

before" Roseanna said shaking her head.

Levicy knew she was probably right. She placed her rough skinned hand on Roseanna's and smiled sweetly. "Don't fret child, you stay with us as long as you need."

Roseanna began to weep. "Thank you Mrs. Hatfield. I never expected such warm hospitality."

"Let's cook us up a batch of cornbread for the troops," Levicy suddenly suggested. "That'll get your mind off worrisome things child."

The young girl dried her eyes with her sleeve. "That sounds like a good idea Mrs. Hatfield."

"For heaven sakes child, stop making me sound like an old woman. Call me Levicy."

While Roseanna visited with Levicy, Johnse was in the company of his father, who wanted to do some fishing. When they arrived at the old man's favorite watering hole, Devil Anse placed a wiggling night crawler on the end of his rusty hook and cast out his line. Johnse, who was less anxious, cut a notch into a old log, dug a hole in the ground and set his rig up so he didn't have to hold on to it.

An hour passed before either man spoke a word. "Looks like the catfish ain't biting today boy," Devil Anse declared.

Johnse didn't move a muscle from his place on the edge of Grapevine Creek. With sleepy eyes half open, his floppy felt hat partially covered his face. "Maybe this spot has played itself out."

Devil Anse reached into his pocket to locate another fishhook. He pulled his line back in and quickly removed the old, rusted hook and replaced it with the new one.

Johnse watched his father for a moment. "I'm sure the fish will know the difference."

The old man sat down next to his son. "Maybe not boy; but your mamma was counting on a fish dinner tonight." He pulled out a small silver flask with the initials CSA engraved on it and took a swig. He put the cap on the container and offered it to his oldest boy.

Johnse quickly grabbed the whiskey and lifted a toast to his father. "Here's to the catfish cooperating." After taking a drink he handed it back.

Devil Anse quickly downed another swig. "I may have more luck shooting me a fish, than catching one today." He tugged on his line a few times.

"Well you've always been a better shot than you were a fisherman," Johnse answered, patting his father's leg.

"Haw, you got that right boy." The elder Hatfield copied his son's procedure, resting his fishing pole up against the log. He yanked a long weed from the dry ground, placed it in his mouth and pulled his hat over his eyes as laid down next to Johnse. "You getting on good with Roseanna are you?" He inquired.

"Yes Pa, she's a real peach ain't she?"

"She surely is." Devil Anse momentarily hesitated. Son, you know I've never been a man to put much store in what other folks have to say about our family."

Johnse rose up into a sitting position. "Yes, I know."

And I would let Roseanna stay with us as long as she likes; but maybe its time to think about marrying her or sending her back to her family."

"I know and I been giving it some thought."

"That's good son and what did you decide."

The younger Hatfield noticed his fishing pole move slightly. "I ain't decided on anything yet; but I'll do a heap of thinking on it."

"Best you not think on it too long. You're putting me between the rock and the hard place with Old Ranel," Devil Anse responded.

Johnse's fishing pole now bent down towards the creek and was nearly yanked out of the hole he had dug. He hopped up, firmly grasping his rig before whatever was on the other end pulled it into the water.

The old mountain man stood up in amazement when he saw his son had snagged something on his line. "Son of a bitch, I can't believe you ain't held on to that all afternoon."

Wading down into the creek, Johnse fought with the fish for a minute, and then slowly pulled in his line to find a sizable bass on the end. "Appears to be about an eight or nine pounder."

"I changed my hook, used fresh night crawlers and I come up empty handed," he said scratching his chin. "That boy does have a gift."

*****

Randolph McCoy was fit to be tied when his daughter had not returned home with his son Tolbert on Election Day. As the weeks passed into months, he became increasingly agitated about the situation.

The area around Blackberry Creek was far from densely populated and most and everyone who lived there knew each other. News of the illicit courtship between the Hatfield boy and Old Ranel's daughter spread like a prairie fire, with neighbors delighting in the bits of choice gossip. Since entertainment was scarce in the valley, discussing the mountain Romeo and Juliet story became the local pastime.

If Johnse had done the right thing and married his daughter after he purloined her from Jeremiah's Election Day gathering, Randolph might have forgiven the infraction against his family. This could have also helped abate the resentment the old man harbored against Devil Anse because he coveted his sizable land holdings. Unfortunately, as more time passed, it became clear to McCoy that the Hatfield boy had nothing but bad intentions.

It was a sweltering, sticky June Morning when Randolph summoned three of his daughters together. Their names were Josephine, who was his oldest, Alifair, who was a year older than Roseanna and Adelaide who was only thirteen. Inside the large McCoy cabin, they collectively wondered why their father had gathered them away from their daily chores. They all watched him intently as he sat in his favorite old chair, arms folded, with a face full of despair.

Randolph stared at his oldest child, evaluating her with his sad murky eyes. "Josephine, you ain't much to look at but you're a good girl and you got good common sense."

Alifair quickly responded. "Daddy" she protested. Pretty and impish, she was always protective of her siblings. "That ain't a very nice thing to say."

He walked over and patted his plain looking daughter on her head. "Well she's pretty near thirty years old and ain't been married yet." The old man realized his was digging himself a deeper hole. "I didn't mean no harm by what I said. What I meant, is that she's a smart girl."

Josephine sighed, shaking off her frustration. "It's all right daddy, charm has never been your strong suit. What is it you want me to do?"

"I want you girls to pack some food and cross the river. Go talk some sense to that sister of yours," Randolph instructed.

The girls were surprised and began to hang on their father's every word. "You fetch her back home and tell her that her I forgive her. Josephine, you're the oldest and she respects you. Remind her that her place is here with us."

"But what if she don't want to come back daddy?" Josephine asked.

Randolph's pale face turned crimson with anger. "I don't care if she does or she don't. I don't care if you have to hog tie her and carry her back on a stake. You just bring her back, you hear."

Josephine walked over to where her father sat, leaned down and kissed his cheek. "Daddy, please don't work yourself into such a state. I'll fetch her back."

He looked up into his daughter's face, attempting to hold back his tears. "I know you will honey."

With the mission of retrieving their wayward sibling, the three McCoys girls left just after sunrise on the following day. Since it was a good eight mile distance between the Hatfield and McCoy cabins, the girls packed themselves a basket full of bread, fruit and traded off toting an old army canteen that was heavy when full of water.

The two oldest girls walked at a robust pace, with Adelaide occasionally running out in front picking wildflowers that sprouted along the road. Fair-skinned Alifair wrapped a scarf around her head, which offered some relief from the baking summer sun.

"Jo, do you think Roseanna is going to want to come back home today?" asked Alifair.

"Ally, do you remember when we were little playing out by the old cemetery? You were toting a big stick you picked up of the ground; and you started poking around a hollowed out tree. Do you remember?" she asked in a raised octave.

"Yes I remember but I'd surely like to know what that has to do with anything."

"I told you about the beehives but you kept on prodding the hives with your stick. When the bees came out stinging the daylights out of you I ran away. I was so scared. Who was it who fetched you out of there when you couldn't move?"

Her sister's recollection brought a smile to her face. "It was Roseanna," answered Alifair.

Josephine's voice resonated with pride. "That little girl ran over, picked you up screaming off the ground, all the while being stung herself. Never making a peep, she brought you home to mama without complaining once. You know she was stung more than a dozen times?"

Alifair experienced a surge of emotion after being reminded of Roseanna's selfless action. "She was so good and I was such a baby."

"Now you asked me if I think we're going to fetch our sister home today. When her mind is made up you can't stop her. If she wanted to be home she would be home now" Josephine concluded.

Adelaide glanced at the canvas bag that carried the pistol their father had provided for protection. "Jo, can you hit anything with daddy's gun?"

Josephine pointed her bony hand towards a distant cedar tree. "See that mosquito on that branch about fifty yards from here?"

Alifair and Adelaide both narrowed their eyes, straining to see what she was talking about.

With a deadpan expression she stopped in her tracks to look her sisters in the eye. "I could take his wings off with this here hog leg."

In unison, the girls broke out laughing.

Walking briskly after eating lunch, the McCoy daughters arrived at the Hatfield cabin by one o'clock in the afternoon. They found Roseanna picking vegetables in the garden with Mrs. Hatfield.

When she noticed the girls coming up the path to the cabin, Levicy quickly stood up and dusted off her white apron. "Roseanna, are those kin of yours?"

"Yes ma'am, those are my sisters." Roseanna was completely taken by surprise at their arrival, as it had been more than a month since she had seen them. "Jo, why have y'all come here?" She asked, embracing all of them one after another.

Roseanna turned to Levicy, who looked a bit uncomfortable. "Mrs. Hatfield, these here are my sisters Josephine, Alifair and the little one here is Adelaide," she said grabbing her young sibling and hugged her tightly.

Levicy smiled and nodded politely. "I am pleased to make all your acquaintances." She didn't want to intrude on family visit and excused herself. "Child, you take your sisters in the house for some refreshments, there's biscuits leftover and lemonade in the kitchen; you know where to find them" she offered hospitably.

"That's alright Mrs. McCoy, we just ate lunch but thank you," Josephine answered. The other girls nodded in agreement.

"Well you all have a nice time" Levicy said, as she turned to walk into the cabin.

Josephine stroked her sisters black hair, and then kissed her aquiline cheek. "Are you alright?"

Roseanna nodded.

"Daddy is all worn out worrying about you little sister, when you coming home?"

Roseanna nervously glanced down at the ground. "I can't, I'm scared bout what he's gonna do if I come home now."

"No need to be scared girl, daddy says he forgives you" Josephine said softy.

"That's awful big of him," Roseanna answered sarcastically.

"But you're shaming us if you stay here" Adelaide quickly

added.

Josephine flashed a look of anger. "This don't concern you little girl, what do you know about such things?" She turned away from Adelaide and gently took Roseanna's hand. "Don't worry about that. You don't know what we're going through. Mama can't sleep at night fretting about what might become of you. And we miss you too. We can leave right now and make it back before sundown."

Roseanna interrupted her sister. "I can't Jo."

"Don't you want to put a stop to all our worrying?" implored Josephine

"I can't come with you right now. I need to sort a few things out in my mind."

"Is it the Hatfield boy? Is that what's holding you here?" inquired Alifair. She put her slender arm around her sister's shoulder. "You can tell us; me and Jo won't say nothing to daddy."

Roseanna leaned into Alifair's shoulder and began to sob. "That's alright sweetie, let it out," she said, wrapping her arms tightly around her distraught sister.

"You love this Hatfield boy?" asked Josephine.

"I know he has a reputation; but if you knew him like I do, you'd know he's a good man," Roseanna answered.

Josephine put her arms around her two sisters. "So you aren't coming home are you?"

"I can't come home until I'm a married woman."

The runaway girl's sibling understood that she had failed her mission. "Well then, it'll be getting dark soon; best be on are way." She embraced Roseanna again. "Don't worry little girl, I'll make it right with daddy."

"I'll pray for you every day," Alifair said, and hugged her sister.

Adelaide ran over kissed and then hugged her older sister. "I'm sorry Roseanna. I didn't mean it."

"That's all right little one." Roseanna brushed the hair from Adelaide's tearful face.

With their goodbyes spoken, the three McCoy daughters quietly walked down the path away from the Hatfield cabin. Their sister watched them until she could see them no longer. She stood for alone for a few minutes and began to weep.

Randolph McCoy was incensed when his girls returned home empty handed. Twice more, he had them return to the Hatfield cabin; both times they would return without his other daughter.

During most of her stay with the Hatfield's, Roseanna believed that Johnse intended to marry her. After she had been a guest for nearly four months, it became exceedingly clear that her lover had no intention of making her an honest woman. He took pleasures with her nubile body but that was the extent of it. Without options, Old Ranel's little girl now felt trapped in a terrible situation. With great reluctance, she left the Hatfield's and went to live with her Aunt in Stringtown.

Aunt Betty Blankenship was a thirty-nine year old widow. She was fond of her pretty young niece, leaving her entirely disposed to take Roseanna in during her hour of need. She was acutely aware that shamed girl would face a firestorm of scorn if she returned to her father's house.

Roseanna's kindly aunt owned a small but cozy cabin, with a porch just yards from the Tug Fork. It was a scant place for a family but perfect for two people. It was entirely a woman's habitat, decorated with fancy hand sewn pillows and white lace in the main room. It was a house full of family antiques that dated back to the Revolutionary War.

Betty had lost her husband at an early age to a cholera epidemic. Though petite, small boned and standing only five feet tall, she was a tenacious woman that knew how to live on her own. She taught herself to shoot a rifle and pistol with precision and hunted her own game. Her reputation as a deadly shot was cemented during one of her nephew's visits. On this occasion, Aunt Betty was able to dispatch a rattlesnake with a forty-four, when the reptile came dangerously close to the child.

Roseanna had been unable to get the Johnse out of her system. The two sweethearts continued their affair because she had not given up her hope on marriage and her suitor was not inclined to let her go. In spite of the continued objections from both families, they kept seeing each other on a regular basis. Their designated point of rendezvous was near a farm owned by Randolph's neighbor Tom Stafford. Johnse would make false promises. Roseanna would apprise him of her perpetual state of ardor. It always ended with the couple doing what their families considered the indulgence of married folk. Their relaxation of the rules became an addiction, for both of them.

By the fall of 1880, the mountain Romeo and Juliet had been illicitly courting for six months. Their romance remained the primary topic for nasty gossip that had permeated throughout the valley. Devil Anse and Levicy, who had become fond of Roseanna thought Johnse was being completely reckless in not marrying her. Randolph was angry, perceiving that he had become a laughing stock for being unable to control his daughter.

On an evening in mid October, the air was chilly and crisp as the sun obscured beyond the horizon. A washed, freshly scented Roseanna was looking forward to seeing Johnse. Days apart from her lover would gnaw at her insides, which alternated with the constant dread over ruining what was left of her reputation and future.

Aunt Betty stood chatting with her niece, while she watched the mountain beauty primping her long dark strands of hair in the mirror. The cabin enveloped the two women with warmth from the blazing fireplace and the widow had poured herself some cider. "You know that Hatfield boy is using you like the neighbor's well."

Roseanna's face cast a frown in the reflective glass. "He's not like that Betty."

Aunt Betty frowned back. "Girl, trust me, this ain't my first barn dance. He's after what all men is after—why can't you find a man that's do you right by you?"

Impatiently dropping her hands to her hips, Roseanna swiveled her chair around to face her well meaning aunt. "You don't know him like I do; I've seen his kind and gentle ways."

Betty rolled her eyes as she sipped her drink. "Did you hear what I said? All men are after one thing and one thing only. And this one's no different. I may be out of practice with men, but I don't expect they've changed much since last I looked."

Randolph had been looking for an opportunity to catch the Hatfield swain unprotected. Upon receiving the word from Stafford that Johnse was meeting Old Ranel's jilted daughter near his farm, he collected his sons Tolbert, James, and Pharmer. By his reckoning it was time to teach the callous young man a lesson in manners.

From the front porch of his domicile, Randolph McCoy looked down at the eager faces of his four sons. "I got word the Hatfield boy is meeting your sister tonight. We're going to put a stop to it."

Tolbert's face lit up like a toothy, smiling Jack o' lantern. "Now you're talking daddy"   "Pharmer, saddle the horses, Tolbert, go get your brothers the shotgun, the Model 66 and the forty-four," Randolph instructed.

Tolbert cocked his head. "Daddy, are we having a shotgun wedding or a necktie party?"

"Son, don't get ahead of yourself. Just get the weapons and just let me do to the thinking."

Randolph had deliberated for weeks on a plan to get Johnse out of Logan County and across the Kentucky border to the town of Pikeville. There the disgruntled father would have him taken into custody. His oldest son James was a local peace officer that was knowledgeable about warrants sworn out against his sister's lover. They included carrying a concealed weapon, as well as brewing and peddling illegal distilled beverages.

The McCoys armed themselves with an array of rifles, shotgun and pistols retrieved by the trigger happy Tolbert. They hastily climbed on the mounts, efficiently saddled by Pharmer and rode towards Mate Creek, which was located a few miles east of Stringtown. There they intended to intercept Johnse and Roseanna at their clandestine rendezvous.

With no moon in the night sky there was pitch darkness, which made the trail difficult to navigate. Randolph led the four nightriders by torchlight, to see the road ahead. His friend Tom Stafford had imparted specific instructions, on where to look for the secret lovers. Randolph followed them to the letter and discovered the young couple underneath a sycamore lying half-naked on a blanket.

Roseanna looked up at her father's face. As the torch flickered she could see his anger. The four men surrounded the couple and levied their guns at their kin's nervous suitor.

"Get up and get your britches on you son of a bitch, before I shoot you where you lay!" Randolph shouted.

"Yes sir, yes sir I will" Johnse replied with his voice cracking.

"Let's kill him now daddy," Tolbert said to his father.

Randolph became rankled with his impatient offspring. "Boy would it kill you to think before you open your mouth. Let's do it my way." He motioned to his oldest son. "Take him."

Constable James jumped off his chocolate Saddle bred, confiscated Johnse's pistol, and roughly tied his hands behind his back. "We're taking you back to Pikeville. You're gonna stand trial boy," he said triumphantly.

Johnse smirked at his captor. "Stand trial for what, seeing your sister?"

"You shut up about my sister or I'll wring your damn neck."

"That would be easy right now," Johnse replied turning his bound up hands towards James.

The young peace officer smirked back. Boy, I got a warrant swore out against you for carrying a concealed firearm and selling illegal beverage." He waived a piece of paper at his prisoner. "See, it's all nice and legal."

"Let me have the chicken scratch so I can wipe my ass with it" Johnse replied.

James puffed out his chest as he assisted his prisoner on to his horse. "You best mind your manners." He pulled his long coat back, pointing to a gold badge. I'm a deputy in this county. I've got every right to kill you if you so much as twitch the wrong way."

Roseanna nervously watched as her brother prepared to take her lover away. "Don't you lay a hand on him James!" she yelled in a shrill voice.

Randolph looked down from his mount with disgust. "I don't even have the words for you right now. But you and I have to go the long mile before too long. Now get on home where you belong." Taking his reins in hand, he rotated his horse around leaving his daughter in a cloud of trail dust.

Hysterical with fear, Roseanna had nowhere to run but to Tom Stafford's place. When she arrived, he felt remorse about informing on her and the Hatfield boy. With eyes flooded with tears, she barely was able to get out a coherent sentence. "Can you lend me a horse?" she stuttered.

The normally gruff farmer's heart melted at sight of the radiantly sobbing, beautiful girl. "Sure honey, I'll saddle one up for you directly," he responded.

Roseanna galloped the borrowed animal as if her own life depended on it. A waterfall of salty teardrops continued streaming down her face as she darted down the unlit trail in the direction of Elias Hatfield's cabin. While engaged in small talk earlier that evening, Johnse had told his sweetheart that his father planned a visit to his younger brother. In spite of the darkness that surrounded her, she managed to see the small bungalow located in a clearing just off the main road. Breathlessly, the despairing girl burst through the door of the cabin where she found Devil Anse sitting with his brother Elias.

In a startled voice Elias inquired "What in damnation do you think you're doing?"

"Mister Hatfield, they got your boy" Roseanna said loudly.

Somehow not surprised, the old veteran calmly folded his hands on the redwood kitchen table. "How many your Pappy got with him?" he asked.

"He's got four of my brothers with him" she answered.

"I appreciate you coming here to warn me honey."

This distraught girl clutched the older man's rough hand. "Don't let them hurt him."

Devil Anse patted her hand. "If they do, they'll be hell to pay."

The Hatfield patriarch wasted no time gathering up a group of his own including his son Cap, his brothers Elias and Ellison, his cousin Jim Vance and two other neighbors that were close by. In spite of their head start, he figured on intercepting his son's captors. No one man in Pike or Logan County knew the terrain better than him. Never had his knowledge been employed with such necessity, then on this fall evening. Using a shortcut that was only known to him, his band was able to overtake the McCoy posse.

Not far from where Sam Stratton had been killed, Devil Anse had his men dismounted, assuming tactical positions along the road to the Poundmill Run. Crouching down behind a dry brown shrub, Devil Anse quickly loaded shells into his Henry Rifle.

Ellison Hatfield checked his revolver to ensure it housed a full load. "I reckon we'll give them boys a real surprise."

Devil Anse smiled back at his brother. "I reckon we will."

The burly Cap crawled along the dirt to where his father was hidden. "Are we planning on shooting anyone?" he asked nonchalantly.

"No they ain't drawn any blood and neither will we. Just the same, you better make sure your Winchester is loaded."

Just barely seventeen, Cap coolly smiled as his father. "I'm loaded for bear."

"We won't kill anybody but that don't mean we won't ruffle their feathers a bit," added Devil Anse.

The quick thinking Jim Vance had instructed Cap and the others roll a sizable log in the middle of the road. Stalled by the huge impediment, Randolph McCoy and his three sons received the jolt of a lifetime, when they rode into the larger Hatfield party. Their shock was heightened when they saw twice their number of guns trained on them.

Devil Anse hooted out from the underbrush. "Evening boys, you got something that belongs to me."

Randolph's dull blue eyes squinted, glancing around at the men who had an array of guns pointed at him. "Don't get nervous with that hardware, I was just fetching your misplaced boy back to you."

Devil Anse gleefully retorted. "Then I better lend you my compass because you were headed in the wrong direction." He pointed over to his son. "Now cut my boy loose and send him over to me."

James slowly walked his mare over to his prisoner and unsheathed his hunting knife. He hastened to cut the ropes that bound his hands together. Johnse cautiously rode towards the Hatfield party without glancing back at his captors

"I wish you'd keep your boy away from my little girl Anderson," said Randolph.

"I think them children got a mind of their own."

"My little girl is my concern; and I don't want your boy trifling with her anymore."

Devil Anse stood up from behind the ground cover and walked out holding his lever-cocked Henry Rifle. "It wasn't neighborly of you to try and take my boy where he don't want to go; but I'll try to see that he doesn't bother your little girl anymore."

Randolph nodded in agreement.

The former Confederate sharpshooter slung the large bore rifle over his left arm, pointing it directly at Randolph McCoy. "Now, I want you to get off them nags and get down on your knees. Then I aim to see you apologize to Johnse."

Jim Vance covered his mouth to keep from laughing.

The McCoys nervously looked at each other.

"I mean now!" Devil Anse yelled.

Randolph, Tolbert and Pharmer all dismounted and sunk down on the dirt ground. Only James remained on his horse.

Devil Anse was surprised when he saw the Pike County deputy refusing to get off his mount. He took several steps forward and pointed his Henry at the defiant man. "What's a matter with you boy, don't have any respect for your elders?"

"I respect you Mr. Hatfield. I ain't afraid of you but I respect you. But I won't crawl on my knees for you," James replied.

Randolph looked up at his oldest boy. "Best do what he says."

The square-jawed lawman looked down at Devil Anse. "I got a bottle of whiskey in my saddlebag, mind if I have a drink before you shoot me?"

Devil Anse roared with laughter, looking back at his supporters as they too began to chuckle. "This boy's got stones; he's the only one in bunch that I got any respect for. All right boy, take as many snorts as you want, I ain't gonna shoot," he said. He lowered the barrel of his rifle away from James and back at the other McCoys.

The elder Hatfield pointed to his oldest son. "You fellers got something to say to my boy" he asked rhetorically.

With more than a half-dozen rifles pointed at his family, Old Ranel cleared his throat and took a bite of crow. "We're sorry for what we did tonight," he said looking over at Johnse.

Devil Anse motioned Randolph and his sons to stand up. "I guess I won't shoot you tonight. Consider this a warning against troubling my family again."

Wanting to leave quickly, the dejected McCoy clan climbed

onto their horses and rode off into the darkness.

Devil Anse turned his attention to his son, as he stood with his arms around Roseanna.

"I should have done everyone a favor and let Old Ranel take you back to Pikeville.
Maybe time in a jail cell wouldn't do you no harm.

Johnse hung his head down.

Devil Anse continued on with his scolding. "You need to thank your uncles, your brother and our friends for helping you tonight. I warned you about this, didn't I?

Johnse kept his head lowered and remained silent in response to his father's lecture.

Roseanna abruptly chimed in. "He's right you know. We can't keep this up any longer. You got to stop pretending you're ever going to marry me Johnse. It just ain't going to hold water no more."

Johnse began to drift off allowing the words of his father and lover to become a distant drone while occasionally nodding in agreement. He had another girl on his mind and would quickly detach himself from the one that nearly got him thrown in jail. He wasn't worried about his father's anger because he was that sure in reality, the old man reveled at outcome of his mission on this cool October evening.

■■■

CHAPTER THREE: DIRE CONSEQUENCES

The McCoys didn't forgive, nor forget Hatfield clan's bold display of arrogant force. They were God fearing men as much as anyone else in the Valley; and didn't mind getting on their knees to pray now and again. Of course they would have preferred it to be out of respect for the Lord and not a Henry rifle. As a result of this insult, tensions remained high, but for a time there were no acts of violence between Randolph and Devil Anse's family.

Two years would pass without incident, after the ill-fated romance between Johnse and Roseanna had abruptly ended. The oldest Hatfield boy plucked another young woman from the McCoy family tree. Her name was Nancy and she was Roseanna's cousin. She was also daughter of the late Harmon McCoy, who had provided human target practice for the Logan County Wildcats.

Nancy McCoy didn't have a father looking over her shoulder and she carried on with Johnse impunity. In spite some minor objections from her mother, the two infatuated lovers were eventually married. Sadly, Roseanna had still held out hope that Johnse would marry her. The news of this courtship and eventual nuptials with her cousin shattered her already damaged heart.

During the days of European monarchies, when a family or a nation was at war with one another, a marriage between the two hostile factions would often bear peace. During this time of heightening strain, this was not the example that was followed by the Hatfield and McCoy clans. The men in the latter family began to resent pretty boy Johnse, exclusively taking after their women. This displeasure would fan the flames of anger and would give hell's lake of fire a run for its money. The Pike County election of August 7, 1882 would be a day this conflagration would begin.

Elections in Pike County were always an occasion for celebration and the summer balloting was no exception. Once again, the polling place was set up at Jerry Hatfield's cabin, because it was concentrically situated, easily traveled to from either side of the Tug River.

It was blistering hot, even for the middle of August. Therefore, for the sake of the voter's comfort, it was paramount to have adequate shade. Jerry's place provided that, with the abundance of Scarlet oak timbers laden with unripe acorns. The neighboring white ash trees bore clusters of spotted blooms that from a distance appeared like small white bouquets. Cool, crystalline water emanating from the Hatfield Branch flowed only a hundred paces away the voting tables.

This particular round of voting attracted a substantial assemblage from Pike and Logan Counties. There was plenty of food and liquor and voters began partaking of the spirits early on. Tolbert and Pharmer McCoy were in attendance and proceeded to consume large amounts of distilled beverages.

Tolbert was a twenty-nine-year old man who some thought carried a boulder on his shoulder in place of a chip. Though less than fair sized, he had a good build for his height. After toiling away in a Pikeville logging camp for two years, he had developed an upper body that was taut and muscular. His facial features were square and rugged, with an oddly broad nose and disproportioned mouth. He was born with a lazy right eye, which made it difficult for him to look directly at someone else. He was acutely sensitive about this feature. It made him troublesome to read and at most times intimidating.

Trouble at the last Pike county election didn't discourage Elias and Ellison Hatfield from attending the festivities. Both residents of Logan County, the two cousins crossed the waters of the Big Sandy to attend the polling party at Jeremiah's cabin.

Elias was tagged as "Bad Lias" because of his generally poor disposition. He swore profusely, displayed no manners around women, never attended church on Sundays and perpetually spit out wads of a foul chewing tobacco that rotted his ferret like teeth.
The gruff man didn't particularly care for anything that didn't involve tipping a whiskey bottle or shuffling a deck. His brother, Deacon Anse, believed in the tenants of the good book. The sinful man teased his well-tempered sibling labeling the scriptures "A nice fairy story." Opposite in every way from his kin, he preferred the company his less refined cousins Devil Anse and Jim Vance.

On Election Day the McCoy brothers nested under the agreeable shade of a century old birch tree. Leaning their sweaty backs up against its huge trunk, the two guzzled several glasses of keg beer. Tolbert observed Elias leisurely enjoying the cover of a neighboring tree, some twenty yards from the polling tables. "See that peckerwood over there?" he asked his brother, pointing his small hand towards the

Hatfield man.

Pharmer didn't move a muscle of his tall, sinewy frame, as he nonchalantly glanced over at the relaxing man. "I'd be blind if I didn't."

Tolbert extracted his razor sharp knife from his buckskin sheath and began cleaning his dirty fingernails "He's kin to Floyd Hatfield."

"That's a disgusting habit" said Pharmer, focusing his opal green eyes on his brother's knife.

He ignored his brother's reproach. "It just gnaws at my innards watching that son-of-a-bitch. He doesn't belong here. Why don't he vote in his own county where he lives?"

"What, are you looking for things to fret about today? Forget about that man; he ain't bothering you. Why don't you fret about getting us a couple of more cold beers?" Pharmer said, closing his eyes and quickly nodding off to sleep. He Left his brother to ponder thoughts about the Hatfield's.

With no one to listen to him, Tolbert began muttering to himself. "Nope, it just ain't right. They take things that don't belong to them. They take up after our women folk like they're sheep. When we objected to Johnse's meddling, that old Devil pointed his Henry at us." Tolbert took a drink of whiskey and washed it down with more beer. Though the alcohol had rendered Pharmer sleepy and mellow, it had the reverse effect on his brother. He became increasingly edgy with each sip, shifting restlessly while he watched his brother snoozing peacefully.

In his mind, Tolbert was looking for a reason to pick a fight. Though obscure, he recalled a minor transaction that occurred between his father and Elias Hatfield. It involved the sale of an old birch wood fiddle, some years earlier. He remembered that Randolph mentioned in passing that Elias still owed him money for the instrument.

"That ain't right," he thought. "That bastard should pay his debts. A man shouldn't go around cheating people," he said under his breath.

In a self inflicted state of agitation, he stood up slowly, dusted his clothes off and glared in the direction of an unsuspecting Elias Hatfield. Filled with strong drink, he wobbled for a moment, took a deep breath, wandering over to the object of his ire. The typically surly Hatfield man was minding his own business, resting comfortably. "Looks like a shit hawk has come a nesting under a shady tree" Tolbert slurred.

Bad Lias raised his faded confederate cap, opening one eye.

"You speaking to me boy," he answered drowsily.

"Yeah you old coot, you ever aim to make good on your debts boy?"

Elias became more wakeful. "Would you mind coming to the point boy, you're interrupting my nap time."

He impatiently scowled at the older man. "You still owe a dollar and fifty cents to my Pa, for the fiddle he sold you."

"Then that's between me and your Pa, so why don't your run along before I thump your ass." He drew his cap down over his face again to ignore the drunken young man.

During his brief logging career Tolbert frequently fought over his size, always with the desire to prove himself against larger men. It irritated him that Elias was attempting to ignore him. He boldly kicked the soul of the reclining man's brown boots. "You couldn't whip me in a month of Sundays," he said.

A rankled Elias abruptly leapt to his feet, taking a hard swing at McCoy. The two men tumbled to the ground, both slinging wild punches. After getting pummeled by several savage blows in his face, neck and arms, Tolbert attempted to get up. The stronger, bigger man pushed the game little one securely back on the grassy soil. When Pharmer and Randolph Jr. saw what was happening, they rushed to the aid of there out matched brother.

A crowd of spectators started to assemble around the ensuing melee. One of them bolted over to inform Deacon Anse that his brother was involved in a serious altercation. The preacher, a man of considerable size, loped over to where the scuffle was raging. Bellowing out at the top of his lungs, his normally temperate face was contorted with anger "Stop this commotion at once!" His bear sized forearm jerked Pharmer, then Randolph Junior off his piled upon brother. Latching onto Tolbert's shirt collar, the big man yanked him violently into a headlock. "Cool down son, just cool down" he said soothingly.

Tolbert was enraged but could feel the sheer strength of the man who now held him tightly in his grip.

"Breath deep son, breath deep and calm down" the deacon whispered patiently. Losing air, the wild young man's body began to go limp as Pharmer and Randolph Jr. stood by watching. Though they wanted to, they dared not raise a finger against Reverend Hatfield. They knew that their father would never endorse such an act of disrespect against his friend. Cautiously, the preacher released the angry lad from his unbreakable hold, scrutinizing the faces of the four younger men.

"What in God's name is vexing you boys today; can't we have a little peace and quiet?" the deacon asked.

In a huff, Bad Lias aimed his finger at Tolbert "That little bastard started the ruckus. I was lying here minding my business."

The Deacon turned to scold his brother. "You watch your mouth Lias, there's women folk around. You're the older man here and you should act like it."

"Save the preaching for your flock, you know I'm headed for damnation."

Anderson Hatfield held to the belief that his wild brother would someday mend his sinful ways. "You should no better than fighting here. You need to set an example." He stood behind his brother and dusted the dirt and loose hay from his back. He then turned his attention to the instigator of the trouble. Placing his arm on Tolbert's beefy shoulder, the deacon walked him away from the still gathered crowd. "Son, I don't know what my brother did to stir you up this way and I really don't care. What I do know, is that you need to stay away from him and make an effort to mind your manners. Can't you just have some fun today?"

Tolbert felt a little foolish as well as impatient at having to endure a sermon about his behavior. He crossed his arms tightly, looking away from the well-intentioned peacemaker. In his mind he was right and anxiously waited for the Deacon to stop talking. "Yes sir Deacon, I'm sorry" he uttered to placate him. After the brief homily, an uneasy calm fell upon the festivity.

The election gatherings had witnessed fights before; but this one caused a fair amount of talk among the growing number of people that were in attendance. Later on that afternoon, the crowd focused their minds back on the celebration.

Tolbert and his brothers went to eat lunch at the wooden picnic tables. Bad Lias resumed napping with his cousin Ellison Hatfield. He was Devil Anse's younger brother and was a large, good-natured man that was well liked by most people that knew him. He arrived at the polling place dressed in torn black overalls and a white cotton shirt. He also sported a preposterously wide brimmed straw hat, similar to the ones worn by the Amish in Pennsylvania. He loved his sun hat and good naturedly accepted a lot of teasing about it.

"Is that your hat or are you carrying a raft on your head" said Tom Stafford.

"Looks like that hat be about ten sizes bigger than your head"

Selkirk McCoy quickly added.

A broad smile appeared on Ellison's darkly complexioned face. His lengthy black beard swayed back and forth, as he walked towards Tom and Selkirk. "Boys, You outta be thanking me. I thought I'd tote some extra hay for your livestock."

At about three o'clock in the afternoon, Ellison stretched his long body out after his restful afternoon sleep. He savored the taste of Jerry's homemade whiskey, while sitting a short distance from the old cabin.

Tolbert still possessed a dose of unfulfilled fury smoldering inside him. He began to take notice of the other mellower Hatfield, who in turn only had celebration on his mind. He sat carefully scrutinizing Ellison's every move, manifesting hateful thoughts in his mind. The more he drank, the more poisonous his deliberation became. He had no reason to give him an argument as he barely knew him. The one thing he knew for certain was that he was Devil Anse's younger brother, which was sufficient.

Tolbert McCoy was now completely intoxicated, with a translucent, dead look in his eyes. The sun simmered down on his face with not a hint of afternoon breeze. A large group of women were engaged in conversation on the front porch of Jerry's cabin. Many of the men were still resting and digesting colossal quantities of food and drink. His hands were sweaty, so he reached down to scoop up a handful of dirt, which he wiped between his palms. He stripped off his shirt, quickly walking over to where Ellison was sitting.

McCoy momentarily stood in front of the unsuspecting man, eyeballing him with a stone cold stare. "Old man, why don't you pull that ridiculous hat over that ugly face of yours" he said.

"What?" Ellison asked, unsure of the younger man's intent.

"You heard me you son-of-a-bitch."

"Boy I don't want any quarrel with you," the older man answered calmly.

Tolbert violently kicked some dirt on to the saddle blanket, upon which rested Ellison's food plate. "Well you got a quarrel you yellow bastard," he shouted.

Ellison strained his patience to remain calm. "Go sleep it off boy. I don't want to hurt you."

"Hurt me, you ain't gonna hurt me. I'm hell on earth." Tolbert's glazed eyes sent a chill down the older man's spine.

Ellison barked back in hopes of scaring the drunken young man. "Get on out of here you little shitbird."

For twenty fearful seconds the two men stood frozen in front of one another. Finally, the young belligerent ended the staring contest. He lunged forward taking a rapid swipe at Ellison's slightly protruding stomach. The larger man noticed a flash of reflective light, while simultaneously experiencing a burning feeling across his stomach. He looked down to see blood beginning to spurt out on his white shirt.

In a red-faced fury, Tolbert charged at Ellison, tightly clutching a blood soaked hunting knife. In a panic, the wounded man attempted to snatch the lethal blade away from his attacker; but the younger man was too agile for him, sticking him again and again.

Pharmer and Randolph junior took notice of the ensuing fight, rashly running to aid their brother. Like Roman Senators who murdered the great Caesar, They pulled out knifes and began slashing Ellison. A group of spectators gathered, watching the altercation in horror but did nothing.

Deacon Anse was resting with his head lowered on a serving table and heard screams coming from just beyond the polling area. He rose up and ran towards the noise. "God Almighty, what is it now?" he mumbled. He quickly jumped in to separate the participants of this new fight. "Jesus, Mary and Joseph are you crazy" he shouted.

A disoriented Ellison was badly injured and lying on the ground. He stood up, staggered for a moment and picked up a large rock. With stone in hand, he wobbled, balanced himself and stumbled towards Tolbert. A loud bang, as unexpected as thunder in the middle of the night, came from behind wounded man. His face contorted with a hideous look of pain and dismay as he crumpled forward and then slammed to the ground.

Standing behind Ellison was Pharmer McCoy. His hand shook as he clutched a smoky barreled forty-five revolver. The young shooter stood with a look of disbelief, almost not comprehending his actions seconds earlier. The preacher stooped helplessly over his cousin, touching his white shirt, which was now red with blood.

Ellison was severely wounded and the McCoy brothers knew it. Making matters worse, there were scores of witnesses to the brutal attack. All eyes fell upon the three young men who perpetrated this savage display.

"You just bought yourself a mess of trouble boys," said Deacon Anse. He looked at them with disgust and disappointment. At that moment, Tolbert realized it was time to depart the polling place. He turned to his accomplices, calmly instructing them to turn around and start walking.

The three McCoys quickly stepped through the gathering crowd, trotting out to the wooded area around Blackberry Creek. When Elias Hatfield realized what was happening, he ran to the edge of the hollow emptying his revolver at the fleeing men.

"Why'd you let em get away Anderson?" shouted Bad Elias.

The preacher waived his hand. "Calm down, they ain't gonna get very far on foot. We'll throw a posse together and fetch em back."

Several distant cousins including Matthew, Tolbert and Joseph Hatfield stepped in to consult with the preacher. They formed a semi circle around him respectfully awaiting his instructions. Joseph had formerly been a deputy in Blackberry Creek. "What can I do to help Uncle Anderson?" he asked.

Looking thoughtfully at the volunteer, Deacon Anse raised his right hand. "Boys, as local constable, I'm hereby authorizing you, to be deputies of Pike County. Try your best to bring those boys back and without any gunplay."

The volunteers gathered up horses and supplies and set out after the McCoys, who were bound for their home by way of the Hatfield stream. Without time to get their horses, the offenders were captured within the hour.

Ellison Hatfield sustained a collection of stab wounds numbering nearly thirty. In addition, there was a large bore bullet lodged in his back. On a makeshift stretcher made of canvass, a group of bystanders carried him to the house of a man named Anderson Ferrell. He lived across the Tug Fork in a place called Warm Hollow, about two and a half miles from Blackberry Creek.

Ferrell was considered by his neighbors to educated healer. He had obtained some medical training during the Civil War, while serving in the Confederate Army. There were no other doctors that were closer than Pikeville or Logan Courthouse. And these towns were both too far away to help the situation. It was determined by the bystanders that if anyone could aid Ellison, Ferrell would be the one for the job.

With an awful grimace on his face, the wounded man moaned in low tones as he was carried over the areas of rough terrain.

The five stretcher-bearers arrived at Ferrell's cabin at four thirty in the afternoon. The puzzled man opened his front door to see the distressed face of Selkirk McCoy. "Can you help him? He's in an awful bad way."

After a cursory glance at the dreadfully sanguine man, the former medic sighed. The situation reminded him of his daughter handing his wife a china dish broken into a dozen pieces and expecting her to repair it. "I can patch him up, but he doesn't have much of a chance," he said grimly.

When the men removed Ellison's now crimson shirt, Ferrell was shocked at what he saw.

During the war he was never required to tend to anyone with so many stab wounds, in addition to a bullet in his back. Summoning all his training, which had been marginal at best, the retired practitioner worked well into the evening cleaning and stitching Ellison Hatfield.

Blackberry Creek buzzed with excitement. It was late in the afternoon but not one person had left Jerry's place. What had earlier been a celebratory mood now became somber as bystanders waited to see what would happen next. After he was informed of the incident, Randolph McCoy arrived at the precinct, to be with his sons. The three nervous men were the temporary custody of Preacher Anse.

The deacon took the Randolph aside to give private counsel. "Ranel, I'm telling you this as a friend and not the law. There's already talk of lynching these boys. So I suggest you let the posse get them to Pike County Jail sooner than later. It's the only way there going to be safe. You need to get them there before Devil Anse gets to you first."

Randolph quickly became angry. "Damn him to hell, he won't touch a hair on them boys" he hollered. Deep down in his nervous gut, he knew this was a threat he could not backup. He anxiously rubbed his hands together, pacing up and down the front of Jerry's Cabin. Turning toward Tolbert he scowled for a moment. "This is a real nice spot you got yourselves into."

His captive son hung his head down. "I'm sorry Daddy" he replied.

Randolph Junior looked towards his father forcing a smile. "We'll take care of those Hatfield sons-of-bitches."

Randolph hardly glanced at his child. "Shut up boy, you've got enough trouble without running your young mouth."

At four thirty in the afternoon, a six man posse departed to safely escort the Hatfield boys to the jail at Pikeville. The small contingent was made up of mostly Hatfield's who lived on the Kentucky side of the Tug Fork. These men had not been involved in any disputes with the McCoys and a few had even intermingled in holy matrimony. Joseph, Tolbert and Matthew were honest men and did not want to see these boys lynched. They intended to see that the prisoners were turned over to the Pike County authorities, but not before stopping for dinner at Floyd Hatfield's place.

Joseph Hatfield, who was only man with experience as a

deputy, was chosen by the deacon to lead the well-meaning posse. After a late afternoon supper at his cousin Floyd's, Constable Joe determined it would be prudent to spend the night at the house another cousin named John. He lived at the northeastern most point of Blackberry Creek. He ignored the preacher's counsel that time was of the essence. To avoid riding all night to get to Pikeville Jail, Joseph decided his men could get a fresh start in the morning.

Late in the afternoon, a vigil for Ellison was underway at the home of Anderson Ferrell. His brother Devil Anse and several friends circled the bed where the wounded man had been placed. The medic had done his best, to tend to his horrific wounds, with the knowledge that damaged man could not be moved. All he and the others could do was watch and wait.

The somber group sat in the candle lit room and remained silent as they watched the wounded man labor to breath. As Ellison's condition deteriorated, it became clear that he was going to die. Standing silently over his brother, Devil Anse softly touched his face for a moment. His impassive appearance gave no hint to the emotions that his quick mind was experiencing. He turned to speak to his son Cap and others in the room. "Let's saddle our horses and get provisions, we got work that needs tending to."

Later that evening, news of his younger brother's dreadful condition reached Valentine Hatfield. He was Devil Anse's older brother and considered himself to be the patriarch of the Logan County clan. His nickname was "Wall," as he was known as a man with unerring good judgment. After hearing of his brother's brutal attack, he rode back to his cabin to assemble a group of handpicked men. This situation was one of concern and the oldest Hatfield brother believed that he should take charge of it. Watching the road with piercing green eyes, his face was nearly obscured by his bushy white eyebrows, beard and a huge silver mane. He impatiently awaited the arrival of his sons-in-law, Doc, Plyant and Sam Mahon and five other friends.

As Justice of the Peace in Logan County, Valentine believed he was endowed with a right to administer justice. While he waited for his aggregate, he gathered up his bedroll, his cap and ball revolver and his most prized possession. This was a recently purchased Winchester, model 1876. By midnight, all eight men Wall summoned stood on his front porch awaiting his instructions. Stepping through the archway of his enormous cabin, he shook his head with approval as he looked into the faces of his well-armed friends. "We'll sleep here for a few hours and ride out at dawn.

Unfortunately for the McCoy brothers, their guards got a late start on the morning following the violence. After a big breakfast, the unknowing posse left John Hatfield's place at about mid morning. En route to Pikeville for less than twenty minutes the small band bumped into Wall and his associates.

Valentine's fourth brother Elias had joined up with him on the way to Blackberry creek. He was the youngest of the quartet of kinsmen, who were leaders amongst the West Virginia Hatfield's. This Elias was known as Good Lias, a nickname that matched his generally sunny disposition and also distinguished him from his nasty cousin.

As the men from Logan County approached Joseph Hatfield's meager group, Wall and Elias slowly walked their mares out front, leaving a distance of about one hundred yards between them and the rest of their men. Wall quickly sized up the opposition before speaking to Joe. He was not directly related to these Hatfield men, who made their homes in Pike County. The Logan Justice of the Piece didn't want to overtly threaten the use of force in taking the prisoners. His objective was to subtly imply that he would if his hand were forced.

Matthew Hatfield who rode alongside his cousin was watching the oncoming posse and leaned over to his cousin Joe. "Who's the big son-of-a-bitch out front?"

"That's Wall Hatfield from Logan County," answered Joe.

The careful old man slowly trotted within yards of the now tense group guarding the three McCoys. Joseph mustered a stern face, as he rode out to meet the approaching man. "What can I do for you Wall?" He softly inquired.

"I want to take your prisoners back to Logan Courthouse. That's why I'm asking hear you and now, to peaceably to hand the boys over to me. I'll make sure they get treated fair; and besides they should be tried here, where the ruckus occurred." Valentine made every effort to sound courteous, while maintaining a confident, yet unyielding manner.

Joe thought for a moment and then spoke bluntly. "How do I know you aren't going to hang them boys, if we turn them over to you?"

"You have my word, that won't happen. And you've always known me to be a man who doesn't ever break his word."

The temporary deputy nodded in polite acknowledgement to the proposition put forth. "Let me parlay with my cousins" he answered.

"Sure you take your time boy."

Joe Hatfield turned his horse, taking his time as he rode the twenty yards back to his group. As he turned away he wiped the nervous perspiration off his forehead. He had already made up his mind on what to do; yet he politely conferred with his cousins. "The old man says he's a going give these boys a fair trial and we don't have to take them to Pikeville. He says they ain't going to hang them."

"You trust him?" Tolbert inquired

"He's law in Logan. I think we can trust him." Joe turned to his other cousin. "What do you think Matt?"

"I think we done what we could to see the law served."

Tolbert Hatfield bowed in agreement.

Joseph wanted to believe what Wall told him, ignoring the nagging voice inside his head. Yet he thought better of tangling with the other posse, particularly when within minutes, they doubled in size.

Devil Anse, also on the trail to Blackberry Creek arrived on the scene just after Wall boldly proposed to take custody of the McCoy brothers. He wore two ammo belts wrapped around his upper body. One was for his shotgun and the other for his Henry rifle. Atop his head was a wide brimmed, felt hat and his neck was hidden by a red bandanna.

Between the two brothers, they had collected nearly twenty armed men. Devil Anse smiled at his older brother and dismounted with the regal splendor of Robert E. Lee. "Who among you is a friend to the Hatfield's? If you are, then step forward and form a line" he shouted.

Between the two groups, every man present moved forward, including Devil Anse's sons Johnse and Cap, Tom Chambers, Charlie Carpenter, The three Mahon brothers, Alex Messer, Moses Christian, Daniel Whitt and several others. These men were all kin or good friends of the family, pledging an excursion into hell if Devil Anse and Wall asked them. He now looked over at Joe Hatfield and his puny band as they sheepishly watched the recruiting session. His dark brown eyes gave no hint of nerves or emotion. "We won't need you boys anymore, we're taking charge."

Joseph felt a knot in his gut as he relinquished custody of the McCoy brothers to the large vigilante group. "Do what he says."

The Mahons quickly transferred Tolbert, Pharmer and Randolph Jr. over to where the giant posse was positioned.

As Joe Hatfield's group headed back to their homes, he turned towards his cousin Matthew. "Do you think we did the right thing?" he asked.

Matt shrugged his broad shoulders. "What choice did we have?"

As they retreated Wall yelled out a warning. "If you or your friends try to dry gulch us on the way out, we will shoot the prisoners."

Joe pivoted his horse around. "Even if I wanted to and I don't, I ain't got the means to bushwhack you today."

"Well just make sure that you stay on your side of the river" added Devil Anse.

The surrogate guards placed the three McCoy brothers into a shaky old corn sled, with their hands bound behind their backs. "Please don't kill us Mister Hatfield" Randolph Junior said looking over at Devil Anse. He felt cold, his voice trembled and he started to sob.

Tolbert nudged his brother's leg with the tip of his boot. "Close your mouth, don't give them the satisfaction of knowing your scared" he said with bravado.

Wall made a disingenuous attempt to reassure the youth. "You got nothing to worry about, unless my brother dies."

Old Ranel, who had remained at Jeremiah Hatfield's home all night, arrived on the scene just in time to witness the Pike County men give up custody of his three sons. He watched them one last moment, as they were carted away in the rickety wagon. His heart ached as the brutal realization of their peril was sinking in. With this in mind, he headed for the town of Pikeville. There he would seek the help of the authorities. The distraught man traveled all morning and most of the afternoon to reach his destination, with hopes of enlisting the service of the local sheriff.

Pikeville was a young, booming Kentucky community. It was attracting a new and professional class of businessmen, with young families that were looking for a prosperous future. Randolph quickly trotted past a large new bank, several stores and a saloon before he finally discovered the office of the sheriff. The old man hastily hitched his horse, to the horizontal post in front of the modest building. He ran inside, informing the clerk he needed to immediately see the Sheriff.

Sheriff Fuller calmly walked out from his tiny office and politely invited Randolph back in. He was a dark skinned, rangy man, who attired himself in a tailored suit, with a gold watch and chain. His choice of hat was a black Derby and he displayed the bearing of a gentleman. "My Name is Sheriff William Fuller," he said extending his long arm out to shake hands.

Randolph gave the lawman an apathetic handshake. "My name's McCoy and I've come to you for help" he blurted out.

Fuller motioned the older man to sit down. "Yes, go on."

Old Ranel plopped down in the chair. "Some armed men have taken my sons as captives. These men call themselves the law, but there not. They're just a bunch of vigilantes."

"What did your boys do Mister McCoy?"

"They supposedly stabbed a man."

"Did they?" Fuller asked bluntly.

"No Sir. That is plain ridiculous. They're good boys and they don't make trouble."

The lanky sheriff fidgeted with his quill pen, repeatedly pulling it out and returning back to its ink well.

Randolph's eyes suddenly became watery. "Their captors aren't gonna give my boys a fair trial, they're just gonna take them back across the river and murder them. You're the law, you have to help me."

The sheriff offered moderate concern. "Who are these people that have your boys?"

"It's the Hatfield's of Logan County. They're being lead by a Devil Anse Hatfield. They got near about twenty guns with them."

Fuller's eyebrows rose. "Devil Anse Hatfield, I've heard of him."

"Then you may know how dangerous he can be when his blood is up."

It wasn't an issue of bravery. However, Bill Fuller wasn't foolish or ambitious enough to send a posse into West Virginia after a group of well armed men. Even if had wanted to, he didn't have the authority to cross the Tug River into a neighboring state.

With a polite smile he explained his position to Randolph. "I'm sorry Mister McCoy, but I don't have any legal right to ride into West Virginia; and even if I did, I couldn't raise a big enough posse to deal with that many guns. Folks around here are store clerks and working folk. They haven't got what it takes, to go up against men like you're after. I'm afraid my hands are tied in this situation."

Randolph had nothing to say in reply to the sheriff, choosing simply to stand up and leave his office. He departed town in a frustrated, exhausted state. There had been very few times during his lifetime that he had felt as alone as on the road back to his home. Assessing that he had no other options available, he decided to wait for news of Ellison's condition.

The large Hatfield posse took them north, across the Tug River. Once they were on West Virginia soil, the McCoys were transported by wagon to Mate Creek. There they remained tied up, held at an old abandoned schoolhouse.

At dusk, the sky became Cimmerian with charcoal clouds, bringing on a powerful storm. The rain began to pound down in terrific waves that produced an ominous creaking on the rooftop of the aged edifice. A lantern was hung on the front of the schoolhouse, which created a glowing, yellowish hue on the wall. Cap Hatfield was chosen to stand the first watch, propping himself against the wall with his big feet resting on the porch rail. His illuminated silhouette reflected off the wall and could be seen from the road.

Johnse bundled up the collar on his navy blue cloth jacket, while walking out to the covered porch way of the schoolhouse. Slight drips of rainwater fell on the rim of his raven colored hat. He set himself down on the thin, wobbly, rectangular board that was laid upon two molasses barrels. Removing a silver flask of moonshine from his top pocket, he handed it to his younger brother Cap who gladly took a long swig.

"Lovely weather we're having isn't little brother?" observed Johnse.

"I like the rain. Makes me feel peaceful for some reason," Cap answered in a low voice. He gave a rare smile to his older sibling. "So offer me some pearls of your wisdom."

Johnse took a drink, reflecting momentarily. "I don't know, maybe if I hadn't taken up with Roseanna, all of this wouldn't have happened."

Cap was a bit surprised by his brother's somewhat penitent statement. "Hell, that's got about as much to do with this as the Rebs firing on Fort Sumter. Nobody forced them boys to call out Uncle Ellison. He wasn't bothering with anyone. If you asked me, they were looking for trouble and trouble is what they got."

Johnse stared out at the heaping amount of water coming down, which began to create a muddy hole in front of the cabin. "Though he ain't showed it, Daddy is plum mad about Ellison. I wonder what him and uncle Wall's next move is?"

"We wait"

"Uncle Ellison is going to die ain't he Cap?"

Cap looked back with sad blue eyes. "Yeah he probably will."

Johnse didn't say anything for a few minutes as he deliberated on the day's events. "I wouldn't want to be one of them three boys inside."

"Neither would I," Cap answered with a sly smile.

Within the schoolhouse, it was dingy and damp, even for the

month of August. The last time it had been used was before Lincoln was President. The shivering cold McCoy brothers were made to lie on the hard wooden floor. Every few hours, a grim messenger would bring a report from Anderson Ferrell's house, where Ellison was growing worse. For the captives, the gravity of their situation was sinking in.

Tolbert and Pharmer were older and attempted to put on a brave face but Randolph Junior was becoming more frightened with each passing moment. "Them fellers aim to kill us" he lamented, and began to cry.

"That ain't gonna do no one no good. You need to buck up and act like a man," Tolbert advised.

"Let him be, he's just a kid; and he's right, we're dead, sure as sunrise tomorrow" Pharmer said in a doleful voice.

Tolbert mustered a forced grin. "Don't think I'm not scared, but Pa ain't gonna let these boys kill us without a putting up some kind of fight."

Across the Tug River Randolph was doing a lot of talking. He recruited not one volunteer outside of his own family that wanted to oppose the large armed band. The worried old man bent a group of sympathetic ears, but that was the extent of it. Although he had two other sons that were old enough to tote a rifle, it would be suicide to go up against the Hatfield's twenty guns. And, with no legal authority to assist him with his dilemma, Randolph resigned the fate of his children to the hands of the Almighty.

At ten o'clock that evening, Sarah McCoy arrived at the schoolhouse with the intention of seeing her hostage sons. She had traveled seven hard miles from her home to Mate Creek, which was located on edge of the West Virginia border. Tolbert's wife, Mary Butcher accompanied her. She was quiet, ordinary looking and carried herself without displaying any signs off worry. Her black dress that was caked with mud from the now flooded dirt road.

Sarah had become unglued ever since the Hatfield's had taken her boys. Dark black, puffy circles appeared under her brown eyes from hours of weeping and apprehension. When the two women arrived at the old schoolhouse, Wall stood on guard duty. Most of the other men were inside the cabin or outside in two nearby tents.

Sarah stepped up to the porch of the schoolhouse but understood she could not enter without permission. I've come to see my boys," she declared, as the rain poured heavily on her long, doughy face.

Wall shook his head. "No Ma'am, best be on your way."

Valentine Hatfield, I've come to see my boys and I ain't leaving lest the rain washes me away."

The silver haired man looked back at the woman with an unyielding eye.

After another few minutes, Devil Anse came out on the porch to join his brother.

Ignoring Wall, Sarah suddenly directed her pleas to him. "Anderson Hatfield, I must be allowed to see my boys. I know you're not scared of nothing or no one. But I'm told that you're a fair man. Why won't your brother let us inside? All you men can't possibly be afraid of two women."

Still attractive at fifty four, Sarah peered into his stern eyes with a deep yearning that nearly penetrated his stoic armor. "You must understand what it's like to be standing in my shoes. You must know that I can't leave without seeing my sons."

Displaying no shred of emotion, Devil Anse remained silent, listening intently to the despairing woman. For nearly a half an hour, the rain gushed steadily down, on the bonnet covered heads of Sarah and Mary. The Hatfield brothers stood like statues, refusing entrance to the two trembling women. With myopic strength, Sarah kept up her pleas, which wore down their resistance. Finally, the two men slowly stepped aside, permitting the soaking wet women enter.

Sarah desperately embraced and kissed her sons frantically as her pent up emotions spewed out. She painfully embraced the notion that angel of death was chasing her boys at breakneck speed. She sat in front of them and began to address the Hatfield brothers. "Please let my boys go, they're good boys; anything they done yesterday they surely don't deserve to die for." Her eyes circled the room, scanning the faces of all the men. Haven't any of you ever made one single mistake? Give my sons a chance and hand them over to the proper authorities."

"If our brother lives, your sons will too" replied a resolute Devil Anse.

The distressed woman began to pray aloud in for the recovery of Ellison. Her voice had an unsettling, banshee like quality. It was affecting the mood of the guards, as most men hated to see a woman in such a state. They understood what they might have to do to those boys. They didn't need to be reminded that they were once Sarah McCoy's babies. At midnight the two women were instructed to leave.

On the morning of August 9, 1882 Ellison's life was slipping away. It was a stunning, clear day after the previous night's downpour. Devil Anse had spent the late evening hours at the house of his youngest brother Elias. Early on the following day, He traveled to Ferrell's home to visit his brother for what he grimly realized would be the last time he would see him alive.

When he entered the darkly lit room, he was saddened to see how poorly his brother appeared. In an amazing feat of final resolve, a dying Ellison weakly recounted the Election Day battle to his kinsman. After this last dialogue, he fell into a deep sleep. His breathing became slower and more labored.

As the visibly shaken man was ready to leave, he turned to speak to Ferrell. "I know you've done everything you could for my brother and I want to thank you for it."

"I've watched many men die during the war and it's never easy or pleasant; but I'm a Christian man and I would do the same for you or anyone" Ferrell answered solemnly. Devil Anse robustly grasped his hand and returned to the old schoolhouse.

Sarah McCoy and Mary Butcher were also drawn back to the schoolhouse, to await news of Ellison's condition. This time they were refused entrance to the cabin. The activity at the abandoned structure also attracted the fascination of many spectators. These people milled about in suspense, speculating and speaking in whispered voices.

On his way back to Mate Creek, Selkirk and his son Albert McCoy had met up with Devil Anse. Ellison Mounts, the bastard son of the dying man also joined them. He was a large, slow-witted man, who was acrimonious about his father's condition.

At noon, Deacon Anse arrived to visit his cousins from across the river. The preacher had conferred with Old Ranel earlier that morning and was on a diplomatic mission on his behalf. He was admitted into the cabin immediately, conducting a brief inquiry with the McCoy brothers. He asked them if they were being treated all right, to which they responded yes. Afterward, he turned his attention to his steadfast relations, to whom he spoke his peace."

"This is no way to meter out the law. These boys deserve an opportunity for justice, in a real court of law. I'm asking you now, before something tragic unfolds, to give those boys over to me. I promise if they're guilty, they'll get what's coming to them."

"Them boys got the same chance my brother got. Besides, they got nothing to fear if Ellison lives" Devil Anse replied sternly.

The doubtful preacher folded his arms and searched his cousin's intense dark eyes for a speck of commiseration. "Vengeance is the Lord's providence."

"Ellison ain't your brother and justice is my providence" Wall answered.

"So if Ellison dies, you're going to murder them boys, aren't you."

Devil Anse turned away from his cousin and walked towards the entrance of the schoolhouse. He stood at the doorway, looking out at the panoramic beauty of his surroundings. Without raising his voice but in an easily audible and calm manner he answered his cousin. "Wall and I don't see things the same way you do. I ain't no preacher but I have read the bible cover to cover on several occasions. I have a certain passage etched upon my mind. An eye for and eye, tooth for tooth, hand for hand, foot for foot, burn for burn, wound for wound and bruise for bruise."

The deacon became irritated with his cousin's interpretation of the scriptures. "That was the Lord's ordinance passed down to Moses the law giver. You can't really believe you have the right to use it the same way."

Devil Anse turned around to face the gentle preacher. "I know you got a good heart and you mean well, but I ain't got any more time to argue."

Walking to where his kinsman stood, the preacher gently placed his hand on his cousin's back. "Then God have mercy on you and them boys," he said sadly. The dejected man stepped out around his cousin and left the schoolhouse feeling like a failure.

At three o'clock that afternoon the Hatfield brothers were resting, when a messenger came to inform them that Ellison was dead. Devil Anse let no emotion stir while receiving the ill tidings. He leaned over his older brother to gently wake him up. Looking down at him he uttered only three words, "We're leaving now." The older sibling rose off his bedroll and put on his gun belt.

"Get them boys up and into the cart, we're riding out of here now" Wall instructed Moses Christian and Tom Chambers.

The McCoys collectively experienced a cold chill running down their spines. They knew their hasty violent actions had taken them to the end of road.

"Where you taking us" Randolph Junior fearfully asked the guards. They grimly ignored his question, roughly placing the prisoners into the wagon.

"Steady boy, it ain't over yet, Daddy won't let us down" Tolbert said with a brave face. Pharmer and Randolph McCoy junior fatefully hung their heads down, for they didn't believe that for a flicker of a moment.

Wall and his brother agreed that they would return the McCoys back to Kentucky soil. About twelve of the twenty men guarding the corn sled left Mate Creek at four o'clock and headed back to cross the Big Sandy. On the way to the river, a man named of Joe Davis rode up to meet the vigilante group.

Davis had dutifully responded, when he got word that the Hatfield brothers wanted to speak to him. Wall immediately ordered the procession of horses stop. He and Devil Anse rode about twenty feet head of the others, to softly engage Davis in conversation.

Joe was a tall, nervous looking fellow, who was dressed gray overalls. He had been at the Election Day celebration and had witnessed the stabbing of Ellison. Wall and Devil Anse had one question they needed answered.

"Joe, Did the young one take part in the killing?" Devil Anse solemnly inquired.
Davis, who normally led a fairly mundane life, suddenly felt important. He understood the power of his testimony word would determine the destiny of a young man. He looked at the two men and paused for dramatic effect. "I'm afraid he did" he answered.

The fate of all three brothers was sealed. They were put into a skiff and transported across the river. Tolbert stared at the wooded terrain, for what he knew would be the last time. He glanced at the amber trees that he so often taken for granted, noticing dozens of black crows descending upon them. The ebony birds cackled in a wild frenzy as if they understood that something ominous was about to happen. His thoughts then turned to his wife Mary, knowing she would be left a widow. That he would not have a child to carry his seed. The hard-edged son of Randolph McCoy felt a frantic sensation and had trouble breathing as he tried to steady himself. He looked at his two brothers with a face wrought with contrition. "I'm sorry, it's my fault. I got drunk and did a foolish thing and now we're all gonna pay for it."

Randolph Junior trembled as if he were experiencing a seizure and could not keep from sobbing. "I don't want to die; I ain't had no chance to live."

"I know, I know" Pharmer said gently. "All you got left is to die like a man." Although his hands remained bound behind him, he managed to lean over and kiss his younger brother's pale cheek.

The skiff came to a stop, just across the river from Mate Creek. "Now we're in Kentucky, lets do what we have to do" Wall impatiently said to his brother.

The McCoys were marched over to some Papaw trees, just

yards from the river. Tolbert and Pharmer walked with a brave, steady stride, but Randolph Junior's legs wobbled, causing him to collapse twice before his last steps were over. Tom Chambers and Cap Hatfield tied the doomed men to fruited trees. They were bound with their hands behind them and their ankles tied at the bottom. The Hatfield men lined up about fifteen feet away from the prisoners and all of them with rifles or pistols in their hands. Devil Anse walked over to where the brothers were bound, making a point not to look directly into their frightened eyes. "Boys, if you want to make peace with your maker, you better do it now," he said, quickly turning and joining the other men.

Pharmer and Randolph Junior began to pray aloud. Tolbert chose to remain silent.

After allowing them a few minutes, Wall stepped in front of the shooting party and began to speak as if he were a town crier reading a proclamation. "As a legal magistrate of the state of West Virginia, I find you three boys guilty of the murder of Ellison Hatfield; and the punishment is death. The sentence to be carried out forthwith, on this day of August 9, 1882. Have you anything to say?"

Randolph Junior was close to hysterical, crying heaps of tears. Pharmer trembled but was silent. Tolbert steadied himself and resigned to his fate. He took in a deep breath, managing one last measure of bravado. "Yeah, I got something to say. I'm sorry I killed your brother, but you ain't nothing but killers yourselves and I'll be waiting for you in hell."

With those final words spoken, Devil Anse instructed the volunteers to raise their weapons and commence firing. The killing party slowly lifted their guns, taking careful aim at the three young men about to be executed without trial.

As the first volley was fired, Randolph Junior screamed out, with a bone-chilling yelp. Tolbert and Pharmer McCoy were ripped apart and killed instantly by the fusillade. Their younger brother stirred for a second, lifting his head. He weakly glanced into the faces of the men who had just fired, as a trickle of blood began to dribble down the side of his contorted face. The shooters thought it inconceivable, that he survived the first volley. The men in line stood completely paralyzed at the unsettling sight of this wounded boy clinging to life.

Cap Hatfield abruptly raised his Winchester, firing a single shot into Randolph's head. "There, the job's finished now." He spoke as if he had just put a wounded animal out of its misery.

The other men in the Hatfield group stood quietly, for about a half-minute after the shooting. "Shall we cut em down?" asked Charlie

Carpenter.

"No leave em, that'll send a message to anyone else who thinks of murdering one of my kin" answered Devil Anse.

The gruesome execution had been carried out with relish by some and strict loyalty by others. The twelve executioners polled back across the Big Sandy River, returning speechlessly to their homes.

*****

James McCoy was Randolph's oldest son. He was thought to be the most affable and levelheaded member of the family. He was also respected by the Hatfield's as the bravest. He alone had once stood up to patriarch of the family. Refusing to get on his knees, even as he faced the barrel of a rifle, he had earned the old man's absolute admiration. Brave but not reckless, he did not possess the firepower needed to rescue his brothers from the Hatfield posse.

At the time of the execution, he was less than a quarter mile away. He had chosen not to remain with his morose father. When the killing party had crossed the river, James had gone to the house of his Uncle Asa. After he heard the rounds of gunfire, his heart sank.

"What was that all about?" Asa said foolishly.

"I think you know" James answered. He and his uncle hastily gathered a couple of friends and walked to where the sound of guns had emanated.

It was early evening when his worst fears were confirmed. As James and his friends rounded a clearing by the Tug, the torches they carried gave light to a hideous sight. The bullet riddled corpses of his three young brothers gently dangled in the warm evening breeze. James walked over and touched the body of his younger brother Randolph, whose top right forehead had been blown off. He ran his fingers through his blonde hair, which was caked with blood.

James stood for minutes without speaking a word. He sat down with his head on his knees in front of his murdered kinsmen and began to weep. The only rational thought he could summon was what that the men who did this to his brothers were evil men. Moments later, he stood up, withdrawing his bowie knife and with the help of his friends cut down the bodies of his dead brothers.

The now lifeless young men were carried back one at a time, the short distance to Asa's cabin. There, they were laid into a wagon, covered with an old saddle blanket, awaiting the final journey to their father's home.

Within minutes after the bodies were taken to Asa's cabin, Deacon Anse arrived to offer his condolences. As he stood beside the wagon with despairing eyes, he bowed his head and began to pray.

"Vengeance is Mine, and retribution, in due time their foot will slip; for the day of their calamity is near, and the impending things are hastening upon them. For the Lord will vindicate his people, and will have compassion on His servants, when He sees that their strength is gone and there is none remaining, bond or free. And He will say where are their Gods, the rock in which they sought refuge? Who ate the fat of their libation? Let them rise up and help you, let them be your hiding place! See now that I am He, and there is no God besides Me. It is I who put to death, and give life."

CHAPTER FOUR: WAGGING TONGUES AND LOADED GUNS

Ellison Hatfield was promptly buried the day after he died, by his three surviving brothers and immediate family. Although it was a solemn occasion, both Wall and Devil Anse felt compensated by their course of action. Conversely, Randolph McCoy was not so contented, with their brand of swift justice.

A violently bitter, miserable Randolph McCoy laid sod upon his three sons on August 12, 1882. His family was devastated by their violent end in the prime of their lives. The funeral was the largest that Blackberry Creek had ever known. To guide their rode to redemption, Deacon Anse was asked to say a prayer over their bodies. Aided by a local church choir, a beautiful rendition of "Shall We Gather at the River" was sung by a crowd of over one hundred people. Though Mister McCoy did not enlist the aid of any of these good folk while his boys still inhaled air, they came out in abundance to pay their last respects.

One uncommonly immense, single grave was prepared. It was located a quarter mile from Randolph and Sarah's cabin. The tranquil site was selected, under the over hanging edge of a lush green, precipitous hill. Sam who was Tolbert's younger brother by one year, constructed three simple pinewood coffins. He started the arduous task of assembling them prior to his brother's executions. When he received word that Ellison had died, he knew that his kinsman would be in quick need of them.

At the funeral, Deacon Anse spoke of the absolute peace that the boys now possessed, as well as their ascension to the kingdom of heaven. Randolph found little comfort in these words. To him, that kingdom was intangible. All he could understand was that his sons were deprived of their time on earth. It never seemed to occur to old man that Tolbert was largely responsible for putting himself and his siblings into their respective graves. He could not and would not believe this; and for this reason he would endure greater suffering.

The McCoy patriarch elected to seek formal adjudication for his unhealed wounds. In the month that followed the deaths of his sons, an inquiry was held at Pike County Courthouse. The honorable Judge George Brown determined that there was sufficient evidence to suggest that Randolph's boys had been murdered. He issued indictments against the twenty men accused in these killings. This included Wall, Elias and Devil Anse, as well as his two sons Cap and Johnse. The judge correspondingly swore out bench warrants, for several people who were sought as witnesses for the state of Kentucky. This group consisted of Deacon Anse, Anderson Ferrell and Sarah McCoy.

Sheriff Bill Fuller was given the task of serving the indictments levied against the Hatfield clan and their supporters. Pikeville was a thriving town that was full of immigrant merchants, stodgy businessmen and young families that had settled there to make their fortune.
The sheriff occasionally had to incarcerate the town drunk or break up a domestic squabble. He was not prepared to take on Devil Anse and his allies. He didn't believe that Randolph McCoy's private war was town business. It was therefore no surprise that he failed to serve one warrant to any of the men involved in the McCoy shootings.

In spite of his obstacles, Randolph was relentless in his efforts to locate an ally for his blood feud against the Hatfield's. He found one in Perry Cline. He was brother in law to the late Harmon McCoy. That fact that Devil Anse was one of the Logan Wildcats who had snuffed out his sister's husband, may have been reason enough for Cline to harbor a Grudge. However, this wasn't the reason for his enmity. His anger was born out of losing four thousand acres of prime land to Hatfield, in a business deal that had transpired some years earlier. This transaction forced Cline to leave his native Logan County and relocate to Pike County. There, the disgruntled man made a living as a Pikeville attorney and part time jailer.

Cline was affable, striking up a great many friendships in new surroundings. His connections and political influence availed him all the legal resources in Kentucky. The law office was tightly adjacent to the County Jail and was nearly Lilliputian. Inside, there was an enormous desk that consumed about half the space in his modest chamber. Behind the desk, there was a rack of unsteady shelves that held stacks of files, which were covered in dust and cobwebs.

When Randolph sat down in the worn out chair in front of Cline's desk, he experienced a sense of claustrophobia. As the lawyer stood up to shake hands, he reminded McCoy of a Praying Mantis. Tall and rail thin, yet the grieving man felt the great physical strength in his grip. He possessed sharp features that endowed him with predatory attributes. His dark, deep-set eyes seemed to absorb every detail, as he greeted the old man with friendship and sympathy.

Cline leaned forward on his desk with his long hands folded together while offering a faint smile. "I'm glad that you came to see me. After all, you and I are family."

Randolph nodded in polite agreement.

"I was awful sorry to hear about your sons and I know that's what brought you here today."

"I appreciate that, you don't know what it's..."

The mournful father was interrupted by the attorney. "I am painfully aware of what it's like to lose someone you love, but you need to play your hand smart. In matters such as these there are legal channels required. It will require time and patience, but together we shall endeavor to seek justice" Cline assured the old man.

"Justice ain't what I'm after. Retribution is what I want."

"The desire for vengeance is born out of anger and loss. You have a right to that. However, anger is a blind passion that clouds a man's thinking. It causes him to make mistakes. The Hatfield's and their rifles may appear to be invincible. Yet the simple stroke of a pen can put an end to a war, put a man in prison or get him pardoned from the hangman's noose. You let me handle this my way and I give you my word, that we'll have your killers brought in and hanged" Cline promised.

Old Ranel felt comfort in the calm and wise counsel of his new found confederate. He longed to unload the responsibility of seeking revenge, upon anyone who would shoulder it. "Violence has taken my boys taken away in the prime of their lives. If you have a way to beat these bastards without..." Tears began to well up in the cheerless eyes of the heartsick old man. "Please, it would be a blessing if you could help me."

Perry Cline reached his long arm out and tightly clenched the sobbing man's hand. "It will be alright. As much pain as you're feeling now, I assure you that your enemies will reap the same, pound for pound, measure for measure.

During the spring of 1883, Randolph made a second appointment to see his newfound friend. He possessed a dangerous habit of imparting his woes to anyone who was foolish enough to listen. Through his loose talk, information of his meeting was relayed to Devil Anse. He too had utilized legal channels to settle several disputes. The careful veteran was aware that a clever lawyer was as dangerous as a loaded pistol. He now was apprised of the recent alliance between McCoy and Cline. It was clear that Old Ranel was never going to let things rest between their families and Devil Anse decided it was time to consider a preventative measure.

He summoned his recently married son Cap back home. As a Rebel sharpshooter, he had performed more than his fair share of killing. He never enjoyed it but surmised that occasionally it was a necessary component of survival. Some men he believed were born to it, embracing it as a natural vocation. His son Cap was one of those men. He wasted no time or sentiment in directing his violent offspring to seek out their tenacious enemy.

Before he departed, Cap's father had advised his son to enlist the aid of his Uncle Jim. He was a man cut from the same deadly cloth. Vance looked upon Cap as a second son and his nephew felt more comfortable around him than any other living soul.

Jim Vance was tall, sturdy as timber and wound as tight as a pocket timepiece. During the Civil War, he had served alongside Devil Anse in Company B of the Forty-fifth Battalion. Towards the end of the conflict, the two men were the principal organizers of The Logan Wildcats. They regarded themselves as a group of home guards serving the interests of embattled Confederacy. Next to Devil Anse, Uncle Jim was estimated to be the deadliest member of the disbanded brigade.

For the job of bushwhacking Randolph McCoy, Cap and Jim recruited three other men to assist them. The five shooters staked out positions on the road to Pikeville just past a secluded stream called Narrow's Branch.

As they took refuge behind three crackling dry hedges, Vance crawled over to where Cap was hidden. "This is a prime spot; we'll catch the old rat in crossfire."

"Hell, we're doing him a favor Uncle Jim," Cap said as he loaded his sawed off shotgun.

Vance cocked his head. "How's that?"

"We're gonna send him up to heaven to be with his boys."

Uncle Jim smiled like a raccoon. "I'm glad you're on my side."

"Until hell freezes over old man."

"How'd you get so mean at such a young age?"

"Daddy says I spend too much time with you," Cap said proudly.

"Maybe that's it" Vance said chuckling.

"If it ain't could be I was just born that way."

"I wish we could breed more like you," Vance concluded.

The hidden assassins didn't have to wait very long. After sitting for just shy of an hour, two horsemen approached from the eastside of the road. Vance signaled the other men with two owl hoots and the group of Hatfield guns opened fire.

With the first volley, two startled horses reeled, violently flinging their riders onto the gravel road. One man quickly jumped to his feet, fumbling to pull his revolver. Before he could raise his pistol, Vance wounded him in the shoulder. In the seconds that followed, Cap got a good look of the two men lying on the road.

"Shit Uncle Jim, neither one of them boys is Old Ranel, he exclaimed.

"Are you funning me?" Vance asked

Cap responded incredulously. "Would I joke about that?"

Vance fired his revolver in the air and with his extended arm made a circling motion. "Let's go boys," he shouted.

On the road back to Logan County Uncle Jim repeatedly shook his head as he trotted his horse alongside his nephew. "I don't like shooting the wrong feller, he said apologetically. It sends the wrong message."

"What message is that?" asked Cap

Folks will start thinking it just ain't safe to travel in Pike County no more."

Cap nodded in agreement. "They will at that; but them boys could have picked a better time to cross our path." His answer, which he hadn't intended to be humorous, elicited a roar of laughter from the entire group. This was welcome relief from feeling embarrassed by their mistake.

Henderson and John Scott were the unfortunate victims of the bungled ambush. As they bore them no malice, Uncle Jim and Cap were relieved to hear that the two suffered only minor wounds. It was strange coincidence that the Scotts were Randolph's cousins, but had never taken any part in any hostilities.

*****

In spite of their recent losses, the McCoy family could claim one small victory. Nancy McCoy was making Johnse one miserable man. Though she was a pretty woman, the newlywed had a tongue that was a sharp as straight razor. After their infatuation had worn thin, the blushing bride decided to become the biggest shrew in Logan County.

As they knew her to be a girl of good character, Devil Anse and Levicy Hatfield would have been pleased if Johnse had married Roseanna McCoy. On the other hand, they held to the notion that their son's new wife was a terrible gossip; and that she was sharing family information about what their neighbors were now calling a feud. However, the failure of their marriage certainly did not fall upon Nancy's shoulders alone. She was correct in discerning her husband's lack of character when it came to his roving eye.

Nancy's sister Mary took great delight in discussing the misfortunes of others. The two sisters visited often and their conversation would frequently turn to the latest feud news. Johnse had a weakness for telling his wife things that would be shared with Mary, who would in turn relay the information to Old Ranel.

The feud gossip between Mary and Nancy, real and imagined, made Cap very unhappy. He hated fact that Johnse was weak and being controlled by his wife. He didn't relish the foul situation that a McCoy woman had in effect infiltrated his family. He resolved that he would put an end to the wagging tongues he was convinced were sharing Hatfield secrets. During the summer of 1882, he decided it was time to teach his new sister-in-law a lesson.

Fundamentally, Cap believed it would be bad manners to personally tangle with his brother's wife. Right or wrong, he loved Johnse and would not bring that shame upon him. Nancy's sister Mary would be the object of his scheme. With her, he would not be violating standards of family protocol. He did not consider her to be his kinfolk in any shape or form.

Cap enlisted the aid of a friend named Tom Wallace. He was an excellent volunteer for the mission, as he had an ax to grind with Mary's daughter Megan. She had recently cohabited with Wallace, but had left him after she discovered her deceiving lover had staged a mock wedding ceremony. She promptly moved back home with her mother and stepfather. Way beyond forgiveness, the young girl was rightfully incensed at this contemptuous behavior.

Megan's loving mother was married to a farmer named Bill Daniels. He was a meek, peace loving man, who like not unlike Johnse was henpecked by his dominant wife.

On the occasion of Cap's visit, Mary, her husband Bill and young Megan were all home doing chores. As dusk came, Daniels was in front of his cabin, brushing down his overworked plow horse. His voice was nearly drowned out by the chirping of crickets, as he hummed out "The Yellow Rose of Texas." The exertion relaxed him, providing welcome relief from the shrill words of his nagging bride.

"Just get your hands in the air Mister and keep them there" a voice ordered.

Unsure of what was happening, Daniels spun around to see two big men that he didn't know. Their faces were barely concealed by bandannas that they wore over their mouths, but he did not recognize them. To make matters worse, he was clueless why they brandished pistols while motioning him into his house.

"I don't want any trouble, I got no quarrel with you mister," he assured the masked men.

Mary heard the sound of loud voices and immediately ran to the front of her cabin. "Get your tail back in the house, before I shoot it off" shouted one of the intruders, who motioned her inside.

Bill Daniels was becoming scared as he focused on the pointed barrel of Cap's forty-five. "What's the problem friend, do I know you?"

Mary recklessly chimed in. "I know who you are Cap Hatfield."

Cap pointed his finger at the woman. "Your problem is that you talk too much. You been talking bout my family's business and I aim to put an end to that."

"Daniels mustered enough courage to speak in a trembling voice. "Hold on friend, you got no call to talk to my wife like that."

Cap raised his pistol, placing it firmly alongside the nervous man's temple. "Mister, I'm told you're a nice fellow; so you just stand there real quiet and don't give me any trouble, you might just live through the night."

With two guns aimed at him, Daniels could do little else but comply with the command of his unwanted guest.

Under his mask, Tom Wallace smiled while he held Daniels and his former fiancée' at gunpoint. They all watched in silence while Cap removed a cow's tail from inside his coat. "This will teach you to keep your mouth shut bout the Hatfield's" he admonished. As those words left his mouth, he shoved Mary up against the wall and proceeded to lash her.

"Stop it" Megan screamed as her mother howled with pain.

Wallace leered at her with sheer sadistic ecstasy, relishing her distress. "Shut up woman, yours is a coming next."

While lightly flogging his victim, Cap began to lecture the woman. "You're damn lucky you ain't a man, or I'd whip you a damn site worse."

As his wife took a beating, Daniels stood helplessly watching. He had to keep taking deep breaths at the sound of his mate whimpering. When Cap was finished with Mary, he held his rifle on Daniels, while Tom Wallace took his turn thrashing Megan.

Though the poor girl had done nothing to him, Wallace took his time beating her back raw with cuts. Megan was the one who had been lied to, yet her spurned man adhered to the concept that he had been the injured party. "I'm done, she's had enough" he informed his partner.

Through his thin mask, Cap glared at poor Daniels. "Mister, we ain't got any fight with you. Just tend to your women and this won't happen again."

The helpless husband returned his captor's icy stare but did nothing. The punishing duo cautiously backed out of the cabin, never removing their eyes from the man of the house. Feeling satisfied, Hatfield and Wallace calmly walked to where their horses were tied and headed off into the night.

The two women were left shaking and humiliated. The markings on Mary's back were not nearly as severe as on her poor daughter. Though Cap had gone lightly, it was not so for his accomplice. Megan's back had several areas of torn flesh, which her mother immediately cleaned and dressed.

In the process of tending to her child, Mary could hardly look at her spouse without the utmost contempt. She felt betrayed and powerless to inflict any retribution upon the two men she considered worse than animals. "What kind of man are you? You should have let them kill you, before you allowed those pigs to touch a hair on our heads" she scolded.

Bill Daniels lowered his head in shame. He knew nothing about guns or violence. He was not foolish enough to pursue Cap Hatfield or Tom Wallace, who did.

*****

Mary and Nancy had a brother. On the day of the whipping incident, he was in the process of hastily packing his saddlebag. Lewis Jefferson McCoy killed some poor soul, by the name of Fred Wolford, at a Peter Creek dance. The young man claimed he was insulted and shot the violator in the neck. Larkin, Jeff's older brother prudently advised him to leave the state of Kentucky.

As he rode out of Pike County his one thought was about where he would end up living. Jeff considered roaming out west to possibly seek his fortune. He had read a handful of dime novels authored by easterners that painted a dazzling picture of scantily dressed dance hall girls, marathon poker games and heroic gunfights. In reality most of these writers had never traveled west of the Mississippi.

Jeff's mind pondered the adventures he would enjoy if he rode to Texas or Arizona but his horse headed towards West Virginia. Nancy invited her brother to come visit any time he pleased; and with his bridges burned behind him, there was no better time to accept her hospitality. He wandered across the state line to his neighboring state, into the welcoming arms of Johnse and Mrs. Hatfield.

The unhappy couple made their home in a place called Grapevine Creek, just under two miles west of Devil Anse. Nancy was churning some butter when she noticed a familiar figure moving up the road. She quickly removed her apron, using it to wipe the beads of sweat from her forehead. Planting her strong hands on her round hips, she smiled broadly when she made out her brother's handsome face.

"You're as pretty as ever little sister," said Jeff. He jumped off his copper colored mare and robustly embraced her.

Nancy grasped his outer arms tightly, gently stroking his cheek. "You're a welcome sight. What are you doing here?"

"I Decided I wanted a change of scenery and that I'd take you up on your offer of a visit."

"You are most welcome. Be nice to have some real family in the house."

Jeff McCoy was tall, good-looking and as vain as a male peacock. As he rested his lean frame on Johnse's comfortable hammock, his sister treated him like the Prodigal Son. He now reflected on why he committed murder only three days earlier. He concluded it was his affable manners and charm with women that brought him to his present circumstances.

*****

Bright yellow torches flickered, surrounding the makeshift wooden dance floor at the Peter Creek Church social. The voluptuous hips of Melanie Nelson swayed to the sweet sounds of the fiddle playing its hypnotic melody. Jeff's head moved in rhythm with the comely young girl who had attracted his stare. After the banjo strummed the last note of the Virginia reel, Fred Wolfed strolled over to retrieve some punch for his date but not before involving himself in a discussion with friends.

With the dispatch of a starving hawk, Jeff quickly seized his opportunity to speak with the object of his newfound admiration. Coming up behind the slender, well-developed young woman, he spoke in a near whisper. "What is a fine young lady doing in the company of the mule I saw you dancing with?" he asked.

All at once, she found herself insulted, attracted and intrigued. She answered without turning around to face him. "Maybe I like mules. They're dumb animals but they're easy to control."

Jeff moved his face within inches of Melanie's ear. "It really sounds very dull. With me it would be a damn sight more exciting. Besides, he dances like a deaf man."

Melanie turned around just as the sound of a medium tempo three-step waltz began to permeate the air. "Why don't you show me how it's done then?"

"Gladly," he said extending arm.

Most of the men she had danced with either had two left feet or at best, did an adequate job of moving. The fine-featured woman felt at ease as the cocky young man twirled her around the dance floor. Every move he made was natural, graceful and without any thought or apprehension about his steps.

When the music ended he beckoned his pretty partner off the dance floor. "My name is McCoy, Lewis Jefferson McCoy, but my friends call me Jeff."

She smiled as he shook her hand. "Well, Mister McCoy, you dance real pretty. My name is Melanie Nelson."

Just as those words left her mouth, angry Fred Wolford interrupted their brief introduction. "Who's this gentleman?" he asked sarcastically.

The slightly embarrassed young woman spoke up immediately. "Fred, I want you to meet Mister McCoy. He just asked me to dance while you were talking."

Wolford gave Jeff a hard look for a couple of seconds. "Well now that you've had your dance why don't you run along?"

Jeff McCoy smiled and shook his head. Wolford thought this was a curious reaction. "What's so amusing Mr. McCoy?"

Jeff looked at Melanie and addressed his response to her. "Well, I guess there is just no accounting for taste."

This elicited a rapid, agitated response from his rival. "What's that supposed to mean?"

Jeff smiled again. "Every time I meet a sweet young gal, they're always in the company of some rude asshole." Jeff McCoy tipped his hat to the lady and then turned to leave the social.

Wolford did not want to appear like a coward in front of his attractive companion. "Hey," he shouted angrily. Grabbing McCoy's shoulder, he spun him around with his left hand and swung a rapid right cross. His rival was knocked on the floor, which caught the attention of the other guests in attendance. He reached his hand up to his mouth, noticing blood beginning to drip from his lower lip.

"That will teach him some manners," Wolford said cupping his fist. He glanced down at Jeff who was slightly dazed, sitting on the ground wiping his face with a handkerchief. Once again a smile came upon his slightly bruised face. Wolford couldn't believe how quickly he composed himself. "You are one curious son-of-a-bitch" he said.

McCoy reached into his boot, extracting a thirty-two-caliber derringer pistol. He abruptly pointed it at his rival, firing a single round into his neck.

The Two Hundred-pound man hurled his hands up to his throat, pressing them tightly in a futile attempt to stem the tide of spurting blood. During the last seconds of his life he stared at his killer with disbelief and fell on the hard floor.

Witnesses watched in shock as the handsome murderer calmly walked over to a teary-eyed Melanie. "I'm sorry I ruined your evening," he said politely. She looked down as the apology left his mouth. The upset young women could not glance at the face of the man who had charmed her so completely just a few minutes earlier. As the cold-blood McCoy walked away, not one person thought of stopping him.

Jeff forgot his troubles for about a week, before he heard about his sister Mary's beating. His other sister reluctantly informed him that Cap Hatfield and Tom Wallace were the ones who inflicted her so-called punishment. She knew that her brother looked calm on the surface but had an explosive temper and was capable of great violence.

It was breakfast and Nancy served Jeff fried eggs with a huge slice of sizzling ham. "Just eat your breakfast and forget about it," she advised.

"I'm not hungry now."

"By that look on your face, you'd think I served you up varmint stew."

"Those two bastards will regret the day they touched my sister," Jeff answered.

Nancy began to get worried. "Don't go and get yourself killed. Cap's meaner than a snake and just as dangerous."

He pulled Nancy's small frame toward his, embracing her for a moment. "Don't worry, I can take of myself."

When Jeff McCoy crossed the border into Mate Creek, he didn't know if the Pike County law was after him. He figured with several witnesses to the shooting of Fred Wolford, it was a safe bet that they were. In spite of the risk of returning to Kentucky, he formulated the curious plan to apprehend Cap Hatfield and his accomplice Tom Wallace. With the assistance of his friend Josiah Hurley, he planned on taking them to the Pikeville Jail. Oddly, it didn't seem to occur to Jeff that he too, would probably be jailed upon setting foot in Pike County.

On a simmering hot, August afternoon, Tom Wallace was working for his friend. He thoroughly weeded Cap's vegetable garden, while Hatfield made a trip to a local medicine man's house. His wife Nancy had taken sick with a severe case of pneumonia, which left her bedridden.

Wallace, who was a tireless workhorse, relished his associate's occasional patronage. He was a hard up sharecropper, who didn't possess the resources of the Hatfield family. The poor man had no luck in reaping a successful harvest the previous season, which left him broke and hungry. He desperately needed a little extra money for the upcoming planting season. Cap would have given his him the money but he knew Tom wouldn't accept charity. He would repay his debt by turning in more than a good day's work. This was before Jeff McCoy and Josiah Hurley paid an unexpected visit.

Tom looked up from his work to see two riders coming up the trail towards Cap's place.

"Get your hands where I can see them shit pockets!" shouted Jeff, drawing a Navy Colt from his shoulder holster.

"Do I know you Mister?" Wallace calmly asked. He continued tilling the soil, looking innocently up at Jeff who remained astride his horse.

The angry McCoy straddled his long barreled pistol across his horse's neck. "No but I know you, you're the brave feller that whips helpless women."

"I don't know what the hell you're talking about boy. You must be mistaking me with some other man."

McCoy cocked back the hammer of his revolver. "No if your name's Wallace, then I believe I'm not mistaken."

Tom placed his large hand atop the handle of the rake, resting his whole weight upon it. "Yes, I'm Wallace, now I'd be obliged if you told me who you are and what hell you want."

McCoy pointed his pistol at the big farm hand. "My name is Jeff McCoy. I'm taking you back to the Pikeville Jail, where they don't cotton to men who whip women folk."

"All right friend, just don't let your finger get jittery on that trigger."

Jeff motioned his gun hand towards the nearby horse belonging to Tom Wallace. "Get your mount boy and be quick about it." Hurley and McCoy waited impatiently, while their prisoner swiftly saddled his horse. "No tricks now boy or I'll splatter your brains on the road."

Wallace's mind raced with thoughts of departing. "These idiots won't get very far with me" he thought to himself. Tom had walked the trail ever since he was a boy and knew every inch of the road from his shack to Cap's place. As the three riders left for Pikeville, his keen eyes waited for the exact moment he would attempt his escape.

About a quarter of a mile down from Cap's place, Jeff and Josiah were chatting complacently. The big farmer saw the perfect spot to jump and run, which coincided with his captor's lack of attention. "Yee haw!" he yelled in a blood curdling voice, which startled his unsuspecting guards. He leapt from his horse, running like a hive of angry bees were chasing him.

Jeff and Josiah both felt stupid, flustered and angry at the same time. McCoy looked over at his friend as if their prisoner's flight was his fault. "Shoot the bastard" Jeff screamed.

"Don't yell at me God dang it" Hurley responded indignantly.

The two men drew rifles from their saddlebags, wildly blasting at the escaping prisoner. Though a sizable, corn fed man, Wallace moved with the agility of a frightened deer. In spite of his speed, he felt a sudden stinging at his side. Pumped full of fearful adrenaline, the runner had managed to a dodge all the shots, save one that grazed his hip.

As he fled across the north side of the trail, Wallace considered his best option, which he decided was going back to Cap's cabin. He ran for the high ground, cutting across a small, narrow ridge to the rear of the structure. The winded man charged inside the unlocked door, quickly barring the entrance to the house. His friend had left his shotgun on a rack over the fireplace and Tom quickly grabbed and loaded it.

Wallace dripped with sweat as he dodged behind the thick wooden door, finally taking notice that his heart was palpitating. Seconds later, several forty-four bullets whizzed through the front window of the cabin. He crouched down on the floor, crawling over to the bed where Cap's wife was laying. "Nancy, I got to get you out of the line of fire" he said gently grasping her hand. Tom gingerly pulled her down off the bed, onto the floor next to him.

"What's happening?" Nancy weakly asked.

Wallace took the outer edge of the linen sheet, wiping the feverish woman's forehead. "You lie still and hush now, everything's gonna be all right." She smiled at Cap's trusted friend and nodded.

"Come on out Wallace. We'll kill you if you don't" Jeff McCoy hollered from outside. Raising the barrel of his Winchester, he blasted off a couple of more rounds. Wallace cowered down just underneath the open window from inside the cabin.

"Why don't you get on out of here, you McCoy son's of whores" Tom yelled back. Just as those words left his mouth, another volley of bullets ripped through the walls and windows of the little house. He placed his shotgun above his head and fired a round through the window.

"Come on out boy. We ain't gonna shoot if you come out with your hands in the air.

Wallace felt responsible for Nancy and didn't want anymore beads flying past her head. "I got sick women in here you chicken shit bastards," he called out.

Hurley and McCoy halted their gunfire, looking at each other with apprehension. "Who's the woman? Jeff inquired.

"Nancy McCoy, Cap Hatfield's missus."

"Is that right, you in there Mrs. Hatfield?" Josiah asked suspiciously.

"Yes," the sick women weakly hollered.

"I told you she was in here you idiots," Wallace chided.

Jeff looked pensively at his friend. "What do you think?"

Josiah mechanically loaded four more cartridges into his repeating rifle. "I think we lost our crack at this bird and I don't want to risk hurting his woman."

"Alright, I don't want no part of that either. That's not what we came here for" Jeff concurred.

The two accomplices had effortlessly captured Wallace and had just as easily lost him while not paying attention. They knew they couldn't rush the cabin or smoke him out without the possibility of injuring the sick woman and so they left empty handed.

When he arrived home, Cap was not a happy man. It was late afternoon as he returned to find his humble abode full of bullet holes. After seeing the damage he ran to his wife, gently kneeling beside her. "Are you all right baby? I've brought your medicine," he said in a soft voice.

Tom Wallace stood in amazement, as he had never seen any such mild traits displayed by his friend. Cap fluffed her blanket and bent over to kiss her forehead.

Nancy weakly reached her hand up, placing it delicately on her spouse's cheek. "I'm alright."

Cap's face was full of rage when he looked up at Wallace. "Who did this?"

Tom knew his friend's anger wasn't directed at him but it unnerved him just the same.

"Another McCoy I never heard of. Say he's kin to Johnse's wife. I think he said his name was Jeff."

He nodded at his friend. "Figures it's a stinking McCoy. They just won't quit while they're ahead." Walking over to a chest of drawers, Cap grabbed a box of shells. "You say this bird's name is Jack?"

"Jeff" answered Tom.

Taking a deep breath Cap pointed toward the stock of his Winchester. "Tomorrow morning I'm having McCoy for breakfast. You want to come along?"

Wallace smiled back at his friend. "Do you have to ask?"

"You're true blue and I'm much obliged to you for looking after my wife." Cap reached out his massive open hand towards his friend and Tom grasped it tightly.

The next day, the two men rode out to see the Logan County Justice of the peace. After hearing Tom recount his story, the judge swore out warrants, for the arrest of McCoy and Hurley. Cap also arranged to get sworn in as special constable, which gave him the authority to take the offenders into custody. This was provided they remained on West Virginia soil.

Cap and Tom took a chance, heading out to the home of Hurley, who lived a half mile down the road from Johnse. Tom couldn't believe his eyes when he saw the duo sitting on Josiah's front steps, leisurely sipping beers. Cap couldn't believe the men that boldly attacked his home were that slack.

"That's him," Wallace said, pointing at Jeff McCoy.

Cap coldly and calmly looked into his new enemy's eyes. "So you're the house killer. I expect anyone bold enough to come after me and my kin to be a hard case. You don't look like much."

"That's funny because I'm real impressed by you," Jeff quipped.

"If I put a bead between your eyes maybe you'll feel different."

Jeff took another sip from his beer. "Maybe"

"Why are you taken up after me Mister?" Cap asked.

"Could be I don't like men who whip women folk."

"Could be some folks can't tend after their women better. Could be I've got warrants swore out against you and could be I'm taking you back to Logan Courthouse."

"What for?" Jeff asked.

"I don't like idiots shooting up my house when my sick wife's inside."

"Mister, I didn't know your wife was there; and left when I learned she was."

"Well you should've learned to never come looking for me."

In spite of the fact that neither Cap nor Tom had drawn a weapon, Jeff and Josiah gave no resistance. They passively let their hands be bound in front of them and let their two guards take them east on the trail towards Logan Courthouse.

Wallace who was usually a quiet man couldn't help but needle Jeff McCoy. "It seems like the shoes on the other foot today don't it boy."

Jeff said nothing back, as the four men trotted along eating trail dirt and enduring hot, humid weather.

After three hours of plodding along towards Logan, Cap was hungry and wanted a rest. He decided to stop at the home of Bill Ferrell, who served in his father's Confederate regiment. Wallace thought his friend's decision to leave the prisoners untended seemed strangely overconfident. Yet they were instructed to remain on their horses, which were tied to a hitching post while their captors went inside to eat.

As Tom Wallace pulled his rifle from his saddle scabbard, he remained skeptical. "You sure they'll be alright if we leave them here?"

"Yes, yes, I'm sure." As he walked inside Ferrell's place, he leaned in and whispered to his friend. "They're too stupid and scared to run," he told him. Cap winked at Wallace. "And if they do run…" he ran his forefinger across his throat making a slashing motion.

Tom's fears of escape were correct. Just moments after they left them alone, Jeff struggled to free his hands from the rope that held them together. The desperate man couldn't believe his luck, when the simple square knot Wallace had secured became loose. He leaped from his horse, bounding like a stag for the nearby Big Sandy River.

When Cap and Tom entered old man's cabin, their noses detected the foul scent of gamy meat. The place was filthy and hadn't been tended to in months. Bill Ferrell was an old widower who didn't usually get much company. He joyfully received his guests, quickly whipping up a batch of leftover rabbit stew and hominy. To their surprise, his cooking was good, so the pair was more forbearing of his smelly cabin and nosy inquiries.

While Tom and Cap busily filled stuffed their faces, Ferrell glanced out his front window. He began to chuckle as he saw Jeff

McCoy dart by. "Ain't that your boy running away?" He asked. The two diners jumped to their feet and rapidly darted outside. They grabbed their rifles, hastily firing several volleys at the fleeing Jeff McCoy; but he now had a two hundred yard head start running for his life towards the Big Sandy.

"I told you we shouldn't have let them alone," Wallace said smirking.

Cap looked up at Josiah who had not moved an inch during the commotion. "Well, at least he's still here." He stood for a moment observing McCoy's shape getting smaller in the distance. "Now I'm really mad at this asshole, I barely got a bite of food" he told Wallace.

Wallace placed his foot in the stirrup of his mount. "You almost ate that whole rabbit by yourself," he replied laughing.

Cap and Tom rode with dispatch after their escaped prisoner. Within a minute they narrowed the distance between them and their man.

Jeff moved his slender frame with breakneck speed across an open field, barely dodging the bullets that buzzed past his head. When he arrived at the edge of the Big Sandy, he slid into the water while taking care to keep his head low. Thrusting rapidly through the gentle current, the fearful man swam with the determination of a slippery trout. The pounding of his heart began to feel like a huge bass drum, as he neared the other side of the river. As he reached the edge, he managed to seek the refuge of an alder shrub that hung deeply into the river.

McCoy waited for what felt like the longest hour of his life. He peeked up to scan across the densely wooded riverbed on the other side of the Big Sandy. He couldn't see Tom or Cap anywhere. His aching body now trembled from being submerged in the cold water.

"I can barely feel my legs. I wonder if they're hiding behind some ground cover. They can't still be there? How could they wait this long?" He thought.

Unable to stand anymore time in the water, Jeff decided to chance a run for it. He looked over his left shoulder, contemplating the hanging branch that was only two seconds away. It beckoned, like a welcoming hand reaching out to grab him. The tentative man hesitated for another two minutes then made the decision to yank himself up out of the chilly water. As his feet touched the safety of the shore, his ears heard an ominous crack coming from across the river. He experienced a hot agonizing pain running up his spine, in union with the strength draining from his body. Trying in vain to keep his grip of the branch, the mortally wounded man fell backwards into the water.

Across the river Tom Wallace was jumping up and down. "You got the son-of-a-bitch Cap!"

Cap just stood coolly, waiting to see if his mark came to the surface. About thirty seconds later, he did, with his head face down in the water. He looked blankly at Wallace for twenty seconds before he uttered a word. "I tried to give that boy a chance, but he didn't let me."

"Sure you did Cap, sure you did." Though he spoke the words, he didn't believe them.

*****

With the exception of a few humid days, the Tug Valley had experienced gentle summer weather, rendering the countryside particularly green and radiant. Abundant varieties of sweetly scented flowers were in full bloom. The tall trees stood healthy and strong, avoiding the ravages of flood or fire. Most families were preparing for the inevitable harvest season. The population inhabiting the Tug River Valley worked their gardens and small crops, looking pleasantly forward to reaping the bounty of their labors. Some would even conceive children, gladly embracing the prospect of creating of new life.

As the summer came to a close, the renewed hostilities between the Hatfield and McCoy clans began to concern the inhabitants of Pike and Logan Counties. They wondered how long the senseless violence would continue. Others prayed that the bloodshed would end soon. Their prayers would not be answered.

CHAPTER FIVE: MIGHTIER THAN THE SWORD

Jeff McCoy had two brothers who were enraged that his life had been snuffed out like a candle. Larkin and Jacob had previously been non-combatants, but now had good reason to enter the Hatfield-McCoy war. They resolved to clean the slate, by seeking out their sibling's killers, Cap Hatfield and Tom Wallace. The former was cautious, never traveling alone or far from his home. He would typically stay in the protective company of his favorite Uncle Jim Vance. Together, they were a pair of exceedingly dangerous men.

Wallace had no such kin to watch over him, being effortlessly captured by the new sprung feudists. Larkin and Jacob could easily have killed him if they wanted to. Fortunately for Tom, their first choice was to operate within the boundaries of the law. The angry brothers opted to escort him to Pike County jail, where he was arrested for murder. His incarceration was short lived though, as he managed to escape from custody after only two days.

Tom's luck was also short lived. A month after he fled Pikeville, his battered body was discovered on the dirt road near Grapevine Creek. Logan County deputies interrogated Larkin and Jacob about their possible role in his demise. "We remember a big man that fit Mister Wallace's description," they informed the law. "But we took him to jail, nice and legal. That's the last time we ever saw him. He must have lit out for some far away place, maybe California," stated Larkin McCoy. No one was ever charged with the Wallace murder.

In August 1887, Confederate war hero Simon Bolivar Buckner was elected governor of Kentucky. This was joyful news, for Randolph's ally, Pikeville attorney Perry Cline. He had supported him, using his political connections to leverage several hundred votes in his hometown. In return for his help, the shrewd lawyer had something he wanted. Cline asked Buckner for assistance in the apprehension of Wall and Devil Anse, as well as the others who participated in killing the McCoy brothers. He subsequently sent the governor documents referring to the details of the Election Day murders. To show his gratitude, Buckner agreed to put forth his full effort in supporting his valued advocate.

The news of Governor Buckner's promise to Cline was a fresh beacon of hope for Randolph. It came shortly after another failed attempt on his life. The incident occurred while he sat on his front porch cleaning his Remington rolling block rife. As he peered down the bore to admire the quality of his work, a stray bullet came whizzing passed his face. The old man fell out of his chair, quickly retreating into his cabin to hide. With all the vegetation surrounding his property, he never ascertained the source of the wayward shot.

The day after the unfriendly fire, an unnerved Randolph paid a visit to Perry Cline. The cool headed attorney listened patiently to his client's ration of fearful complaints.

"I just can't take this much longer Perry. You have to do something about these bastards." Randolph nervously ran his fingers through his hair. "It's getting so I can't even set a spell on my own porch" he said excitedly.

Cline thought for a moment before speaking. "This is just what your enemies want. Just remain calm my friend, don't let them buffalo you."

McCoy impatiently raised his hands in the hair. "They ain't shooting at you Perry."

"Do you think if Cap or Devil Anse was shooting at you they would have missed?" Cline began distractedly writing on a piece of paper, which annoyed Randolph.

"Am I boring you?"

"Of course not but I had a thought that I needed to write down." Cline pushed the paper away looked directly at Randolph.

"I need to know that something's being done so I can sleep at night."

"How long do you think it will take for the Hatfield's to come after me when they find out I have the governor's support, eh?" Cline reached behind his desk to pour himself and his guest two cups of stale coffee. "You're just going to have to hang on a little while longer. Stay out of sight as must as possible so you don't make yourself a target for bushwhackers."

"You know what really bothers me?"

Cline sipped his coffee. "What?"

"You're telling me to be patient when I don't even know who's a shooting at me. I may not be around long enough for your legal remedies." Randolph's voice became louder. "I get warrants issued by the Pikeville judge that your cowardly sheriff won't serve. And even with them trying to kill me twice, the law says that he can't do a thing to touch the Hatfield's."

Cline looked at his pocket watch to check the time. "My Lord, look at the time," he said. The old man was talking in circles and the busy lawyer was growing tired of listening. He now spoke more firmly. "You need to stop this constant fretting. You must stop complaining and start believing that it's going to work out and you're not going to die. Any other notion is a useless waste of thought." Cline lowered his voice and spoke slower and enunciated more. I'll say this one more time so you understand. The wheels of justice are in motion. They may roll slowly, but they're moving in our favor. I'm going to see the governor in two weeks and he'll issue warrants for them boys. We have right on our side, we have the law on our side; and we now have the governor on our side."

Randolph managed to smile. "Perry, I just hope I live long enough for the wheels of justice to roll over the Hatfield's."

"You'll live to see them behind bars or hanged."

The efforts of the Pikeville attorney did not go unnoticed by the people involved in the McCoy shootings. News of Governor Buckner's active interest in the case somehow leaked out of his office. The information filtered into Logan County, where the Hatfield supporters lived. These twelve men deemed their course of action as justice. When Devil Anse beckoned for their help, all of them had stepped forward without hesitation. Nor did any of them flinch when they sent Old Ranel's murdering sons to meet their maker.

The Logan County Hatfield supporters gathered for a secret meeting. They resolved to scare Cline off with a threatening letter that was posted to his home in Pikeville. The content of their message was short and sweet, stating "Hands off or will hang you." The ambitious bureaucrat did not concern himself with this threat as he was walking around in the company of two hired bodyguards.

Perry had also dispatched a telegram to a man well qualified in metering swift justice to hard men. He was a native Kentucky man who was presently unemployed, residing in the town of Louisville. Frank Phillips had spent the previous two years as a deputy sheriff in Dodge City establishing a reputation as an unstoppable lawman. He was self educated, well read individual who possessed affable manners and determination that bordered on madness.

In 1882, Dodge City was a rollicking cow town. Sprawling fields, of bountiful wheat stalks surrounded the outside edge of the community. The dirt-lined streets were populated with greasy hash joints, opium dens, dry goods shops, whorehouses and a modern firehouse. There were several fancy Hotels, such as the Drover's Cottage and the Merchant's Palace, which sported an abundance of red velvet and gold trim.

The town had no shortage of saloons, where a person with a mind to could drink, gamble and get cheap entertainment. There were little mud hole taverns, which appealed to the lowest form of compulsive gambler and drunken rummies. There were also high rolling places such as Balder and Laubner's and The Long Branch, which attracted the largest crowds after dark.

One night during his service as town deputy, Frank Phillips was having a quiet dinner at the Saint James saloon. He sat alone at his table, minding his own business. There was a pouring rain outside, which had not ceased for several hours. He looked up from his food to catch a flash of lightening silhouetting the images of three unfamiliar drovers that came strolling into the room. These cowpokes wore long, white linen dusters, while nervously clutching their rifles.

The Saint James was a long narrow saloon that offered an ornate, hand carved, wooden bar stretching thirty-five feet long. On the ceiling, there were two very large, crystal chandeliers that provided only dim light. The bar was crowded with patrons, who were happy to be out of the wet, muddy weather.

Phillips sat at the far end of the saloon, facing the entrance. He was an experienced lawman, never sitting with his back to the door. That was a mistake made once by the famous Bill Hickok, who paid for it while playing a hand of poker. Frank kept his eye on the men when they walked into the Tavern. After having a round of beers and sizing up the situation, the cowboys began to walk towards him.

Armed to the teeth, the strangers stepped across the room, forming a half circle around the deputy's table. The men were dripping from the storm, which caused small pools of water to form on the floor of the saloon. All eyes in the place now focused on Phillips and the drovers. However, not one bystander intended to get involved. Most of the patrons didn't like the deputy because he was a good gambler, a good fighter and a women stealer.

"What can I do for you boys?" Phillips calmly asked.

"We come to tend to some business with you deputy" said the man on Frank's right. He was tall, hard-featured and had a lengthy knife scar on his cheek.

Phillips smiled, which somewhat unnerved the men. "What kind of business?" The steady man cut a chunk out of the sirloin steak, laid in front of him and prepared to place it in his mouth. "Why, would you have business to settle with me? I don't even know any of you.

"You're Frank Phillips. You dry gulched a friend of ours" said the man in the middle.

The deputy finished chewing his meat and took a large swallow off of his beer. "That's right, I'm Frank Phillips. Now, may I know the name of man you say I dry gulched?"

The man on his right side took a small step forward. "Does the name Tom Ellis mean anything to you?" he asked.

The deputy looked up towards the ceiling of the saloon, feigning contemplation. "Tom Ellis, Tom Ellis, let me see...nope, doesn't mean a damn thing to me." Phillips tilted his head as if to signify deep, thoughtful reflection. "Wait a minute, I remember him. He howled like a dog when I stuck a knife in his liver."

As the words left Phillip's mouth, the faces of the cowboys brimmed with anger. The lean man on the deputy's left rapidly reached for the gun that he carried in his belt. Frank had practiced his speed and accuracy thousands of times. His precision was nearly automated as he drew his colt revolver, shooting the man square in the head. The wrangler's body propelled backwards, slamming into the saloon's roulette wheel. Before he knew what hit him, Phillips fired at the drover in the middle. He too, never cleared his leather, collapsing to the floor with a bullet through the heart.

The third cowboy was a heavyset man who was frightened beyond any reason at the split-second timing of the lawman's gunplay. He turned his stocky frame around, running for the exit as fast as he could move. Phillips nearly let him get to the swinging door of the saloon, before he coolly shot him in the back. The mortally wounded man stumbled, crawling on his belly to get to the front door of the Saint James. The portly cowboy died face down in the street, in exterior of the entrance.

The incident was over in about fifteen seconds. This was all the time it took for the angel of death to whisk off three more souls. The St. James Patrons gaped in awe at the speed at which Frank Phillips dispatched the young cowboys. They watched with equal astonishment, when he sat back at his table and finished his supper.

During the year 1882, the able Bat Masterson was sheriff of Dodge City. The well-known fire eater performed a brief investigation of the shooting and determined that two of the drovers had pulled on his deputy. Nonetheless, he asked him if it was necessary to shoot the third man in the back. After all, he was running away. "I killed him tonight, so he wouldn't come back on another night to kill me" Phillips explained. Though he believed that he had crossed the line, Masterson found it difficult to fault his cold blooded logic. All three shootings were determined to be in self-defense.

*****

Several years after the incident, Phillips was hired as a special deputy in the town of Pikeville. This was on the recommendation of Perry Cline, whom he had befriended upon his return to Kentucky. Frank was designated, as the man who possessed the requisite abilities to track and capture the Logan County Regulators.

In September of 1887, Cline and Phillips traveled to the state capital at Frankfort, to have an audience with the governor. Buckner issued a proclamation and a five hundred-dollar reward for the capture of Devil Anse Hatfield. The charge was murder in the first degree, for the 1882 killings of the McCoy boys.

A formal request was made for his extradition. It was sent directly to the honorable E. Willis Wilson, Governor of West Virginia. It demanded that the fugitive be delivered to the commonwealth of Kentucky, for a trial to be conducted in Pikeville. The telegram received no reply.

Twenty days after the first petition, Perry Cline sent a letter politely asking for status on the extradition of Devil Anse and the other men named in the indictments. This letter also received no reply. Twenty additional days passed before Cline finally received a response from the Secretary of State's Office. The answer stated that all but two of their requests had been fulfilled. The two that were not honored were for Elias Hatfield and Andrew Varney. These men had presented their side of the story to Governor Wilson. They convinced his office, that on the day of the murders, they were miles away from where the incident took place. The Secretary of State assured Cline, that the warrants for the others would be issued, upon receipt of fifty-four dollars. This fee was to cover the administrative costs of the State of West Virginia.

Cline believed that the request for the filing fee was another way for West Virginia to slow the process of extradition. "So that's their game, well there's more than one way to skin a polecat, especially one from West Virginia," he snorted to Phillips. Cline went to the Pikeville courthouse, securing bench warrants for all the men accused in the McCoy killings. With these warrants, and in spite of the fact he didn't have the West Virginia authorization, the clever attorney sent Frank Phillips across the state line.

Phillips immediately retrieved his first captive. Of all people, it was Selkirk McCoy. Though it had been nine years since the hog trial, Old Ranel never forgot that he had decided in favor of Floyd Hatfield. Both he and his son occasionally worked for Devil Anse as employees of his timber business. He was also present when the three young McCoy brothers bought the farm; and of course this had been an unwanted sale.

Poor Selkirk was taken to the Pikeville County jail and was held without bail. On that same day, Frank Phillips decided to personally write to Governor Wilson. Rather than enclose the entire fifty-four dollars, he went ahead and enclosed the tidy sum of fifteen dollars. This was for five people named in the murder indictments that he wanted most. They included Devil Anse, Cap and Johnse, Jim Vance and Tom Chambers. The Governor of West Virginia was annoyed that a lowly Kentucky peace officer had attempted to correspond with him for such a demand without going through proper channels. He sent back an angry response immediately after receiving Frank's letter.

In his response to the deputy, Wilson claimed a reliable source had informed him Perry Cline was involved in unethical activities. That he had used his political influence, to pressure Governor Buckner into offering large rewards for Devil Anse and his supporters. The letter further stated that the governor was aware of a clandestine deal that transpired with a certain party in the Hatfield family. That the Pikeville attorney had promised A.J. Auxier, a colleague representing Johnse that he would use his influence to get his indictment reversed. Auxier signed an affidavit, that he had accepted the sum of two hundred and twenty five dollars. This money was paid to Cline, for wielding his so called judicial power.

Governor Wilson believed that Cline was contradicting himself. He had tirelessly lobbied for justice to be rendered against Devil Anse and his supporters. Yet he had recently accepted monetary compensation for the purpose of eliminating certain indictments. The governor ended his letter with the following statement:

"Warrants were issued by the State of West Virginia for the purpose of serving justice and for no other reason. Furthermore, I assure you that there will be a full inquiry into the actions of Mister Cline."

Deputy Phillips paid Perry a visit to share the letter with him. He walked in and laid the unfolded document on top of his associate's desk.

Cline was puzzled when he saw the document. "What is this

Frank?"

     Phillips looked back with a wide grin. "It seems that his Excellency, Governor Wilson that is, feels that we have abused our posts." It also appears that the Governor has implied, that you have used these Hatfield warrants to extort funds for your own personal gain, he said mockingly.

     Cline responded with righteous indignation. "The only thing I've done is to consider that money will sometimes ensure that Justice is metered out correctly."

     On December 31, 1887 Governor Buckner made what soon after nicknamed "The Bad Apple Speech." It had come to his attention that some disagreeable men from West Virginia had murdered citizens of Kentucky. And that these violent men were in wanton disregard of the laws of the state. Although he didn't say so directly, he was referring to bad men that resided in Logan County. He explained that these "bad apples" would threaten all of Kentucky; and therefore the commonwealth must take action to weed them out. The Hatfield's and their sympathizers considered this speech to be a threat and it vexed them.

CHAPTER SIX: GOOD INTENTIONS

"That old man has got to be stopped," Said Cap.

"He's right you know, let's go ahead and finish it," agreed Jim Vance.

"Maybe we should put the old bastard out of his misery," said Devil Anse.

The three men were gathered at the home of Anderson Hatfield. It was a frosty, clear New Year's Day in 1888. The twelve-month term was only seven hours young, born of fresh hope and full of possibilities. Icicles fashioned slender, white stalactites that tapered on the windows of the cabin. A thin layer of new fallen snow blanketed the landscape. Nearby, a pack of wolves cried out a howling, melancholy daybreak song.

The trio of kinsmen gathered inside the warm kitchen enjoying the comfort of the inviting fireplace. They sipped their fresh brewed coffee and hungrily waited for the hot breakfast that Levicy was cooking for them. The solid, round-faced woman clutched the handle of a cast iron skillet with her chubby hands. She flipped nine eggs over, quickly moving to another pan, where sizzling strips of thick sliced bacon fried to a perfect crispy brown. Moments later, the obliging Mrs. Hatfield presented each of the men with a heaping plate of food including steaming grits and buttermilk biscuits.

Uncle Jim sucked down his food with the speed of a voracious lion. "What about this Cline, him writing to the Governor and all?" He asked, exposing a mouth full of food.

"I don't know if he'll keep going if Old Ranel is gone. His notions go down deep as his pockets. I reckon he's proven that he can most likely be bought off," Devil Anse replied with disdain.

Cap fashioned an egg sandwich with one of his mammoth biscuits. "Daddy, I think you might just be forgetting one thing. What about that crazy son of bitch Frank Phillips?"

Devil Anse dipped his doughy biscuit into liquid egg yoke, sopping up what remained on his plate. "Yes son, he's crazy like a fox and from what I've seen, meaner than hell. But I think he'll do what Cline tells him to do."

Vance stood up and stretched, wiping his mouth with the sleeve of his torn flannel shirt. He looked over at his cousin with an expression seeking culmination. "That all brings us back to the same fork in the road. Last summer, when I found a gopher in my vegetable garden, I put a siphon hose down the hole and flushed that old boy out. When he popped up with his long yellow teeth, I smashed him with a hoe. You see where I'm heading?"

"Its time we flush ourselves a gopher" Devil Anse replied.

"When?" Cap quickly inquired.

His father didn't answer him and instead walked over to the pine wood rack, which held his rifles. Uncle Jim smacked his nephew on his meaty back and began cackling. "Boy, when your daddy grabs his guns, folks better be fixing to dig some holes."

*****

The Hatfield's held to the notion that there was no time like the present to rid themselves of their old foe. Devil Anse asked Johnse to ride along with Tom Chambers for the purpose of recruiting volunteers for a raiding party. Since Frank Phillips had made his recent incursions into West Virginia, Hatfield supporters had begun to dwindle. Chambers had been present the day the McCoy brothers were executed. He had stood by his friends even though it was becoming increasingly dangerous to do so.

As the two men rode out from his father's cabin, cold foggy mist spouted from the nostrils of their saddle horses. "Let's go get ourselves a Cottontop" Johnse instructed. He referred to Ellison mounts, the slow-witted, illegitimate son of the late Ellison Hatfield. Devil Anse wanted him for the raid because he was obedient, mean and proficient with a long rifle. He stood over was six feet tall, weighing two hundred pounds and all of it solid brawn. With a full head of unusually fine, prematurely white hair, he was given his nickname.

Mounts was in the process of mending the roof of his cabin, when Johnse and Tom rode up to his porch. "What the hell you doing boy, it's Sunday. You should be taking life easy on the Lord's day" Johnse jokingly advised.

The big man looked down at his cousin with dull green eyes, which gave no indication of a contemplative being. "I didn't know, and I ain't much for religion" he replied apologetically.

Johnse smiled at his cousin's explanation. "I was just funning you. You know I ain't much of the church going sort either."

Cottontop carefully climbed down the half-broken, makeshift ladder alongside of his dilapidated cabin. He tucked his ragged blue shirt in and adjusted his belt. "Where are you boys going, you ain't going coon hunting are you?"

Tom Chambers nodded no. "Nope, but we are off to kill us a varmint."

Ellison gave a puzzled look. "What manner of varmint are you after cousin?"

"This critter is the two legged kind. He's the kind of varmint that put your daddy in his grave. I thought you might want to come along. I know you're a damn good man and we could use your help."

The usually deadpan Ellison slapped his leg, howling like a stray dog. "God dang, you boys wait here, I'll get my Springfield." Cotton took less than a minute to retrieve his breechloader and his bedroll. He saddled his gray mare as economically and eagerly accompanied the two other men back to the Hatfield home. There, Devil Anse, along with his sons Elliott, Cap and Robert E. Lee were mounted and ready to join them.

The seven man group proceeded on to Floyd Hatfield's home. Though almost ten years earlier, his disputed ownership of a wild pig had put a spark to what had become a long string of hostilities. The riders cantered their horses for another mile down the road, where Charlie Gillespie and Doc Ellis joined them. Cap had visited their homes earlier that morning. He had easily recruited them as members of the raiding party. The still enlarging band quietly rode a half-mile down to Thacker creek, finally stopping at the home of Jim Vance. There, all of the men dismounted to conduct a parley.

Devil Anse looked at the faces of every man who circled around Vance's front porch. "I want you all to listen to my cousin Jim, because he's got something important so say"

All eyes in the band focused on the other old veteran. "I think you all know what were doing standing out here, freezing our asses off. We got to finish things with Old Ranel, once and for all. We got to burn him out; and his seed if need be. In your guts you all know that I'm right. With this Kentucky lawman breathing down our necks, we're running out of time." Pausing for a moment, Vance slowly looked each man in the eye. "When was the last time any of us had a peaceful night's rest? For my part, I can't remember a night, when I wasn't rousted by the cracking of a twig or gotten jumpy from the hooting of an owl. I can't speak for anyone else, but I'm tired of sleeping with my gun under my pillow and wearing my boots to bed."

Uncle Jim's words struck a chord with all the men. They also had grown weary of resting with one eye open. They too were getting tired of traveling in groups. These men all feared that they would be the next one apprehended by Frank Phillips and his posse.

After patiently letting his kinsman do the talking, Devil Anse suddenly spoke up. "If any of you boys haven't got a taste for what's going happen today, I'll understand."

Tom Chambers looked thoughtfully over at his friend. "We got into this pretty near the start and we ain't going to quit now, not before the job's finished." The other men all stood in silent accord with this sentiment.

At noon the eleven Logan Regulators mounted their horses, directing them towards Pike County. Not since the War between the States, had Devil Anse and Jim Vance departed on a mission with such purpose. Most of the band had been there when the McCoy brothers were tied to the Pawpaw trees and executed. By their reckoning, this final raid seemed the only way to abate the violence between the Hatfield's and McCoys.

As the riders approached the edge of Logan County, Devil Anse became violently ill. The aggregate of men stood silently watching as repeatedly vomited. He weakly looked up at his friends and kin with a face as pale as a ghost. "I can't make it today, I want to, but I can't. I'm sorry but I'm going back home."

Devil Anse looked over at his four sons. "You pay attention to what Uncle Jim tells you to do—you hear. He'll get the job done." He was barely able to put his foot into the stirrup of his horse, climbing slowly back into his saddle. His associates would later come to realize that they should have interpreted his sickness as a premonition as to how the day would end.

Jim Vance was now in command of the impending raid against Randolph McCoy and his family. Devil Anse had the utmost confidence in his cousin's keen ability handle disagreeable situations. The wiry killer was one of the founding members of the Logan County Regulators. During the Civil War, they had rid the territory of unwanted men before and with extreme precision.

The raiders crossed the shallow waters of the Tug River, going by way of Poundmill Run. As they quietly passed Jerry Hatfield's place, several of the men somberly reflected upon the Election Day stabbing of Ellison. The memory that lingered there would reaffirm in their minds, the purpose of this day. After stopping to eat dinner, they reached Randolph McCoy's cabin shortly before ten o'clock in the evening.

About one hundred and fifty yards from the house, Johnse, Cap and Jim Vance tied up their horses and covered their faces with masks. The seven others did not bother to hide their identity, following quickly behind in a single file line. The men were alert, feeling a sense of excitement, as they approached their objective.

The sky was overcast with dark clouds, which entirely obscured the half moon. It had not snowed all day but a thin layer of frost remained on the ground. Johnse and Cap carried coal oil lanterns, which helped to navigate the underbrush. A peaceful calm infused the chilly nocturnal air, with no one to disturb it except the crickets and the occasional cry of a nighthawk.

The McCoy's home stood quietly atop a heavily wooded hill. It was a large place by mountain standards, with a two story house next to a one story back house. The two buildings were joined together by a rectangular covered passageway. Next to the house was a small barn, which housed the family livestock.

Jim Vance's plan was a carry out a basic siege. It called for the regulators to surround the cabin and for its Inhabitants to surrender. He was sure that they would comply, in light of superior Hatfield strength. When the McCoys exited their home, Vance and the others would shoot down Old Ranel without blinking. And, if a few other family members got in the way or happened to catch a stray bead, that would be acceptable.

Vance stopped within a ten yards from the cabin. He placed his index finger to his mouth, to quiet the noisy footsteps of his nephew. "Jeez Elliot, why don't you blow reveille so they know we're coming," he said sarcastically. He motioned all the regulators to form a circle around him. "Now boys, old man McCoy and his wife are the last living witnesses to the Election Day business. We finish them off tonight and they'll be no one else to make any trouble."

Seven souls in the McCoy home slept comfortably in their warm beds, unaware that the Hatfield raiders had surrounded them. They hovered outside with thoughts as dark as the looming snow clouds. Poised for attack, they would be as unstoppable as a plague of locust descending on a wheat field. Vance instructed the ten men to group into firing positions around the cabin.

"Cap, you and Cottontop go cover the kitchen. Johnse, you and me will go round to cover the throughway to the main house. Tom, Charley, Floyd and Doc will watch the front door of this shit hole" Vance told the others. The four men ran towards the main entrance and paired off, covering the entire periphery of the McCoy sanctuary.

Elliot anxiously asked "What about me Uncle Jim?"

Vance thought about where he could put his young nephew. "You and Bobbie Lee cover the door from the small house to the throughway" he instructed.

As Elliott and his brother began to walk away Vance whistled at them. "Don't do anything stupid and don't fire off your guns till I give the signal."

Vance gave one last look around the perimeter of the cabin to make sure all of his men had taken up their designated spots. After he was satisfied that there was no escape, he ended the tranquil evening serenity with his booming voice. "Randolph McCoy, you get on out here now.
You and your kin are prisoners of war." The taut faced killer removed a gold watch from his front pocket and checked the time. "You got five minutes to come out or will burn you down."

Randolph lingered in a state of half sleep, until Vance's shrill threats began to permeate his unconscious thoughts. When he realized he wasn't dreaming, he rose up in his bed and shook his sleeping wife. "Woman, you get the girls together and stay out of harms way," he instructed the confused Sarah.

Outside, Vance continued to holler his threats. "You hear me you McCoys? Get on out here or will light you up like a cracker box."

The shouting awakened Calvin McCoy, who warned his sisters to stay hidden. He reached under his bed, grabbed his Winchester, a handful of shells and climbed the stairs of the main house. Carefully poking his head out the upstairs window he couldn't see anyone.

Randolph remained on the first floor of his house, arming himself with his Remington. Hovering down, he hastily pushed a chest in front of the main door. This was the attack that he had dreaded for months. However, even the old man never thought the Hatfields would assault a house full of women at night. Nevertheless, Randolph would not surrender his family or his home without a fight.

Uncle Jim anxiously glanced at his watch again. "You got two minutes to surrender, or else we're coming in" he bellowed.

Johnse, though not a coward, did not have much of a stomach for fighting. He began to get jumpy when he thought he saw something move by the upstairs window. He nervously aimed his rifle and accidentally squeezed off a round. After that, all hell broke loose when the other raiders started firing.

A tempest of bullets blew through the doors and windows of the McCoy home. The shots shattered several dishes, which hung on mantelpiece above the downstairs fireplace. Without a spare weapon between them, the defenseless McCoy woman cowered behind the beds in the main house.

The two McCoy men furiously answered the Hatfield gunfire. Johnse was the first casualty of the battle when Calvin's bullet nicked him in the leg, while he ran for cover. He ducked behind the barn, pulled up his pant leg and noticed that the wound was bleeding profusely. Remembering the trick his father had taught him years earlier; Johnse tore a strip of cloth from his shirt and applied a tourniquet.

An exasperated Vance checked the perimeter, watching his men rapid-firing into to the cabin. "Stop shooting, stop shooting goddamn it! Don't any of you idiot's fire until I tell you to." The men outside held their fire while he began to talk again. "All right, you had a fair chance and now I aiming to warm you up." Suddenly he bolted over to the side of the McCoy home.

Uncle Jim quickly searched the area, looking for something he could use to get a blaze going. His keen eyes gravitated to a pile of cotton lying in a wooden crate and he struck a match to it. Grabbing a big piece of fire lit cotton; he stuffed in a floorboard at the base of the house. He took another piece and wedged it into a deep crack that was in the front door. "Yahoo!" he cried out, running for cover behind a tree.

Tom Chambers observed Vance lighting the fires and got into the spirit of things." Why should you get all the fun," he hollered at Vance. He picked up fallen two foot branch from a dead tree and wrapped a rag around it. Retrieving Cap's lantern, the firebug poured some coal oil on it, creating a rough-and-ready torch. He gleefully jaunted over to a big pile of logs, stacked by the rear door of the house. Stumbling briefly Chambers managed to advance onto the roof.

Randolph heard footsteps overhead, pointed his shotgun up towards the sound and fired. The blast exploded through the roof, knocking up shingles and creating a big dust cloud. The debris blinded Chambers and he experienced a profound throbbing agony on his right palm. As the smoke cleared, Tom was focused his eyes on the reason for his pain. He lifted his hand in terrifying disbelief, when he noticed that three digits were missing. The horrified man let out a banshee wail, fell off the roof and plunged onto the ground. Running for the woods, shaking his hands and howling like a coyote, he was not seen until hours later.

The McCoys also had their share of troubles. Although Chambers had failed to light a fire, Vance's little blaze was rapidly spreading through their home. Calvin placed his rifle out the second floor window and began rapid firing. His volley was answered in spades when the Regulators began to fire without orders from Vance.

"Get some water on that blaze" Randolph shouted. His three oldest daughters had remained crouched in the main house but now the smoke was beginning to choke them. Josephine threw open the front door, in an attempt to chuck water on the spreading inferno. The stalwart young woman was immediately repelled by Jim Vance's Winchester fire.

"If they're coming out, shoot the women," Uncle Jim yelled to Cap and Cottontop.

Josephine, Alifair and Adelaide used all the water they had, finally tossing a pail of buttermilk from inside the cabin. In spite of their desperate efforts, the fire continued to spread.

Alifair was frightened and mad at the same time. She stepped just outside the flaming front door, shouting at the attackers, "I know your voices Cap and Johnse Hatfield. You're nothing but yellow livered trash and a pack of cowards."

Cap became infuriated at her insults but did not have the stones to fire upon her. "Cottontop, Shoot her, shoot her!" He shrieked.

"No!" cried Johnse Hatfield. He raised his arm towards the muzzle of Ellison's Springfield, in a futile attempt to prevent him from firing. Impervious, Mounts blasted away with deadly accuracy and hit his mark. As bullet penetrated her heart, Alifair never knew what hit her. She stood for two seconds staring at Cap, Johnse and Ellison, and then fell forward.

Johnse reached his hands up to his head, frightfully yanking his long hair back on both sides. "Cottontop, What have you done?"

Josephine sensed that something terrible had happened. She popped her head outside the cabin and called out for her younger sister. "Alifair, are you all right?" Glancing out only briefly, she had enough time to see her sister lying sideways on the cold ground.

"Josephine, Alifair, what's happening down there?" Sarah inquired.

"Oh my Lord, oh my Lord, they've killed her, they've killed Alifair" Josephine wailed hysterically. As soon as she heard her daughter's words, Mrs. McCoy rushed outside to aid her little girl.

With rifle in hand, Jim Vance abruptly bounded towards her. "Get back in or I'll kill you where you stand."

Sarah ignored his words and knelt down over her dead child. She looked up at Vance with eyes brimming with defiance. "Then you'll have to kill me, because you ain't keeping me from my baby."

Jim Vance had no shred of compassion for Sarah or her daughter. His heart was now filled with violence, as if he were at back Missionary Ridge or Cold Harbor. He pivoted his rifle butt around, striking Sarah with a solid thrust to the rib cage. The savage blow knocked the wind out of her, throwing her back away from Alifair. In spite of her terrible pain, she propped herself up on her hands, crawling in the direction of her murdered daughter. "Please, let me tend to my little girl. Oh please, can't you see she's dying?"

As he sat watching Vance's cruelty, Johnse held his aching leg and nervously rocked back and forth. He could no longer bear to witness Sarah's pleading. Running to where she sat, he started to violently shake her. "Goddamn it, will you please shut up. Just shut up." His actions only caused the poor woman to become hysterical. He attempted to cover her mouth as he pulled out his revolver. Tugging on her long silver hair, he clubbed the back of her head with the butt end of his pistol. Sarah fell unconscious on the ground, lying by Alifair's side.

Flames completely engulfed both stories of the McCoy home. Calvin, who was suffering from smoke inhalation, came running downstairs. He stooped down behind the old chest that his father was hiding behind. "Daddy, we're finished in here. You and the girls got a slim chance if I create a diversion."

Randolph shook his head. "I don't like it. I say we all stick together."

"That ain't going work Daddy. My minds made up. I'm going head for the corn shed and draw their fire. When I do, you light out for the woods to go for help," he instructed.

He smiled at his son, noticing a tear welling up in his left eye. "I love you daddy," he told his father. The old man looked at him for a time without saying anything. After a moment to gain his courage, Calvin shook his father's hand, grabbed his rifle and dashed outside. The agile young man discharged his Winchester in rapid succession, running backwards, away from the house. Halfway between the cabin and the corn shed, Ellison Mounts stood in his path.

Calvin McCoy stopped ten feet in front of Cottontop and cocked the lever on his repeating rifle. He fired twice, hitting the big man in the shoulder and in the thigh. Ellison yelped like on hound when the second bullet tore into him. Calvin dry fired his rifle, which was now out of ammunition. He tossed it on the ground, reaching down for the Arkansas toothpick that he wore at his side. With a running jump he plunged the long, narrow blade deep into his adversary's burly shoulder. Ellison again squealed with ear splitting pain.

Cottontop was now on the offensive. He reached up with his giant hand to block the next deadly thrust of Calvin's blade. In a rage of anger and pain he snapped the bone in his attacker's wrist. McCoy heard the sound of his arm breaking, turning his face white with pain. He was now a helpless rag doll in Ellison's grip. Mounts quickly brought both his hands up to the younger man's head; one holding his chin, one wrapping around the back of his skull. In a quick sweeping motion, he broke the brave young man's neck.

Calvin's sacrificing diversion, gave his father and sisters ample time to escape. As his son fought Cottontop, Randolph McCoy ran as fast as he could, retreating to the cover of the dark forest. Something inside told him his son was dead, flooding his eyes with salty tears. As he ran further away from the house, he could see the flames rise up above the tall oak trees. Bright yellow-orange in color, it was as if the sun was rising in the middle of the night. The old man's thoughts turned to his wife and daughters whom he had left behind. Josephine, Adelaide and Fanny McCoy had managed to escape the inferno, hiding just a few yards away.

When the house began to collapse Jim Vance had the realization that Randolph had somehow escaped. He threw his arms up in the air and began to scold his kinsmen. "You dumb bastards, you let him get away."

Ellison Mounts covered his shoulder wound with a piece of torn cloth. "How you know the old man still ain't inside?"

Vance raised his voice. "Because you big, dumb bastard, he ain't stupid as you are. He wouldn't stay in there and burn up. He got away." He now turned to Cap and Johnse. What'd we come here for?" He repeated himself slowly "What, de we come here for? We came here to get the old man." Uncle Jim quickly recovered his composure, giving instructions to his nephews. "Cap Set fire to the barn and will make for the river straight away." He looked over at Johnse and Ellison who stood with their heads lowered. "Come on children, get your mounts. God help us, we're going home."

The dejected raiders retrieved their tired horses and swiftly retreated back home. Vance was still upset over the outcome of the assault. "You had to fire your gun you damn fool. I told you to wait for the signal, didn't I?" he said looking over at Johnse.

Johnse in turn began to scold his cousin Ellison. "Why did you have to go and shoot the girl for?"

"Because I told him to you asshole; we should have killed them all. Now that old man's never going rest till we're all in the ground" Cap answered. He glared at Johnse as like wanted to shoot him. Neither brother spoke another word for the remainder of that terrible evening. The raid that was supposed to end the conflict would now undoubtedly exacerbate it.

Randolph McCoy had eluded his attackers by hiding out in a neighbor's pigpen. When he was sure it was safe, the cold, mud-covered man ran back to discover his still burning home. Though suffering from a mild case of shock, he had survived an attack that was meant to kill him. The old man had mournfully agonized after his three sons were killed. Nevertheless, there was nothing in the world that could have prepared him for what his eyes saw upon his return home.

"Sweet Lord Jesus" said Randolph, when he located the body of his son Calvin. He was lying with his twisted head looking up at the evening sky. His face possessed a fixed expression of lifeless terror that his father would never forget. After he stood for a minute staring down at his murdered son, the old man took two weak steps and fell to his knees. He stood up and continued on until he came to the front of his burned out home. Smoke and embers continued to flicker on the rubble of the place he had built with his bare hands.

In back of the burned up debris, he found his three daughters freezing cold, hunched over and sobbing. They had built a small fire for warmth, doing their best to comfort their severely wounded mother. Randolph kneeled down to caress his wife's battered face. Jim Vance had smashed her ribs and Johnse cracked her skull. She was somewhat conscious, hazily looking up at Randolph. The dazed woman was barely able to form the word, "why?"

Randolph rubbed his fingers on his aching temples and spoke softly. "It's my fault. I brought this wrath down upon my family and God forgive me for it."

The furious gunfire, accompanied by the nighttime blaze, had not gone unnoticed by Old Ranel's neighbors. They quickly gathered to give aid to the terrified McCoy family. A couple of men picked up Sarah and carefully loaded her into a wagon. They transported her along with the three surviving daughters, to the house of James McCoy. Randolph stayed behind at the wreckage of his home.

The old man's despair was still not complete. He slowly walked over to where his daughter Alifair was lying. He sobbed like a child, when he looked at her pretty and now lifeless face. Her long, curly blonde hair was frozen to the icy, hard ground.

Randolph pried his dead child up off the freezing soil, cradling her in his lap. His thoughts drifted off for minute. He remembered a beautiful, fair haired child running into his arms and hugging him. She had just had a terrible nightmare and her father assured her he would always be there to protect her. In his anguish, Randolph cried out into the night. "Oh my baby, my child, what have I done, what have I done?" Like a pale apparition, he sat there on the ground exhausted and beaten, crying until the tears on his face became drops of crystal.

■■■

CHAPTER SEVEN: THE WIND CHANGES DIRECTION

On January 3, 1888 The McCoys buried two more children. Calvin and Alifair were laid to rest in a grave next to their three brothers who also died violently. Randolph was inconsolable about suffering nearly a decade of violence and loss. In addition to the destruction of his home, his beloved wife Sarah was barely clinging to life. With no one else to turn to, He moved his family into the home of his one and only ally, Perry Cline.

The day after his children's funeral, Randolph went to spend time with Cline at his office. During the morning hours prior to his visit, he wandered the streets of Pikeville, imparting his woes to several good folk who happened to cross his path. The old man received sympathy in abundance, from outraged citizenry who were appalled at the Hatfield assault. Upon reaching his friend's office, his eyes were flush with tears. With a face wrought with sadness, he opened up his soul to his sole supporter.

"She couldn't even be at the funeral. Sarah loves her children more than life itself and would have gladly died in place of any of them," said Randolph.

"She doesn't know about Calvin too, does she? Cline softly inquired.

"No, off course not; but she knows about our little girl. She was lying next to her you know."

A look of sympathy was on the lawyer's face. "I know my friend, I know all the details." He paused, measuring his words. "This has all been an awful mess. You've suffered greatly, more than anyone should have to endure. But now you must look ahead. You have a wife that needs tending to. She's going to need lots of care and rest."

Randolph leaned his head back in his chair and exhaled a protracted sigh. "Five Children lost in as many years. No father should have to endure that."

"I know, but you must realize that's what's done is done and you have other children that are depending on you." Cline's face suddenly became strangely solemn in appearance. Now I have to something to tell you," he said gravely.

"What is it Perry?"

"Your Daughter Roseanna came to see Sarah today," Cline said pausing for a moment. "And Martha and I have invited her to stay."

*****

Perry Cline owned a two story Victorian house located in the middle of Pikeville's residential district. His comfortable home was now inhabited by McCoys, including Sarah and four of her Daughters. Perry and his wife Martha had no children of their own and were actually pleased to have the battered family stay at their ample residence. Martha, the former widow of Asa Harmon, treated his daughters like a loving aunt would.

If she were to ever recover, the badly injured Sarah would require constant attention. Martha already had her hands full with maintaining her home and six mouths to feed. Roseanna had not attended her sibling's funeral but she was not going to leave her mother in the care of others. The morning her father went into town, she came to visit the Cline home and offered to care for Sarah. Martha immediately prevailed upon her to stay on, in spite of her father's possible objections.

In the years that followed her romance with Johnse, Roseanna had sometimes stayed with her family but her father never forgave her transgression. Most of the time, she lived with her Aunt Betty in Stringtown. After she retrieved her meager belongings, Roseanna was brought to see her badly beaten mother, who had been moved into the main guestroom of the Cline household.

The upstairs room of the Cline house was exquisitely decorated with two antique tables that were overlaid with white lace. A spacious four poster bed with a fringe canopy was located in the center of the room. On top of the feathery bed with satin bedspread, lay several embroidered, silk pillows. Martha's cedar wood hutch stood on the left side the large room and was covered with flowers and plants. By the open windows, a gentle wind fluttered back the white linen curtains, allowing Kentucky sunshine to pour in.

Roseanna studied the face of her injured mother and started to cry. She tiptoed to where she lay, sitting down in the chair next to the bed. Touching her swollen face, she ran delicate fingers through her matted hair. Sarah's blue eyes squinted, smiling at the sight of her favorite daughter. The slender, ghostly woman began to speak softly. "Momma I'm here now, I'm here. Everything's going be all right. I'm going stay and take care of you."

Shortly after his estranged child entered, Randolph quietly

walked up to the doorway of the guestroom, silently observing his daughter's actions. Sarah opened her eyes wider and looked at her child with motherly concern. In a barely audible voice she began to speak. "Child, you look too thin and pale."

Roseanna smiled at her mother, ignoring her statement. "Don't worry bout me Momma, I'm feeling as fine as a June day. You need to let me worry about you for a change." She abruptly altered the topic of conversation. "Who did this to you?" Some folks say it was Johnse. Was it Johnse that did this to you?"

Sarah began to sob. "Yes, he hit me."

Roseanna's sick heart sank further when her mother confirmed what her Aunt Betty had told her.

As she stood up and turned to walk out of the room, her father was waiting for her in the hallway. Seeing her after so many months caused him to experience a surge of emotion. "Hello baby, it's good to see you," he said.

Randolph's beautiful girl glanced down at the hardwood floor and then shyly into her father's face. "It's good to see you too Daddy. Tears began to well up in her father's recently dried eyes. "I've come to tend to my mother's wounds" she explained.

He nodded in acknowledgement. "That's good child, your mama needs you and I need you too." Randolph put his arms around his daughter, embracing her tightly. The old man finally understood that he had his hands full with one feud and needed to have peace among his own.

*****

All of Pike County was buzzing with talk about the savage New Year's assault perpetrated against the McCoy family. Local newspapers carried some badly written, somewhat exaggerated reports about the attack. These articles favored an editorial style that slammed the Hatfield men, stating "They were no better than wild dogs." People the Tug Valley were appalled to learn that innocent women were being killed and beaten by nighttime marauders.

The citizenry in Pikeville were particularly outraged by the News Year's incident. The town was growing larger, more prosperous and did not want to see the violence continue. The growing class of businessmen thought that it reflected badly on the people of Kentucky. It made them appear as little more than savages.

When Randolph McCoy had cried his last tear, he became angry. Once again, he called upon Pikeville Sheriff Bill Fuller to take action. Once again his demand was ignored. He conveniently informed the distraught man that without papers of extradition, he could not enter West Virginia. Fuller was relieved that he wouldn't have to leave his comfortable office in Pikeville.

Perry Cline didn't need the services of the less than ambitious Sheriff. He called on the talents of former Dodge City Deputy, Frank Phillips. He had no such reservations about going into West Virginia to administer justice. "Bring them back alive or draped over their saddle." Just get the job done Frank" Cline instructed his friend.

Phillips smiled, shook his head and headed for the door of Cline's office. Before he left, he turned around, confidently leaving his associate with his promise. "You just make room at that jailhouse of yours, because you're going have plenty of occupants."

When it came to rounding up the Hatfield gang, there was one small detail that he completely ignored. He had no legal authority to ride into West Virginia to capture fugitives from Kentucky justice. In spite of this obstacle, Phillips had a plan to pose as an agent for his home state. With a giant posse of twenty-seven volunteers, he boldly rode to Logan County with the intention of capturing Devil Anse, Wall, Cap, and anyone else who stood with them.

With this mission before him, Frank was in his glory. He loved to hunt men and was good at it. Before transporting his posse across the Big Sandy, the deputy carefully planned his routes, gathering intelligence on the locations of each man he was after. In his professional opinion, Cap Hatfield and Jim Vance were the most dangerous of the group; and that's who he went after first.

On January 12, 1888, Frank Phillips crossed the Tug River into West Virginia. His posse headed directly up Thacker Mountain, towards Cap's place. At the base of the steep hill, the anxious peace officer dusted himself off while he addressed his sizable group. "Gentlemen, most you are city boys. The men were after are extremely dangerous. When I tell you to keep your heads down, for God sakes, keep them down. When I order you to fire your weapon, try not to hit me." Phillips leaned in on his saddle towards his men. "And try not to shoot the man next to you either. You listen to everything I tell you to do and we'll have these birds in custody before supper."

Vance and Cap had spent the previous days shooting at raccoons. After the hunt, the two hunters returned to Uncle Jim's cabin quickly gutting and skinning their fresh game. Jim's wife Mary dutifully prepared the meat they brought back, and the pair ate their fill.

Shortly after licking his fingers clean, Vance began to experience the after effects of his meal. "God dang I got the worst bellyache I ever had. The coon meat must have been a little ripe when the misses' cooked it" he told Cap.

"Maybe it you didn't stuff your fat belly so damn full, you wouldn't feel so bad," Cap advised.

During their outing, one of Uncle Jim's neighbors advised him of the imminent arrival of the Kentucky posse. Cap wasn't sure whether or not this was a rumor, but he thought it best to be near Devil Anse. "Instead of lying around like a couple of stuck hogs, why don't we head back to the old man's place? Maybe walking all that game off will make you feel better," he suggested. Vance felt well enough to travel, so he, his nephew and his wife Mary set out for the safer place.

Walking the path adjacent to the Big Sandy, Uncle Jim rubbed his sinewy arms. In spite of the thirty-six degree temperature, he didn't wear a coat over his denim shirt. "I don't know who wants to kill me worse, Old Ranel or my wife with her cooking" he complained.

"Leastwise Old Ranel don't sleep in the same bed with you" Cap replied. The two men laughed at Mary's expense.

The dowdy Mrs. Vance was tired of taking jabs about her cooking from her nauseous husband. She decided to leave the men to their wisecracks and walk up the hill by herself. When she reached the top of the bluff, she glanced down catching sight of something that chilled her bones. Frank Phillips, along with his large well-armed posse was midway up the other side of Thacker Mountain. The fearful woman quickly bounded back down the south side of the steep hill. "They're coming—they're coming, a whole company of law dogs!" Mary said excitedly. Uncle

Jim soberly looked at Cap, grabbed Mary by the arm and the trio retreated to find the best position to fight from. They sought quick refuge behind a wall of rocks that lined the left side of the mountain trail. The two kinsmen rapidly crammed extra shells into their Winchesters.

"How many of them are there?" Jim calmly asked.

Mary nervously shook her head. "More than I can count."

Vance cocked the lever on his repeating rifle, took a deep breath and laid his back up against the side of a gray shale boulder. He didn't want his wife or his nephew to remain with him any longer. "Cap you take Mary down to your place where it's safe. I'm too old, too sick and I don't feel much like running today."

"Yeah, what are you aiming to do?" Cap inquired.

Vance cautiously stood up in a crouching position and peered out over the huge stone. "I'm aim to make a fight of it. I ain't gonna skedaddle from no Yankee lawman."

Cap smiled at his Uncle Jim. "Aunt Mary, Can you make it down to see my Misses by yourself?"

Vance flashed a look of disapproval. "What are you talking about boy?"

"I ain't leaving you behind by yourself you old coot."

"I'll be fine father" Mary said.

"Alright then mother," Vance replied shrugging his shoulders. His wife kissed him on the cheek, got up and within moments became a speck on the mountain trail.

The Hatfield kinsmen were temporarily safe behind ground cover, about two hundred yards from the top of the hill. They did however have two problems. First, they had nearly been taken by surprise, leaving them with no time to ascend to the high ground above. Second, they were overwhelmingly outnumbered, with no chance of outfighting their opponents.

In spite of the circumstances, Uncle Jim's spirits were good as he acted as if he were about to embark on a turkey shoot. What we'll do boy, is make them think that there's a heap o' fighting men down here," he said in a whispered voice.

Cap nodded his head in acknowledgement of this suggestion. "Good Uncle Jim. That's a real good plan but how you aim to do that?"

Vance shrugged his shoulders. "Spread out and use you're repeating rifle. That's why Mister Winchester made them so you can load on Saturday and keep shooting till Sunday."

"Shoot fast, that's your plan? Cap asked. He had somehow anticipated a better answer. "All right captain, you and me are a whole battalion." He saluted his uncle and the two men diffused out fifteen yards apart, waiting for a clear shot at the posse.

Five interminable minutes passed before the Pikeville vigilantes cleared the top of Thacker Mountain. As they began to descend the hill, a volley of Winchester fire knocked two men of their mounts. The others quickly dove from their horses and scurried like mice to any available cover.

"Jesus, Mary and Joseph, I think they're expecting us," said a man named John McKnight. He was a puffy Scottish blacksmith who had come along with Phillips for some excitement. He ducked alongside the veteran after the initial fusillade of shots.

Phillips rolled his eyes. "If nothing else Angus, you have a talent for stating the obvious."

The name's McKnight, John McKnight. What do you think

deputy, sounds like there are half dozen guns up there?"

"That's an old mountain recipe boy. That's what those Hatfield boys are cooking up, nothing but an old mountain trick. There ain't any six men up there you tinhorn."

While serving a short stint as an Army Scout in New Mexico, a Native American agent taught Frank an abundance of tracking techniques. During his two years in Dodge City, Masterson used his talents to trail nearly a dozen fugitives, which Phillips either killed or captured.

The Special Deputy from Pikeville instructed his men to span out across a forty-five degree flanking line, cautiously advancing towards the direction of the gunfire. Cap and Vance kept shooting at the pressing company but were able to do little to prevent them from steadily gaining ground.

Though most of the men in the posse were not professionals, Phillip had brought a sharpshooter that managed to get a spot above Vance, obtaining a clear shot at him. The Logan Regulator saw a puff of rifle smoke, followed by the forbidding sound of a Sharps rifle. A split second later he felt a pulsating stomach pain. This was a hundred times worse than the bellyache he had experienced earlier.

"Cap, I'm gut shot boy," Vance cried in anguish. "Gawn, get out of here boy, run while you still got a chance."

The usually stony cold man felt his eyes fill with tears. "I ain't leaving you Uncle Jim."

"Get on out of here boy. I'm finished and you got a chance." The badly wounded managed to give one last smile. It ain't your time yet boy, so get on out of here before I shoot you myself." He looked down at his nephew and nodded his head for him to go. Cap hesitated for a moment, touched the old man's shoulder, turned around and ran like hell down the mountain.

Jim Vance was dying from his belly wound. Clutching his stomach, he propped himself up against the massive gray rock, waiting for Phillip's men to close in. He bowed his head and began to pray aloud "Dear lord. I know I'm about to meet you. I done a lot bad things and I'm begging your forgiveness."

Carefully peeking over a hedge, Phillips caught a glimpse of the older man praying. He cautiously came out in the open, firmly leveling his forty-five at the bleeding man. "Well now Mister Jim Vance, you look like your feeling poorly."

"Why don't you kiss my Confederate ass" Vance replied, squinting up in pain.

Phillips laughed, slowly stepping over to where Vance was sitting, placing the muzzle of his gun to the wounded man's wrinkled forehead. He grinned for a moment, as if he were about to make pleasant conversation. "You know old man I was too young to fight in the War Between the States. But my father was a proud Union man who hated you rebel scum. It'll be my pleasure to send you to hell."

Vance looked directly into Frank's steel blue eyes without flinching. "I suspect we'll meet again in the hereafter Yankee," he said. Just after those words left his lips, Phillips mercilessly fired a bullet into his head.

Moments later, McKnight walked up behind Phillips. With smoke still emitting from the barrel, the deputy leaned his head against the side of his revolver. For ten seconds, he blankly stared down at the dead man. Frank suddenly pivoted around to see who was standing behind him, which startled the blacksmith. "That son-of-bitch won't bother any more women" he said. Patting the volunteer on his strong back, he began to walk back towards the large posse. McKnight stood there looking at Vance's corpse with morbid curiosity. Phillips stopped and smiled back at the man. "What's the matter Shamus, haven't you seen a dead man before?"

The tall blacksmith answered in a heavy brogue. "No sir, I never have."

"Well that bastard's deader than General Custer. Now let's go eat some supper."

Phillips had stated an undisputable truth. The very capable Jim Vance was now lying as dead as the aforementioned Civil War hero and unsuccessful Indian fighter. Cap had been blessed to escape the Phillips posse and he knew it. Not very many things ever gnawed at his conscience, but leaving Uncle Jim behind to die would now be one of them.

When he caught up with his Aunt Mary, Cap took the hysterical woman back to his home. There he collected his wife Nancy, who was able to give little comfort to the newly widowed woman. With his perception that Phillips would not rest on his laurels, the resilient man immediately left for his father's home.

After making the brief trek south to the Hatfield cabin, Cap found his parents preparing dinner for his younger brothers and sisters. His adrenaline was still up when he ran into the main room of the cabin and blurted out the news. "Pa, they got Uncle Jim, that son-of-bitch Phillips got him."

Not wanting to further upset his wife and children, Devil Anse invited the distraught Mrs. Vance in to try to eat a bite supper. "Levicy will tend to the women," he informed Cap. He then motioned his son outside to discuss the day's events.

Devil Anse rested his forearms on the rail of his front porch. Cap reached into his pocket for some tobacco and began to roll himself a cigarette. "Son, you generally never give me cause for shame but that was a dumb thing you did coming in and upsetting Mama and the kids." He rested his hand on his son's arm. "You know better than that."

"I wasn't thinking too clearly. You're right, I should've thought better of what I done."

Devil Anse grimly looked at his son. Your Uncle Jim, is he dead?"

"Yes Pa, they gut shot him and I believe he must be."

"You don't know for sure?"

"No Pa, I wanted to stay with him but he wasn't having any of it. You know how I feel about the old coot. I'll never have another friend like him." Cap took a long drag off his smoke.

"You can't worry about that now. He's probably dead and you're alive and I reckon that's all that matters. Damn it to hell. I knew this would happen. We missed our chance on New Year's I knew there would be hell to pay; especially with the little McCoy gal getting killed."

Cap shrugged his big shoulders. "I reckon that's not a point for argument."

Devil Anse took out his pipe and stuffed it with a wad of tobacco. "How many men has Phillips got with him?"

"Well at least twenty I reckon" Cap replied.

"He'll probably wait a day or so before he comes after us. That may just give us enough time to raise our own posse.

Nodding in agreement, Cap hung his head town and appeared like he was about to cry.

Seeing his son's eyes well up with tears was nothing something Devil Anse had ever recalled. He put a lit stick to his pipe. "What's the matter son?"

"I shouldn't have left him there."

"Did you have a choice?"

"There's always some kind of choice. I don't think he have done the same."

Devil Anse raised his eyebrows. "Well he's dead and you're alive, so you'll have a long time to mull it over." He paused to inhale his pipe. "But if you ask me, you done the right thing."

"We ain't even gonna get a chance to give him a decent burial." Cap threw his cigarette on the ground and violently stomped it out. "I'm gonna kill that son-of-bitch Phillips if I get a chance."

His father nodded in agreement. "You'll have to stand in line."

After an evening of rest and planning strategy, Anse and Cap set out for Logan Courthouse. Upon their arrival, the wealthy timber merchant had no problem getting his friend, State Senator Floyd to get a warrant issued for the arrest of Frank Phillips. Through that same connection, he was able to secure the assistance of Joe Thompson, who was the Sheriff in Logan County. He informed the McCoys that he was the rightful law and didn't appreciate any two-bit Kentucky men invading his county.

For a week straight, Frank Phillips raided West Virginia without opposition. He successfully captured several men wanted in the McCoy indictments, delivering them to Perry Cline's Jail at Pikeville.

On January 19, Sheriff Thompson, along with Devil Anse assembled a posse of their own numbering thirteen men. They took the field intent on finding the Kentucky interloper and capturing him before he could illegally kidnap anyone else. The special deputy from Pikeville was also on the move. With the plan of taking Cap Hatfield into custody, he entered West Virginia with a fresh of posse of eighteen volunteers. Late in the afternoon, the two groups met alongside the Tug Fork and were not happy to see each other.

Arriving at the trail junction at the same time, the rival companies wildly commenced firing on one another. The Phillips men seized a favorable position behind a four foot high stone wall, while the Thompson men scrambled for the cover of a muddy ditch. Nothing but a small tributary called Grapevine Creek separated the two hostile factions.

In an attempt to get an advantage, three of Thompson's men made it to the nearby woods. The climbed up into the thickly covered trees and took up sniper positions. For several minutes afterward, the air was thick with the exchange of bullets.

Cap was still hot over his Uncle Jim's killing, drawing a vengeful a bead on Bud McCoy. In an attempt to get a clear mark of his own, he was foolish enough to stand up over the protection of the stone barricade. As Sam McCoy warned his cousin to get down, Cap's well aimed bullet found its way to Bud's chest. His cousin knelt down over the half conscious man. "You damn fool! Don't ever stand out in the open when a Hatfield man is shooting at you."

Frank Phillips crawled over to where Sam was sitting. As he

held his cousin in his lap, the deputy shook his head. "What happened to him?"

"The fool doesn't know how to keep his head down."

"Shit, them sons of bitches got us in a Mexican standoff" said Phillips, leaning over to Sam's ear.

Sam had spilled the first real blood ten years earlier, when he killed Bill Staton a few months after the hog trial. After that initial incident, he had not participated in the escalating violence. When his favorite cousin Alifair had been killed, he felt he had stood by and watched long enough. For his part, Big Sam was one of the few men in the posse that Phillips respected. As he tried to peek over the wall, his hat got nicked by a forty-four forty shot. "Damn, that was close. This is a Mexican standoff."

"I'm open to suggestions big man," answered Phillips.

Aiming his rifle, Sam propelled a bead at one of the snipers. "I say we just wait it out, or try to get some men around behind them" he answered, yelling into Frank's ear.

Phillips poked his head over and also managed to get his Stetson nicked by a Hatfield slug. Quickly sitting down behind the protection the one foot thick stone, he put his finger through the hat hole. "I don't know how we could get behind these assholes. We ain't got any way of getting across the trail, not without getting cut to pieces."

Across the road, the Logan Sheriff sought to the counsel of Devil Anse, the old professional. "This is getting us nowhere Mister Hatfield. We got them pinned down pretty good but we'll pay hell flushing them out" Thompson observed.

The former Confederate sharpshooter carefully searched the perimeter of the battle site, in an attempt to find a weakness in Phillip's barricade. "You're right sheriff we ain't gaining no ground here. Besides, there's too many of them. Best we pull out before some good men get shot full of holes."

Sheriff Thompson whooped a loud call, revolving his finger in the air to get the attention of his men. "On your mounts boys, we're pulling out" He yelled.

Retreating to the cover of the woods, the Logan men encountered heavy fire. With such a fusillade of lead, it was a miracle than only one man was hit. His name was Bill Dempsey and Sam McCoy had managed to shoot him out of his saddle. From a distance of two hundred yards, he had hit the poor West Virginian in the shinbone. With a badly broken leg, the wounded man crawled to a corn shuck pen, howling liked an animal in a snare. "Someone please give me some water, I'm so thirsty" he yelled, as he lay there helpless.

Frank Phillips, Dave Stratton, Sam and Jim McCoy surrounded the young man, taunting him with pitiless abandon.

"You don't need water boy, you need to sprout wings and fly away" said Big Sam.

"Looks like this boy's had a bellyful of our hospitality for one day" added Jim.

Tears began to stream down Dempsey's anguished face. "Don't shoot me no more" he pleaded.

Frank Phillips was suddenly possessed by a wild eyed look, blissful in his malice. Walking over to where hurt man lay, he kicked him squarely in his wounded leg. The young screamed out with a hideous shriek.

"Damn Frank, that was harsh," Sam remarked.

With raised hand, Phillips motioned him to be silent. "I'll handle this my way." With a frightful look of anger he kicked the poor man again. "What you got to say now boy?"

Between his spurts of sobbing Dempsey attempted to explain. "Sheriff Thompson told me it was my duty to ride along with him," he stuttered for a moment, "to pursue the Kentucky law breakers."

Phillips believed he was an avenging angel and did not appreciate being referred to as a criminal. "You pathetic little bastard, you're the only one breaking the law," he said, pointing his Colt at the terrified man.

"No!" begged Dempsey.

Completely unmoved, the deputy took slow deliberate aim at the trembling man, shooting him squarely in the head. "That's one less useless peckerwood sucking air," he said appraisingly. He calmly spun his peacemaker around, holstering it with the grace of an orchestra conductor.

Sam and Jim McCoy were dumbfounded at Frank Phillips summary execution of Bill Dempsey. They too had done their share of fighting and Big Sam was not unfamiliar with the taking of a man's life. As the harsh lawman walked away from his handy work, Jim spoke to his cousin in a near whisper. "Damn, Frank sure likes killing a man. Maybe more than anyone I've ever seen."

Big Sam gave Jim a nod of agreement. "Yeah, but you should leave it alone cousin. Just leave it be."

Jim McCoy did not heed his cousin's advice and hollered out at Phillips. "Did you have to kill him? Why couldn't we have taken him back to Pikeville?"

Frank nonchalantly turned back around. "I brought you along because I thought you had the stomach for this."

Jim responded back with indignation. "I do."

"Then pack him on his horse and we'll take him back and see if there's some reward," Phillips instructed.

Devil Anse had also seen Dempsey fall and took refuge behind God's timber to observe his fate. Like Jim McCoy, he too was sufficiently convinced that Frank Phillips was as cold blooded a man as he had ever seen. Though tempted to take a long rifle shot at the deputy, he stood powerless to save the young man from his early grave. After the fatal bullet was fired, he somberly mounted up and caught up with the other West Virginians.

In his fifteen day campaign, Frank Phillips had struck deep into the heart of the Logan Wildcats. He had successfully apprehended Wall Hatfield, Tom Chambers, Doc and Plyant Mahon, Moses Christian, Elias Mitchell, Andrew Varney, Sam Mahon and L.S. McCoy. All these prisoners were known to have been present, at the killing of the McCoy brothers. In the town of Pikeville, Perry Cline, with the assistance of a colleague named Lee Ferguson, busily assembled evidence for an impending trial.

Frank was not only successful at hunting men but he proved to be adept at the art of courtship. He established once and for all, that Johnse Hatfield married the wrong McCoy. His chosen wife, the former Nancy McCoy, first and foremost had always remained loyal to her family. As hostilities between the two clans reached a fever pitch, the already weak marriage collapsed entirely. The morning after the New Years raid, Nancy packed her belongings and her two children into a small hay wagon. Without looking back once at her tidy home, she headed for Pikeville. She was resolved to be forever be finished with the weak willed Johnse.

In Pikeville, the attractive and recently separated Mrs. Hatfield met Phillips at the Starlight Palace Saloon and quickly fell head over heels in love. Unlike her first husband, Frank was not irresolute nor was he the philandering sort. He recognized how to still Nancy's sometimes high-strung personality. Her fondness was built upon his inner calm and strength; a rare trait that he shared only with her.

Johnse finally realized that he should have married Roseanna. She was devoted to him, above anything or anyone. Now it was far too late to do anything to remedy his mistake. While she was nursing her mother back to health, hers was slipping away. Roseanna began having dizzy spells, taking sick, with what was thought to be the measles. Only a month after her arrival at the Cline home, she lay dying in the same bed that her mother had occupied. For one last time, it was Sarah's turn to take care of her daughter.

When Roseanna had taken a slide for the worse, Sarah gathered her four surviving daughters in the den. A married Lilburn McCoy traveled from Louisville to be with her younger sister. Together the five women watched their beloved girl slip father into an unknown realm of bleakness. Randolph could not bring himself to sit in the same room as his dying child, electing to wait downstairs in the main room.

In her heart, Sarah understood that child was already gone, but she continued to talk to her as if she would snap out of her dire condition. "Come on child, you've got to fight this sickness. Don't you know you've got your whole life ahead of you?"

Roseanna clutched at her mother's hand. "I got nothing ahead of me Mama, only dark days. For five hellish years that's what I've known, long dark days. Why should I want to live for that?"

Sarah began to cry at her daughter's lamenting declaration. "Don't talk like that child. I've been to hell and beyond and I'm still here. Don't leave me now baby, don't leave your family."

Sarah's beloved girl was breathing slow, wheezing breaths. She weakly glanced around the room, looking first into the face of her favorite sister Josephine. She smiled briefly, and glimpsed upon the teary eyed expressions of Lilburn, Adelaide and Fanny. For a half a minute she did not answer her mother pleas. Finally, in a voice that was hardly audible, she spoke once more. "There's one thing that could have made me happy Mama," she said pausing for a moment. "And that was taken away me." After a few more slow breaths, Roseanna McCoy was dead.

Over the past decade, Randolph and Sarah had lived to see six of their children die. She had not perished from a bullet, but she too, was a casualty of senseless conflict. It was a family dispute that had now claimed the lives of twelve people. Some Romantic souls in Pikeville and Logan Counties compared Roseanna and Johnse to Romeo and Juliet. Star crossed lovers, who because of bitter hatred between their respective families had been kept apart.

When confronted with the news of her death, Johnse cried like a child. He had not been told of Roseanna's illness and would have liked to seen her one last time. Perhaps he could have held her hand, stroked her hair or touched her face. Perhaps he could have given comfort, as she began her journey to the afterlife. These thoughts plagued him like ghosts tormenting troubled souls.

It was little consolation when Devil Anse informed his son Johnse that he had made a mistake about the quality of their mountain romance. "I was wrong about things. I should have forced you to marry that girl. She was a great soul," he said.

■■■'

CHAPTER EIGHT: WAR BETWEEN THE STATES

A northern newspaperman by the name of Charles W. Haynes traveled to Pikeville, all the way from Pennsylvania. His publication was the first from another state, to take an interest in the Hatfield-McCoy troubles. He spent only three days in Pike County, interviewing local townsfolk about the well known feud. Though his visit was brief, the reporter now believed he knew everything there was to know about this epic conflict.

Haynes first met with Randolph and Sarah McCoy. Randolph he said "Was a poor haunted soul who suffered from the weight of his loss. A man that only once gave a thought, to taking revenge against the Hatfields." The writer also hastened to speak with Frank Phillips and Perry Cline. In his article, he pronounced them "Crusaders of justice that sought to rid the land of the murdering Hatfield gang."

The writer's slant, was that the McCoy family, were victims of a vindictive Hatfield reign of terror. That Devil Anse was the evil mastermind behind a campaign of unprovoked murders. When someone brought him a copy of this article, reprinted in *The Louisville Press Journal,* the Hatfield man had this to say:

"When a silver dollar lies on a gambling table, one side of the coin remains hidden. Heads or tails, you only see one side. This was the same as that newspaper man's opinion of me; a man that he never personally met, or knows anything about."

An article by a West Virginia publication rebutted the story written by Haynes, In addition to several others coming from Kentucky. This particular writer took great umbrage with the article written by a journalist who was perceived as a Yankee trespasser. His Newspaper, *The Logan Bulletin* made the following statement:

"It seems that the reporting in Pennsylvania, has colored the prolonged hostilities in favor of the McCoy faction. It has been falsely reported that the Hatfields have been solely responsible for the proliferation of violence. This Northern account paints a picture of West Virginians as being no more well behaved than Outlaws. This outrageous slander professes that violent West Virginia men are a poor reflection on their state.

It seems that this so called correspondent must have failed to perform his research properly. If he had, he would discover that this is a feud, which has its roots in Kentucky. It was born out of incident that occurred at a polling place in Pike County, near the Kentucky border. This biased report has clearly reflected poorly upon his sovereign state, not ours."

It was becoming obvious, that Kentucky had their side of the story, as did West Virginia. The feud was not just a conflict between two families; it was now much bigger than that. It was increasingly cleat that it was becoming a war between two states. The governor of each respective territory would soon be compelled to pickup the gauntlet of this unavoidable fight.

Governor Buckner of Kentucky was outraged when he read about the New Years day killings of Calvin and Alifair McCoy. On January 9, 1888 he was moved to write a letter to Governor Wilson of West Virginia. He requested that the responsible parties involved be delivered into the hands of Kentucky justice.

The Gubernatorial leader of West Virginia had his own interpretation of events that had transpired and his evaluation differed from Buckner's. In swift reply to his neighboring state, E. Willis Wilson countered with his own righteous indignation. He sighted what he considered to be the illegal atrocities perpetrated at place called Grapevine Creek. Wilson explained that his sources had provided him with eyewitness statements, that Frank Phillips had willfully and unlawfully murdered one William Dempsey. That he was an officer of the State of West Virginia and was killed during the commission of his sworn duties.

In addition, Governor Wilson confirmed the testimony that Dempsey carried legal warrants sworn out against Phillips and several McCoy family members for the recent murder of Jim Vance. The governor further stated that the West Virginia men being held at Pike County Jail had been arrested without proper warrants.

Thus began a series of back and forth correspondence between the two governors. These honorable men dispatched their respective representatives on a fact-finding mission about the feud. It was not surprising, that the Kentucky agent informed Governor Buckner that the hostilities were the sole responsibility of the vindictive Hatfield clan.

The agent from West Virginia blamed Perry Cline for stirring up the recent outbreak of problems. He went on to inform Wilson that the lawyer's actions were motivated strictly by financial gain. That he was well aware that the Hatfields were men of property and that he used his position of authority to extort money from them.

Wilson came to the conclusion that his war of words with Buckner was at a stalemate. He sent an aid named Colonel Mahan to personally gain audience with his Kentucky counterpart. The representative carried with him a one final letter from Wilson. The text of the memorandum firmly demanded the release of the nine West Virginians that were being held at Pikeville Jail. It tersely delineated Wilson's contention, that these men had been seized without legal authority.

In his immediate response to this exacting dispatch, Governor Buckner claimed the following, "I cannot release these men, as the court of Kentucky, and not I, has jurisdiction over them." Wilson was not satisfied with his neighbor's answer. His next move was to summon the foremost legal mind in West Virginia. He was the State Attorney General, a short, scholarly man named Alfred Caldwell.

After considering the details of the case against the eleven West Virginians, Caldwell sent Governor Wilson a short note:

"Your Excellency, the State of Kentucky has a very good case and we have a rather weak one. The murder of the three McCoy brothers was committed on Kentucky soil, as was the raid on McCoy home. The Commonwealth of the State of Kentucky therefore has the right, to hold and the try these nine men for these alleged crimes. You are correct in your belief that the nine West Virginians were seized illegally. However, once these men were on Kentucky soil, their legal authorities were empowered to arrest and hold them for trial.

In addition, though Frank Phillips did not have legal authority to arrest and detain citizens of our sovereign state, this will be overridden by the right of Kentucky to try them for murder. It is my considered opinion that the state of Kentucky will eventually prevail in their right of extradition and subsequent trial of these men. By litigating with them at this juncture you are merely going to prolong an inevitable victory for our neighboring state." After reading this statement, Governor Wilson elected to ignore Caldwell's advice.

Wilson sent for another one of West Virginia's most eminently qualified lawyers. He was a former member of the United States Congress, named Eustace Gibson. When he arrived at the governor's office he received a hearty handshake and listened to an abundance of flowery words.

"Sir you are now to take up the noble cause of state's rights. West Virginia is the home of the forever loved Stonewall Jackson. We joined the lamented Confederacy to defend these very rights of our sovereign state. We shall now not permit our citizenry to be kidnapped from our commonwealth and taken without due process," Wilson advised Gibson.

Two days later on Sunday February 8, 1888, Gibson was on board a train bound for Louisville Kentucky. He consumed several cups of coffee while reviewing his defense for the nine West Virginians. With a case strongly in favor if Kentucky, the lawyer knew he was going to be fighting an uphill battle. He felt akin to the embattled salmon that fights off the effects of a strong current. He remembered the promise he gave to the Governor Wilson just before leaving his office. "Your Excellency I shall do more than my best to resolve this matter in favor of our citizenry."

The United States District Court at Louisville was a stately place. The city fathers had spared no expense when constructing it. The main courtroom was furnished by magnificent dark ebony tables and benches that stretched out with opulence. The floor was a mosaic of marble tiles, leading up to the Judge's Bench. Behind that, stood two, large and impressive stone pillars, where the state and federal flags were hung.

The Hatfield-McCoy feud had emerged from the wooded mountain terrain to transform into a political battle. However, the impending hearing would be somewhat more complex than the hog-trial that was conducted at Deacon Anse's cabin.

Eustace Gibson was a tall, lean, dignified looking man in his late fifties. For his day in court, he wore a black suit of clothes, with a black stovepipe hat. The morning of his appearance, he made an early appointment to see one of the town barbers. He had his gray streaked hair, beard and mustache groomed and his face sprinkled with cologne. Afterward, he felt more than fit to go before the honorable Judge John Watson Barr, to present a motion for writs of Habeas Corpus.

During his years in the legislature, Gibson had established a pre-eminent reputation as an eloquent speaker. He understood the only defense that would save his clients, would be to establish that the Hatfield defendants were being held illegitimately. That the illegal capture would preclude the commonwealth of Kentucky from charging these men with any crimes. Hence writs of habeas corpus would be utilized as a method to gain their freedom.

The Second District Court began business promptly at nine o'clock in the morning. The large chamber was nearly empty except for the presence of those who were in attendance to administer the proceedings. After Judge Barr initiated the hearing, the former congressman was the first man called to speak before the bench. Gibson stood up and slowly walked to the middle of the large courtroom and began to talk in a booming voice.

"Your honor, the State of West Virginia is here today to request that writs of habeas corpus be admitted in the case before the bench, and to dispute the apprehensions that were conducted in our state. The arrests in question were performed by a man that had no legal authority to enter our commonwealth. Mr. Frank Phillips, this so called constable seized citizens of West Virginia, transporting them across the state line, without the benefit of due process. Not only does the Commonwealth of West Virginia believe that these men have been deprived of their rights as citizens of our state; we also contend that by holding them in Pikeville, that these men face the constant danger of assassination. We therefore believe, that in the interest of justice, the prisoners in question should be immediately released into the custody of legitimate authorities representing our state."

After Gibson had completed his opening remarks, he took his seat flipping his long coat tails behind him. The state of Kentucky was represented by their Attorney General, a man named Parker Watkins Harden. He was in his early forties, appearing simultaneously righteous and stern. It was now his turn to argue on behalf of his state. Harden called upon his excellent memory, having taken mental notes, while listening to Gibson's argument.

"Your honor, in this case, the issue of habeas corpus so clearly defined by the esteemed Mister Gibson just doesn't hold water. He seeks to cloud the real issue of this case, attempting to render it a legal argument over state's rights. This case is not about state's rights. Your honor, the decision before you, is whether or not writs of habeas corpus should be admitted in this particular case. Our esteemed Governor Buckner has utilized all the proper procedures, in his attempts to see this matter through to its conclusion" said Harden. He momentarily stopped speaking, taking a sip of water. He turned to face his opponent and resumed his argument.

"Mister Gibson has stated that these men were illegally captured, by an unauthorized agent of the State of Kentucky. Even if this was the case, which the state believes it is not, this does not overshadow that fact that the commonwealth of Kentucky believes that these men are guilty of the gravest crimes. They are not accused of kicking a dog or spitting on the sidewalk. They stand accused of murder; and if Mister Gibson had his way, we would have to permit all criminals the right to hide out in another state. Your honor, if we allow these writs of habeas corpus, these men will never come to trial. Especially in the State of West Virginia, where they are men of prominence" Harden concluded.

As he approached his chair Mister Harden politely nodded to his opponent. Eustace Gibson was impressed by his adversary's speech. "He isn't a bad lawyer. I'll have to kick his tail around a little bit" he thought to himself. His reflection was interrupted by the sound of the judge's voice.

"Mister Gibson, you may now present your closing arguments," he announced courteously.

Gibson took the floor, moving with the contemplation of a well-maneuvered chess piece.

"Thank you your honor. It is esteemed leader of West Virginia, the honorable Governor Wilson that has followed all proper Procedure and not the esteemed Governor Buckner. The well meaning governor has not answered the issues presented to him by our Governor Wilson. He has shamefully avoided the courtesy of receiving papers of extradition from the commonwealth of West Virginia.

In addition, let me pose these questions for your consideration. Why did of the commonwealth of Kentucky, wait over five years to charge our citizens with the 1882 killings of the McCoy brothers? Your honor, it is my contention that this is clearly a matter of bad faith. Why has the State of Kentucky made such a protracted decision to charge my clients? Surely, with all the great power that your great commonwealth has at it disposal; the power of your executive, the power of your judicial and your military; and the power to protect your citizenry, from crimes committed against them. I say again, why did you wait five years? Why did Kentucky wait, until a lawyer of questionable ethics named Perry Cline manipulated your Governor into offering the attractive sum of twenty five hundred dollars reward?

For the record, let me state that this reward is nothing but blood money that was offered for the illegal capture of West Virginia citizens, by bloodthirsty men of questionable authority. In the case before the bench today, it seems to me that the choice is clear your honor. The State of Kentucky should review and admit the writs that I have presented today." Gibson stated. He bowed his head before the judge and walked back to his seat.

After a short recess, the honorable Judge Barr rendered a decision on the case. He allowed the writs of habeas corpus to be admitted and returnable by February 20, 1888. The press in West

Virginia commended Judge Barr for his impartial decision and praised
Eustace Gibson for his admirable services. The Kentucky press had
also began to take notice of the case and had a field day with the
judge's decision. *The Louisville Press-Journal* published the following
statement.

"It is a sad day when the press and not deputies of the state, are
to be the ones to protect our citizenry from the crimes of evil men. It
seems that angry citizens must carry the trident of justice until men of
our judicial branch choose to render proper decisions. Our
commonwealth has chosen instead, to protect the rights of white
savages, whose atrocities have been unequaled in our state's history."

To add insult to Kentucky's temporary injury, Governor Wilson
issued his own request of extradition. He wanted the eighteen men
involved in the Dempsey killing, to stand trial in West Virginia.
Governor Buckner was incensed at was he interpreted as a petty tit for
tat maneuver, choosing to ignore Wilson's request.

*****

West Virginia had won the first legal engagement but it was
certain that the War Between the States would continue. Devil Anse
had avoided capture by Frank Phillips and observed the outcome of this
judicial battle with a watchful eye. He was fearful that he too might be
apprehended and taken to the Pikeville Jail. He was stunned at the
capture of his brother Wall and the other eight men. He decided to
move his wife and family closer to Logan Courthouse. There, he was
under the protection of the local authorities. For the first time in his life
his was scared, as the situation had grown way beyond his control.

CHAPTER NINE: HABEUS CORPUS

"Are you some smartass, big city reporter?" asked Wall Hatfield.

No Mr. Hatfield, I'm on the up and up. My name is John Mitchell of the Louisville Press-Journal. Our readers would like to hear your side of the story. I'll give you every opportunity to explain your situation without any cheap shots. Are you at liberty to speak?"

"You're damn right I am young man."

The journalist was an educated, serious young man of twenty-eight. He was dressed professionally, polite and carried himself with the bearing of a man beyond his years. At his side he held a thin, brown, leather notebook with a thick wad of paper stuffed inside. He removed a pencil from his shirt and prepared to take notes from the solid looking man. His newspaper had dispatched him to get a line on the violence for their anxious readers.

"What is your role in what local citizens are now calling a feud between your family and the McCoys?"

"I ain't got no role. I'm not involved at all young feller. I don't know anything about the things they say I done and neither do the other men in jail with me. Them other fellers got no more to do with any ruckus, than I do" replied Wall convincingly.

The reporter quickly jotted down a paraphrased version of the previous statements. He glanced up from his notepad for a moment. "Then why were you arrested Sir?"

Wall frowned for a split second, which was rapidly replaced by a wide grin. "A large posse, toting a heap of guns, came to my home and told me I was going to Pikeville. I thought better of being contrary, since they had their rifles pointed at my nose. Besides, I got nothing to fear. I'm innocent of anything they say I done. As far as I know, the men who did any killing ain't the ones on this train."

The reporter again took pause from his note taking. "Mr. Hatfield, how is it possible that so many of the wrong men were arrested?

The older man looked at him in earnest. He spoke in a low voice, as if he were imparting a secret. "These posse men, led by this fancy law dog Frank Phillips were afraid to go after the real killers. It was easier for them to come to our places instead. We were tending to our homes and our farms peaceably, not hiding out from anyone. Once these jokers got us cross the Kentucky State line, they said we were under arrest."

"How has your treatment been?"

"I got no complaints. Most of the time, I ain't been locked up. Mister Perry Cline, the jailer, has let me go wherever I pleased, as long as I came back at night. Some town folk made threats against us here in the jail, but Mister Cline said 'They'd have to kill him first, before they'd get to us'. This gave me some comfort, for he seems to be a man of his word." Wall paused for a moment and then continued on with a soft voice. "However, Old Ranel McCoy said he was gonna blowup the Pikeville jail, with us in it; and he could have done it, big as he pleased; especially, because we ain't going nowhere. He's got plenty of folks taking his part and I'm awful sorry for the man. I know that he lost his sons and a daughter but I ain't got nothing to do with none of that."

Earlier in the morning on February 16, 1888, the nine members of the accused Hatfield gang had been removed from Pikeville jail and were being escorted under heavy guard. A Louisville Marshal named J.V. McDonald had arrived in town to take charge of the prisoners. Judge Watson Barr gave him the task of transferring the accused murderers from Pikeville to the District Court. The lawman presented Jailer Cline the order of release and transfer to Louisville, to allow the prisoners to be present for the upcoming habeas corpus hearing.

The accused men were instructed to gather their meager belongings in preparation for their impending trip. With McCoy sympathizers growing in numbers, there had been numerous threats made upon the lives of the accused. There was also a rumor of a possible attempt by Hatfield supporters to liberate the jailed West Virginians. For these two reasons, Cline insisted that the care and safety of the incarcerated men was his ultimate responsibility. He told Marshal McDonald that he would like to personally take charge of guarding them until they were safely delivered to their destination. Although he would accompany him, the officer was more than happy to hand over that duty.

The prisoners were delivered to the Pike County train depot, for transport aboard the Chesapeake and Ohio Train. By Cline's reasoning, this would minimize any danger of escape or ambush. For their short trip, the attitude of the West Virginians was surprisingly good. They were happy to be saying goodbye to Pikeville. These normally free roaming men had been cooped up in jail for more than a month.

The entourage traveled in a Pullman Train car and most of the captives enjoyed a chance to experience the scenic countryside. Some, who had never been on a train before, were amazed by the speed at which they traveled. The men were also in good spirits, because they firmly believed that they would soon be released from captivity. With the likes Governor Wilson and Eustace Gibson fighting their cause, there was little chance of prolonged jail time.

Mitchell spoke to several other prisoners, who were all more than willing to share their stories. At the end of the passenger car, sat a tall, older man with white hair and a droopy mustache. He was quiet and sullen and had been watching the reporter interview the prisoners. The writer acted on his curiosity.

"Sir, would you be Randolph McCoy?" Mitchell asked, sitting himself down next to the older man.

"Yes I would."

Mitchell grabbed his notepad and flipped to a fresh page. "I'm sorry for your loss sir, but my readers would love to hear your story. Can you take a moment to make a brief statement" he said, barely containing his excitement.

McCoy shifted in his seat and cleared his throat. "I ain't much in a talking mood son. Besides, them Hatfield men have been flapping their jaws pretty steady."

"Anything you say, no matter how brief would be appreciated."

Randolph's arms folded tightly. "You see, I'm on this train to see justice done, good and proper. I've lost six of my children at the hands of the Hatfields and their friends. I've done nothing to provoke these killings, nor have my kin. Less than eight weeks ago, I lost three Children and I nearly lost my wife. By the mercy of the Lord, she will recover." Randolph paused and took a deep breath. "My home was burned to the ground and my livestock was run off. And I aim to see all the men responsible pay for their crimes."

The tall, sad looking man gazed out the open train window, watching the as the gorgeous Kentucky landscape quickly passed by. Mitchell was impressed by what he perceived to be a calm, articulate man that had suffered great wrong. "Mr. McCoy, what about your daughter Roseanna, did she die of a broken heart?"

Randolph' face became red with annoyance. "I would rather not talk about that subject. What I will tell you, is that was another insult against my family. Johnse Hatfield trifled with her affections and left her high and dry, and then had the unmitigated gall to marry her cousin

Nancy."

The Chesapeake and Ohio train arrived in Louisville at seven thirty in the evening. The Louisville station was mobbed with city dwellers, that all wanted to get a gander at these savage mountain men. "They don't much look like vicious killers" said a bystander. Most of the people there were surprised to see a group of clean, well dressed prisoners. The curious crowd closed in tightly as the marshals and jail guards walked the captives off the train and towards the lockup.

The guards were experiencing difficulty in navigating the gathering crowd. Within a short distance, the slow moving procession came to an abrupt halt. In a voice ringing with authority, Cline yelled loudly at the assemblage. "Would you folks back up and give us some breathing room. Come on, the circus isn't in town today." Begrudgingly, the crowd slowly parted in the middle, leaving a narrow path open. The file of men now continued on, followed by the spectators that watched every move as the West Virginians were walked the five blocks to the Louisville Bastille.

The jail was a large, ornate building with Greco-Roman architecture. At the front of the structure, was an inlaid iron door that stood some twenty-five feet high. On each side of the massive entrance there were two large rectangular pillars, atop which rested stone, hand chiseled gargoyles.

As the West Virginians approached the building, their jovial moods changed to a sense of impending dread. They were processed, and then marched down the long hallway to their cells, which were cold and dark. After that, the men were placed into quarters with strange inmates and for the first time, some of them felt truly trapped. "Don't fret boys, we'll all be out of here soon enough" Wall informed the Mahon brothers.

A group of reporters from various Kentucky and West Virginia newspapers gathered at the front of the jail. A man named Lee Ferguson was there to greet them. He was another Pikeville attorney, who was an associate of Perry Cline. He was also a member of the security force guarding the prisoners traveling from Pikeville to Louisville. Being well acquainted with his colleague's gift of gab, Cline appointed him to speak to the press.

Ferguson was a tall man with a loud voice and bulging stomach. He was flamboyantly attired in a vermilion colored suit. His big, baggy trousers had white stripes, which were held up by red suspenders. His ensemble boasted a matching top hat, red and white shoes and at his side he carried a black cane. It was carved from mahogany wood with a gold eagle at the end of it."

A newspaperman towards the rear of the group whispered to his colleague, "Is this fellow a lawyer or a ringmaster?"

"Mister Ferguson, what's your reaction to the Hatfield claims of innocence?" asked John Mitchell?"

The rotund attorney placed both his hands on the sides of his unbuttoned coat. "Gentlemen, these men that were brought here today are guilty of the most heinous crimes. We intend to see that they pay for them. In spite of their efforts to use bribe money to avoid extradition; our aim is to see that these killers stand trial in Kentucky, where the murders in question were committed."

"What about Devil Anse Hatfield, When are your men going bring him in?" Another reporter inquired.

Ferguson put his hand over his mouth to cover a yawn. "Devil Anse Hatfield is the next man on our list. He most of all, should be here today. My esteemed colleague Mister Cline is convinced that he is the leader of this bunch. It seems that he has avoided capture by selling off his land and moving near Logan Courthouse. There, the local West Virginia Authority protects this criminal. We are certain that his financial resources are considerable. By selling off five thousand acres for half its value, he was able to pay for his protection" replied the lawyer.

"Mr. Ferguson, what is your opinion about the incarceration of Wall Hatfield? I interviewed him this morning, and he claims to have no knowledge of the crimes for which he is accused."

Ferguson rolled his eyes. "Wall Hatfield is profound liar. This is a man that claims to have five wives and thirty-five children. He told me that he apportions his time between a quintet of lucky women. What kind of man could have five wives and not be liar?" Ferguson asked rhetorically. The crowd laughed in response to the lawyer's remarks.

The Hatfield prisoners were divided up into two large cells that were located side by side. For the first couple of days, they kept to themselves, avoiding conversation with the other inmates. Later, they warmed up to their surroundings, discovering that their fellow cellmates were curious and friendly. The Louisville prisoners also enjoyed the company of unusual guests. Particularly Wall Hatfield, who was an adept story teller.

After nine days of restless Louisville hospitality, the mountain men were treated to their first day in court. On Saturday February 25, Judge Watson Barr would consider the case for habeas corpus. The experienced adjudicator was bald and bespectacled, appearing small behind the huge wooden bench. The Courtroom was filled to the rafters, with every seat taken by reporters and spectators. The accused men sat impassively while the lawyers from the battling states proceeded to present their long winded arguments.

Following the endless verbosity of the opening statements from the prosecution and defense, Judge Barr recessed the proceedings at noon. After the court clerk passed him a note, he informed the room that the hearing would be resumed on Monday. This was to allow time for an honored dignitary to arrive. The Sunday edition of *The Louisville Press Journal* received the information and carried the following headline, "Windy Wilson to Visit Louisville."

The neighboring luminary arrived the next day without pomp or ceremony. Governor Wilson was a short, tightly wound looking man. His face was well lined, with a pale white pallor. It was painfully obvious that his thin hair had been dyed bright red, in addition to his mustache, which was trimmed in a handlebar fashion. Spectators in the courtroom noticed that he chewed on it nervously and continuously. In spite of his odd appearance, the audience was collectively impressed by his presence. They understood for him to be in attendance, this case had to be significant.

John B. Floyd, Wilson's close confidant was also in attendance. He was a State Senator from Logan Courthouse who was a friend to the Hatfield family. Devil Anse had served under his father's command during the Civil War. The two men had come to Louisville to assist and strengthen West Virginia's already able legal team. Prior to the proceedings, Governor Wilson briefly addressed his legal contingent.

"Gentleman, I'm sure that you understand why I'm here today. The integrity of our state is in your hands and your hands alone. However, I am putting myself at your disposal for any additional counsel that you may require. John and I have brought applicable case records and some legal volumes, with precedence cited from a similar case. Now let's win this one, so we can bring our men back home."

The Commonwealth of Kentucky was first to argue their case. As co prosecutor, Parker Watkins Hardin recruited J. Proctor Knott, the former Governor of Kentucky. Since West Virginia had their chief executive in attendance, the Attorney General wanted his own prominent politician to assist his side with the case.

Knott was an imposing man. At six feet four inches, he towered over most of the spectators that jammed the courtroom. For his appearance, he wore a white cotton suit with tails, a white ruffled shirt and black bow tie. When the former Governor stood up to make his opening statement, all eyes in the room focused on his giant frame.

"It is more than an overstatement to say that the State of West Virginia is well represented today. They have brought with them their best legal minds to present their case. Even their esteemed Governor has graced the city of Louisville, as well as this courtroom with his presence. It is however unfortunate that the issue they argue today can only be summed up as trivial.

Our honored counselors from West Virginia have stated that Frank Phillips did not have the proper warrants or delegated authority to arrest the nine men sitting in this courtroom. Let me state for the record that Deputy Phillips did not, act as an agent for the Commonwealth of Kentucky" Knott loudly proclaimed. This brought a loud gasp from some of the spectators in the courtroom.

"Because Mister Phillips acted as an individual, not a legal agent, this nullifies any involvement of our great state. Therefore, Kentucky is not responsible for Mister Phillips or the actions of any men that followed him. Our state is not responsible for how the arrests in question were made. However, Regardless of Frank Phillip's actions and his possible violation of procedures, the State of Kentucky had every legal right to arrest these wanted men, once they were found to be within our borders" Knott said. The former governor went on to cite other cases that would support his assertions.

After a half hour of legal argument, The Kentucky lawyer sat down to hear the opposing argument. Once again, the eloquent Eustace Gibson would present the West Virginia case. He sat at his table for thirty seconds reviewing a note the Governor Wilson had passed over to him during Knott's statement. When the dramatic lawyer strolled out onto the middle of the courtroom floor, he had a facial expression that displayed nothing but confidence.

"Your Honor, The State of Kentucky has perpetrated an abominable miscarriage of justice. Frank Phillips is nothing more than a Charlatan. He misrepresented himself as an authorized agent of your commonwealth, acting without proper authority. This has been clearly stated by the honorable Mister Knott. He has attempted to illustrate his points, by citing what he claims to be similar cases. Your honor, I can assure you that none of those cases apply to the issue at hand. There has been no such precedent where men were taken illegally, until a proper officer of the law could arrest them. These men were held for twelve hours before they were served with legal warrants.

Mister Perry Cline of Pikeville is also in collusion with Mister

Phillips in this disgraceful affair. By summoning all the magistrates as witnesses, he prevented them from hearing the case against the accused men. These men have not administered justice; they have merely fiddled with it."

When both states had finished their arguments Judge Barr finally spoke. The bookish little man declared in a loud voice. "Gentlemen, I am not prepared to render a decision today. As far as I can determine, this case has no precedent and I will therefore consult with experts on the constitution. Thank you gentlemen; court is now adjourned." The counsels for both sides looked at each other in amazement at the lack of any resolution for this case.

"Your honor, if it pleases the court. May I beg your indulgence for a moment?" asked Gibson, stepping up in front of the Judge's bench. "My client Wall Hatfield has taken sick, while being held here in your Jail. He is an older man and his health is not good. His incarceration and poor diet has brought on his ill condition. I would ask your honor, that he please receive immediate medical attention."

"Your request is granted. A physician will be brought over to him immediately" replied Barr.

The Judge finally announced his decision on March 3, 1888. He resolved to let the Supreme Court of United States make the decision. Considering the time he took the judge's statement was incredibly brief. He answered, "This is a matter of dispute between two states. Therefore, a decision on the right of habeas corpus can only be made by the High Court of the United States."

The nine prisoners bowed their heads, appearing gravely disappointed. They had counted on a solid resolution on this matter. Instead they were handed over to the Kentucky authorities, to be taken into custody. This was not before an attempt by Gibson to obtain bail for the men.

"Your Honor, I request that bail be granted for the nine men in custody. They all have families and are responsible men," he stated with conviction. "The commonwealth of Kentucky has nothing to fear by granting this request."

Judge Barr slammed his gavel down. "Mister Gibson your request for bail is denied. This is not an offense for which I would accept a motion of bail; and even if I was to do so, I suspect most of these men would take flight to West Virginia."

A moment after those words left his mouth Andrew Varney stepped forward. "Judge I want to go back to Pike County" he said.

Barr looked impatiently at the West Virginian. "Mister Varney you have able counsel representing you."

"I don't expect I know what them lawyers is saying but I want to go back to Pikeville."

Judge Barr was stopped in his tracks, perplexed by Varney's request. "Mister Varney, please tell me why you want to go back to Pike County?"

"Cause, they're gonna hold court next week and I want be there to prove I'm innocent."

Judge Barr quickly determined Varney wasn't the swiftest horse in the pack and was trying to remain patient. "Mister Varney, let me remind you of one reasonably significant detail. If your lawyer had not made the request for a writ of habeas corpus, you would be in Pike County now."

Varney shook his head in disagreement with the judge. "It weren't on my account I was brought here. I didn't know what they was doing till I got here."

"Mister Varney, I sympathize with your plight. I only wish I had known before, but now it's out of my hands" the judge told him.

Varney cocked his head. "Whose hands is it in then your honor?"

"Gods I'm afraid, it's in God's hands Mister Varney," Judge Barr answered. He quickly stood up and exited to his chambers.

That evening, Gibson was having a hefty meat loaf dinner at his hotel. At his table, several newspaper reporters approached him. "Congressman what did you think of today's decision?" one of them inquired.

"I think it was a poor one. It is the worst kind of buck passing. However, I am this very evening going to prepare an appeal to this decision. And let me tell you another thing. Some of the prisoners have requested to return to Pike County. I believe that someone has tampered with these men. It appears that they have been given false hopes about making bail if they return to Pikeville. The last thing I want to see is these men returned there, as I firmly believe great danger awaits them" Gibson answered.

"What's your opinion about Knott and Hardin?" asked another reporter.

Before answering the question, the attorney took a bite of his sizable meal. "Our side's been treated terribly. Your newspapers have been against us from the moment we got here and have treated us badly; and we have not been given a bit of courtesy from the opposing lawyers." Gibson picked up his napkin and daintily wiped his mouth.

"But in answer to your question, I'm not terribly impressed by Hardin or Knott as men. They have both been rude and uncooperative."

After his brief statements, all but one reporter departed Gibson's table. John Mitchell from The Louisville Press Journal had remained to ask one more question. "Mister Mitchell," Gibson said impatiently. "What can I possibly tell you that you don't already know?" He asked cynically.

Mitchell smiled at his sarcasm. "Congressman, forget that I'm a reporter tonight. This is off the record. I was in court today and I listened to all the legal mumbo jumbo."

Gibson tapped his fingers impatiently on the table. "Is there a point here?"

"I'm curious to hear what you really think of opposing counsel?" The reporter asked softly. Mitchell leaned forward to await the lawyer's answer.

The old politician turned, glancing to his left side and then his right. "Off the record, they're not worth the powder to blow them to hell."

On Monday, March 5, the Louisville courtroom was again crowded with spectators. Governor Wilson had returned to personally argue the appeal for the nine West Virginians. Although he was thoroughly confidant in Eustace Gibson in the handling of the case, he felt that his final oratory would have a dramatic effect on the judge. A perfect hush came over the chamber when the diminutive governor took the floor. The spectators agreed his stature was small indeed but his loudly spoken words had fire in them.

"Your Honor, I am standing here today in this courtroom, because I believe that the reputation of West Virginia has been impugned. As governor of my beloved state, it is my responsibility to protect the honor of our commonwealth. Therefore, I, more than any man, am responsible for representing and protecting the people that live there. These are my primary reasons and concerns and this is why I chose to be here today.

I believe that the issue that stands before this court is of paramount importance to my state. You will decide if kidnapping is a legal means to an end. Yes your honor, because that's exactly what Frank Phillip's and Perry Cline have perpetrated. They have kidnapped citizens of the state of West Virginia, for the purpose of rendering their distorted version of justice. I say you must not allow this to transpire your honor," Wilson concluded.

The Governor's closing argument achieved the desired result.

That afternoon, the state of West Virginia won a minor victory. After a short deliberation, Judge Barr granted an appeal to a higher court. However there was a minor point of contention. Barr ordered the prisoners to be returned to Pikeville jail until their appeal could be heard. In spite of his team's legal victory, Attorney Gibson was outraged by the judge's decision to move the prisoner's back to Pikeville

"The determination to move the men is an outrage; those men are not safe in Pike County and will most certainly come to some harm. There have been a plentitude of threats on the lives of these gentlemen" Gibson told the judge. His warning fell upon deaf ears.

In regards to the defense counsel's remarks, *The Louisville Press Journal* printed the following statement:

"Apparently, Mister Gibson believes that the only fair and honorable people in the country live in West Virginia. This couldn't be more of a myth than the legend of the fountain of youth. Let us assure him, that not only will the prisoners be safe in Pikeville Jail but also they will receive a fair trial. Our commonwealth has no hidden agenda here. We seek only the administration of justice, pure and simple. The great state of Kentucky does not make a habit of convicting innocent men."

Most of the West Virginians were happy they were returning to Pikeville. There they would be closer to friends and family, who could provide them with tobacco, candy, fresh clothes and moral support. The mountain men were now homesick and would have to wait ten days until the Pikeville authorities could come to retrieve them.

On March 15, Perry Cline arrived in Louisville with an entirely new problem to contend with. The lawyer had been presented with a bill for over nine hundred dollars. This was for the expense of transporting the captives from Pikeville to Louisville. Authorities from the larger city informed the jailer that the debt was his town's responsibility. He was furious over this bureaucratic trickery and decided to personally take the matter up with Governor Buckner. Only a day after arriving in Louisville, this situation compelled him to take a trip to the state capital.

The miffed jailer quickly set out for the town of Frankfort. Cline let his mind wander for a few minutes while he rode along the magnificently scenic of the Kentucky River. He slowly traveled past the exquisite old mansions of a town that had been established at the end of the Revolutionary War. He thought about the political boost he would receive from the high profile case that was now unfolding before people of his state. And that perhaps he would one day be able to live in one of those great old homes. That one day he might be elected to high office by those who valued his diligence in bringing the dangerous Hatfield gang to justice.

The city itself was built in center of Kentucky's Bluegrass Region, which was abundant with corn and tobacco crops. As he approached the state offices, he admired the splendor of the structures that surrounded him. The Capital building was encircled by Doric marble pillars that had a thick colonnade with an opulent marble roof.

Perry Cline waited only twenty minutes before being shown in to see the head of state. Governor Buckner's office was about ten times the size of his, which induced his admiration and envy. The walls were decorated with portraits of President Grover Cleveland, former governors and famous frontiersman Daniel Boone. The floors were covered with rich looking bronze colored tiles and Buckner's enormous desk was made from the finest polished oak.

A minute after he entered his stately office, a robust looking Buckner strode briskly over to the attorney to shake his hand. Physically opposite in every way to Governor Wilson, he was a tall, good looking man with dark hair, blue eyes and a rugged, square jawed face. The former Union Army hero had been monitoring the habeas corpus hearings with a watchful eye, wishing to offer Cline every courtesy.

After giving his guest a cigar, the governor plopped down into the plush leather chair behind his desk. He motioned his guest to also take a seat. "Mister Cline how can I be of service?" asked Buckner.

The Pikeville attorney bowed his head respectfully. "Your Excellency, I appreciate you seeing me on such short notice, so I shall come directly to the point. In compliance with the writs of habeas corpus that I was served with, I was presented with the dilemma of transporting nine dangerous men from Pikeville to Louisville. I was also confronted with the possibility of a violent ambush by Hatfield supporters if we were to travel by horse and wagon."

Governor Buckner looked thoughtfully for a moment after Cline had spoken. "Yes I can see how that might be a problem" he responded.

Cline bowed in agreement. "Yes indeed. Therefore, I chose to transport the prisoners by train, which brought them directly to the Louisville train depot without incident."

The governor nodded approvingly. "So obviously you were successful in your endeavor. Now how can I help?"

Perry Cline reached into his well-worn briefcase to remove

some itemized invoices. "There were expenses incurred in transporting the West Virginians your Excellency. The Train Company has presented me bill for a sum of nine hundred dollars, which is due in thirty days. I have asked the city of Louisville to foot the bill, as it was Judge Barr that summoned the men to that location. I have received no cooperation from Louisville officials in this matter. They told me that Pikeville should pay the bill. Sir, Pike County is no more anxious than Louisville, to pay these traveling expenses."

Governor Buckner listened to Cline's recap for several minutes, without comment. He genuinely wanted to help a man who had helped him to be elected. "Your Excellency, I am a poor attorney who merely wants to see justice prevail; but if don't get help from the commonwealth, I will be forced to foot the expense out of my own pocket. This would put a great hardship upon me and my family" explained the lawyer.

"Mister Cline, the Commonwealth of Kentucky appreciates what you have done so far. I am also quite sympathetic to your dilemma. I will endeavor to seek the help of the legislature to pay for the costs of transporting the men. I believe that I can safely assure you today that you will get the money needed to cover your traveling costs. Incidentally Perry, I want you to know that folks in the state capital are watching this trial with great interest. You get these West Virginians put away and I think there's a good chance you'll taking up residence here in Frankfort," said Governor Buckner.

The two men shook hands and Cline was walked out into the lobby of the Capital. The Pikeville man was elated because in addition to having the Governor's word about being reimbursed, he knew he could be on the fast track to elected office. In celebration he ate an expensive meal and booked a nice room to rest before he returned to Louisville, to once again transport the prisoners.

While waiting for Cline to return from the state capital, Wall Hatfield granted an interview to *The Louisville Press-Journal*. Once again the paper dispatched John Mitchell, who had previously interviewed the West Virginia prisoner on the train to Louisville. With pencil in hand, the well-dressed reporter was escorted into Hatfield's jail cell. The rank smell of human waste permeated the nostrils of the newspaperman. Although the Bastille was considered a modern facility, Mitchell was still appalled at the dirty conditions, which the prisoners had to endure.

"Mister Hatfield, do you and your fellow West Virginians still maintain your innocence?"

"That's right, not a man among us had anything to do with the killings. There's no one here that harmed no one neither." Wall replied.

"Who did then? The reporter couldn't help notice that the old man looked pale and thinner than he did on train.

Wall stretched out on his jail cot. "It was my brother Devil Anse and his sons Johnse, Cap and Bob and four or five others. They're real bad men. That's why they got me in here, because I'm his older brother and no other reason."

"Our readers want to know your reaction to Lee Ferguson's accusation, about you having five wives? Why do you think a Pikeville District Attorney would make up something like that?"

The inmate sat up in his cot. "I wish you reporter fellers would contradict that story. I ain't ever had but one wife and wouldn't want no more. That Ferguson must be crazy if he thinks I could handle more than one gal at a time. You boys are sure going to get me in trouble with my old gal."

On April 5, the case of habeas corpus was taken before Judge Howell E. Jackson of the United States Circuit Court. After a brief deliberation, Howell upheld the opinion of the lower Court. He subsequently granted the defending attorneys an appeal, before the Supreme Court of the United States. The family feud that began with a hog trial in a log cabin was now to go before the highest court in the nation.

Newspapers in Washington D.C. picked up the story this historic battle over the rights of habeas corpus. All the editorial sections ran articles about the legal significance of this confrontation between two states. The pieces stated that two former members of the House of Representatives would argue on opposing sides of this high profile case.

On April 23, 1888, the final act of this legal drama was to be staged, which would bring down the curtain the protracted battle over state's rights. On the high court docket, the case was identified as, "Plyant Mahon vs. Abner Justice, jailer of Pike County."

Eustace Gibson was the first to argue his before the nine judges of the Supreme Court. The experienced litigator was confident, well prepared and convinced that he would bring home a victory for the State of West Virginia. For nearly two hours, his voice boomed with the polished oratory of a skilled politician.

"Your Honors, this is a most historic day, for you on this venerated court have the opportunity to right a wrong and to correct a great injustice. Plyant Mahon and the eight others were treacherously kidnapped from the state of West Virginia. After their unlawful detainment, they were illegally transported across the state line into Kentucky. This is the plain and simple truth. There is no other way to describe the devious acts committed by the so called 'Special Deputy' Frank Phillips. They were the actions of a lawless man who invaded his neighboring state. His foul deeds were committed without proper warrants and procedure; and his actions are clearly indefensible.

Mahon's fundamental, constitutional rights have been violated. This great document clearly implies that 'There shall be no resort to force, for the purpose of capturing persons charged with a crime and fleeing to another state'. This rule of the constitutional law was clearly violated by Phillips and the other Pike County authorities. Your Honors, I beg you to do what is legally and morally right. Honor the writs of habeas corpus and return these men to West Virginia," Gibson concluded.

J. Proctor Knott now had his opportunity to rebut statements made by his former congressional colleague. The unusually tall attorney walked to the center of courtroom and while gathering his thoughts, stood silently for twenty seconds. His long hesitation added dramatic effect to his cause. Unlike Gibson, he was refreshingly brief, taking only twenty five minutes to argue his point.

"In the words of William Shakespeare, "This is much ado about nothing." I do not understand why the commonwealth of West Virginia has chosen this proceeding to secure redress in this matter. It would be much better for them to file a direct suit against the commonwealth of Kentucky.

Their actions remind me of a ride I recently took on a train. While my friend and I stood at the rear platform, we noticed a small yellow dog jump out of the bushes. With all his might, this scrawny mongrel ran to try and catch our speeding train. As the excited dog was quickly left behind us, my friend said. 'I wonder if that dog really thought he could catch this train; and if he did what he would have done with it.' And with that quote, Knott's argument was finished.

On May 15, *The Louisville Press Journal* stated, "The legal battle between Kentucky and West Virginia is now over and our brilliant attorney, former Governor Knott has prevailed. Our nation's highest court has upheld the decisions made by the honorable Judges Barr and Howell. This August body has stated that there are no legal means established, for the mandatory return of individuals illegally taken from one state by authorities in another state. It is now clear that nothing stands in the way of the administration of Kentucky justice.

The nine West Virginia men will remain in Pikeville Jail, until their day in court arrives."
■■■

CHAPTER TEN: THE FORTRESS

The sizeable office of The New York Globe was overflowing with the pecking sound of Hammond Typewriters. Twenty newspapermen busily worked at their desks, scrambling to meet deadlines for the morning edition of the publication. The aroma of stale cigar smoke and burnt coffee engulfed the office, as copy boys and typesetters plodded in and out of the hectic, rectangular room.

Thomas Randolph Kelly purposely sat at his cluttered, banged up desk putting the finishing touches on his latest expose. "Another God damn masterpiece," he thought to himself. The proud writer had spent the previous three weeks investigating allegations of corruption at Tammany Hall, the whore of the Democratic Party political machine, wielding a tremendous influence over the city and state of New York.

Kelly's muckraking news article stated that under the new leadership of Richard Croker, little had changed with this crooked establishment. The hard nosed reporter concluded that the new regime had simply developed more sophisticated methods in maintaining a network of payoffs. Though it was now twelve years since the conviction of the infamous Boss Tweed, the tenacious writer had dug up some compelling evidence to suggest that New York should embark upon a new legal crusade to once again clean up Tammany.

Kelly was a short, brawny man who was first generation American born, from Irish decent. Like many others from Celtic roots, his dirt poor parents had immigrated to the United States during the great potato famine of the late eighteen forties. He had grown up in the toughest section of the Five Points district, where decaying tenements like Gates of Hell, Jacob's ladder and The Old brewery housed thieves, miscreants and murderers. With a drive to succeed, he had not grown up to be one of them.

"Tom, the boss wants to see you," yelled one of Kelly's coworkers. With a slight feeling of dread, he rapidly walked down the narrow, dark hallway to the editor's office. Bill Blaylock was a quick tempered man of few words He managed all the reporters and had a reputation for frequently shouting at them. He had spent thirty years with the Globe working his way up from teenage floor sweeper to reporter and finally to Editor and Chief. Having been one of the best writers at the paper, he never missed a trick. Kelly understood from experience that when he dealt with his boss he better his facts straight and his work on time.

The editor's office was dim and dusty with the blinds closed, even though it had an excellent view of the city. Bill Blaylock sat in a huge swivel chair, while chewing on the end of a Partagas cigar. Obscured in a cloud of smoke, he furiously jotted down some notes while Kelly stood at the entrance of his workspace. Kelly waited for his supervisor to acknowledge his presence before entering his office.

Blaylock motioned the reporter into his office. "Come on in Tom, I got a new project for you." "Do you like to travel, a working vacation?" the editor asked in a jovial tone.

The seasoned writer suddenly felt a sense of excitement at the prospect of leaving New York. "A change of scenery is good."

"Then you should be happy Tom—pack your bags, you're going to West Virginia," Blaylock informed him.

This news somewhat astonished him. "West Virginia, what's in West Virginia?"

The editor puffed out several smoke rings. He looked up in the air as if he were speaking to someone else. "Why West Virginia he asks."

Kelly nervously smiled. "Yeah, why do you want me to go to West Virginia?"

"There's a little war going on between some mountain roughnecks living on the border of Kentucky and West Virginia. I've read dispatches about scores of men and women being murdered.

"Who are these idiots?"

Blaylock open a small humidor and offered his writer a Cuban cigar, which Kelly quickly grabbed. "These idiots are the Hatfields and McCoys. They've had a blood feud going on for over ten years. Newspapers in Washington D.C. and Pennsylvania carried a story about the Supreme Court getting involved with the arrest of nine murder suspects that were illegally held in Kentucky."

Kelly eagerly listened while puffing his smoke. "Sounds like a Saturday night in the Five Points."

Blaylock nodded in agreement. "Yeah, except you won't find any Plug Uglies in Logan County. I want you to locate a man named Devil Anse Hatfield and get an interview with him."

"What's a Devil Ants?" Kelly asked with a puzzled look.

"It's Devil, A-n-s-e; he's the leader of the Hatfield men. He's one mean, murdering mountain man, that's wanted by the state of Kentucky, real bad. And if you can get to him, you'll have done what no other reporter has been able to do."

The writer had a smirk on his face. "You mean no other reporter has wanted to do. He'll no doubt try to kill me if I try to find him?"

The editor chuckled. "I got news for you. There are plenty of people in town that want to kill you already."

"They'll be a lot more after my Tammany story."

Leaning back in his chair, Blaylock flopped his large feet on is desk. "Then now is the perfect time to get you out of town."

Kelly stood up to leave his boss's office. "If someone wants to shoot me, it may just as well be in West Virginia."

"That's why I like you Kelly, always a positive attitude," Blaylock answered.

*****

After two wearing days of train travel, followed by a half-day stagecoach ride, Kelly arrived in Logan County, West Virginia. When he checked into his Spartan room at Bunce's Hotel, he was tired, hungry and grouchy. This preceded a minor case of culture shock after the writer surveyed the size this small rural town. In less than four days, he had gone from the noise and excitement of a fast paced metropolis, to a town with narrow streets with nothing more than a few dozen unpainted wood and brick buildings. By his quick reckoning, this ramshackle hamlet was no more than a flyspeck.

The following day Kelly immediately went to work talking with local townspeople, to determine whom to interview for information about the Hatfield's. He was informed that John B. Floyd would be the man he wanted to see. He arranged to have a meeting with the State Senator, whose office at the county seat was only two blocks from his hotel.

Floyd was an old Hatfield family friend. During the habeas hearings, he had accompanied Governor Wilson to Louisville. After his introduction to the reporter, the senator arranged a meeting with Devil Anse's brother Elias. In sending him to West Virginia, Kelly's editor knew he would work quickly and without trepidation. After leaving New York only five days earlier, he was now about to meet a real live Hatfield.

"You look like a city boy. You must be that writer from New York City." said Elias Hatfield. His voice boomed from the entrance of the Morgan's cafe. Clad in overalls, boots and a straw hat, he sauntered over to the table where Floyd and Kelly's were sitting. "The senator tells me you're buying lunch today." The robust man extended his long arm.

"It would be my pleasure sir" replied Kelly. He stood up, firmly clasping the big man's hand. Floyd had brought the visitor to the local Logan eatery, for the purpose of making an introduction. The reporter with impressed by his size and strength. He also sensed an honest quality when he looked into the dark blue eyes of this Hatfield clansman.

Elias sat down across from the newspaperman. "You're a long way from home Mister Kelly. I hear New York's the biggest city there is."

Kelly sipped a blazing hot cup of coffee. "I don't know of any bigger."

Elias narrowed his eyes. "What I can't directly figure out, is why folks from your parts would be interested in the affairs of my kin."

"Well then, I'll come directly to the point Mister Hatfield. My paper thinks that the feud between your family and the McCoy family is news worthy. We believe that our readers would very be interested in the Hatfield side of the story. And why enmity exists between your families," Kelly explained.

"That's a real hive of hornets Mr. Kelly." Elias looked over at Floyd seeking affirmation.

"It's alright Elias, Mister Kelly seems to be an honest fellow," Floyd said.

What exactly would you like to know about?" asked Elias.

"What's your involvement in the feud Mr. Hatfield?"

Elias shook his head. "I ain't been involved in any of that. All I want is to be left alone. If folks just leave my family alone, then they got no quarrel with me. If they don't, then watch out. That's my code of life Mister Kelly. I just mind my manners and my business."

"What about your brother? Kentucky newspapers say he's the brains behind the killings of several McCoys."

"I don't expect my brother would want me spouting off about his affairs. I suspect maybe you should ask him that question yourself Mister Kelly."

Kelly looked Elias straight in the eyes. I'd like nothing better. In fact, that's why I am down here Mr. Hatfield. I want to tell his side of the story, fair and square. I'll give your brother a voice and a chance to be read by a quarter of a million New Yorkers."

Elias shook his head in amazement. "You say that many folks read your paper? Dang, I couldn't imagine that many souls. You must be piled on top of one another."

That's right Mister Hatfield. It's real crowded there. But I tell you in earnest that it's so. Now, Can you take me to meet with your brother?" Kelly anxiously asked.

Elias thought about it for a moment. "I suppose there wouldn't be no harm in it. All the papers in Kentucky have done nothing but write lies. And my brother deserves a chance to tell his side of things."

"I aim to tell the truth Mister Hatfield."

"Then we'll leave directly Mister Kelly," said Elias.

Thomas Kelly thanked John Floyd for his help and then rented a trail horse from the Logan livery stable. He and Elias would have to ride for a few hours through isolated country, before reaching the new home of his brother. The fugitive's old house by the mouth of Peter Creek was no longer a safe haven because it was too close to the Kentucky border.

Devil Anse Hatfield learned from the mistakes made by several of his associates, who currently took up residence in the Pikeville Jail. He was resolved to not be taken into custody, not by Frank Phillips or any other man. He purchased two new parcels of land, between Logan Courthouse and his old cabin. His new abode was wedged inside of a small valley, with its back up against the highest mountain in Logan County. This eliminated any possibility of a rear assault from anyone who wanted the old man. He could see anyone approaching for miles from his new location. If someone tried to capture him, they would have to come straight at him.

As Elias Hatfield and Kelly approached the narrow valley, they could see a structure that looked like a small fortress. It was a curious rectangular building that was short and flat looking. It was constructed from huge logs that were each two feet round, stacked up six high. At the front of the, was thick oak door that looked like it could stop a train. Open portholes all around the periphery gave the inhabitants a view of all points in the valley.

"Is that your brother's house?" asked Kelly.

"No, that's 'The Unwanted Guesthouse' replied Elias.

The curious reporter pulled out his handkerchief to wipe the sweat from his forehead. "Unwanted guests?"

"The kind that a come toting Winchesters." Elias pointed to the building. "See them holes surrounding the place?"

"Yes, it looks like an ironclad."

"Those are gun ports. They come in mighty handy if any bead planting comes necessary."

"Bead planting, what's that?"

"That's when a man shoots another feller Mister Kelly. He draws a bead on him. Ain't you ever heard that expression?"

"Where I come from most people are shot in pubs or street fights and at close range with a pistol." Kelly flashed Elias a sly smile. "We call that drilling someone."

Elias motioned Kelly to halt his mount. "Although he already knows I've brought company. I need to go parley with my brother to make sure I can bring you up to the house." Elias shrugged his shoulders." That's just good manners around these parts.

Kelly nodded in agreement. "Yes, of course."

"You wait here. I best make sure that no one takes a shot at you" Elias instructed.

"Yes please, no bead planting in my Irish field. I'll stick here like glue."

Elias smiled and turned his horse up the hill. Kelly waited on his trail nag, intently watching his guide go past homemade fort, up the steep ridge. He could barely see a cabin, about a hundred yards up behind the Unwanted Guesthouse.

The reporter waited for about ten minutes but Elias had still not come to retrieve him. His thoughts turned to New York and the small apartment where he lived. How different his life style was, from these rugged mountain men. A week earlier, he was in the largest city in the country, alive with the noise of carriages, streetcars and rush of humanity.

His day dreaming was abruptly interrupted, when from behind came a large hand yanking his suit jacket and pulling him down off his horse. From the ground Kelly looked up to see a tall, sturdy looking young man. He jumped to his feet, managing to duck a punch that was thrown by the youthful stranger. Kelly countered with his own short left jab in his attacker's face, followed by a swift uppercut to the body.

Kelly stood only five foot, seven but both his punches connected solidly. The stunned but much larger mountain came at the Irishman again but was hit with a combination right hook to the chin and rabbit punch to the side of his head. The young man fell to the ground and started to lift himself up, until he heard the sound of gunfire. A startled Kelly and his attacker turned around to see Elias standing with another big mountain man who brandished a Henry Rifle.

Devil Anse walked toward his son. "Bobbie Lee what the hell do you think you're doing? That man's our guest." He extended his hand out and Kelly immediately shook it. "I'm sorry for my son's bad manners young feller. My name is Anderson Hatfield."

Robert E Lee Hatfield slowly stood up and dusted himself off. His reached his hand out to shake Kelly's like nothing had happened. "Mister Kelly, that's my nephew Bobbie Lee" said Elias.

The young man hung his head down with embarrassment. "Pleased to meet you Mister Kelly; I'm awful sorry I took a swing at you."

"That's all right. I just wish I hadn't worn my new suit. Paid twenty dollars for it last summer," Kelly said, wiping the dirt off. "Why did you come at me kid?"

"He thought you were a Hawkshaw Mister Kelly," answered Devil Anse.

The reporter noticed Bobbie Lee's mouth had a trickle of blood. He reached into his coat pocket and handed him his handkerchief. "Here kid, your lip's bleeding. What's a Hawkshaw?"

"It's a bounty hunter" replied Elias.

Bobbie Lee walked over and gently patted Kelly on the shoulder. "You really gave me a good walloping. Where did you learn to fight that way Mister?"

"I learned to fight in an Irish gang, at a place called the Five Points. It's a little slice of heaven where you'll find the toughest mugs on earth. And I also did a little boxing at college" answered Kelly.

"I'll be damned," replied Bobbie Lee.

After the men trudged up the ridge to the Hatfield cabin, their guest was introduced to Levicy and the children. Devil Anse was thrilled to have a reporter all the way from New York City. He wanted to impress Kelly with some real West Virginia hospitality. "Sweetie, cook up a mess of vittles, Mister Kelly is staying for dinner" he hollered.

Kelly found Devil Anse to be a forthright, entertaining conversationalist. The affable West Virginian told his side of the story in a clear and concise way. He spoke about the origins of the feud, stating that he had wished no harm upon The McCoy family. He informed the journalist that he even helped influence a decision by Logan jury to acquit Sam McCoy of killing Bill Staton.

"What about all the other killings? What about the three murdered brothers and the New Year's raid on McCoy family home? Kelly bluntly inquired.

"You heard about that all the way in New York, did you Mr. Kelly?"

"Yes, my editor became interested after he read about the

arrests of the men that supposedly rode with you and your brother during the violence against the McCoys ," answered Kelly.

"Those so called boys murdered my brother Ellison in cold blood. That's what they done. But I'm not a vengeful man. I had nothing to do with their killings. My brother Ellison had a lot of friends that were mad bout him being bushwhacked; and them boys wound up dead. That's all I know about it. But if you want to know how I feel, my brother never harmed a fly and those three McCoys took his life for nothing. No sir that was justice" replied Devil Anse.

"What about the New Year's incident?"

"Honestly Mr. Kelly, I don't know much about it. I wasn't there."

"I would be inclined to believe you Mr. Hatfield, but what troubles me is while I was in Logan Courthouse, I read an account of things in a Louisville newspaper. It stated that your own brother Wall blamed you for the raid and all the McCoy killings" Kelly said boldly.

Devil Anse poured a shot of whiskey for his guest. "Here's to you. It's real sad. Right now he'll say anything to protect his own hide. I feel sorry for him. But he's making up stories for the newspapers and that's all there is to it. I wasn't anywhere near Old Ranel's place on New Years. I reckon it was my Cousin Jim Vance but he's dead now. He was murdered by Frank Phillips and his posse of hired killers."

"Is that why you're hiding out up here?"

"Yes, that's part of it. Them Kentucky men led by Frank Phillips are coming into our state, kidnapping folks right out of their own homes."

Kelly kept steadily writing on his note pad. "Who is this Phillips I keep hearing about?"

"He's Perry Cline's hired thug," Devil Anse said shaking his head. "I seen him in action and he's a stone cold killer."

"Mister Hatfield, tell me about the Unwanted Guest House, is Phillips the reason you built it?" His question prompted a laugh from his host.

"Like I told you before, a man ain't safe in his own place no more. Even our Governor Wilson couldn't stop them. Took it all the way to the Supreme Court he did, but them sons of bitches didn't lift a finger to help. So I built this place and let me tell you," Devil Anse pointed his finger at Kelly, "ain't nobody getting up the hill that don't belong. The front of the guesthouse is a foot thick. I got three thousand rounds of ammo squirreled away and enough food to outlast the siege at Vicksburg. You see Mister Kelly, I intend to protect my family and myself; and if anyone's going to try taking me, they best send a regiment of men." After speaking to him for five hours, Kelly was convinced that it would take a whole army to capture the old rebel.

*****

Other fugitives in the Tug Valley region not were as smart or prepared as Devil Anse Hatfield. During the summer months of 1888, rewards for remaining fugitives added up to nearly eight thousand dollars. This attracted so-called detectives and bounty hunters, from all across the United States.

Kentucky and West Virginia became a popular place for these enterprising gentlemen. Anderson Hatfield was the most wanted feudist of them all. His fame was increasing because newspapermen from around the country were coming to the Tug looking for a story. His capture would not only bring a bounty hunter a fair sum of money but it would also bring great notoriety. The Hatfield-McCoy feud was becoming national news and Devil Anse and Randolph became the primary focus of this ever growing saga.

Local authorities in Kentucky and West Virginia were going wild offering rewards. Governor Wilson was filled with vengeance when his state lost the habeas corpus case that went before the Supreme Court. He was not about to let Kentucky lawbreakers tread through his state, going unpunished. To reduce the chance of further incursions, he offered a five hundred dollar reward for the capture of Frank Phillips. Additionally, the state indicted the crafty lawman, along with twenty-five others, for the murder of Jim Vance. These men also had a price on their heads but it was a lesser amount of one hundred dollars each.

The Valley was being flooded with intrepid bounty hunters looking for a quick payday. Area inhabitants were becoming increasingly irritated by the influx of these outsiders.

"A most unwanted kind of plague has fallen upon our valley," began a short Kentucky editorial. "They are called detectives but they are far from the like. These men are not real lawmen, not like the ones that serve your county. These men are not concerned with justice of any kind. It doesn't matter a damn to these mercenaries, whether they arrest a Hatfield or a McCoy. Their primary concern is how much money that can be made in the transaction.   It should be the goal of our citizens to hang these detectives and drive off anyone that does not belong in the valley. When that happens, people that live here can get down to the business of planting crops and cutting timber before the spring rains. Furthermore, I have a suggestion that could possibly end hostilities between the McCoys and Hatfields. Offer nice rewards for these detectives, and enough honest Hatfields and McCoys will unite to rid the valley of these vultures in less than two weeks."

The first branch cut off the bounty bush was a man named Dave Stratton. He was with Frank Phillips, the day Bill Dempsey was ruthlessly killed. This Kentucky man had taunted the poor West Virginian, before the ice cold Frank Phillip's put a bullet in the terrified man's head. To catch him, The Eureka Detective Agency of Charleston West Virginia dispatched three agents to capture the fugitive. It was an easy day's work for the hawkshaws, who located their man asleep under a pleasant green tree. One of the detectives simply placed his Walker Colt at the side of the sleeping man's head. "You don't give us any trouble and you might just make it to Logan Courthouse alive" he instructed detective.

Mid October was Harvest time in the Logan County, but there was different kind of bounty being gathered. Young Charlie Gillespie was captured in Virginia, taken to Cattlesburg jail, and then transferred to Pikeville. The colorful Lee Ferguson escorted him under heavy guard. Gillespie had voluntarily gone along with the Logan Wildcats on the ill-fated New Years raid. He talked about it freely and was more than happy to put the blame on them.

In Pikeville, Thomas Randolph Kelly interviewed the young man while he was incarcerated. His piece was carried in the Globe, as well as several other publications, which were read across the country. The story stated Charlie was a nice looking gentleman with jet-black hair and piercing blue eyes. The reporter wrote that this youthful Hatfield associate was a real fine fellow, hardly being a man that looked like an outlaw.

"Some Pinkerton man got the drop on me, while I was tending to my chores," Charlie said. "He put his hog leg up to the back of my head and told me to raise my hands. I told him, you got the iron in your hands mister and you can kill me if you want to, but I ain't gonna throw up my hands for no one. If you treat me like a man, I'll go along peaceably with you."

"Why did you go with the Hatfields on New Years Day?" asked Kelly.

"Cap Hatfield tricked me. All he told me was that we going out for ride and that we was gonna have some fun. It was Cap, Johnse, Jim Vance and those other fellers that began the ruckus and did the killing. That big fool Cottontop killed the McCoy girl."

Kelly looked up from his notes. "Who is Cottontop?"

Gillespie cleared his throat and spit on the floor of visitor's room. "Ellison Mounts killed the McCoy girl named Alifair. He was mad about his Daddy's being stabbed and shot by the McCoy brothers."

"Is that why the men you rode with attacked the McCoy home?"

"Vance said that we had to kill Randolph McCoy, because he was the only living material witness."

"Witness to what?"

"He was the only witness to the killing of the McCoy brothers." As he spilled the beans, Charlie nervously shifted in his chair. "Vance said he was tired of sleeping with his gun under his pillow. He told them other fellers to fill the McCoy cabin full of holes, until them folks came out. I didn't do any of that. All I did was stand guard by the horses. Honest mister, I wouldn't have gone along, if I knew they was do any of that," Charlie answered.

Two weeks later, a pair of bounty hunters came looking for Ellison Mounts. They were a couple of hard nosed gunmen, named Dan Davidson and Trevor Gordon. The two men were good friends who had met while serving in the United States Cavalry. After leaving The Dakota Territory they both worked for Allen Pinkerton's detective Agency in Chicago. Normally they specialized in breaking strikes but also had experience in tracking men.

Davidson was big, mean and didn't talk much. Gordon was friendly and did enough talking for the both of them. The two detectives had read newspaper reports about the large rewards being offered for the Hatfield-McCoy feudists. They had been unemployed for a few months, which motivated them to ride into West Virginia.

To obtain their first reward, the nearly broke ex-Pinkerton's chose to go after Cottontop. Some local folks in Logan County had informed them that he wasn't too bright and would be easily apprehended. The skilled hunters traveled to Mate Creek and staked his cabin. Waiting outside all night, they decided they would stay until they caught sight of him.

"This sure isn't Chicago is it Dan," Gordon commented.

"Chicago, this isn't even Deadwood," Davidson answered in a monotone.

"That's for sure. It's almost like being on a deserted island. The beefy little man rested his back up against a tree. "I'll say one thing though; it is peaceful and quiet out here."

"Yeah it would be, if you stop flapping your jaws for a minute but that would be like asking a crow not to peck at a cornfield." Davidson pulled a small whiskey bottle from his top pocket, took a swig and handed to his partner.

Trevor wiped his lips and took a drink. "If I didn't do the

talking then who would? You're the quietest man I've ever known."

"I talk, when there's something important to talk about" Davidson responded indignantly.

Gordon crossed his arms and looked in the air. "Now let's see, when's last time you started a conversation? I know it was when Garfield got killed by that agitator."

As the two were talking, Ellison came out of the front door of his small cabin. He climbed on his mare and quickly galloping off Grapevine Creek.

Davidson watched the large man as he mounted up. "He's one big, ugly son of a bitch, ain't he Trev.

"Dan I'm proud of you, you actually started a conversation all on your own."

As they untied their horses, Dan smiled at his partner. "Let's go collect our reward on this big son-of-a-bitch."

Most people acquainted with him thought that Cottontop was a slow-witted young man. However, he was smart enough to know when he was being followed. Choosing not to show his alarm, Ellison continued to ride his horse at a steady pace. Davidson and Gordon tentatively followed behind him for about twenty minutes.

As he attempted to lose them traveling through some rough terrain, the detectives grew impatient. The two men began to close the gap between themselves and their prey. "Hey kid, stop" yelled Gordon. Cottontop ignored the man and kept riding. "Hey kid, I know you can hear me. Just stop for a second, we ain't gonna bite you."

Ellison Mounts halted suddenly, veering his horse around to face the two bounty hunters. He yanked his Springfield rifle out of his saddlebag, slinging it across his arm. "Why you following me, what do want Mister?"

"Me and my partner have ridden a long ways. I've got kin folk round these parts," answered Gordon.

"Is that a fact?" asked Mounts.

"That's a fact. They live near Logan Courthouse. You wouldn't happen to know if we're on the right road would you?"

Ellison sat expressionless, staring at the two detectives for ten seconds. "I asked you a question boy, do you know the way or not?" Gordon said in a hostile tone.

"Oh yeah, I know the way" answered Mounts. He abruptly pointed his gun and fired a round at talkative man.

"God damn it" yelped Gordon after the hot bead smashed into his leg. Both detectives slid off their horses, with Davidson quickly helping his associate take to the cover of the forest. "That blonde prick ain't as dumb as he looks" the wounded man said in a shaky voice.

"You ain't lying," replied Davidson. He pulled out his hunting knife and cut his leather holster strap off. He quickly used it to tie a tourniquet around his wounded friend's leg. "It doesn't look so bad. Looks like the bullet went clean through."

Davidson reached for the flask out of his coat pocket and took a swig. He poured the rest on his wounded partner's leg, which caused him to wince with pain. "That's a waste of good whiskey Dan."

"Don't worry about that, we'll buy a case when we're done here" answered Davidson. The quiet detective looked his friend over for a moment.

"What? I don't like that look on your face, you've been thinking again, haven't you?"

"Trev, You love to talk, don't you?"

Gordon shrugged his shoulders. "You know I do."

"Well, here's you're golden opportunity." Davidson inserted several cartridges into his Winchester. "You keep this asshole distracted and I'll double back on the dumb bastard. Who knows, maybe you'll bore him into giving up."

"Haw haw, it's not bad enough the kid tried to kill me, now you're gonna torture me with your bad jokes."

Davidson grabbed his rifle, crawled out behind his associate and disappeared out into the underbrush. "Hey kid, you might as well give up now and save us the trouble of taking you back draped over the saddle" Gordon yelled.

"Kiss my ass you Pinkerton bastard" Ellison yelled back, as he fired off a round towards his pursuer.

"Hey boy, that's real funny; you calling me a bastard. I heard tell that you're the one who has no daddy. I hear that your daddy looked like Swiss cheese after the McCoys got through with him."

"Just keep talking Yankee, so I can draw on bead on you." Between yelling, Ellison took time to load his Springfield.

"Draw a bead? You couldn't draw water from a full well" yelled Gordon. He fired a couple of wild shot back at Mounts.

"Shot good enough to hit you mister" Ellison yelled proudly.

"Sure, when I was standing still and right in front of you. Why don't my partner and me come over and hold still for you? How'd that be kid? You can pretend you're shooting ducks at the shooting gallery."

Davidson's smart mouth tactic worked perfectly, providing him ample time to get a position behind the unsuspecting Cottontop. Taking care not to make noise with his big frame, he crept up on the side of a burned out hickory tree, planting the barrel of his Spencer rifle astride a branch. "Hey moron, surprise" Davidson said in a whispered voice.

A startled Ellison turned around to see a large bore, center fire rifle pointed at his heart. "Damn hawkshaws," he muttered, throwing his rifle on the ground. The brawny detective had Mounts put his hands in the air, calling out to his talkative partner to come and put steel handcuffs on their prisoner.

The former Pinkerton's transported Ellison to the Pikeville jail, turning him over to the loving arms of Perry Cline. After receiving their reward money, the tenacious detectives took a few days off. Gordon quickly rebounded from his leg wound and along with his partner Davidson, was back on the trail of another fugitive.

Alex Messer was a hard case, and considered a dangerous man by reputation. He was a former lawman, claiming to have twenty-six notches on his Remington, forty-four, forty. He stood six feet tall and some said he was strong enough to pull a plow without a mule. Boasting to his friends, he said that unlike Devil Anse, he wasn't about to run from any detectives.

One brisk but sunny November day, Messer left his fortified cabin early in the morning. He drove his wagon to Lincoln County, for the purpose of picking up some needed supplies. It was a small, sparsely populated town, not too far from the West Virginia border. Messer was not aware two cautious and dauntless detectives were trailing his every step.

While in the Lincoln General Mercantile, Gordon struck up a conversation with the local mountain man. He passed himself and his partner off as city boys that needed some advice on the right kind of feed for their chickens. He actually told the unsuspecting Messer, that he and Davidson went by the name of Smith and Jones.

Gordon was such an affable fellow, that he got himself and his partner an invitation to Messer's place. He lived alone in a small one room cabin, which was two miles north of Lincoln. The three men were sipping some of their host's fine homemade whiskey, when the conversation turned to firearms.

"That's a good looking hand gun you got there Mister Jones, what make is it?" Messer asked.

"Why it's a nickel plated, Pearl handled, forty five Colt, Sheriff's model. Would you like to take a look at it?" Gordon slyly asked his host.

"Sure" Messer replied enthusiastically.

Gordon handed his loaded pistol over to Messer and let him examine it. He unloaded the barrel, spun it around, cocked and dry fired it. "This gun has a beautiful action to it Mister Jones." The trusting man reloaded the firearm and handed it back to the small detective.

"What's the make of the hog leg you're carrying in your holster, Mister Messer?" Gordon asked innocently.

"This?" Messer asked, easing the revolver out of its holster. "Why this is a Remington, model eighteen seventy five, forty-four. Frank James owns one just like it." He handed the weapon over to his newfound friend and told him to try the action.

"Yes sir, this is a mighty fine gun you got here Mister Messer and I appreciate you handing it over to me. Now my partner and I have something we'd like to share with you."

"Yes, what is it Mister Jones?"

Gordon smiled at Messer, with a grin as wide as a river crossing. "Sir you are now in the custody of Trevor Gordon, that's me and my friend over there is Dan Davidson."

"Nice to meet you" Davidson quickly added.

Messer's jaw dropped when he found out that he had invited bounty hunters into his home. He was even more irritated and haven given over his gun without a shot being fired. As a result of his over confidence, the careless fugitive now found himself making an unplanned trip to the Pikeville jail.

Not all the detectives who visited the Tug Valley were as cunning as Gordon and Davidson. This was particularly true of two from Pennsylvania, who claimed that they would be the ones to capture Devil Anse. They sat around at a tavern in Logan Courthouse, telling patrons they would also shoot Cap and Doc Ellis. This information was relayed to the Hatfields, who in turn got arrest warrants issued for these arrogant northern detectives.

These loud mouth bounty hunters soon found themselves locked up in the Logan County Jail. But not before they provided Cap and Doc some minor amusement. On their way to jail, the two detectives were forced to cross a stream, with the Logan men astride their captive's backs. "I never stayed so dry or had so much fun crossing a stream before," Cap reflected for the local newspaper.

CHAPTER ELEVEN: KELLY VISITS MABELS

"We rode our old trail horses over rocky terrain and steadily up endless sloping ridges. Before we reached the mountain, I became anxious as we passed fewer and fewer dwellings in this already meagerly populated territory. As we trotted peacefully down the narrow trail, I observed a few of the robust inhabitants of the region. They watched us too as we traversed the terrain and signaled our impending arrival by hooting out birdcalls to their nearest neighbors. I'm sure our host knew of our upcoming visit long before we arrived.

When I first saw the mountain man, he struck me as a mysterious and imposing figure. He stood six feet, two inches tall, with his blue jeans tucked into his knee high boots. The long gray coat that he wore fluttered like a battle flag in the wind. Exposed, was the Army Colt revolver that he wore holstered at his side.

I could not help but stare at his prominent features and his powerful frame, which was remarkable for a man of fifty. His good manners and warm hospitality immediately eradicated my initial trepidation at our introduction. After all, this amicability was coming from a man with a notorious reputation for violence.

He beckoned me to sit and chat on his front porch, all the while surrounded by his children and grandchildren. We all hung on his every word while he wove a colorful tapestry of fascinating stories. I sat entertained for several hours listening to his version of the violent events that have already taken a dozen lives. These were the same actions that had reinforced his fierce reputation. I will now recount to you our readers the story of Devil Anse Hatfield."

These were the opening passages from Thomas Randolph Kelly's article, which appeared in the New York Globe. Bill Blaylock sent Kelly a telegram informing him his Hatfield story was generating a good deal of interest. He instructed him to prolong his visit to get a follow up story about the ill-fated romance between Roseanna and Johnse and to use the Mountain Romeo and Juliet angle.

A day after wiring back his story, Kelly received another telegram from Blaylock. The message surprised him, as it instructed him to travel to Pikeville, Kentucky. His Hatfield-McCoy articles were helping to sell more newspapers. He had done his job too well and now had been now been recruited for the long haul. The big city newspaperman was going to rural Kentucky to report about the impending trial of Wall Hatfield.

When he arrived in Pikeville, Thomas Kelly was somewhat relieved. It wasn't New York, but it was a lot more of town than Logan Courthouse. Since he would be spending many weeks there he hoped that the town met his required criteria. In between his writing chores, he was happy to discover minor distractions to pass the time. This included gentleman's clothing store, a smoke shop, a good barber, some decent eateries and two saloons.

Pikeville also had something that Kelly thought every self respecting town should have, which was a Bordello. It was on the outskirts of town but it was still within walking distance from his hotel. After only a few days in town, he decided to make use of its services.

Kelly wanted to doll himself up for his first big night in town. He put on his dark gray suit accompanied by his 14-carat gold watch and chain. He wore a pristine Bowler Hat that he had purchased at the men's store in town. As a finishing touch, the fancy dressed man splashed on some toilet water that smelled like lilac.

During his afternoon visit to the barber, the New Yorker asked one of the local boys where Mabel's fancy house was located. He was properly instructed about its whereabouts and who he needed to see. Kelly found it amusing that the place was called Mabel's, as there was no one there who went by that moniker.

In his conversation at the barber's, Kelly was told to ask for "Big Brenda." When he first laid eyes one her, he understood why she was called by that name. The reporter was a well traveled man but never recalled seeing a woman with such large breasts and broad shoulders. She was a haggard looking redhead in her late forties, who wore her makeup caked on like plaster. On her lips she painted on the reddest lipstick Kelly had ever seen, and on her right check she had a mole the size of a June bug.

When Kelly knocked on the door at Mabel's, the gregarious, strong-armed Madame immediately yanked him inside. "Hey sweetie, you ain't from around here are you?"

"No you gorgeous creature, I'm from New York City" Kelly answered.

A broad smile appeared on Brenda's face, exposing a missing front tooth. "Gorgeous, ah ha, ha, you smooth talker" she roared. "Go on with you now, are you really from New York?"

"Yes Ma'am and a kind local gentleman informed that this is

the finest house in all Kentucky" Kelly said, with a hint of Irish accent.

"You got it right honey—you came to the right place."

"When I came in I could see that right away. Kelly says I, that fine fellow who led me here, did not lead you astray."

"Let's hope not; leading you astray will be my job." Brenda winked at Kelly. "Now let me get you some whiskey and we'll get down to business."

After Kelly forked out the tidy sum of fifteen dollars, Brenda led him into a dimly lit room where three available working girls sat playing poker. To his surprise, all three were fairly attractive. His choice included two washed out blondes and compact looking brunette. The dark hared girl was the one that smiled back at him, so he selected her. His new acquaintance at once escorted him to one of the upstairs rooms. She was young woman in her late twenties, with milky white skin and a short shapely form. Her eyes were dark and sultry, with lips that were full and sensuous. Though employed in a brothel, the man from the Five Points thought she had style.

As they entered the room, Kelly's eyes darted around to quickly glance at the plush red carpeting, which smelled like a mixture of spilled beer and cheap perfume. He glanced at the brass bed and ran his open palm over the satin bedspread. His eyes were then drawn to the wall where several paintings of beautiful naked women were on display.

"Hell, this room's got everything any self respecting Ne'er do well could want."

"I hope so, especially with little old me here to keep you company. What's your name darling?"

"It's Thomas."

"Well Thomas, my name's Debbie. Would you like a drink?"

"Does a beaver build dams?"

"Well this one doesn't" she answered, pouring him a glass of inexpensive brandy. "A lot of my customers are married men, traveling salesmen and the like. Are you married Thomas?"

"No, my job takes me all around God's creation for long stretches of time. That's no kind of life for a woman. So I don't have much to offer a perspective bride."

"I doubt that, you don't look so bad to me." The petite prostitute looked her client over for a moment. "In fact, you're pretty damn good looking," she declared.

Her compliment caused the Kelly to blush momentarily. He knew it was probably just happy talk, but it sounded good. "You don't have to flatter me" Kelly quickly replied.

"I'm not, I mean it. You're quite nice to look at and I'll prove it to you." The young woman took off her silk housecoat and stood seductively in her black lacy underwear. She slowly stripped off her French brassiere, exposing her small but shapely breasts. Glancing at her client seductively, Debbie gracefully slipped out of her undergarments. Except for sheer, black silk stockings and garter belt, she stood completely and gloriously naked.

Though experienced with professionals, Kelly shyly sat back in his chair sipping his brandy while enjoying the brief strip tease.

"Why are you still sitting over there? Come over here and get what's coming to you," she said in a sultry voice.

"And what's coming to me."

Debbie motioned him over. "You'll have to come to me first." Kelly quickly complied and walked over to the inviting young woman. He stood before her for a moment, soaking in the curves of her figure. "Do you like what you see Thomas?" He looked her up and down and nodded. "Yes I do very much." "Then show me."

In the thirty minutes that followed, Thomas Randolph Kelly was in a blissful state. He worked for several months without so as minor social engagement. With precious few days off in between, there had been no doubt in his mind he had needed the companionship of a woman but not the kind with strings attached. After their paid session was over, Kelly laid comfortably with Debbie's arms wrapped around him.

"Are you a satisfied customer Thomas? You know us girls at Mabel's aim to please," she said softly, running her fingers through his black hair.

Kelly thought about it for a moment. "Does a horse eat oats?"

"You sowed these wild oats eh?" Debbie answered slapping her thigh. "Are you going to be in town for awhile Thomas?" she suddenly asked.

"Yes I'm here on business and I suspect that I'll be here for several weeks."

"Good, then I'll be expecting another visit from you soon."

Kelly stood up and began to slowly get dressed. "I can assure you of that Miss Debbie."

An hour later, Kelly lay awake in his lumpy hotel bed, staring at the portrait of Daniel Boone, which hung on the wall directly in front of him. He thought about Debbie and how curvaceous her body was. He pictured her long brunette hair hanging down on his face while they made love. His body still had her scent on his skin and he thought about how good it felt to have a pretty woman's delicate fingers touching his hair. Even though he knew that to her, he was only John that had only once crossed her path, he wished that she was lying next to him.

Kelly thought it would be nice to settle down with a woman as attractive and accommodating as Debbie. Maybe he and his future wife, whoever she was, could get a small house with a white picket fence; and he could move out of his tiny, cluttered apartment. Possibly, they could have a couple of kids and start living like other young families. With a life like that he wouldn't have to seek his companionship in a house of ill repute. After deliberating those thoughts for some time, his better judgment took over. A few minutes later he was sleeping peacefully.

∎∎

CHAPTER TWELVE: WALL FALLS

Hot, hot, sticky and miserable. It was the third week in August of the year 1889, and the trial of Wall Hatfield was about to begin. After his little diversion from the previous night, Thomas Kelly had slept peacefully. He ate a large breakfast at his hotel, checked for messages at the telegraph office, then promptly walked four blocks down to the office of District Attorney.

Lee Ferguson was a Pikeville lawyer and associate of Perry Cline. Taking on the role of information liaison, he had conducted a press conference on the steps of the Louisville Bastille. This was after the arrival of the West Virginia prisoners for their habeas corpus hearing. When he learned that he was assigned to be the prosecuting attorney for the Hatfield case, the big city reporter set an appointment to interview Ferguson.

Kelly entered the District Attorney's untidy office and momentarily awaited the arrival of the busy man. The observant writer glanced at the wall and admired the beautifully framed law degree. It stated that the University of Kentucky had awarded it to Mister Ferguson in 1872. In the center of the floor, was a worn out Persian rug that laid underneath a beat up maple desk. On top of the small table were piles of papers and files related to the upcoming legal contest. There was also a basket containing a few stale doughnuts and a half eaten sandwich, as well several empty sarsaparilla bottles.

A portrait of the well known Daniel Boone, early Kentucky settler also hung on the wall. "That's the same picture that is on the wall of my hotel room," Kelly thought. He stood up to read the gold nameplate that was at the bottom of the portrait. "Daniel Boone" he mumbled; "Boy they sure love him around here. He must have been some kind of big shot."

A tall, heavyset man entered the room, briskly walking over to shake hands with the reporter. "Sorry I'm late Mister Kelly, but I'm getting kind of busy. The trial starts in two days and I'm wrapping up some loose ends" Ferguson stated.

Kelly smiled, turning on his charm. "I fully understand and appreciate you taking time out of your busy day to see me."

"Not a problem at all, though your certainly not the first reporter that's been in here to see me." Ferguson opened a file and began to read its contents.

"That's been the story of my life. Always I'm a day late and a buck short."

"Can I offer you some coffee Mister Kelly?"

"No, I had some at the hotel." Kelly sat back down in the chair in front of the desk.

The lawyer looked up from his reading. "Of course you are from one of the largest newspapers in New York. That carries a lot of weight with me. Yes sir, mighty impressive."

Kelly removed his note pad from a leather satchel. "I'm just an Irish kid from a hell hole called the Five Points. And I'm lucky enough to make a living stretching the truth."

Ferguson nodded and smiled politely. "Well Sir, what can I tell you about the case?"

"With the convoluted twists and turns of this legal contest do you think you'll get a conviction against Wall Hatfield?"

"I'm quite certain of it." Ferguson paused, folded his hands and leaned forward in his big chair. "I've got witnesses that will place him at the site of the murder, and I have something better than that."

"Oh yes and what would that be?" Kelly asked the prosecutor.

"I've got a signed confession from Wall's nephew, the bastard son of his late brother."

"Yes, what's his name again?"

"Ellison Mounts."

Kelly nodded. "That's right, old Cottontop.

"Yes indeed Cottontop. And he has provided us with irrefutable testimony about the murders of the three McCoy brothers."

"What method did you use to extract this confession? Did you employ a blackjack like one of our Manhattan Policeman?" Kelly said jokingly.

"No, we don't quite conduct our business like that down here Mr. Kelly."

"I certainly didn't mean to imply anything."

"Don't worry Sir, you didn't offend me. I know you're being droll. We may not be as sophisticated as you New Yorkers, but Pikeville isn't exactly full of backwoodsmen."

"Kelly nodded in agreement. "No, I can see that."

"Ellison Mounts isn't the smartest wolf in the pack. After detectives brought him to town, I began working on him with my interrogation techniques. He started off by trying being a real hard case;

but I got him to spill the beans by telling him that the Hatfields had hung him out to dry" explained Ferguson.

"So what did you do when the kid began to crack?"

"When Mounts was ready to spill his guts, I got Perry Cline, the Sheriff and a secretary in our holding cell to hear his confession. I couldn't believe the details this kid remembered, After all, he's considered an idiot. He's named Gillespie, Carpenter, Messer and Old Wall Hatfield himself. The whole bunch was there when the McCoy brothers were killed. Wall swore them all to an oath of secrecy. Of course I'm still missing the nastiest ones in the batch, Devil Anse and his sons Cap and Johnse" Ferguson said, with a slight tone of frustration.

"How many men are you bringing cases against Mister Ferguson?"

"Call me Lee," replied the large attorney.

"Thank you I will. But in return I expect you to call me Kelly, that's what my friends call me."

Ferguson smiled politely, bowing his head in response to the reporter's courtesy.

"I have assembled cases against seven men including Wall. And I have a strong body of evidence and witnesses to support the charges against them."

"Who are the other men Lee? Are they mostly Hatfields?"

"No, they're mainly friends of the Hatfields. Charley Carpenter is one of them. He tied up the poor McCoy brothers before the others murdered them. Alex Messer is another. We also have the Mahon brothers, Doc, Plyant and Sam. Those three are Wall's son-in-laws. And lastly of course, we also have Ellison Mounts, my star witness. Mister Kinner has dismissed charges against two men, in exchange for their testimony against Wall Hatfield."

Kelly finished writing down the attorney's previous statement and briefly looked up from his notepad. "And who might they be?" He inquired.

"Two brothers we arrested, Dan and Jeff Whitt. They were both present at the murders. All of the other men were shooters in the killings. But the first man up before the bench will be old Wall. He among them was surely the ringleader; he along with his murdering brother. If we only had his brother, if we only had that old Devil" Ferguson concluded.

*****

The Pikeville Court house was a two story, red brick building, with wooden windows painted with white trim. At the front of the second floor was a small balcony with French doors. This brought welcome relief if a spectator needed to get some fresh air or have a smoke. The courtroom itself was filled to capacity with people who sat in the darkly stained wooden benches that furnished the municipal building.

Many of the local townspeople had taken the day off, for the purpose of watching the first day of this historical proceeding. Newly designed electric ceiling fans brought minor relief to the people that were present on this hot, humid day. Also in attendance were reporters from newspapers around the country, including Thomas Randolph Kelly.

At the front of the courtroom, at opposite ends, were two oblong tables, along with large leather chairs that were provided for the defense and prosecuting attorneys. Representing the Sixteenth Judicial District, for the commonwealth of Kentucky were S.G. Kinner and Lee Ferguson.

Wall Hatfield had retained Confederate war hero Braxton Gaynor for his defense. He was the first litigator to take the floor of the jammed packed courtroom. Known as the "Fighting Confederate," he was the youngest man to rise to the rank Brigadier General in the rebel army. He had been a dashing young cavalryman who forged his reputation under the command of Stonewall Jackson, at the Seven Days campaign and the battle of Chancellorsville.

Gaynor was fifty-two years old and had put on a fair amount of weight since his glory days. He was a tall, handsome man who carried his extra pounds well and walked with the confidence of a man of privilege. His suit was richly tailored and Confederate gray, as if to remind all present of his valiant deeds during the War Between the States.

"Gentleman of the jury, Let me ask you a simple question." He paused to look at the face of each man in the box. "What are we doing here today? My client is an innocent man. He has been wrongly accused of three murders that he did not commit. In fact, never in my estimation, has such an innocent man been so wrongly accused of a crime he could not and would not commit. Yes, he was present when the young men were taken, but his only concern was for their safety and just treatment.

Gaynor walked over to where the jury foreman was seated and leaned in smiling at him. "Wall Hatfield is not a murderer. He is far from that and the evidence that I will present will prove that conclusively; and we'll all be able to go back to our homes and businesses. And you the jurors can return this upstanding man sitting before you, back to his home and back to his life. It will be my job to convince you, the twelve men of this jury that what I'm saying is the absolute Gospel truth and it will be your job to exonerate Wall Hatfield. This must be done in the name of what we understand to be justice in this country. It must be done in the name of what we know is the right thing to do."

The attentive jury was sufficiently impressed by the impassioned words of the former war hero. After all, most of them considered themselves loyal southerners. It was now the prosecuting attorney's turn to speak his peace and he had the hometown advantage.

The honorable Judge John M. Rice was chosen to preside over the Hatfield trial. With the countenance of a thoughtful, scholarly man, he looked the part of a distinguished magistrate. This was a now an extremely high profile case with considerable political ramifications for those involved. Governor Buckner selected Rice, based upon his reputation of honesty during his many years of service on the bench. "You may present your opening remarks Mister Ferguson" he instructed.

Having had several months to prepare for the case, Ferguson was ready for his initial argument. He confidently walked to the center of the courtroom and stood in front of the jury. Dressed in a blue, pin striped suit, with his hands clasped behind him, he began to address the twelve men sitting attentively before him.

"Gentlemen, Wall Hatfield is a heinous murderer. This is the plain, common sense truth. You are all intelligent men who want to hear and see with your own eyes what is the truth is in this case. The truth is that Wall is a cold, calculated killer and the commonwealth of Kentucky will prove it to you. He kidnapped two men and a boy, with the intention obstructing real justice from being carried out." Ferguson pointed his index finger directly at Wall. "That man sitting over there, with malice of forethought played judge, jury and finally deemed himself as chief executioner. Motivated solely by vengeance, he took the law into his own hands. Now he must pay for it.

You, the jury have the opportunity to right this wrong and provide this man with a chance for real justice, which is infinitely more than he provided for the poor McCoy brothers. You, the men seated before me today, have an opportunity to send a message out to lawbreakers in our great state. You, the men seated here today can send out a warning that our state will not tolerate lawless men and vigilante justice. That our state will meter out the law like a swift and decisive thunderbolt sent down from the heavens. That our state will be a safe place for its men, women and children; and will be governed by the law and only the law."

Lee Ferguson finished his statement, quietly walking over to pat his associate, S.G. Kinner, on his shoulder. With opening remarks made, Kentucky was ready to present their case against Wall Hatfield, and called their first witness. "The state calls Randolph McCoy your honor," the prosecutor announced in a loud voice.

Dressed in a white shirt and black pants, a sixty four year old Randolph McCoy stepped into the witness box. His white hair, mustache and beard were peppered with a few streaks of his once darker color. His once smooth skin was now well lined with years of suffering from the loss of his six children. He was tired and battered, but not beaten. The old man had waited years for his day in court, a real court. Now that day had finally arrived.

Lee Ferguson gave Randolph his opportunity to tell his version of events that transpired on Election Day 1882. When he completed his well rehearsed testimony, Gaynor then had the opportunity to cross examine the witness.

"Good afternoon Mister McCoy, I'm Braxton Gaynor, how are you today sir?" asked the defense attorney.

"I'm fine" Randolph declared sternly.

"Good, that's fine sir. I know it was a long time ago, but can you tell me the names of the men who took your sons into custody?"

Randolph folded his arms tightly. "Yes, Devil Anse and Wall Hatfield."

"Who else was present sir?"

"Cap and Johnse Hatfield were there too."

Gaynor moved in a little closer to the witness. "Who else was there sir, can your remember their names?"

"I don't recollect."

"You don't recollect?" The lawyer repeated loudly for the jury to hear.

"No sir, I don't."

"You don't recollect who was there, but yet you know Wall Hatfield was there?"

"Yes sir, that's right."

"Mister McCoy, who shot your boys on Election Day?" Gaynor asked suddenly.

"I don't know for sure, I wasn't there when they shot them"

answered Randolph, squirming in his chair.

"You don't recollect who killed your boys, yet you know Wall Hatfield was there. What else don't recollect?"

Lee Ferguson abruptly looked up from his note taking. "Objection your honor, Consul may have set a new world record badgering a witness."

"Your objection is sustained Mister Ferguson. Mister Gaynor, you must please confine yourself to specific questions and refrain from extemporaneous commentary" Judge Rice instructed.

"Yes your honor—"Mister McCoy, in your testimony to Mister Ferguson, you stated that Wall Hatfield and several other men whose names you can't remember overtook the men transporting your sons back to Pikeville."

"Yes, that's what I said" Randolph answered somewhat impatiently.

Gaynor again moved closer to the witness. "Do you remember the names of the men, who attempted to take your sons back to Pikeville?"

"Err…um…I think it was Joe and Matt Hatfield."

"Yes and what were the names of the other men who were with them?"

"I can't recall."

"Well, since you testify being with these men, do you recall what Wall Hatfield said when he took custody of your sons Mister McCoy?"

"Yeah, he said something about that my sons should be tried in the place where the crime was committed."

"Tried, tried for what Mister McCoy?"

"Tried for killing Ellison Hatfield"

Gaynor turned towards the jury, increasing his volume. "You did say tried and not murdered, didn't you Mister McCoy?"

"Yeah, that's what I said, what's a matter are ya deef?" Randolph replied. The courtroom exploded with laughter.

Judge Rice slammed down his gavel. "I will have order in my courtroom at all times," he admonished. "Mister McCoy, you will please confine your answers to a yes or no."

Gaynor regained him composure and resumed his cross examination. "Mister McCoy, as you stated before, you really don't know who killed your boys?"

"Yes sir, I didn't see it happen, but I know who did it" Randolph rebutted.

"And since you weren't there, you really can't say that it wasn't Wall Hatfield's intention to give your boys a fair trial?"

"I know that wasn't his intention."

"Mister McCoy, just answer yes or no. You can't say for sure, that it wasn't Wall Hatfield's intention to give your boys a fair trial?"

Ferguson stood up from his chair. "Your honor I object. Now learned consul is asking the witness to speculate about the defendant's intent."

"I'll allow it," Rice immediately replied.

"Mister McCoy, I'll repeat the question. Can you say that you know for certain that Wall Hatfield did not intend to give your sons a fair trial?"

"No, Since I wasn't there, I can't say for sure" answered Randolph, hanging his head down.

"No further questions for the witness your honor," the defense attorney announced.

The courtroom suddenly buzzed with the sound of low talking voices. "Ladies and gentleman, we must have silence in my courtroom at all times" Judge Rice warned. "Mister McCoy, you may be excused from the witness box.

The prosecution had not faired well with Randolph at their first witness. Ferguson and Kinner hoped to rebound with the testimony of Sarah McCoy. In spite of her frail appearance, she had fully recovered from the wounds she received from the New Year's Day attack. All eyes in the court were now glued and all ears attentive as the old woman began to testify.

The burly court bailiff stepped up and administered the oath to Sarah McCoy. "Do you so swear to tell the truth, the whole truth and nothing but the truth, so help you God?" He asked.

"Yes, I do" Sarah said softly, taking her seat before the judge and jury.

Lee Ferguson walked over towards the witness stand, stopping only two feet in front of the witness "Mrs. McCoy, how many of your children have died violently during the feud between your family and the Hatfield clan?" Ferguson boldly asked.

Outraged by his question, Gaynor stood up and yelled loudly in his Virginia drawl, "Your honor, I strongly object to my esteemed colleague's question. What possible relevance can it have to the case in hand?"

"Objection is sustained. Mister Ferguson, you will please confine your questions to ones regarding the case before the bench," instructed the judge.

"Your honor, I think my question has the greatest bearing on this case. It establishes the motive for the on going hostilities between the two families" Ferguson fired back.

"Mister Ferguson, I've already made my ruling." Judge Rice looked over at all the attorneys. "Counselors, I hope to not have to warn either one of you again, about sticking to the case before the bench." Gaynor, Ferguson and Kinner all nodded in agreement.

The prosecutor turned away from Sarah, walking over to where the jury was seated. "Let me re-phrase my question. Mrs. Hatfield, how many sons did you lose, as a result of the Election Day incident in eighteen eighty two?" Ferguson asked.

"Three, I lost three of my boys, Tolbert, Pharmer and Randolph junior."

"And how old was Randolph Junior Mrs. McCoy?"

"He was just sixteen."

Ferguson shook his head. "Yes sixteen, and I'm sure were all very sorry about this tragedy. Mrs. McCoy, please tell the court, what happened on the night of August Eighth, Eighteen eighty-two."

"Well, Mary Butcher, my son Tolbert's wife and I, walked a fair distance to the old schoolhouse in Mate Creek. That's where the Hatfields, were holding my boys."

"Please tell the court what occurred next, Mrs. McCoy," Ferguson instructed.

"When we got to the abandoned schoolhouse, it was late in the evening, about ten o'clock. Wall Hatfield stood at the entrance, blocking Mary and me from seeing my boys. It was downpour, the likes of which would've caused Noah to build another ark" described Sarah. Her remark elicited slight chuckles in the courtroom.

"Go on dear, you doing just fine. What else occurred?"

"Wall Hatfield stood there all high and mighty and he wouldn't let me see my boys. It was his brother Devil Anse that let us pass."

Lee Ferguson knew that Sarah's testimony was being taken in earnest by the jury. He observed that they were hanging on her every word. "Mrs. McCoy, what condition were your sons in when you entered the cabin?"

"They was cold, tired, tied up and a scared to death. I begged the Hatfield brothers to let my boys go so they could get a fair trial. Wall said that if his brother Ellison lived, then my boys would live too. But if he died, my boys would too."

The prosecutor smiled at his witness. "What happened after that

Mrs. McCoy?"

"Wall and Devil Anse told us to go. They said that they couldn't stand to hear me wail no more. I'm sure that what they couldn't stand was their own murdering guilt eaten at their souls," Sarah said in a raised octave.

"Objection your honor, the witness is speculating on the thoughts of the accused," Gaynor concluded.

"Objection sustained. Mrs. McCoy, please just stick to the statements of fact and not your opinions."

"Yes your honor, I'm sorry." Sarah again looked at Lee Ferguson. Well Sir, me and Mary were forced to leave…and…and that was the last time I saw my boys alive" said Sarah, choking back her tears.

Ferguson paused for a moment to give his question the proper dramatic effect. "Sarah, who do think killed your boys?"

Before she could answer Braxton Gaynor loudly objected. "Your honor, the prosecuting attorney is asking the witness to speculate on this question, as opposed to making a statement of fact."

"Objection sustained, Mrs. McCoy you will refrain from answering that question. Mister Ferguson you know better than that."

"I withdraw the question your honor. Thank you Mrs. McCoy, I have no further questions," Ferguson said indignantly and took his seat.

The defense now had the job of cross-examining Sarah McCoy. He sat at his table thinking for about 30 seconds before speaking. "Good morning Mrs. McCoy, how are you today?"

"I'm fine, but I'd be better if you got on with it, so we can get this over with" Sarah quipped.

The courtroom broke out with laughter causing the lawyer's face to red. He composed himself, smiling politely. "Mrs. McCoy, you stated to Mister Ferguson that, Wall Hatfield blocked your entrance to the old school house. Is that not correct?"

"Yes that's correct."

"Mrs. McCoy, that was almost eight years ago. How can you be sure it was Wall and not his brother Devil Anse?"

Sarah McCoy blurted back her answer petulantly. "I've known the man for thirty years; I think I know what he looks like."

Gaynor now knew Sarah's memory was much clearer than Randolph's was. "Mrs. McCoy, what are the names of the other men who were with Wall and Devil Anse at the cabin?"

In spite of the lawyer's attempt to tax her memory, Sarah rapidly rolled off the names. "It was Cap, Johnse, Alex Messer, Charlie

Carpenter, Dan Whitt; and several other men were outside in tents."

Gaynor turned away from the witness and faced the courtroom audience. "Mrs. McCoy, didn't Wall Hatfield come to visit you at the home of Perry Cline after you had been badly beaten and didn't you mention to him, that your late son Tolbert had told you at the cabin, that Wall had been kind to them?"

"No!" yelled Sarah in a shrill voice. "I never made any such remark. My son's was scared to death that man was gonna kill them. He told them, that He was gonna fill them full of more holes than a sifter bottom. That's what I remember."

The defense counsel was momentarily shaken. Like an inexperienced second lieutenant that was caught in an ambush, he decided to cut his losses and retreat. "I have no further questions for this witness your Honor."

At the end of Sarah McCoy's damaging testimony, Judge Barr adjourned the proceedings for the day. During the first day of the Hatfield trial, Thomas Kelly had taken several pages of notes. He had every intention of going back to his hotel room, to begin working on his next dispatch. However, as he walked into the lobby of the Pikeville Court House, something distracted him. He bumped into his paid companion from the previous evening.

"Thomas, what are you doing here?" asked the shapely brunette.

"Oh, hello there, I'm here reporting on the trial for the New York Globe."

"New York Globe, what's that?"

Kelly rolled his eyes with mock indignation. "It's only one of the largest newspapers in the country."

"Oh, my goodness, I didn't realize you were such an important man."

"I'm not. I'm just an extremely talented man that gets a decent wage for reporting the news. And when I don't get the facts straight, I just make them up."

Debbie chuckled at the reporter's wit. "Is the Wall Hatfield trial news in New York?"

"Yes, New Yorkers love to read about other people's misfortunes. It takes their minds off their own troubles." The reporter tucked his leather satchel with his notes under his arm. "So we know why I'm here, what the devil brings you in here today?"

"I have the day off, so I decided to see what all the fuss was about. I've been reading about it in our town newspaper for months."

Kelly suddenly had a whim. "Since you have the day off, would you do me the honor of joining me for supper?"

Debbie Ferris hesitated for a moment, as she normally made a rule to not go out in public with clients. "Yes, I would like that very much. I don't get to hob knob with many big city newspaper men."

Kelly smiled and extended his arm. "I'll try not to be a disappointment."

Debbie wrapped her arm around her escort. "I'm sure you won't be."

The reporter and his companion enjoyed a steak dinner at the Starlight Palace saloon. It was a Wednesday evening and the tavern quiet and dimly lit. They sat at a secluded table, making small talk about the differences between big city and small town lifestyles. Kelly talked about his love of journalism and told Debbie about some of his recent work. Unlike his dinner date, he had traveled around the country and had twice journeyed to Europe.

Debbie had lived Louisville and Pikeville all of her life. Although she had only had a limited formal education, Kelly found her to be intelligent and stimulating conversationalist. She in turn viewed Kelly as attractive, worldly and a pleasant change from the men she met while practicing her evening vocation.

"I suppose your wondering why I became a prostitute." Debbie blurted out.

Kelly nearly choked on his dinner. "No, I was just enjoying the company of an intelligent, vibrant woman. Your reasons for how you make your living are your business. But since you did bring it up, why are you?"

"I like you and I want to tell you anyway."

Kelly bowed in modesty at her comment. "Thank you"

"My husband and I met in Louisville. I was working at the grocery and he used to come in and bring me fresh flowers. He would tell me I was the prettiest thing he had ever seen."

"I can see why he said that. Your husband was a man with good eyesight. What happened, did you leave him?"

Debbie looked down and began to blush. "Hell, we were just kids and he was as sweet a man as there ever was. Clarence was his name. He had a job with the Wentworth coal mining company, outside of Louisville. It paid pretty well and he loved doing it. I had only known him a short time before we were married. Six months after we got hitched, he was killed inside the mine, which was nearly three years ago."

"I'm terribly sorry, what happened?"

"It was an accident, nobody's fault really. He was setting a dynamite charge on a clogged chute. The charge blew too early and twelve tons of coal suddenly gave way and buried him alive. Clarence loved everything about mining and setting explosives. He used to drive me crazy at dinnertime with all his talk about that damn coal mine. I guess he died doing what he loved." Debbie shook her head. "Funny isn't it? Someone who loves being down in a deep hole in the ground like that."

"Men are funny that way and maybe he liked the seclusion. I guess I love my job too. And sometimes I wind up going to some real hellholes." Kelly paused as the barmaid delivered to drinks to the table. "Well it's awful he got himself killed, must have been hard on you."

Debbie slowly sipped the glass of champagne her companion had ordered for her. Reflecting upon her past had an effect on her that she had not anticipated. She sighed softly. "Anyway, I was in bad shape and I became a drunk and whore. I've never been much for working in a store or a cafe. When Clarence was alive, I stayed home and took care of him. We almost had a kid right before he died, but I lost the baby. Probably just as well, I wouldn't have made much of a mother after he died."

"You've had a tough time and I'm sorry for your loss" Kelly replied.

Debbie's tone of sadness gave way to a more cavalier one. "Don't going playing the violins for me. I'm twenty-eight years old and I'm doing what I want. It's not so hard what I do. After all, I perform a service for the community. I even got a judge and the mayor coming to visit me on a regular basis." She lifted her glass, toasted the air and drank it down.

Kelly stared at the young woman for a moment, trying not to look her with pity. To him her life seemed sad and empty, but this attracted him even more. His life had an aspect of emptiness too.

Debbie abruptly changed the subject. "Hey lets see some of these stories you write."

"Now, you're kidding right?"

"Yeah now!" she answered. The couple left the saloon and window shopped, occasionally kissing while walking back to the Hotel. The newspaperman showed his date the story he had written about Johnse and Roseanna. For fifteen minutes Kelly watched as Debbie quietly read his article without saying a word. When she finished she laid the paper down on the night stand and looked into Kelly's eyes. "You're a real romantic sort."

"I'm just writing what people want to hear." Kelly grabbed the bottle of Whiskey on his dressing table and poured a drink for himself and his guest. "Besides, it was a juicy story, real Shakespearean drama" he replied cynically.

"I don't know about any of that flowery clap trap but you're good. This is much better than the things they write in the local paper."

Kelly tipped his Bowler and spun it on his forefinger. "Why thank you Madame, my first critical success in Pikeville."

Debbie suddenly leaned over and kissed Kelly on the mouth.

"What was that for?"

"I don't know, I like you" she replied.

"Is that apart from your professional feelings?"

"Shut up and pour me another drink."

Thomas did as he was instructed and served the pretty girl another shot of bourbon. The couple drank several more while talking until two o'clock in the morning. They both fell asleep for a short time and when Kelly awoke two hours later, Debbie was gone.

*****

Thursday morning the trial of Wall Hatfield was promptly back in session. The second day of testimony brought out another large crowd to see James McCoy take the oath. He was the oldest son of Randolph McCoy. Once he stood in front of Devil Anse's Henry Rifle, refusing to pay homage before the older man. He was still ruggedly handsome at forty years of age with a demeanor was strong and forthright. His voice had a booming masculine timber, which all helped make him sound like an earnest witness.

"Mister McCoy, please tell us what happened on August 9, 1882. This was day your three brothers were murdered," asked Lee Ferguson.

"Objection your honor, the demise of the McCoy brothers has not yet been proven to be a case of murder in a court of law" Gaynor stated indignantly.

Ferguson turned to the judge, raised his hands in the air and smiled sarcastically. "Well your honor, if they weren't murdered then it was the worse case of suicide I have ever seen." The courtroom erupted with laughter after the prosecutor's remark.

Judge Rice had to cover his mouth to hide his own laugh. "Mr. Gaynor, I think we can safely say the McCoy brothers met their demise at the hands of others. Your objection is overruled."

Ferguson repeated his original question. "Mr. McCoy, please tell us what happened on that terrible August Day."

"I remember the day Sir. I tried to stay close to my brothers all along but the Hatfields had so many men guarding them. I couldn't get in to see them and like everyone else I waited."

"Waited for what?"

"I waited for news about Ellison Hatfield."

"Why, Mister McCoy, what news were you waiting for?"

"News about whether or not he was going die. You see Wall and Anse Hatfield were sitting around like vultures waiting for the man to die. That way they figured they could kill my brothers with a clear conscience."

"Objection your honor," Gaynor loudly interrupted. "The witness is speculating on my client's thoughts and motivations."

"Objection sustained. Mister McCoy, would you please give your testimony based on statements of fact and not opinion" the Judge advised.

"Anyway, when the Hatfields heard the news about their brother, they were on the move. I went to my uncle's house, waiting to see what would happen next. On the road to my Uncle Asa's place, I saw Wall and Elias Hatfield, Ellison Mounts and one of the Mahon boys. I wished that there had been some way to help my brothers, but there was too many of them," James explained. As he sadly looked down at the floor for a moment, the courtroom sympathized with his sense of loss. "While I was waiting at my uncle's place, me and him heard shots fired; about fifty of them."

"Asa and me gathered up a couple of men and we went over towards where the shots was fired. That's when we found them."

"What did you find there Mister McCoy?"

"My brother's dead bodies, that's what we found. They were tied to some paw paw trees and hanging in the wind.

The sound of low talking voices buzzed through the courtroom. Ferguson confidently looked over at his opponent. "Your witness Mr. Gaynor"

The large attorney walked over, and in an attempt to intimidate him, looked James straight in the eye. "Mister McCoy, did you see who shot your brothers?"

"No sir I didn't. I did see Wall and Elias Hatfield, Ellison Mounts and Plyant Mahon headed for Mate Creek, about twenty minutes before the shots was fired. I don't expect they was headed for a barn dance," answered James.

"Whether or not they were attending a barn dance, a church social or picnic is not my concern. Now I asked you if you saw who saw shot your three brothers. All I need is a yes or no answer to that question."

James McCoy's face became red with exasperation. "No, I did not."

"I have no further questions for this witness at this time your honor" Gaynor said. The defense attorney was satisfied that none of the witnesses had been able to place his client at the scene of the shooting. The eldest McCoy brother was now excused from the witness stand. His testimony had done little to impress the jury either way.

The commonwealth of Kentucky called several other people, who re-stated what the three
McCoys had testified. Late that afternoon, Joe Davis was sworn in to give testimony regarding his brief encounter with the Hatfields.

"Mister Davis, you met Wall and Devil Anse Hatfield on the road to Mate Creek on August ninth didn't you?" asked Lee Ferguson.

"Yes I did Sir." Davis answered.

"What were the circumstances of this meeting?"

The Hatfield brothers got word to me, that they wanted to talk."

"Talk, talk about what Mister Davis?"

"They wanted to talk about the killing of their brother. You see, I was at Jeremiah Hatfield's place on Election Day and saw what happened with Ellison. Wall wanted to know if the young one took part in the stabbing."

Ferguson walked towards the jury box. "The young one was referring to Randolph McCoy Junior?"

"Yes sir" replied Davis.

"And what did you tell him Mister Davis?"

"I told him that he did."

Ferguson now stepped over to the jury box and placed his hands on the railing. "Mister Davis, why would Wall Hatfield ask you such a question?"

"He needed to know because he was fixing to shoot the other two brothers and he didn't want to shoot the boy if he didn't have no part" Davis replied.

"Of course, how noble of him" Ferguson quickly responded.

A red faced Gaynor now stood up yelling. "I object your honor, in the strongest possible terms. The prosecutor is providing commentary on testimony in the most mocking and frivolous way. A statement I might add, that is purely conjecture and not a matter of fact."

Judge Rice banged his gavel to silence the courtroom.

"Objection sustained, Mr. Ferguson please refrain from any more melodramatic remarks during the remainder of this proceeding. Mister Davis, the commonwealth appreciates your testimony today but I need you to only stick to the facts of the case."

Ferguson bowed to the judge. "My apologies your honor; I have no more questions for this witness."

Gaynor maintained his strategy, repeating the same question he had asked all prior witnesses. He remained at the defense table, seated next to Wall Hatfield. He looked down at his notepad, never making eye contact with Davis while he doodled with his pen. "Mister Davis, did you see Wall Hatfield shoot Tolbert, Pharmer and Randolph McCoy Junior?"

"I did not."

"Did Wall Hatfield ever state that he was going to kill those boys, without a trial?"

"No sir, he did not" Davis replied.

"So you really can't say for sure, why Wall Hatfield asked you about Randolph Junior's complicity, in the killing of Ellison Hatfield, can you Mister Davis?"

"No, I can't be absolutely positive."

"Thank you Mister Davis, I have no further questions for this witness" The defense attorney said confidently.

Thus far, Gaynor had been able to prove to the jury, that Wall Hatfield had not been at the scene of the shooting. That was until the Whitt brothers took to the witness stand. Dan and Jeff had gladly cut a deal with commonwealth prosecutor selling out the Hatfields to save their own skins. For this testimony, second chair prosecutor S.G. Kinner took over from Lee Ferguson.

Jeff was the first up, testifying that Wall Hatfield was at the murder scene and he swore the participants to an oath of secrecy. "He threatened every man there with a necktie party, if they broke that oath," said Jeff. After his testimony, came his brother Dan.

While Kinner questioned them in great detail, Gaynor carefully observed the testimony of the Whitt's. They were a very real danger to his client, as they were the only people on the witness list that had actually been at the scene of the shooting. Gaynor sat at his table listening intently to the brothers, looking for a hole in their statements. After several hours of grueling testimony, he found was he was looking for.

For their day in court, Kinner had both the brothers dress up in pressed white shirts with black suspenders. They were young, clean-shaven and appeared like fine upstanding young men. It was the intention of the prosecutor that they were perceived by the jury as contrite, misguided lads led astray by the Hatfields. The reformed Dan and Jeff could now correct their mistake by testifying against Wall and the others.

Braxton Gaynor was now ready to perform his cross examination. In mind his he was still every bit the young cavalry officer and it was his goal to outflank each hostile witness during their testimony. He was a born strategist and he loved to fight; whether it was his glory days on the battlefield or his time in the courtroom. For him winning was everything and if justice were served that was all the better.

"Mister Whitt, you stated that Wall Hatfield was on the Kentucky side of the Tug Fork, near Mate Creek and that he was present at the killings of Tolbert, Pharmer and Randolph McCoy," Gaynor restated for the record.

"That's right sir" Whitt answered with a nod.

"You further state that Wall swore you and the other men present to an oath of secrecy. Is that correct?"

"Yep, that's what I said."

"Well that all seems clear enough. Mister Whitt, you have stated that Wall Hatfield was going to exact revenge if his brother died," Gaynor paused for a response from the witness.

"Yeah, I said that too."

Mister Whitt, why did you ride along with the Hatfields that day?"

Before the witness answered, Kinner spoke first. "Objection your honor, Mister Whitt is not on trial today."

"Mister Kinner, I'm going to allow the witness to answer that question. Objection overruled," Judge Rice informed the surprised prosecutor.

"In other words, you had no ill feelings towards the McCoys."

"They killed a man, who was kin to my friends."

"But the McCoys never did anything to you to make you want to kill them?"

"No sir, they didn't" responded Whitt.

"Yet by your own sworn testimony, you stood by and watched the boys get killed" Gaynor stated.

"Yes sir, I did and I'm sorry for that."

"Did you shoot the McCoys yourself Mister Whitt?"

"No sir, I told you, I just watched" the witness answered, with a hint of irritation.

"You just stood there, when all the other men started blasting away? Come on Dan, I've been in the battlefield many times with guns and cannon blazing away. It's exciting when a man has a loaded gun in his hands. Didn't you want to shoot those boys too?"

"Your honor, I must object to this line of questioning. The defense counselor is being argumentative. The witness has already answered the question and is now being prodded into admitting to something he didn't do," Kinner protested.

"Counselor, as his client is on trial for murder, I'm going to allow defense counsel the greatest possible latitude in his cross examination of this witness. Mister Whitt you will please give an answer to Mister Gaynor's question.

"I'll repeat the question." Gaynor slyly smiled. "With all the other men firing their weapons, didn't you want to shoot those boys?"

"No sir! I did not" Whitt answered indignantly.

Gaynor briefly lost his train of thought. He walked over to his table, looking down at his notebook for a moment. He turned around, looked at the witness and paused.

"Mister Gaynor, do have any further questions for the witness?" asked Judge Rice.

"Yes your honor I do," The defense quickly rebounded. "Mister Whitt, who shot the McCoys?"

"I recollect it was Devil Anse, Cap, Johnse and Bill Tom Hatfield" answered Whitt.

"Who else was there?"

"If I recall, it was Alex Messer, Tom Chambers and Charlie Carpenter."

"Did Wall Hatfield fire upon the McCoys?"

"No sir, but he gave the order to."

"Mister Whitt, your brother Jeff testified that four men left before the shooting started. Do you recall the names of these four gentlemen?" Gaynor innocently inquired.

"Yes, it was Joe Murphy, Moses Christian, Plyant and Doc Mahon" Whitt responded confidently.

Gaynor moved towards the witness. "Joe Murphy, Moses Christian, Plyant and Doc Mahon; and you're absolutely certain that's who left the scene at Sulphur Creek?"

"Yes Sir I am."

Interestingly enough Mister Whitt, your brother Jeff testified that it Sam Mahon who left the scene. Are you sure it wasn't Sam and not Plyant Mahon who left?"

"Well, I think so" Whitt tentatively answered.

"You think so, but you're not absolutely certain, are you Mister Whitt?

"I reckon not."

"You reckon not. Still, you can say with absolute certainty that my client was at the sight of the killings?" Gaynor asked mockingly.

"Yes Sir."

The defense attorney once again walked over to read his notes, as there was one more question he wanted to remember. "Mister Whitt, would you tell the jury, how you have avoided prosecution for your complicity in this affair?" He petulantly requested.

"Yes sir, I made a deal with Mister Kinner over there, in trade for me spilling the beans about the Hatfields" Whitt replied. The courtroom spectators responded with thundering laughter when they heard his honest answer.

Lee Ferguson quickly stood up and interrupted the proceedings. "Your honor may I speak to this issue?"

"Make it brief counselor, its Mister Gaynor's nickel," Rice answered.

"Gentleman of the jury, the Whitt's have been granted immunity in exchange for their testimony. However, the commonwealth of Kentucky believes in the integrity of their testimony; otherwise we would not have granted them exemption from prosecution."

"Thank you for your endorsement of Mister Whitt's testimony counselor. Now, may defense counsel finish his cross-examination of the witness?" Judge Rice asked rhetorically.

"Oh course your honor," Ferguson said shrugging his shoulders.

Gaynor looked up from his seat and addressed the judge. "I think the jury understands what this man's testimony is worth. I have no further questions for him," he said contemptuously.

Back at his hotel, Thomas Kelly put the finishing touches on his daily dispatch. He was supplying reports about the trial to increasing numbers of fascinated Globe readers. "Today Braxton Gaynor demonstrated why he is nicknamed 'The Fighting Confederate'. He ably dispatched the so-called eyewitness for the prosecution, a good-looking young man named Dan Whitt. It looks like the Prosecution will have to work a little harder to get a conviction in this case," he concluded. After he finished with his work the reporter walked down the street to get some dinner.

Kelly decided to have supper and a drink at the Pikeville Station, which was a local saloon and eatery. He sat alone at the huge, inlaid, iron bar that overlooked the restaurant. His wandering thoughts turned to Debbie Ferris, but he knew that she was probably working.

While he awaited his roast beef sandwich, Kelly looked across the room and noticed a short, handsome man wearing a deputy's badge. He was dressed in black jeans with a beautiful gray button flapped shirt. His feet were adorned by black cowboy boots with silver studs and at his hip, he wore short barreled Colt revolver.

Though he had never met him in person, the reporter recognized Frank Phillips from his photograph. The tough looking man was in the company of an attractive young woman in a long blue dress. She had soft features, surrounded by silky brown hair. Kelly quickly drank his shot of bourbon, grabbed his beer and walked over to where the couple was sitting.

The blue eyed deputy calmly looked up at the New Yorker, as he approached the table. "You must be Frank Phillips" Kelly said excitedly.

"Yes I am; who the hell are you?"

"I'm Thomas Kelly of the New York Globe. May I join you and your companion?"

Phillips hesitated for a few seconds then motioned to Kelly to sit. "Sure, why not, seeing as how you're here all the way from New York." Phillips gently touched the woman's shoulder. Mister Kelly, this is my fiancée Nancy McCoy."

The anxious reporter reached out to lightly grasp the hand of the former Mrs. Hatfield. "I'm charmed to make your acquaintance Miss McCoy" he replied. Kelly couldn't help briefly staring at the woman, as he was impressed with her good looks. He remembered from his research she had once been married to Johnse Hatfield. He could not help but think that she was the woman that came between him and Roseanna McCoy. And worse yet, that they were cousins.

"Would you like a drink Kelly?" Phillips politely asked.

"Mister Phillips, the only time an Irishman says no to a drink, is when you ask him if he's had enough" Kelly answered.

"Ha! I'll take that to mean yes Kelly. Two whiskeys and a glass of wine Rebecca," Phillips yelled at the waitress. "Now, what can I do for you?"

"My readers would like to hear from the man who captured the Wall Hatfield and his men. After I get done telling the readers about you, you'll be a household name." The reporter boasted.

"Sort of like Sears and Roebuck eh?

"More like Buffalo Bill."

Phillips raised his whiskey glass. "Except I don't wear a white hat."

"Who really does in this world? Now tell me about how you rounded up the Hatfield Gang."

"Well Kelly, there's not much to tell, most of them so called bad men came along as gentle as lambs."

"Not all of them?" Kelly asked, flipping open his note pad.

"No, not all of them. Jim Vance gave me a bit of an argument. However, his uncooperative disposition was greatly improved after proper ventilation."

"Is that the instrument of ventilation?" Kelly asked, pointing down at Phillip's revolver.

"Plays quite a tune Kelly, you should hear it sometime."

"I understand several men have heard that tune Mister Phillips."

"Now were exchanging metaphors eh Kelly? I know you're a fancy East Coast newspaperman but what you mean to say is that I've killed a few men." With a deadpan face, Phillips looked straight into the reporter's eyes.

Kelly nervously nodded in agreement. "Sorry if I gave offense."

"Don't worry Kelly I'll sleep like a baby tonight. I didn't shoot anyone that didn't need killing." 0

Kelly had not expected Frank Phillips to be so articulate or direct. "I was told about your shoot out with three drifters in Kansas. Perry Cline told me the story. He says that you killed all three without getting up from your dinner."

"You can't believe everything Perry tells you, he has a habit of spinning a yarn."

"You must be pretty fast with that gun of yours," Kelly said like a schoolboy.

"I'm faster than most but what counts is that I hit what I aim for. When I look down the barrel of another man's gun, I don't think about getting killed. Are you afraid to shake off your mortal coil? I hear you newspaper boys' lead dangerous lives."

Kelly laughed nervously. "Yeah, I'm gonna leave this world kicking and screaming. And the only hazard I face is whether or not my grammar's good. What about the men you're still looking for? What about Devil Anse? When are you going after him?"

"I don't know. He's a real hard case, that son of a bitch; and he's much smarter than the rest. Built himself a little stronghold, out in the middle of nowhere; and from what I've heard, it could only be taken by a frontal assault with a lot of guns. I don't much like the odds. You would have to catch him off guard and that's not likely to happen" Phillips replied.

The waitress came to the table to drop off a round of drinks. Kelly reached into his wallet and Phillips quickly motioned his hand. "Drinks are on me tonight."

Kelly bowed in acknowledgement of the deputy's gesture. "To your health sir and you too ma'am," he said turning to Nancy. "I think you're right Mister Phillips. I was up at his place a few weeks back. I talked with that old man for about four hours. I wouldn't want to tangle with him."

Phillips quickly downed his bourbon. "Oh, you're the one who knocked around one of his boys. I heard about that. I knew there was something I liked about you Kelly" he said patting the writer on his back.

Kelly began to blush and quickly changed the subject. "Mister Phillips, don't take offense by this question, but how do you feel about being a wanted man in West Virginia?"

"It's ridiculous. Sort of the pot calling the kettle black isn't it? I'm a lawman who did his job and did it well. Now West Virginia says I'm a wanted man for going into their state to arrest a bunch of killers, ridiculous. That's a job they should have done."

Nancy McCoy had sat quietly, listening to the two men chat. She began rubbing her new fiancés shoulder and decided to join in on the conversation. "Mister Kelly, I don't know what you're fixing to write in your fancy newspaper; but I'll tell you one thing, you're sitting next to a man, a real man. I happen to know the difference between a man and a boy."

"You mean Johnse Hatfield, don't you?" Kelly boldly asked.

The pretty girl grinned with satisfaction. "I sure do; and I'm happy to say, I fixed that little mistake. All the Hatfields are scared to death of my man, but I know the truth. He's just a pussycat." The smitten woman kissed her lover on the cheek.

Phillips shrugged his shoulders and smiled. "What can I say? I aim to please, but don't print that part about me being a kitty cat in you're paper Kelly. Not unless you want your name in…what do they call it when you pass on?"

"The obituary column," Kelly answered obligingly.

"Yes, the obituary column," Phillip agreed.

*****

The following day, the Pikeville District Court was back in session. Braxton Gaynor conferred with his client, who wanted to take the stand in his own defense. "Wall, I think it's a mistake putting you up on box. We got them on the run and we don't need your testimony," he protested.

"I think the jury wants to hear me speak my peace. Otherwise they'll think I'm afraid. They want to hear me say I ain't guilty; and that's what I aim to tell them" Wall replied.

"You may just be the instrument of your own undoing, but it's your neck. If you insist on going up on the stand, I'm not going stop you."

After months in jail, Wall's frame looked fit and sturdy, although his gray hair and bushy eyebrows gave him a kind, grandfatherly appearance. He laid his hand on the bible and swore to tell his version of the truth.

Gaynor paced the floor with the nervous energy of a caged panther. "Mister Hatfield, would you tell the court the events that unfolded on August Eight and Ninth, Eighteen Hundred and Eighty Two" he asked loudly.

"Well, after my brother Ellison was stabbed and shot, I assembled a group of eight men for the purpose of arresting the three McCoys. I took charge of them but only with the intention of taking them in for trial." Wall looked out at the jury and the courtroom spectators, making eye contact with several of them. "You see, some men I didn't know too well or trust were fixing to take them boys back to Pikeville. I couldn't let that happen. It was much too dangerous to take those boys back to Pikeville. My wounded brother had a lot of friends who were mad about what the McCoys did to him."

"Your honor, I object. What the McCoys did or didn't do to Ellison Hatfield was never proven in a court of law," said S.G. Kinner.

"Your honor, if it pleases the court, the defense can produce at least a dozen sworn statements from people who witnessed the McCoy brothers stab and shoot Ellison Hatfield," Gaynor quickly responded.

"Your objection is overruled Mister Kinner" Judge Rice answered.

"Mister Hatfield, please continue your testimony" Gaynor instructed.

"Well, I told Mathew, Tolbert and Joseph Hatfield, that the McCoys should be tried in Blackberry Creek, cause that's where the ruckus occurred" Wall explained.

"So you did confer with the volunteer posse about your

intention to see justice served."

"Yes, it was always my intention that these boys get a fair trial" Wall answered, hanging his head down for a moment. "I was awful sorry things didn't work out that way, but I didn't have nothing to do with that. I figured the trial should be held in Blackberry Creek, So that testimony could be taken from several witnesses."

"When did your brother Anderson Hatfield get involved?"

"He came along with his sons Cap and Johnse and they was armed with Winchesters and Colts. They also had some other fellers with them. My brother told all the men who were friends of the Hatfields to stand in line and take his part. He told me that he wanted to take the McCoys to Mate Creek, to an empty schoolhouse." Wall again hung his head down. "He didn't give me any choice; he said he was taking them. I wasn't happy with the idea, but my brother's not a man you want to argue with, especially if he's carrying a Winchester. Besides, he had enough men to back his play on anything he wanted."

The defense attorney turned towards the court audience. "In fact, didn't you try to save the McCoys from your brother's vengeful wrath Mister Hatfield?"

"Yes I did. I told him them boys had to get a fair trial, after all I am a justice of the peace."

"So you never made the statement that if your brother died the McCoys would too?"

"Never, I kept telling my brother that he shouldn't take the law into his own hands. After all, I am a justice of the peace" Wall repeated.

Kinner stood up from his table. "Objection your honor; the defendant has now twice stated that he is a justice of the peace. His so called vocation is not relevant to this case. Especially in light of the charges he stands accused of," Kinner said indignantly.

"Your honor, my client's profession is very relevant to this case as it goes to demonstrate his authority as a magistrate for what he deemed to be a local matter "Gaynor argued.

"I'm going to allow the testimony as it stands Mister Kinner, your objection is
overruled," Judge Rice said in a monotone.

Gaynor barely concealed a smile at the judge's decision. "To the best of your recollection, please tell the court what happened on August 9, 1882."

"My brother kept the three McCoys at the old schoolhouse and our cousin the Deacon came over for a visit. He talked about having a fair trial for the McCoys. I agreed with my cousin and told my brother that we needed to take the boys in to town. When Ellison died, he just wasn't gonna listen to reason. He said he was gonna take them boys back to Kentucky soil and finish it. There was nothing that I could do. I headed back Mate Creek, towards my home. My other brother Elias came along too. When we were near Sulphur Creek, he had to answer the call of nature."

There were snickers from several spectators in the court after Wall's remark. Having been momentarily distracted, Gaynor missed what he had said. "I'm sorry Mister Hatfield you said something about nature's call. Did your brother hear a bear or wolf?"

"No sir, I said he relieved himself" Wall replied. The Pikeville courtroom exploded with laughter. Judge Rice was smiling too but he still banged his gavel, asking for order in the court. Gaynor turned a bit red but began laughing along with everyone else. He composed himself and asked Wall to continue his testimony. "Please continue telling the jury what happened sir."

"Like I said, my brother answered the call of nature. While I was waiting on my horse, I heard about fifty gunshots coming from about three hundred yards away. I knew I shouldn't have left them boys but I hadn't the ways or means of stopping my brother." Wall again scanned the courtroom. He did his best to appear sincere and make eye contact with people. "He's a powerful hard man to reason with when he makes up his mind to do something."

"So you had nothing to do with killing those three boys, did you Mister Hatfield?" Gaynor asked loudly.

"No Sir I didn't."

With feelings of trepidation, the Fighting Confederate looked over at the jury and slowly turned towards the Judge. "I have no further questions your honor."

"Your witness Mister Kinner," announced Judge Rice.

S.G. Kinner was dressed in a white suit with a black bow tie. His manners reflected his decidedly southern bearing and he spoke in a slow, deliberate way. Standing up from his chair, he walked over to the witness box and with a distance of about eighteen inches; he stood face to face with Wall Hatfield.

"I'm sure were all quite impressed with your valiant attempts to serve Justice Mister Hatfield" Wall remained silent, but bowed his head in agreement. "Mister Hatfield, on August ninth 1882, Randolph McCoy claims that you told him that 'If my brother dies, your sons will too' Mister Hatfield, is he a liar?"

"He most certainly is lying about that because I never said no such thing!" Wall adamantly declared.

Kinner displayed no emotion to the defendant's righteous indignation. "Uh huh, I see. Mister Hatfield, on the same evening, Sarah McCoy claims you made that very same statement to her. Mister Hatfield, is Sarah McCoy a liar?"

"She's lying too. What do you expect, she's married to Old Ranel; and her boys were killed by my brother" Wall replied with his voice slightly raised.

"That's very interesting Mister Hatfield, because Mary Butcher has made the same statement. You remember Mary Butcher, don't you? She was married to the late Tolbert McCoy. You know, he's one of the men that you stand accused of killing. Now she says she heard you make the same statement Randolph and Sarah heard." Kinner reached down on the table and lifted three envelopes in his hand. "I have all of their sworn statements in my hand. Sir, Is Mary Butcher a liar too?"

"She must be lying, because I never said anything about killing those poor boys."

"Why would Mary Butcher lie about that Mister Hatfield?"

"I don't know. I know she lost her husband and I'm sorry for that; but they're blaming me for something I didn't do. I'm telling you, it was my brother's doing!"

"Mister Hatfield, the court has heard the testimony of Dan and Jeff Whitt. Both of these men said you were present at the killings of the three McCoys. Both men say that after the murders, you demanded that the participants swear to an oath of secrecy. Mister Hatfield, are both of the Whitt brothers lying as well?"

"Of course they're lying. They're lying to save their skins. I swore no man to any oath."

Kinner stood with his back to Wall Hatfield, facing the twelve men in the jury box. He began to speak in a slightly louder voice. "Mister Hatfield, the commonwealth has the sworn statements of a dozen witnesses who saw you riding with your brother Anderson Hatfield towards Kentucky. All of the statements indicate that you were riding towards Sulphur creek during the time you had custody of the three McCoy brothers. This was approximately twenty minutes before these young men were shot. The commonwealth also has a signed confession from your nephew Ellison Mounts."

"He's not my nephew!" shouted Wall Hatfield.

Kinner calmly ignored the witness, continuing his cross examination. "As I was saying, the commonwealth has the signed confession from Ellison Mounts, stating the he participated in the murders; and that you yourself, gave the command to kill the three McCoy brothers. Now are you going to tell me that he's lying too?" he asked in a raised octave."

Wall held himself in check and calmly answered the prosecutor. "What you have, is a confession from a half-witted boy that's trying to save his own skin."

Braxton Gaynor was unable to help his client. He wanted to object to Kinner's cross- examination, but he had no grounds to for doing so. All he could do was sit by and watch the defendant be dismantled piece by piece.

For dramatic effect, Kinner once again moved in close to Wall Hatfield's face. "The commonwealth of Kentucky has three eye witnesses to the murders and several witnesses who heard you threaten the lives of Tolbert, Pharmer and Randolph McCoy. Can it possibly be that all these people have banded together, to orchestrate one big, fantastic story? Is it conceivable that these people lying Mr. Hatfield?"

Wall looked him straight in the eye and answered. "They must be," he answered.

Kinner again turned his back to Wall and stood before the Jury. "Thank God that we have you to tell the truth Mister Hatfield." He turned slowly away from the jury, looking at the defendant with disgust.

The next day, the Braxton Gaynor called several character witnesses to speak in Wall's defense. By the end of the day, the lawyers were ready to present their closing arguments.   Wednesday morning of the following day, the opposing attorneys spoke for one hour each. They both presented their arguments in a clear, eloquent fashion. Both sides felt confident that they had won the hard fought case.

The Judge imparted instructions to the jury and they began their short deliberation. After only four hours of examining the evidence, the twelve men reached a verdict. Wall Hatfield was found guilty and was sentenced to life imprisonment.

■■■

CHAPTER THIRTEEN: POOR COTTONTOP

After the Wall fell, so too did the friends of the Hatfields. Doc and Plyant Mahon, as well as hard case Alex Messer, received life sentences in jail. All of these Logan Wildcats were pronounced guilty of the 1882 murders of three McCoys. However, Wall Hatfield and three other men were granted appeals.

Another trial followed for the 1888 Murders, of Calvin and Alifair McCoy. With the exception of Jim Vance, most of the men indicted for these crimes had been fortunate enough to avoid capture. These lucky souls included Cap, Johnse, Robert, Elliot and their father Devil Anse. Once again, his family had remained remarkably untouched by the tragic events that had unfolded during the feud.

Two other men were not as fortunate as the Hatfield boys were. Handsome young Charlie Gillespie was sentenced to life imprisonment for his role in the New Years Day killings. And then there was poor Ellison Mounts, the last man ever tried and convicted of violence against the McCoy clan. He had expected to receive a lighter sentence for cooperating with Pikeville authorities. The less than brilliant man had confessed to Lee Ferguson in front of several other witnesses. They all heard him freely admit that he had been the one to shoot pretty Alifair McCoy. Like the farmer that locks the barn door after the cow escapes, he had made one mistake. He forgot to make a deal for clemency before confessing to his crimes.

The jury felt nothing but sympathy for the teary eyed Sarah McCoy, when she testified that Cottontop had so mercilessly shot her poor child. When the frail woman recounted her story in vivid detail, the twelve-man group was brought to tears. These jurors were anxious to see someone pay for this terrible crime and that fate would be relegated to Mounts. After his conviction, Judge Rice sentenced him to die on the gallows.

September 5, 1889, was a gloomy, rainy day. This was particularly depressing for the convicted men who were headed for a long stretch in jail. To await the outcome of their appeals, Wall Hatfield, Alex Messer Doc and Plyant Mahon were being transferred to Lexington Kentucky. The rain came down for two days straight, rendering the roads muddy and treacherous. The Pikeville jail wagon carried the melancholy prisoners the thirty miles to a small railroad depot. The four men in the wagon remained silent but desperate thoughts of freedom raced through their heads. Rumors of a rescue party led by Cap had been relayed to Sheriff W.H.

Maynard. Along with James McCoy, Frank Phillips and a man named C.T. Yost, the seasoned lawman was charged with escorting the condemned.

The four prisoners kept their watchful eyes on the trail, hoping for their liberators to strike at any moment. In some small measure, this was how the McCoy brothers felt on their wagon ride to Sulphur Creek. As in the case of the ill-fated trio, no rescue party ever came.

Early on the morning of the following day, the caravan arrived in a town called Richardson. The twenty-five townsmen that helped to guard the wagon were sent on their way back to Pikeville. All that remained were the four appointed deputies transporting the prisoners by train to the Ashland station. There, the convicted men could be taken to Lexington on the last leg of the journey.

Once again, the Hatfield prisoners traveled on board the Chesapeake and Ohio train to their place of confinement. On that sojourn, the men had high hopes of being delivered back to welcoming arms of West Virginia. This time however, their chances of ever seeing freedom were growing dimmer.

At the Ashland Station, the deputies shackled the captives to a hitching post. The lawmen were hungry, exhausted and there was a small cafe and bar right next to the train depot. James McCoy stayed to watch the prisoners while the other three deputies went for coffee.

The grill was warm and inviting, so the lawmen grabbed a cramped table. Sitting in front at the wooden counter, was a young man Frank Phillips thought he recognized. "I know that kid," he told the two other men. "That's Jim Vance's boy. I need to pay my respects," he added.

"Be careful Frank, that boy may not feel obliged to want your respect," warned Sheriff Maynard. Phillips paid no attention to his companion's advice, strolling over to where the young man was sitting. He audaciously sat down next to him and ordered coffee from the cafe's proprietor.

The Vance boy was tall, sinewy and wore a felt cowboy hat over his long dark hair. His gray duster was unbuttoned, which revealed the large forty-four-caliber pistol strapped to his lean body. The quiet young man sat with his eyes looking straight ahead, while sipping his blazing hot coffee.

"Hey kid, are you Jim Vance's boy?" Phillips asked, in an affable manner.

"Yeah, I'm James Vance, but I ain't no boy" the young man tersely replied. He spun around on his stool, quickly glancing at Phillip's short-barreled peacemaker.

"Sorry James, I didn't mean any disrespect. I'm Frank Phillips. I just came over to introduce myself because I met your father."

"You met him and then you killed him. I don't exactly call that being properly acquainted you scum sucking bastard." Vance put his hands on his hips. "You must be all nerve to show your face to me," Vance said in a raised voice.

"Now hold on kid, just take it easy. I was just trying to be friendly," Phillips answered, with his open hands in the air.

"You got to know that you got no leave speaking to me. No leave at all. The only business I have with you don't involve conversation." He stood up from his stool, getting up into Frank's face. "Hear you're pretty fast with that hog leg, why don't you give me a demonstration?" Vance said fearlessly.

Phillips was not remotely frightened of the young man but he didn't want any trouble. Just as that thought crossed his mind, Sheriff Maynard and Deputy Yost stepped up behind Vance.

"Well you yellow trash, I asked you a question. You gonna show me how fast you are?" hollered Vance.

"Not tonight kid, I just don't feel like pulling on you" Phillips answered. The veteran peace officer turned away and began to drink his coffee.

Young Vance felt a storm of rage rising up inside. This was a hatred that went deep down to the bone. He now had what perhaps was a one-time opportunity. There, sitting before him, was the man who ended his father's life. He hard looked Phillips for about twenty seconds. The deputy sat placidly at the counter, while drinking his warm brew. Maynard and Yost also stood frozen behind Vance, watching for his the next move. After a moment of contemplation, his hand reached for the pistol that was in his belt. Before he could level his forty-four, two large hands grabbed him from behind.

"Not tonight kid. We've have enough killing over this stupid feud" Maynard said. While Phillips finished his coffee, the two peace officers escorted James Vance out of the establishment. Maynard and Yost spent fifteen minutes lecturing the upset Vance and talked him into going home.

Later that evening, the prisoners were safely loaded on train that was headed for Lexington. Maynard and Phillips sat across from one another, in the hard wooden seats of the passenger car. Phillips peered out the window, while the rhythm of the train tracks had a relaxing effect on him. The Pikeville Sheriff looked over at his colleague, watching him without speaking for a time. He had been a friend to the enigmatic man for several years, being one of the few men that were not afraid of him.

"That was a close call earlier, I thought that kid was going get himself killed" commented Maynard.

Phillips continued looking out the train's window, without being too interested in what his friend had to say. "Yeah well, everything worked out all right" he answered apathetically.

"Why did you do it Frank? Why did you even bother talking to that kid? Did you really think he was going shake your hand for killing his pappy? Maybe you thought the kid would let bygones be bygones and throw his arms around you."

Turning towards the sheriff, Phillips gave him the oddest look he had ever seen. "I don't know why. I just felt I needed to be nice to the kid. I wasn't looking for a fight. I just wanted to pay my respects" Phillips answered in a strangely sensitive way.

"You can't shoot a man and expect to be cordial with his son" Maynard in a fatherly way.

Phillips again vacantly peered out the window, observing the wooded shapes that were quickly left behind in a dark void. "I suppose you're right. I don't know what I was thinking."

The following morning, the four convicted murderers were turned over to the authorities in Lexington Kentucky to await the outcome of their appeals. On November 9, 1889, the appellate court of Kentucky rendered a decision on previous convictions. Wall Hatfield, Alex Messer, Doc and Plyant Mahon would definitely be spending life in prison.

Wall was sick and discouraged when he arrived in Lexington two months earlier. He had plenty of time to contemplate the loss of his freedom but he kept a shred of hope that the conviction would be overturned. After that was taken completely away he became despondent. Wall had been a justice of the peace, an administrator of the law. In the case of the Election Day murders of the McCoy brothers, he had even considered himself above the law. Now he believed the law had cheated him. Six months after his appeal was denied he died alone in jail.

*****

One man in West Virginia had avoided capture and incarceration for his involvement in the McCoy killings. It was Devil Anse. The fact that he was smarter, tougher and richer than Charlie Carpenter or his own brother was one of the reasons he was still free. There were plenty of bounty hunters in Kentucky and West Virginia, who wanted him badly.

In spite of his luck avoiding any capture, the now famous West Virginian was about to about have his own experience with the justice system. The reason for this courtroom appearance had nothing to do with murder or feuding. His legal problem pertained to selling whiskey without paying taxes on it.

Dave Stratton was a McCoy family ally. He had participated in the so-called battle of Grapevine Creek. Along with Sam and Jim McCoy, he had taunted Bill Dempsey. He too watched the wounded man suffer, refusing to give him water from his own canteen. Standing on the sidelines, he witnessed Frank Phillips put a bullet in the poor man's head.

This enemy of the Hatfield clan was now causing problems for its leader. Rather than tangle with the man in person, he had a more covert plan that required much less potential for danger. His clandestine strategy involved going to Charleston, West Virginia. There he presented evidence against his foe, to a grand jury located at the state capital. Stratton's testimony resulted in a warrant being issued for Hatfield's arrest.

An honest Marshall by the name of Bill White was given the chore of capturing the man with the most notorious reputation on the West Virginia border. He went directly to Island Creek, having little trepidation about visiting the well-armed mountain stronghold. The Marshall was familiar with social mores of men like Devil Anse. White had a proposition that he thought would interest the clan leader. He signaled up with a hooting call and was permitted to venture past the fortress that guarded the Hatfield cabin.

Upon his arrival at the fortified house, The Marshall was cordially invited in to sit by the warm fireplace. With a hound dog at his feet and surrounded by several of his host's children and grandchildren, he patiently explained the situation to the well known feudist. "The State of West Virginia has issued a subpoena for you to come into court and answer some questions. Let me assure you, this isn't a state matter. It's about selling whiskey without paying taxes, which is a Federal offense," he advised.

"Is that a fact?" Devil Anse asked.

"That's a fact. However, all I want is for you to come back to Charleston, to tell your side of story regarding Stratton's accusation about operating an illegal still. It will be a fair and square hearing and I promise there won't be any tricks. You'll have the protection of the Federal Government. What that means, is that no state authorities will bother you."

Devil Anse raised his eyebrow. "From Kentucky neither?"

"Not from Kentucky neither.

The Marshall fidgeted with his gold badge on his shirt. "You have my word you'll be given a fair shake; but what I need to know, is what your answers going to be? Do I have your word that you're coming down?"

"I believe you're an honest man, particularly since you took the trouble to come up here alone and in peace. I'll come down to Charleston to answer this trumped up lie but I'm gonna bring my own bodyguards with me."

"I don't see any problem with that Sir" White answered. He extended his right hand and the old rebel shook it. We'll look forward to seeing you next week," the Marshall said turning to leave the cabin.

On November 19, 1889 Devil Anse rode into the capital city of West Virginia. His entourage included his sons Johnse, Cap and Robert. They were armed to the teeth, with an array of big bore rifles and pistols. With long bandanas flying in the wind and ammo belts across their chests, the rugged looking quartet looked like they could have served with Bloody Bill Anderson.

As they entered the outskirts of Charleston, the Hatfields admired the architectural splendor of aristocratic mansions surrounding the state capital. Johnse jumped off his horse to fully appreciate the opulent Sunrise Mansion. "Would you look at this place Daddy," he said with his mouth agape.

"That's more house than I'll ever need" replied Cap.

"That's more house than any of us will need put together," added Devil Anse

"I wonder what it's like to be that rich." Johnse pondered aloud.

"We are rich son," said Devil Anse.

"Huh?"

"That's right son. We're rich in family, rich in friendship and rich in acreage. That's the kind of riches that means something." As he remounted, Devil Anse pointed his finger back at the huge home. "I wouldn't know what to do with a fancy place like that. Could hardly let the hound sleep inside or have the grand kids run round like wild banshees."

Cap defiantly spit on the street in front of the mansion. "Why not? A house is a house, no matter how big."

"Folks round here ain't like that son. That ain't considered good manners. Folks around here wouldn't appreciate our ways," Devil Anse answered.

"Well, I'll change my ways for that big house on the end," Johnse said pointing his finger at a large yellow Victorian home.

"I'm with you Johnse," young Robert chimed in.

"Hell, you couldn't even afford a good outhouse Bobbie Lee," Cap quipped. His remark caused a cackle of hysterical laughter.

Charleston was the largest city in West Virginia. The Hatfields were unaccustomed to all the people and activity that surrounded them.

The city itself had anticipated their arrival, carrying a big article in the local paper about the upcoming moonshine trial. In keeping with his promise, Marshall White assigned a group of twenty deputies, to guard the already heavily armed Hatfield clan.

The confined room at the Charleston State courthouse was brimming with spectators, all of whom wanted to get a gander of the notorious feudist. Two lawyers ably represented Devil Anse, one of whom would become Governor of West Virginia. The crafty attorneys shot holes in the case against the clan leader. They easily proved that the charges were purely fabricated and a flimsy attempt to lure the old man out of hiding.

Stratton was exposed as a colossal liar with an axe to grind. Motivated only by self-interest, he had conspired with bounty hunters to capture the much sought after clansman. With those facts working against him, the jury took less than an hour to deliberate their verdict. Unlike his brother Wall, who was sentenced to a prison term, Devil Anse was found not guilty.

"The defendant has been found not guilty of the charges put forth in the indictment. No one in the state of West Virginia shall lay a hand upon this man. In addition, to ensure his safe passage, I am assigning twenty-five special deputies to escort Mister Hatfield and his bodyguards to the train depot. When he gets back to his home, I do not have any objections to anyone who is foolish enough to try to arrest him" said Judge John Jackson. The crowded courtroom laughed in response to his statement.

Miles away, in the town of Pikeville, another member of the Hatfield family was not as lucky at Devil Anse. Though there was a pound of flesh about to be collected for past crimes, he would not be the one to remit it. Ellison Mounts was the poor scoundrel who would pay that debt. For the murder of young Alifair McCoy, he was bound for an appointment with the hangman.

At the end of November, Mounts received a visit from Thomas Randolph Kelly. Before returning to his home in New York, this would be was to be his last assignment for the newspaper. The Pikeville Jailer obligingly led him to the eight by nine foot cell where Cottontop was in kept. The reporter was surprised to find the prisoner in reasonably good spirits and happy to grant an interview.

With notebook in hand, Kelly sat on a short wooden stool in front of Ellison's jail cell. "A pleasure to meet you Mister Mounts" Kelly said. He extended his hand through the bars of the cell.

"Likewise" Mounts replied, giving Kelly a weak handshake.

Kelly thought that Cottontop was actually a handsome young man with his nearly white hair and strong build. "How are you sir?" He asked.

He answered the reporter's question in a monotone vocal cadence. "As well as can be expected I guess. I mean it's me that's gonna be hanged, when others did the real killing."

"Mister Mounts I've come all the way from New York to cover the events that have transpired during the recent trials, including yours and Wall Hatfield. I represent The New York Globe, which is one of the largest newspapers in the world. It has just over a quarter of a million readers. I can't imagine how difficult this must be for you, but our readers would be grateful to hear why you're the man being punished for the murder of Alifair McCoy. I'll understand if you can't talk about it."

"Don't worry about that Mr. Kelly. I ain't got much cause to be shy about that no more. A quarter million that sure is a lot of newspapers" replied Ellison with a half smile. "Well since nothing's gonna stop me from swinging pretty soon, I might just as well complain to as many folks as will listen. And well sir, a quarter million's a lot" he paused as if to calculate the number in his brain, "a damn big lot. Well, where should I start Mr. Kelly?"

"At the beginning Ellison, at the beginning."

"Well, as folks say round here, I got the shaft but not the mine. After that poor McCoy girl got shot, I got snared by a couple of sneaky detectives. I gave them a fight, but they got me after a while. They brought me here to Pikeville for the reward money and that was that. Then Lee Ferguson told me they was gonna hang me unless I cooperated, which I did. A lot of good it done me, they're gonna hang me anyways" Mounts lamented.

Kelly stopped writing, glancing up from his notebook with a puzzled look. "Why did you ride with the Hatfields then Ellison?"

The condemned man became irritated at Kelly's question. "Yeah, I rode with them but they forced me to."They came after me two times because they know I'm real strong. Cap and Johnse said that since the McCoy brothers killed my Pappy, I had to avenge his death. I was there when they met their makers but it wasn't me that pulled the trigger. I can tell you that before God."

"Who did then, who pulled the trigger Ellison?"

Cottontop rolled off the names in quick succession. "Devil Anse, Cap, Johnse, Alex Messer, Charlie Carpenter, The Mahon's and the Whitt's; they did the shooting."

"Everyone but you" Kelly replied with a slight tone of sarcasm.

"Yeah, that's right Mister Yankee newspaper man, everyone but me. I ain't got any of their blood on my hands."

"What about Sarah McCoy's testimony? She says you're the one who shot Alifair."

"That's a bald faced lie. She never did see me shoot her little girl, I don't kill women folk. Besides, there was so much of a ruckus going on. If she'd had really known who shot her daughter, she had known it was Cap Hatfield." Now all those other fellers are getting jail and I'm fixing to get myself hanged.

"Yes, it seems so Ellison and I'm sorry for that" Kelly replied.

"Well nothing you can do. I'm already a forgotten man. My lawyers came last week to talk at me but that's the last I thing I heard. Why should they care no more? Those vultures thinking it's a lost cause. Why should they care? They can go home to their families. I'm gonna sit here biting my nails until they open the trap. Messer, the Whitt's and Wall Hatfield, they're a heap guiltier than I am. But I'm the one that's gonna die. Well, I guess it's the luck of the draw."

"You were definitely dealt a bad hand."

"You got that right, from your lips to God's ears Mister Kelly."

*****

Thomas Kelly had been in Pikeville for three months and was anxious to return to the chaos of New York. Before he headed back, the small town offered Kelly something he wanted; something he thought would make him contented. It was a petite little woman named Debbie Ferris who was currently employed in a brothel. The traveling reporter was ready to settle down and raise a family and he wanted to do it with her.

During his time in Kentucky Purgatory, he had spent as much time as he could with the wayward woman. On her evenings off, they would discuss the trial, New York and life in general. On those agreeable occasions they would never make love. If Kelly wanted that he had to pay for it; and pay for it he did. During his stay in Pikeville, he had visited Mabel's frequently. He would always request the company of the little brunette who had first caught his eye, some four months earlier.

On his last evening in town, Kelly escorted Debbie to the Pikeville station. On this midweek night the usually noisy eatery was quiet. A musician sat playing soft, melodic tunes on the restaurant's newly acquired upright piano. Kelly ordered two glasses of champagne, accompanied by roast chicken for himself and his companion. His dinner date had two hours before she had to be at work practicing her profession.

To Kelly, the thought of Debbie being with other men was growing increasingly distasteful. His dinner companion wore a new red dress, with a black velvet choker. Kelly liked red, thinking there was no better or more sensual color for a pretty woman. To him, she was more radiant than anyone he had known. He no longer wanted to share her warmth.

"You're looking at me funny, something wrong?" Debbie asked.

Kelly set down his drink. "I'm sorry, I was just thinking to myself, how beautiful you are tonight. Red is definitely your color. It's a color of passion, a color of life."

"Thank you, you're not so hard to look at either."

"I'm not very good at this so I'll come directly to the point. I want you to come back to New York with me. You make me feel good about things. When you're with me, I don't give a damn about anything else. The world could tilt on its axis and that wouldn't bother me." Kelly took Debbie's hand. "I want to make a life with you and it'll be a good one. No fairy tale ending but a good life with kids, dogs and church on Sundays.

"I really don't know what to say to that" Debbie replied. She was caught completely by surprise. She knew that Kelly liked her, but not on the level he had just revealed.

"Say yes, that's all. I have given it a great deal of thought and I know you would love New York. The money I make will support us both comfortably."

She felt strange, defensive feelings welling up in the pit of her stomach. "Thomas Randolph Kelly, I suppose you think you're my Irish knight in shining armor. You've come to this little hick town on the border of Kentucky to save me. You think you're going to rescue me from my worthless, dirty life as a whore!"

"What?"

"I suppose I should get on my hind legs, like a dog and beg to be taken to New York."

Kelly's face turned red, with wrinkled lines of agitation appearing on his forehead. "Nobody is asking you to beg like a dog, jump through a hoop or sing 'The Battle Hymn of the Republic'. Yes, I know what you do for a living; and it doesn't matter to me one damn bit. You would think I asked you to drink a cup of hemlock" he responded.

Debbie's face became icy cold and she folded her hands tightly on the table. "Well, that's mighty big of you Mister Kelly. A fine, high and mighty writer you are and you don't mind being seen with a whore" she replied angrily.

Kelly remembered his college days in the boxing ring. Like a fighter who used the wrong tactic he began to counter punch. "Look, you got it all wrong, I think about you all the time, even when I'm working. That isn't like me, I like my work. I want you and I need you. I'm not saving you from your life, you're making mine better and perhaps you and I together will amount to something that's really good. I'm thirty-five, I've never been married and I'd like to have a family. I want to have a family with you Debbie. Come back to New York with me. Come back with me on the next train out of this place," said Kelly. All his thoughts were laid bare and he felt good about it.

As Debbie listened intently to his slightly unorthodox proposal, tears began to well up in her brown eyes. Any hardness or anger in her face had now dissipated, as she too was ready to speak from her soul. "I'm sorry Thomas. I was very hard hearted a moment ago. I should be flattered, and I don't deserve a chance at being with a man as decent as you." She ran the tips of her fingers gently across Kelly's face. "I just don't know if I can allow myself to care about you like that. It's not that I don't want to, but I'm afraid to."

Kelly moved closer to put his arm around Debbie's slim shoulder. "You don't have to be afraid of anything. Just come back with me. I won't let anything ever happen to you. If you hate New York, I'll buy you a first class ticket back to Pikeville—I mean it" he assured her.

Debbie grabbed her silk handkerchief, wiping the tear smeared makeup from her face. "Look at me, look at what I've done to myself. I'm a prostitute and I drink too much. Is that what you want Kelly? I'm unclean, is that what you want?"

Kelly knew that he did want her. "Hell, I drink too much, gamble, smoke and have whored around the world, what does that make me? You think I'm bucking for sainthood? I'll have to be your knight in tin can armor."

Debbie laughed and wrapped her arms around him and kissed him repeatedly. "You can be like that windmill chasing knight we read about..."

"Don Quixote" Kelly blurted out.

"Yes, that's the one." She kissed him on the cheek again. "Yes, I'll go back to New York with you. We'll make babies together, you can write great newspaper stories and I'll keep a nice home for you. One where I'll always be there when you come home."

*****

On the outskirts of Pikeville, there was a special construction job underway. Sheriff Maynard had contracted several local workmen to build a gallows for Ellison Mounts. Public executions were illegal in the state of Kentucky. Making money however, was not. A good hanging was real entertainment and Pikeville hadn't had one in over forty years. The chamber of commerce had suggested to the mayor that the execution of

Ellison Mounts would attract thousands of spectators. Therefore, this would bring in thousands of dollars in revenue.

The city fathers being law biding men wanted to observe the state code regarding public executions. They decided to build a wooden fence around the gallows that would prevent anyone at ground level from witnessing the hanging. This did not thwart the Mayor from having the gallows constructed in a valley at the bottom of a hill.

Governor Buckner had set a date for the hanging, which was scheduled for February 18, 1890. As the day approached, rumors of fighting Hatfields, arriving to liberate Mounts from jail were circulating around Pikeville. These erroneous reports even gave Cottontop a glimmer of hope, for a while anyway.

A week before the execution, Ellison went on a hunger strike and began acting crazy. Hatfield supporters told Sheriff Maynard that he was losing his mind. They protested that he was in no condition to be hanged. "He didn't have much mind to begin with, and he'll have mind enough to be executed as scheduled" Maynard replied, to all who considered themselves concerned parties.

The Reverend James J. Price was pastor of the First Baptist Church of Pikeville. He came to visit Ellison nearly every day before the execution. He knew he couldn't save Cottontop in this world but he was bound and determined to help him find redemption. Ellison was happy to have visits from anyone, including the preacher. Price brought him some black licorice sticks that he had purchased at the general store.

"Hello Ellison" Price greeted.

"Hello preacher man" Mounts responded.

"Are you going to get right with the lord today, we haven't got much time left."

"No, I ain't got much time preacher but you got all the time in the world."

The tall minister grabbed a cigar from his shirt pocket and struck a match against the bar of Ellison's jail cell. "Aren't you afraid of dying? Wouldn't you like the comfort of knowing that you're going to heaven? I mean knowing that you are going to have a place in paradise." Price took a several puffs off his stogie. "All you got to do is say the words boy."

"What words are those? How about these, dear Lord come spring me out of this shit hole!"

"Don't mock God son. Don't turn your back on salvation. You're gonna die, that's for certain. Why don't you trust the Lord? What have you got to lose? Say the words, accept Jesus Christ into your heart as your savior and you'll be forgiven. Do you want to die with that girl's blood on your hands?"

Ellison spit the licorice out of his mouth. "I ain't got her blood on my hands. Her blood was spilled by the Hatfields."

"You were there boy, you were there. You're knee deep in it, boy." The Reverend pointed his finger. "No matter how you twist it or turn it around, you're knee deep in blood."

"You're just full of good cheer today parson" Mounts said flippantly.

"Go ahead and make jokes. Hell is full of souls who were unrepentant. Remember the day of the crucifixion. Our lord Jesus was executed with two other criminals. One man mocked the Lord and was unrepentant; 'If you are the King of the Jews, then save yourself' he said. And the other man said 'Jesus, remember me when you come in your kingdom'.

'This day you shall be with me in paradise' Jesus told him." The preacher thought he had finally made a point that Ellison could not deny.

"Paradise? That man wound up in a hole in the ground, just like I'm gonna be. Thanks for the licorice parson, I'll see you tomorrow."

The Pikeville Chamber of commerce had been correct in their business prediction. The upcoming hanging was attracting thousands of visitors to town. The Hotels were booked, the restaurants were standing room only and the local merchants were doing brisk business. Visitors in town were in a festive mood, spending money freely. Everyone in town was excited and happy, everyone except Ellison Mounts.

Sheriff Maynard also had his hands full. With several thousand extra people in town, Pikeville was a pretty crowded place. The sheriff had taken Frank Phillip's advice, posting guards at several corners of the town. He also had sharp shooters stand watch on the second floor of the jailhouse, as well as across the street. In spite of the temporary swelling population, the newly arrived town guests were well behaved, causing no increase in the crime rate. The only outbreak of trouble came from the most unexpected of people.

On the Monday evening before the hanging, Sheriff Maynard received a complaint about a disturbance that was taking place at the Starlight Palace. It seemed there was a drunken man waving his pistol, firing shots at the glass chandelier. The intoxicated patron was scary and dangerous. It turned out it was Frank Phillips. The bar was full of customers but no one dared to tangle with him, especially when he tight as a drum. While he toyed with his revolver, his blue eyes were becoming blurry. He began to rant and rave about the Hatfields to anyone who would listen. People watched with a frightened fascination, as he began to temporarily unwind.

As he leaned up against the edge of the oak wood bar, Phillips turned to talk to the man standing next to him. The nervous looking gent was short, plump and certainly didn't look like a fighting man. "Hey, you know who I am?" Phillips asked.

"Yes sir" the man replied timidly.

"Well, then say my name fat boy" Phillips ordered, pointing his pistol at the man.

"You're Deputy Frank Phillips."

"That's right" Phillips said, smiling enthusiastically, "I'm Frank Phillips; and what's your name boy?"

The customer's voice trembled a bit. "My name is Carson, Don Ca...Carson."

"I'll tell you something Don. I'm the man the brought in the Hatfield Gang. No one had the guts to stand up to them boys, except me. And I brought them in, including the boy they're fixing to hang tomorrow." Several other uneasy bar patrons closely watched his every move. Glad he was focusing his attention on the man next to him.

Phillips looked up above him, at a copy of Gainsborough's "Pinkie." "Don, see that picture of that woman up there?" he asked, pointing up towards the portrait.

"Yes sir, I do" answered Carson.

"You want to see me shoot the eyes out that old gal?"

Carson carefully measured his thoughts before he answered. "As much as I would like to, I don't think it's such a good idea Mister Phillips."

Phillip's became angry. "Maybe it would be a better idea, if I cut your liver out. How about that?" He reached down into his boot and pulled out a sizable knife. At that moment, the sound of a familiar voice called out from behind him.

"That'll be enough Frank, leave the man alone," Sheriff Maynard instructed in a calm voice.

Phillips quickly turned around, leaning up against the bar. The lawman had several deputies and militiamen to back him up but none of them made any sudden moves.

"Hello sheriff, can I buy you a drink?" Frank asked his friend.

"No, I'm working. There is something you can do for me though. You can give over that pistol and toothpick you're carrying" The sheriff answered.

"I'm afraid I can't. Man's got to protect himself. That's because I'm the one. I'm the one ain't I? I'm the one who brought in the

Hatfields."

"That you are Frank, that you are" Maynard said reassuringly.

"That's right! I should be running this town now, shouldn't I?"

Maynard was surprised to see his friend in such a state. The confident man he knew had never been seen like this. "You pretty much run things already Frank, but I can't have you waving guns around. You're scaring people."

"Let them be scared, they're all worthless cowards" Frank answered belligerently.

"That's right Frank, some of them are afraid, but not everyone has guts like you. Now just give me your gun Frank." The sheriff quickly nodded to Deputy Yost, and several armed men quickly rushed the intoxicated deputy. One of the half a dozen men got Frank's gun away from him, forcing him to lie face down on the floor. Another of the deputies handcuffed Phillips, with his hands behind him. The drunken man turned his face up sideways and screamed loudly. "Get your hands off me you bastards. I'll gonna remember all your faces."

"Take him down to the jail and let him sleep it off" Maynard instructed.

No charges were filed against the special deputy. When he sobered up, Phillips apologized to Maynard, Yost and the five other deputies that had subdued him the previous day. He also sought out the nervous Don Carson to ask his forgiveness. Everyone understood that he had one too many and respected him for being man enough to say he was sorry.

At noontime on the following day, Sheriff Maynard arrived at Ellison's jail cell to escort him to his execution. Mounts, was having consul with Reverend Price, who was still attempting to save his soul. The sheriff looked grimly at Mounts, withdrawing a death warrant out of his back pocket. "It's to get this over with," he said somberly.

Ellison looked up nervously at Maynard, continuing his puff his cigar. This was a farewell gift that Reverend had brought for him. For obvious reasons, Mounts was a wreck. He had not slept a wink the night before. Price assured him that very few men could or would want to sleep, the night before they're about to die. With the preacher standing alongside him, the prisoner was escorted out of the Pikeville jail for his trip to the scaffold.

Sheriff Maynard shackled Ellison's feet together, as well as handcuffing his hands behind him. The sun was a glowing hot ball of fire, baking the ground like a brick oven. It was perfect weather for the spectacle that was about to unfold. Like the poor souls during the French revolution, Mounts was placed in a wagon sitting atop his own wooden coffin.

It was Tuesday afternoon and the streets of Pikeville were deserted. Stores were locked up like it was a holiday with the town's activity at a standstill. Almost all of the inhabitants and newly arrived guests were now gathered at the outskirts of the community, patiently awaiting the appearance of the condemned man.

The wagon carrying Ellison Mounts was surrounded by thirty militiamen and four sheriff's deputies. With twelve mounted men at the front of the procession, twelve at the rear and five on either side of the wagon, Maynard was confidant that nothing would prevent him from delivering his prisoner.

Riding along in the death wagon was Reverend Price. He sat on the coffin right next to Ellison, with an opened bible. He began to read Psalm twenty-three, in a soft comforting tone. It occurred to the preacher that he didn't need to have the bible open. He knew this prayer by heart. It was surely appropriate for Mounts, as he was clearly headed into the Valley of the Shadow of Death.

When Price finished the Lord's Prayer, he implored Ellison. "Boy, you still have time. Don't go before the Lord without being saved"

"Do I parson? Do I have time? I'm scared of dying, real scared. Can you save me?" Ellison asked. He started to cry while his face looked longingly for an answer.

"Yes you can be saved. I can't save you, but with his infinite grace the Lord can. Bow your head now son and come to know the Lord. Tell him that you want to take him into your heart; then when you go before the God who stands in judgment of all, you'll be forgiven."

Ellison quickly complied with Price's instructions, praying in desperation for the forgiveness of a God he had previously denied. "I'm still awful scared reverend," he said trembling.

"I know you are. The difference is now you have the Lord walking beside you. He'll be standing on the scaffold with you. His hand will lift you up to the place of eternal life" Price assured him.

"He will?"

"Yes my son, he will."

The wagon slowly drove through the main streets of Pikeville, then past the houses at the edge of town. It proceeded out on the hard dirt road towards the small valley where the gallows stood patiently waiting. Desperate thoughts surged through Ellison's brain, like the gush of a raging river. He thought about how short his life had been which caused his breath to become short and his heart to pound faster. He kept recalling the words of the parson. "The Lord will be with you, he will guide you into his kingdom."

In spite of finding salvation, Ellison contemplated and feared the pain he would endure on his remaining time on earth. It was only minutes away from the moment when his neck would snap like a twig. That was only if the noose was placed properly, for a clean break. What if he dangled there for a while and choked to death slowly? This was the thought that plagued him.

Cottontop couldn't believe his dull green eyes when he saw the eight thousand spectators, covering the hills around the gallows. There they sat perched like vultures waiting for something to die. This was the moment that they had all come to see; the curious, dreadful sight of witnessing a man die.

In spite of the cruel reality of waiting to witness an execution, the throng of humanity was giddy as if they were going to the circus. Two clever food vendors were on the scene, selling peanuts and soda pop to the hungry crowd. Some spectators even brought picnic lunches, laying inviting blankets out on the side of the hill.

The wagon with the procession of militia guarding the condemned man finally came to a halt. The twenty-minute ride was over. To Ellison it passed like seconds. He looked up to see the solidly constructed murdering monster that awaited him. A twenty-two foot high, wooden fence had been built around the scaffold. The wall of lumber was configured as a forty foot square, leaving ample room on the interior the structure for Pikeville dignitaries. Inside the fenced area were a dozen folding wooden chairs, where the Mayor and members of the city council were seated. They all agreed, that the contractors had done a first rate job building the gallows and fence.

Sheriff Maynard motioned to his men fix bayonets on their rifles and to surround the perimeter of the execution sight. He, along with the remaining six deputies escorted Cottontop into the killing structure. He stood for a moment glancing up above the fence, on to the hill that faced the entrance of the compound. Among the thousands of eyes that fell upon him, Ellison could not extract a shred of pity or comfort.

Alongside the condemned man, Reverend Price spoke loudly in prayer, attempting to calm him. None of Ellison's family or friends was allowed to be inside the complex. Like everyone else they watched from the surrounding hills. Maynard walked over to the mayor, asking for his permission to commence with the execution. "Proceed sir, this crowd has waited long enough" replied the mayor.

The Pikeville Sheriff quickly stepped over to Mounts, informing him it was time. The tense guards awkwardly turned the prisoner around, helping him ascend the ten steps up to the hangman's noose. Ellison walked dauntlessly up the wooden tiers, turning to face the mass of so called humanity.

Right behind the condemned man, Price walked up the steps and firmly grasped his right arm. "Fear not, the Lord is with you and I'm with you" he said, stepping down from the scaffold. Maynard stood with three other guards on the platform of the large gallows. He formally read the charges for which Mounts had been convicted.

Deputy Yost and another guard had the condemned man positioned over the center of the trap door, placing the large noose around his neck. "Don't worry boy this is an art form and I know how to do it; you won't feel a thing" Yost told Ellison.

"Are you sure?" Mounts asked, as tears welled up in his eyes.

The deputy gently patted his shoulder. "Sure I'm sure."

"Ellison Mounts, The Commonwealth of Kentucky has found you guilty of the charge of murder in the first degree. The sentence of death mandated by the Sixteenth District Court shall be carried out immediately, this day February 18, 1890. Have you anything to say before the sentence is carried out?" asked Maynard.

Deputy offered the condemned man a blindfold, which he declined. Ellison Mounts stood for a moment, looking around the hills at the throng of morbid spectators. Dressed in new jeans, with a beautiful hand embroidered blue shirt, his blonde mane blew backward from the breeze. "I ain't gonna make no speech; but I hope all my friends remember me and that I'll get to see them in heaven. I want to thank the sheriff for being kind to me and the Parson for saving my soul."

For one last moment of spiritual reassurance, Ellison looked down at Reverend Price. As tears began to fill his eyes the preacher nodded back at him, and mouthed the words "God Bless you," which comforted the doomed man.

"That's all," Ellison said, nodding to the sheriff.

Maynard walked over to the large handle that was built to spring the trap door of the deadly scaffold. Just as he stood poised to pull the lever forward, Ellison yelled to the surrounding crowd. "They made me do it! It was the Hatfields that made me do it!" For that moment, it was quiet enough to hear the grass grow in the valley.

In one swift, powerful thrust, Maynard pulled the lever forward, activating the precisely weighted pulley, dropping Ellison's large frame down through the trap door. As his neck snapped, the large crowd sounded out a loud, collective gasping noise. His feet bobbled for a few seconds but he died quickly as Yost had promised.

Ellison's lifeless body hung for about ten minutes, as a reminder to anyone who might consider themselves above the law in Kentucky. The crowd of people began to slowly disperse. Their ghoulish curiosity, the desire to see someone die, had been fulfilled without a hitch.

The heavy, lifeless body was cut down and loaded into the flimsy wooden coffin that been supplied by the town of Pikeville. He was to be buried at a pauper's graveyard, just yards away from the place of his execution on the hill overlooking the gallows.

Fifteen minutes later, Sheriff Maynard surveyed the landscape around the stark plank wall. The huge crowd was gone and heading back to Pikeville or their homes in other surrounding towns. The undertaker and his assistant placed the lid on Ellison's simple pine coffin and proceeded to nail it shut.

Maynard jerked a whiskey flask from his jacket pocket and took a stiff drink. This whole affair had caused him days of stress and he was glad it was over. He walked over to the hill where the undertakers had carried the body. He took another swig of the strong bourbon as he watched the two men hastily cover the coffin with dirt. "Poor dumb bastard" he mumbled.

■■■

CHAPTER FOURTEEN: STRANGE GOINGS ON

Dave Stratton was stinking drunk. On the evening of May 14, 1890, he went into town and proceeded to swill ten pints of beer. In the good company of his tavern cronies, he spoke at nauseam about his disdain for Devil Anse. Unfortunately, his plan to frame his enemy in Federal Court for operating an illegal still had unraveled in a Charleston Courtroom.

At approximately ten o'clock in the evening, Stratton decided it was time to walk home. It was a dark, May evening with a thick layer a fog that blanketed the ground, making it nearly impossible to see. Since Dave was already impaired, he decided to follow the railroad tracks back to his home. For a man in his condition, his simple idea to travel a linear path was quite logical.

Stratton, a West Virginian, was a friend and ally of Randolph McCoy and his friends on the Kentucky border. He lived near Logan Courthouse, less than half mile from where the new railroad mail depot was located. So close in fact that on most evenings he could hear the Chesapeake and Ohio train pass by his home.

On his way home, the intoxicated man began to have a one way conversation. "That old Devil thinks he's real foxy," Stratton muttered. He tripped on one of the railroad ties and fell on his hands and it took him about twenty seconds to get up. "What makes me so sick is no one in his home state can lay a hand on him. Well, if he ever comes around my neck of the woods, I'll show him. I'll put a Goddamn bullet in his head. I'm awful tired; hope the misses won't be too put out at me tramping in so late. Yep, thank the good Lord for these tracks, or I'd never find my way back to my place."

After his initial fall, Stratton cautiously walked along for some distance. He was fine up until his knee high boot got caught in a one of the cracked wood slats. This caused him to plunge forward, soundly hitting his head on the iron rail. He was now rendered unconscious, laid out perfectly in the path of the next on coming locomotive.

Mrs. Stratton did not rest easy that evening because her man had not returned home. Lily climbed out of bed at six in the morning and quickly dressed. She was a petite woman, though far from delicate. Her long thin legs carried her lean frame at a quick pace, while her opal blue eyes darted up and down the trail. "Where was her husband?" she thought.

It was a perfect spring morning as the haze was just beginning to lift. The wooded area near the flowing creek was alive with the music of a thousand birds. Their song was augmented by the sound of the countless bees that performed their ritual of pollination. The warmth of sunlight crept through the trees with beaming rays of white light and the scent of the flowering vegetation infusing the atmosphere.

If she hadn't been so worried, Lily would have found her walk more enjoyable. This morning she was having terrible thoughts. It wasn't like her man to disappear or miss sleeping in their bed at night. Dave had stayed out late before, but he had always come home. Mrs. Stratton was painfully mindful of the fact that her husband had enemies. Perhaps he encountered one of them on his way home and was hurt or killed. After walking for ten minutes, she arrived at the railroad tracks. She slowly stepped along them for about five hundred yards, until she came to where the mangled body of a man was lying.

*****

About a month earlier, a man named William O. Smith was sleeping soundly in his snug, warm bed. He was a former Confederate Army Colonel, whose nickname was "Rebel Bill." At fifty-six years old his body remained trim and strong from his recent tree farming job for the Norfolk and Western Railway. This was a profession he added to a long list of trades he had performed during his lifetime.

Smith was in deep, restful sleep when the door of his small cabin suddenly burst open. In a half sleep, he sat up in his bed to see the silhouette of man standing in his doorway. Before he could stand, this dark figure rushed over and pummeled Rebel Bill with his fists. Because the shadowy attacker wore a mask, he could not be identified.

After multiple blows with his fists, the intruder unsheathed a large hunting knife, attempting to stab Smith several times. In spite of the diligent effort by this would be assassin, the old lumberjack resiliently rolled around to avoid the knife blows. During the struggle, he managed to reach over to the small table by his bed and grab his revolver. With the butt of his pistol, Bill struck his attacker in the head, causing him to retreat for the door.

This nighttime assault might have gone unnoticed or unreported, except for one thing. It was rumored that Frank Phillips had been the assailant. This story was not verified, but it spread like a prairie fire throughout the Tug valley. The day after the attack, Smith was well enough to ride his horse to the justice of the peace. He secured an arrest warrant sworn out against Frank Phillips. Though Rebel Bill had legal paper in hand, it was merely a formality. He had no intention of taking him into custody; he wanted him dead.

As the rumors spread through Kentucky and West Virginia, people wondered why these two men wanted to destroy each other. Some accounts stated that during the war, Rebel Bill established quite a standing as a fighting man. Local myth stated that Smith single handedly outfought a company of Union soldiers that pursued him after he raided their bivouac.

Another account circulated about Smith launching a Guerilla strike against James Garfield's brigade, as they attempted to raft down the Big Sandy River. In the years that followed, Garfield became President of the United States and Rebel Bill wound up cutting logs. He did however manage to outlive the successful politician by several years.

It was rumored that Smith's celebrated career as a soldier is what caused Frank Phillips to seek him out. Apparently the special deputy's father was a second lieutenant under the Garfield's command. After his successful assault, Rebel Bill took him as prisoner, resulting in his death by starvation at the infamous Andersonville Prison in 1864. It was said that when Phillips discovered where the old man lived, he vowed revenge for what had been done to pappy.

All the speculation aside, Phillips said he had an air tight alibi. He claimed that he was miles away at the time this alleged attack took place. This did not matter because Rebel Bill had his warrant and was sure that Frank was lying.

Some of Smith's neighbors thought it was strange that anyone managed to survive an attack from Frank Phillips. When the man set his mind on killing someone that person generally wasn't around long. This time the deputy had apparently not been so lucky. The man who had shot Jim Vance and several others had met his equal.

On April nineteenth, a month after the attack, another rumor circulated that Rebel Bill had surprised Phillips at Peter Creek, killing him as dead as Stonewall Jackson. Another story stated that Phillips was killed as John's creek on April twentieth. That seemed strange because of the logistical improbability involved in dying at two different places on two successive days.

The town Pikeville buzzed with the news of Frank Phillip's untimely demise. He was a hero to most of the people that lived there. After all, he was the man that brought the Hatfields to justice. He had been the only man with the intestinal fortitude required for that distasteful job. The townsfolk were even more surprised when the dead man rode into town. This was two weeks after he had been reported killed.

Frank Phillips stopped in for a drink at the Starlight Palace, shaking hands with several patrons. He held his sinewy arms opened wide to show the patrons that he was unharmed. "See for yourselves boys, I don't have a scratch or a mark. Take a good look, because if I'm dead, then I'm the liveliest corpse you've ever seen" he said in a jovial tone.

In the town of Charleston West Virginia, it was also reported that well known lawman was very much alive. An internal revenue agent had seen him just two days earlier on his way out of Pikeville. It was also proven, that William "Rebel Bill" Smith had been attending court on April nineteenth and twentieth. Both the calendar days he was supposed to have killed Phillips.

Yes, Frank was very much alive, but poor Dave Stratton was very much dead. When his wife had found him on the morning of May 15, he was in horrendous shape. His head had been cracked open, along with his chest caved in. The poor soul died just hours after his wife discovered his body lying by the railroad tracks.

After the grisly find, Mrs. Stratton was justifiably beside herself. She wondered who could have done such a thing to her husband. Who would have been despicable enough to leave a man in such a state? Some of his friends suggested that Dave had fell victim to Hatfield Vengeance. After all, the man had bravely brought testimony against Devil Anse in a Charleston Courtroom. One friend even surmised that the violent clan had trampled Stratton with their horses.

A couple of days before Dave Stratton met his maker, another interesting event occurred in Pikeville. This was more than a wild rumor. On a May morning three months after Ellison was hanged, deputies at the Pikeville jail prepared for their normal shift change. The daytime jailers came in with their coffee cups in hand, greeting the nighttime guards who were tired and ready to go home. The early shift was informed that all was well and that it had been quiet, boring graveyard watch.

One young deputy performed his daily ritual of distributing breakfast and taking a head count of the prisoners. To his dismay, he discovered one of his men was missing. It was young Charlie Gillespie, who was no longer where he was supposed to be. After a fruitless search around the facility, it was determined the young mountain man had somehow escaped.

"That little son of bitch was smarter than he looked," said one deputy.

"Yeah, smarter than we were," quipped another.

Gillespie had accomplished something that not one of the other convicted Logan Wildcats was able to do. He avoided serving any real jail time for his involvement in the killing of the McCoy family members. Pikeville never sent any posse after him and he never served another day in jail. In the years that passed, no one ever figured out how he got away.

*****

Eighteen Ninety was indeed a year of strange goings on. It was also a year of relative peace between the Hatfield and McCoy clans. Other than rumors of violence that titillated the hungry press, nothing really happened. The earlier part of the year had seen Ellison Mounts executed but beyond that, there was nothing new for the newspapers to write about.

During the year, not a week had passed without an article about the now legendary conflict appearing in one of the local publications. It was true that these stories of violence excited the readers but there was also one positive article that was printed by *The Louisville Courier Journal*.

"The famous Hatfield-McCoy Feud is at long last at an end. There has been a wholesale slaughter of many souls on both sides of the feud. Numerous men have lived as fugitives from the law, with prices on their heads and detectives on their trails. Some men were lucky, daring and cunning enough to avoid capture. Although many were apprehended, several were imprisoned and one was hanged. There were too many senseless incidents of violence on both sides of the feud. Families witnessed their young men die in the prime of their lives and their older kin murdered, with nothing gained for the blood spilled and nothing good accomplished. It finally appears that the Hatfield and McCoy families have both agreed to let the matter rest."

Both West Virginia and Kentucky were happy to see the cessation of hostilities transpire. They both did their part to contribute to the peace that had been initiated that year. The new governor of West Virginia was a man named A. Brooks Fleming. He withdrew the reward money that had been offered by former governor E. Willis Wilson. This meant that Frank Phillips and his Kentucky deputies were no longer wanted in West Virginia.

In Kentucky, the Pikeville officials weren't exactly knocking themselves out to go after Devil Anse or his sons. This meant that several men didn't have to look over their shoulders all the time. Even more ironic was that fact that Lee Ferguson was now in trouble. The man, who so vigorously pressed the cases against the Logan County Wildcats, was now himself facing several indictments. They included stealing government pensions from unsuspecting war veterans.

After the two trials were over, the foundations of peace had been laid between the Hatfields and McCoys. However, just when people started to get comfortable with the idea of the two clans not shooting at one another, the body of Bud McCoy was discovered. His friends found him lying face down in a pool of blood, near a lumber mill in Peter Creek. As a result of the eighteen bullet holes in his body, foul play was suspected.

No one in Pikeville denied that Bud was a nasty piece of work. He was a drunk, a bad gambler and he liked to start fights with no real cause to do so. In spite of his flaws, his family was upset because he was the second son of Harmon McCoy to die violently. The keen eye and proficient shooting of Cap Hatfield had taken the life of his brother Jeff. It was therefore not unreasonable for the shadow of suspicion to fall upon Island Creek clan.

After further investigation, it was found that normally ill-tempered Bud was actually killed by one of his own. Ples McCoy, along with man named Bill Dyer killed him after a drunken quarrel. Though very few people in Pikeville were pleased about Bud's untimely ending, they were happy that the bead didn't come from Hatfield rifles.

During 1890 there had been many rumors and unexplained occurrences attributed to the feud. Dave Stratton was dead and his wife and friends had all assumed that is was a case of foul play. The simple truth was that he was unceremoniously run over by the Chesapeake and Ohio train. It was mighty peculiar that Frank Phillips had been killed and didn't even know it. Nor did he have the decency to admit he was dead, upon receiving the news that such was his fate. It was truly a mystery that no one at the Pikeville jail could figure out how Charlie Gillespie sprung himself from his cell. And, after years of fighting, it was downright uncommon to see a member of the Hatfield and McCoy family engaged in pleasant conversation with another; yet it happened on a main thoroughfare in Pikeville.

Finally, the strangest thing of all was the communication received by *The Wayne County News*. The letter was from a man considered by many, to be one of the most violent participants of the long feud. The note was addressed to the editor of the publication and went as follows:

"Dear Sir, I am asking you for space in your valuable paper, to print these few lines. An amnesty has been declared in the feud, between our family and the McCoy family, and I wish to declare the following sentiment. I do not wish to keep the old feud alive and I am sure that everyone, like me, is tired of hearing the names Hatfield and McCoy. I'm also sure that the states of West Virginia and Kentucky are tired of the border warfare that has existed in a time of peace. The war spirit that I once carried like a torch has been extinguished; and I now rejoice at the prospect of peace. I have devoted my life to the sword and I now say openly that I regret this decision. There has been a terrible loss of noble lives and valuable property, in the struggle between our families. We being like Adam, not the first transgressors. Now I propose to rest in the

spirit of peace and I sincerely hope that others will do the same."
The letter was signed, Cap Hatfield.

■■■

CHAPTER FIFTEEN: DEVIL ANSE MEETS BUFFALO BILL

"Hey mister you lost?" asked an unfamiliar voice.

Detective Bill Baldwin was startled, quickly twirling his horse around to see a towering figure of a man standing before him. The stranger was lean and robust. His black beard was spotted with gray streaks, creeping down his shirt almost to his stomach. Attached to his waist, two revolvers dangled from a black leather holster. Standing in brown, well-worn boots, his dirty brown duster flapped in the wind.

"I'm not exactly lost Mister. I've got a map with me. Would this be Island Creek?"

"Yes it would. Are you just passing through?" asked the tall man.

"Yes, that's it exactly. I'm just traveling through and thought I'd have a look see."

"Is that a fact?"

"Yes that's certainly what I thought I'd do. I heard this is rugged beautiful country" answered Baldwin.

My name's Anderson Hatfield. It'll be getting dark soon, you best come back with me and spend the night at my place."

Baldwin reached down to give the mountain man a firm handshake. "I am pleased to make your acquaintance Mister Hatfield. My name's Tom Harper; sure I wouldn't be putting you out?"

"Nope, my kin loves having company. We don't get many visitors around here."

Detective Baldwin followed on horseback, while his host walked up the road a quarter of a mile. Up a short grade, the detective noticed an odd looking structure that was surrounded by gun ports. "What's that place for" Baldwin asked.

Devil Anse acted nonchalant. "Oh that, that's in case we get nosy strangers or detectives coming around making trouble. After my boys and I ventilated a dozen or so of them fellers, they stopped coming around anymore. It's been so quiet lately, now we mainly stock firewood in it."

The seemingly lost traveler raised his eyebrows and chuckled to himself. His host hitched up his brown mare and packhorse, motioning him inside his newly built cabin. "Don't be shy Mister Harper I want you to meet my family."

It was five o'clock in the afternoon and several people milled about the cabin. Devil Anse merrily introduced his guest to his wife and children. "Mr. Harper, these are my children Elias, Troy, Joseph, Rosada and Willis. The two-year-old over there is my youngest one Tennyson."

He looked around the room at his large family. "Kids, this here gentleman is Mister Harper and he's gonna stay the night with us."

"Pleased to meet you Mister Harper," said several children's voices in unison.

"You have a beautiful family Mister Hatfield" Baldwin agreeably told his host. He was now reasonably satisfied that his real identity had remained unknown to him. Although he knew by reputation that Hatfield was nobody's fool, it seemed that his befuddled manner had succeeding in deceiving him.

William Baldwin was a partner in the very successful Baldwin-Felts Detective agency. He was forty-two years old, possessing an abundance of experience practicing his trade. He was formerly chief scout during his hitch in the army where he learned about hunting men. Now he met the most famous feudist in America and with little effort was sitting in his home. As the he sat comfortably in the best chair in the house, Baldwin experienced a slight twinge of guilt accepting Hatfield's warm hospitality. The detective had journeyed to Island Creek to apprehend two of his older boys for distilling illegal alcohol.

In spite of his clandestine mission, Baldwin was impressed with Devil Anse and his family. For dinner, his wife Levicy prepared a meal of wild duck, vegetables, mashed potatoes with gravy and fresh biscuits. Sitting at the head of the table enjoying the fine meal that was prepared for him, he couldn't help but be entertained by his notorious host. All the things he had heard about the man's bloodthirsty reputation now seemed totally unwarranted.

"Mrs. Hatfield, I want to thank you cooking up such a fine dinner. And to put me up as well, no weary traveler could ask for much more than that," Baldwin said with a polite nod.

"We love having guests, don't we Levicy" Devil Anse loudly proclaimed.

"We sure do father. As my husband said earlier, we're kind of hidden away in this valley. We don't get much company."

After dinner, the old patriarch served his guest some fresh coffee, imparting several amusing yarns, which kept him laughing most of the evening. At about ten o'clock, he showed Baldwin up to the upstairs loft. Inside the upper room there was an inviting feather bed, which was made up with fresh linen.

"You have a nice rest Mister Harper." Devil Anse pointed over to a nightstand that was beside the bed. "You can use that pot on the table, if you have to rid yourself of water. My wife will cook you up some breakfast in the morning."

"Thank you Mister Hatfield, you've been most kind" Baldwin replied.

"Good night Mr. Harper," said the old man as he closed the trap door to the loft and went down stairs.

Detective Baldwin had won the confidence of his mountain host and would snatch Robert and Elliott under his unsuspecting nose. Not only was he in the middle of enemy country, he had actually been invited to stay under their roof. With pride in himself and his plan, he placed his revolver under his pillow and quickly dosed off to a peaceful sleep.

At about four in the morning, the noisy sound of creaking wooden stairs began to permeate the detective's sleep state. "Oh Mister Baldwin, Mister Baldwin, you need to get up," a voice said loudly. The surprised detective stirred in his comfortable bed. Quickly rising up from his warm mattress, he peered out the window of the loft and noticed it was pitch dark. "I know its early Mister Baldwin, but you need to get up and get your breakfast" the voice instructed.

The detective focused his eyes on a big head, popping up inside the opening of the loft. The sleepy man now suddenly realized it was Devil Anse, who held on to coal oil lantern. "Mister Baldwin, if you dress quickly, the wife's cooked up some ham and eggs for you. If you eat them fast, I can probably get you out of here before my older sons come up. They're mean sons-of-bitches and if they catch you here, they may want to shoot you. You know they have peculiar notions and they don't much like detectives."

Baldwin shook his head in amazement. "I'll be right down.

"How's your breakfast Mister Baldwin, everything tasty?" Devil Anse asked courteously.

The nervous man wolfed down his food. "Oh yes, no complaints here."

"The wife made up some coffee for you to take with you. Don't expect we'll be seeing you anytime soon, ain't that right Mister Baldwin?"

The detective nodded obligingly. "No, I don't think you have to worry about that. You can safely say that I won't get up this way again."

It was just before dawn when the two men finished their hot morning meal. Devil Anse saddled up a mount, quickly escorting his guest down the ridge about a mile down the trail. "Well, this is where we part company, good luck Mister Baldwin. Come back when you can't stay so long."

"Thanks, I'll remember that" the detective answered. He looked at crafty old bird and hesitated for a moment. "Well I sure out smarted myself on this one. I'll say one thing though."

Devil Anse turned his horse around. "What's that Mister Baldwin?"

"I wish that you were working for me."

The older man smiled, waived to his deceiving guest and trotted off towards his home. Baldwin hastily brought his horse to a gallop, riding back to Logan Courthouse empty handed, but alive.

*****

The violence of the Hatfield-McCoy troubles was now three years in the past. The people of the Tug Valley had other things on their mind during the late spring of 1893. The biggest spectacle in the world had arrived in Pikeville. Buffalo Bill Cody's Wild West show was in town for four days, which was expected to attract thousands of visitors. There had not been such a multitude of humanity in Pikeville since the Ellison Mounts hanging.

Nobody as famous as Buffalo Bill had ever come to Pike County Kentucky. He was a celebrated figure across the country even before his famous show ever existed. His exploits though greatly exaggerated, were known throughout the world. This was largely due to the colorful dime novels written by an eastern writer named Ned Buntline. William Frederick Cody was even awarded the Congressional Medal of Honor, for his heroic participation as a scout during the war against the plains Indians.

The town was cleaned up from top to bottom, with a gigantic banner strung across the center of the main street. In big red, white and blue letters, it read "Pikeville welcomes Buffalo Bill's Wild West Show." The Mayor, the Sheriff and the City Fathers would be on hand to present the great hero with the key to the city.

On the day the show arrived there was a parade led by the famous frontiersman, who continually tipped his hat to the crowd. At the center of the town square, Buffalo Bill's horse kneeled down and Cody recited some flowery dialogue that had been scripted by Buntline. Before performing in his Wild West extravaganza, Bill had played the part of himself in several one act melodramas. The crowd roared with approval after he delivered his wooden lines about shooting buffalos, fighting savage Native American warriors and taming the Wild West.

Falling in behind Buffalo Bill was a preview of the upcoming show. Several thousand spectators lined the streets of Pikeville, gleefully awaiting the titillating sample. The sight of blue coated cavalry, rowdy cowboys and real live Sioux thrilled children and adults alike. Toward the end of the noisy procession rode the beautiful Annie Oakley. Dressed in a white fringe suit with silver studs and pristine white cowboy hat the queen of the show waived and smiled at the sea of wildly cheering faces.

At the middle of town the Wild West parade came to a halt. First, expert stunt riders mounted atop gorgeous Palominos performed fancy rope tricks. Next a group of circus clowns tossed dinner plates that were blasted out of the air by three pistol sharpshooters. Finally, Sitting Bull, the famous medicine man ambled slowly past the crowd without cracking a smile.

At a giant lot at the edge of town, the Wild West extravaganza assembled its red, white and blue tents. On Thursday evening June 15, it opened for business. The bleachers in the main pavilion were packed as tight as a sardine can. There were also a few standing room only tickets that were sold to people lucky enough to get them.

The show opened with a scaled down rodeo, as several cowboys roped steers, wrestled calves and performed some bronco riding. A histrionic recreation of The Battle of War Bonnet Creek was staged, where Buffalo Bill led the United States Calvary to victory against the warring Native Americans. Hundreds of young boys in attendance were awestruck by sight of the great star; all of them wishing that they could be him, if only for a moment.

The climax of the show was an exhibition of marksmanship that featured Annie Oakley, the thirty three-year old sharp shooting sensation. Dressed in a yellow sparkled, fringe cowgirl costume with matching yellow boots, her short, shapely figure was complimented by long brown hair and brilliant green eyes.

Oakley began her career as a marksman at age seven, hunting game to feed her family. She had already toured the United States with Buffalo Bill and was considered by many to be the greatest shot of her time. Next to the star himself, she was the most popular attraction of ninety minute program.

For her first trick, the arresting sharpshooter blasted one hundred clay pigeons out of the air. One after the other, without a miss, they exploded before the dumbfounded eyes of the sold out arena. Next, Annie had an assistant toss a playing card into the air, which she hit nine times with a rifle before it hit the ground.

Before the grand finale, featuring all the performers in the show, Buffalo Bill offered to match targets with anyone in the grandstand. Typically speaking, this was an offer that in most cities or towns was rarely acted upon. Devil Anse, along with his children and grandchildren had attended this particular performance. For the man from Island Creek, this was a challenge that could not be turned down.

The tall, stoop shouldered man sauntered out into the center of the ring, to shake hands with Cody himself. Buffalo Bill dressed in a stunning white, tailored suit of clothes, with a beige Stetson atop his head. He was tall and good-looking, sporting long silvery blonde hair, with a perfectly trimmed mustache and beard. On his hands he wore spotless, white, buckskin gloves.

As he stood next to the celebrated marksman, the mountain man proudly smiled. "It's an honor to meet you Buffalo Bill," he said excitedly.

"The pleasure is mine sir" Replied the showman.

A couple of targets were placed at the far end of the circus tent, with a white wooden table set up on the opposite end.

"Have you had much shooting experience sir?" Cody asked with slight condescension.

"A little bit" Hatfield replied modestly.

"Winchester Model Ninety Two's all right?"

"Anything you like Buffalo Bill. I'm honored just to be standing up here with you." Devil Anse giggled nervously. "I just hope I don't make a jackass of myself."

"Nonsense Sir, I'm sure you'll do your town proud."

Cody called for an assistant, who laid two spanking new Winchester Rifles on the white table. The show announcer walked to the center of the ring carrying a hand held megaphone. "The great Buffalo Bill Cody will now match targets at one hundred yards, with the gentleman from Island Creek. The crowd applauded with wild approval. By local legend and newspaper accounts, they were familiar with Devil Anse's reputation as a marksman.

The targets were small, measuring twelve by ten inches. "Mister Cody, you mind if I wear my spectacles? My eyes ain't as good as they used to be."

"No, by all means, wear them," Buffalo Bill politely replied.

The guest marksman reached into the pocket of his flannel shirt and put on his glasses.

"Would you like to shoot first?" asked Buffalo Bill.

The mountain man motioned Cody to pickup one of the Winchesters. "No, it' your show, you go first."

Buffalo Bill obliged him, quickly aimed and fired his first shot.

"It's in the number ten ring; right side of the bull" shouted the ring announcer. The spectators applauded enthusiastically. Devil Anse grabbed his rifle, aimed as quickly as Cody and fired. "In the number ten ring just to the left of the bull" the announcer shouted. The audience hooted, whistled and clapped for the local man.

"Pretty damn fine shooting sir" Cody said, somewhat surprised.

"I had to get used to your Winchester; shoots a little high," responded Devil Anse.

"The shooters will now fire six rounds in rapid succession," said the announcer.

Devil Anse pointed his open palm towards Buffalo Bill's Winchester. "Go ahead Mister Cody," he said politely. The famous cowboy smiled and tipped his hat. Picking up his Winchester, he fired off six rounds as fast as he could pull the lever.

In an excited voice the results were declared. "All six rounds are in the number ten ring; with four in the bull," said the announcer. The throng of people loudly approved with whistles and applause.

Buffalo Bill now cordially pointed down at his competitor's rifle. "Now it's your turn sir."

Devil Anse, took a deep breath, picked up his Winchester and swiftly fired his own six shots. The ringmaster walked over to the West Virginian's target and looked it over twice. "All six rounds in the number ten ring, with five shots in the bull," he announced. This time the crowd came to it feet, cheering uncontrollably. Buffalo Bill took off his white Stetson and graciously bowed to his victorious opponent.

As a reward for his shooting prowess, Cody walked over the table and handed Devil Anse one of the Winchester rifles. The wily sharpshooter quickly grasped the gun, raised it into the air and listened to the sound of thunderous applause. Afterwards, Buffalo Bill walked over to the show's announcer to ask him a question. "Who the hell was that man?"

"That's Devil Anse, the leader of the Hatfield clan. You know the Hatfield-McCoy Feud?"

Cody shrugged his shoulders. "Oh, I'm not sure I ever heard of him."

The ringmaster smiled politely. "I guess you haven't read the newspapers lately. He's pretty well known around this part of the country."

Buffalo Bill removed his expensive Stetson and set it on the table next to the remaining Winchester rifle. "Well, I'd hate to shoot it out with that son-of-a-bitch."

■■

CHAPTER SIXTEEN: ECHOES OF THE PAST

Dave Monarch leaned against the chipped wooden rail of the Pikeville Ferry. As he crossed the lake, rays of red hot sun burned his pale skin. With nothing else to do, he studied the curious old man who operated the Ferryboat. "What a melancholy face," he thought. Out of boredom the farmer made the mistake of initiating small talk with the old trail raft operator.

"Hey, what's your problem today Mister? You look like someone killed your dog," he said.

"What's my problem you say?" the old man asked in an agitated tone. "Do you know who I am Mister?" he added.

Monarch shrugged his shoulders "I have no idea sir, I hadn't given it much thought. I'm just making conversation."

"Well I'll tell you who I am. I'm Randolph McCoy, now you heard of me?"

"Yes, I've heard of you."

The tall old man walked over to his passenger, standing closer than socially acceptable. "I suppose you've heard of all the wretchedness the Hatfield family has caused me?"

"Yes I've read a little about in the newspapers."

"Newspapers, now there's a waste of paper and ink. Let me tell you the truth young man" Randolph insisted. He cared little, whether or not the nicely dressed gentleman was interested in his troubles. "Devil Anse and his foul seed have brought me to where I stand today; yes right here on this old ferryboat you're standing on mister."

"How's that so Mister McCoy? Aren't we the masters of our own lives?"

"Masters of our own lives you say? That's a load of cow manure. I'll tell you why that ain't so. Because I stood up against the Devil's kin in Blackberry Creek; that's what started this mess. His cousin stole one of my pigs. Since you've just purchased them fine animals you're transporting today, you out to know what a pigs worth."

The passenger nodded his head in agreement.

"That's right, they rigged the jury so I wouldn't get back what's mine and that's what got the whole ball rolling. After that, Johnse Hatfield took up with my daughter Roseanna. He led her on and then didn't do the right thing by marrying her.

"Well that's not right..."

Randolph wouldn't let his passenger get in another word. "Fact is he added insult to injury, thumbing his nose at everyone by marrying Rose Anna's cousin Nancy instead. That broke my little girl's heart it did. That poor girl was nearly dead inside and when she took sick with the measles, she had no heart left to fight for her own life. She died a broken heart. Yes sir, she died of a broken heart. And all because of that smug faced Hatfield boy."

About half way across the lake, Monarch pulled a watch from his vest pocket and checked the time. What had been a short trip now seemed interminable.

"Outta be about two thirty, right mister?" asked Randolph.

"That's right Mister McCoy."

"Yep, I'm just like clockwork. Do the same ride bout six times a day. By the way, I didn't catch your name mister."

"It's Monarch, Dave Monarch."

Randolph continued to pull the rusted chain of ferryboat while his mouth worked harder than the raft. "Well, while we still got a little stretch of time let me tell you what happened next. Election Day of 1882 is when all hell broke loose in my life. The Hatfields picked a fight with my boy Tolbert. He defended himself and his brothers and they killed all three of them. My three boys, Tolbert, Pharmer and Randolph junior; good boys, they were all put in their graves on the same day; and who by? By Devil Anse and his kin, that's who."

The normally easy going farmer was growing somewhat impatient as the ferryboat headed closer to the shore at Pikeville. His pleasant mood was beginning to fade. He had only wanted some polite small talk and instead he received a long sob story.

"Mister Monarch, I don't suppose you read about the New Years raid on my home did you?"

"No, but I'm sure you won't mind telling me."

"I sure as hell don't mind" Randolph answered obliviously "Cap Hatfield and Jim Vance brought a whole gang of murderers to my home. They killed my brave boy Calvin. He drew their fire, so I could run for help. Those bastards bashed my wife's head in and killed my baby Alifair. Then, if that weren't enough, they burned down my house and chased off my livestock."

"That' awful, just awful Mister McCoy…"

"Thank God for my friend Perry Cline, God rest his soul. He and his good wife took in my family and me. Otherwise, we would've had no place to go. If it weren't for Perry, I wouldn't have this job running this here ferry. Now he's gone too." Randolph sighed. "You don't get many friends like that in your life."

"No I'm sure you don't" agreed the bored passenger.

"You know that Devil Anse Hatfield and his sons are still free. They never served one day in jail for their crimes. That old bastard never lost one of his children and I lost six of mine." Just as those words left his mouth, the old wooden transport reached the landing at Pikeville.

The ferry passenger hastily untied his livestock, paying the old man for his fare. All the while Randolph continued to prattle on about his troubles.

"Well, you take care" Monarch said politely. He tied his newly purchased oxen to the rickety wooden cart that his wife and son had dutifully brought to the landing. After the wagon had traveled about fifty yards, the farmer quietly turned to speak to his spouse. "God that was the most annoying man I've ever met."

Mrs. Monarch smiled, giving her husband a curious look. "Who was he?" she asked.

"That old man was Randolph McCoy. No wonder the Hatfields wanted to kill him; after spending fifteen minutes with him, I wanted to kill him too.

*****

Although Randolph's hatred of the Hatfields never diminished, the long feud between the families was finally over. The old man had few friends, fewer of which cared to listen to his ramblings. His best friend and ally, Perry Cline had died in 1892. This left him alone with his choleric memories. Not even his wife Sarah cared to hear his bitter, myopic conversation. His enemies had sworn that they wanted to live in peace. The Hatfields no longer wished to dwell on the unfortunate tragedies of the past. They chose to look ahead towards a new beginning.

On November 4, 1896, the town of Matewan prepared for the presidential election. Located in West Virginia, the small hamlet was only a stone's throw from the Tug Fork River. It was also only a short trek away from where the McCoy brothers were killed some fourteen years earlier. That was a day that was long past but not forgotten.

Established by a group of businessmen only a few years earlier, Matewan was proud of their rapid development. The local citizenry realized the sound value of land near the tracks of the Norfolk and Western Railroad. The inhabitants of this tight knit community hung flags and banners, making arrangements for a day of voting and peaceful reveling.

One well known resident from Island Creek decided he would come to town to cast a vote for his chosen candidate. This man of reputation was Cap Hatfield. His participation in the Election Day killings of 1882 was permanently etched on all those who lived within a fifty-mile radius. The town's folk were aware that this once violent man was now practicing the ways peace. Yet his mere presence made some people nervous enough to keep a watchful eye.

Though he had vowed to lay down his sword in general, Cap did not ride into town unarmed. With him he carried his weapon of choice, a Winchester Rifle. On his hip, he also holstered a colt revolver. Though he wasn't expecting trouble, experience taught him to never travel unprotected.

Riding along with Cap was his favorite stepson Joe Glenn. Though only an adolescent, the boy's big lanky frame made him appear much older. He too rode into town with a loaded Winchester in his saddlebag.

The outcome of this election would decide whether William Jennings Bryan or William McKinley would be the next President of the United States. Cap was a Democrat, as were most loyal southerners. This particularly applied to sons of former Confederates. The offspring of ex-rebel fathers would never vote for a Republican. Lincoln had been the first member of the party elected to the presidency and these men remembered him the Boss of the Yankee army.

One thing for certain, was that William J. Bryan could count on getting votes from the recently formed Mingo County, which was split off from Logan County. In fact, Bryan would carry the state of West Virginia, as well as several other southern states. However, Bill McKinley would be the one who got elected. Bryan did however have two more opportunities to run for the presidency, losing both times.

It was nearly nine years since the Battle of Grapevine Creek. The people in town often discussed the famous feud and Newspaper photographers had recently come to Island Creek to have the Hatfields dress up and pose with their guns. Yet there was little concern over Cap's visit since he no longer had an ax to grind with the McCoy family.

The townsfolk were far more concerned about a recent grudge of undisclosed nature, between Cap and a man named John Rutherford. Residents of Matewan all agreed that Cap was older, wiser and more inclined to control his famous temper. Nevertheless, the new Mayor decided it would be prudent to have a word with the celebrated feudist, to guarantee his intentions remained peaceful.

Matewan was experiencing the effects of an Indian summer. The week before the election had been one of record temperatures. The air on Election Day was dry, without a shred of breeze and the ground was hot as a skillet. As Dr. Rutherford saw Cap ride into town, he stepped out of his office and onto the wooden walkway. "Hello Cap."

The big man dismounted his horse, tying it to the mayor's hitching post. "Hello Jim, how the hell are you?"

"I'm so good I can hardly stand it. Who is that fine looking young fellow with you today?"

Cap proudly pointed at the tall, dark hared youth. "This here is my boy Joe and I thought I'd bring him to his first election celebration."

The mayor extended his hand. "I'm Pleased to meet you young man."

"I reckon the pleasure is mine." Joe Glenn responded shyly.

"He's a nice young man Cap. It's good to see young people with decent manners these days." The smile on Rutherford's face gave way to a more serious look. "Cap, I'm happy you decided to be with us for election" the Mayor began.

"You got something else on your mind?" Cap asked, interrupting Rutherford.

"But we don't want any trouble here today" said Jim.

"Who would I have trouble with?"

"Come on son you know with who, my boy!"

"What can I do to put your mind at ease Jim?"

"There is one thing you could do."

"What would that be?"

"You can leave your guns with me" The mayor said boldly.

Cap's icy blue eyes unnerved the Rutherford for a moment. This often occurred when people he engaged in conversation looked directly at his left one, which had a pale discoloration. After an uncomfortable pause, Cap smiled. "Sure Jim, I just came to have a few drinks and vote for my man."

Rutherford pointed towards Hatfield's side arm. The well known feudist handed over his Winchester and his pistol to the relieved mayor. He smiled again and changed the subject. "You think us Democrats got a chance of getting our man voted in?"

"I don't know son, those northern boys are putting an awful lot of money up to back this McKinley fellow. Bryan's the candidate for the poor man. He's fixing to mint more silver and inflate the greenback, which helps get folks to get out of debt easier," Rutherford explained.

The big man cocked his head sideways for a minute. "You sure know your stuff Jim."

"Just simple economics my boy" said Rutherford.

"That all that sounds mighty good, but I'm voting for Bryan because he's Democrat" Cap concluded.

The former feudist did just what he promised. He voted for man and sought refreshment at the local tavern. So that he could keep reasonably sober for the ride home, he intended to only have a few drinks. After bumping into some friends and downing five shots of Jack Daniel's Old Nunber 7, he had changed his mind.

Joe Glenn patiently waited outside the tavern as he was too young to drink bourbon. Being the affable young man like his Uncle Johnse, he was found some adolescent girls to talk to. They were milling about the crowded streets, so he offered to buy them ice cream with some money that his stepfather had given him.

John Rutherford woke up with a terrible hangover but reached for the half finished glass of warm beer, which sat on his night table. The big man wobbled over to the wash basin, quickly splashing some cool water on his sweaty, unshaven face. On the table next to his personal items sat a quarter pint of whiskey. With his shaking right hand he grabbed it, swallowing what remaining contents the narrow mouth bottle had to offer.

By the time he reached mayor's office he was half drunk. Stomping heavily in through the front door, the intemperate man knocked over the coat rack as he entered. Jim Rutherford glanced up from his lunch to see that his son had odd sneer on his face. The younger man plopped himself heavily into the chair that sat before his father's desk.

"You been drinking a lot son?" asked Dr. Rutherford.

"Yes Pa, I have been drinking a bit."

As he sat down, the mayor happened to notice his son was wearing his holstered revolver. What's on your mind boy?"

I saw Cap Hatfield ride into town after I got up, did you talk to him daddy?"

"Yes, I talked to him and he came in to vote with his boy. He gave me his guns and he gave his word that he doesn't want any trouble."

"Oh he doesn't want trouble and you believe that?" John replied sarcastically.

The mayor spoke in a firm tone. "Yes I do believe him. I don't know what happened between you two. I suppose if you had wanted me to know you would have said something."

John raised his voice. "Yeah that's right. My business with him is my business."

"That's fine with me son but I don't want you going tweaking his nose. Just stay away from him today. That man has put near a half dozen men into their graves; just leave him be."

"Don't worry about me daddy. I'm going to have a few friendly drinks with some friends and if he stays clear of me, I'll stay clear of him."

"Why don't you stay here with me? I'll make you a sandwich.

Besides, you look like death warmed over. Why don't you get some food in your stomach before you commence to celebrating?"

"I don't want anything daddy." He stood up from his chair and began walking out of his father's office.

"At least let me hold your revolver until Cap leaves," the mayor added.

As he reached for the knob of the entranceway, John stopped and turned towards his father. "I'll say it again your honor. If he doesn't mess with me, I won't mess with him." He left slamming the door on his way out.

Although hundreds of people came to celebrate that afternoon, things remained calm all day. The restaurants were busy, the saloons were full and money was being spent freely. With the exception of a few drunken revelers firing their pistols in the air, the party continued on peacefully. After speaking with the sheriff, Mayor Jim Rutherford was satisfied that he hand avoided any potential trouble.

About an hour before sunset, Cap Hatfield gathered up his stepson and prepared to leave the village. He had consumed a fair amount of whiskey, which had a mellowing effect on his already low key demeanor. Hatfield had kept his promise by staying clear of any incident. On the way out of town he stopped off at the mayor's office. Cap and his stepson retrieved their guns then trotted their horses through town one last time.

As they approached White's general store, Cap noticed a group of men that gathered in front the entrance. Big John Rutherford was among the assembly. He was drunk, agitated for no legitimate reason and ready to fight. He had just informed several bystanders that he was prepared to demonstrate that Cap's reputation was merely hot air.

One of John's friends was a heavyset man by the name of Kyle James. He was the kind of man who enjoyed stirring people up. As Cap cautiously rode closer to the middle of the street, Kyle seized the opportunity to agitate his friend. "John, what were you saying about Hatfield? Cause here's your boy now. What are you going to do about it? You gonna just let him ride out of here?"

As James egged him on, Rutherford emerged to the front of the group and began yelling at Cap. "Hey boy I got something for you" he bellowed. He drew a thirty two caliber K-frame revolver from his holster firing a round at Cap's head.

As John's badly aimed shot flew past him, Cap fell sideways off his horse, clutching for his pistol on the way down. His frightened horse kicked up enough dust, to momentarily obscure his whereabouts. Though slightly woozy from drinking, he stood up, quickly taking aim at the crazed attacker. He fired two shots that missed and one that didn't.

John tossed his pistol down in the dirt, jerking his hand up to grab his Adam's apple. The large man began choking on his own blood, feeling a jolt of extreme pain for a split second. As quickly as his brain processed this sensation was as long as it took for his body to topple to the ground.

Henderson Chambers was John's brother in law. Just moments before, he had entered White's store to purchase some tobacco. Upon hearing the commotion, he ran to the front of the store just in time to receive a bullet in the center of his forehead. One of the stunned onlookers was Rutherford's cousin Elliott. With a revolver in each hand, he blazed away, charging like an oncoming bull. Cap fired back twice hearing the terrible clicking sound of his empty revolver. Without looking behind, he ran with the fear of God in him. He moved fast, managing to dodge all of Elliott's wild shots taking cover behind a railroad bridge. The daring man who had been through many violent scrapes now desperately attempted to reload his forty five.

"Looks like you're short of lead Hatfield," yelled Elliott. He leveled his pistol at Cap's belly and began walking toward him. "This time I ain't going to miss boy."

Cap threw down his pistol, glaring straight at the young man who now had the drop on him. Elliott deliberately aimed his revolver at Cap's head, but decided to have one last word. "You ain't so much are you Cap Hatfield?" As those words left his mouth, a puff of smoke appeared from a distant sycamore some fifty yards behind the railroad-bridge.

Elliott experienced an agonizing pain from the middle of his back. He weakly held on to his pistol without firing, slowly turning around to see the face of young Joe Glenn. The agile adolescent quickly bounded towards him with a Winchester in his hands. The wounded man reached up his hand behind his back, touching his torn bloody flesh. In utter disbelief, he looked at his own blood soaked fingers. "I'll be damned," he said, going down face first into the ground.

Joe glanced down at the body of the young man he had so accurately shot down. "Is he dead?" he asked in a quavering voice.

"Oh yeah, he's definitely dead. You killed him good and proper." Cap placed his hand on his stepson's shoulder. "You did what you had to do son. Now we best be on our way. Folks ain't gonna be too happy about this," he advised. Having little time gather their horses, the pair opted to run for the cover of the nearby wooded area.

Shortly after the gunfight, Mayor Rutherford gazed upon the body of his fallen son. "Damn him, I knew he'd wind up like this."

Matewan Sheriff N.J Keadle had no problem inducing volunteers to join a posse going out after Cap. The Rutherford's had plenty of friends who were upset over John and Elliott's thrust into the afterlife. The sheriff also dispatched deputies out to cover the local train depots, as well as the main roads that led out towards Kentucky.

In spite of his efforts, it wasn't any of Keadle's posse that apprehended the Hatfields. The men responsible for that were a pair of Pinkerton's named J.H. Clark and Dan Christian. These experienced law dogs were familiar with the territory. In addition, an informer had provided a tip on where they might find their fugitives. Two days after the killings, the detectives discovered Cap and Joe Glenn sleeping on the side of a mountain near Grapevine Creek.

Though ink used for stories about the Hatfield-McCoy feud was long dry, interest remained high across the country. For that reason alone, local newspapers in the bordering states of Kentucky and Ohio jumped on the story of the Election Day shootings. It had involved a well known participant of the aforementioned hostilities, along with a stepson who was labeled a cold blooded killer in training.

Clark and Christian were hailed as heroes. They had captured the notorious Cap Hatfield without spilling a drop of blood. The two highly paid detectives happily reported that the fire eater had come along "Without a lick of trouble." Cap stated that "He hadn't tried real hard to escape justice." He claimed he would have turned himself in right after the shootings but was afraid of getting lynched.

In April of 1897, Cap and Joe were brought before the Circuit Court Judge in Williamson, for the charge of multiple murders. Several friends of John Rutherford testified that Cap fired the first shot on Election Day. Three other witnesses testified it was the other way around. After four days of testimony, the jury decided that both men had been partially responsible; and concluded they fired their weapons within seconds of one another.

Cap and Joe were found guilty of the crime of involuntary manslaughter. Since their actions were motivated primarily by self preservation, they received a lenient sentence. After escaping Frank Phillips and the long arm of Kentucky justice for his involvement in several killings, Cap would have to spend a year in Mingo County Jail. His stepson Joe was given a one year term at the reform school in Pruntytown.

After serving only six months of his sentence, Cap was released from jail. While incarcerated he reduced his hours of monotony by studying law books. The once marginally educated man decided to attend Law College in Tennessee, but only for about six months. Though he never completed his term of education, he passed the bar exam, eventually practicing law in West Virginia. He was also elected as Deputy Sheriff, holding that office for several terms. Two of his children followed their father in the practice of law. His daughter had the distinction of becoming the first female lawyer of Mingo County.

*****

The year 1898 brought dramatic changes into the lives of a pair of famous feud participants. Frank Phillips was spending most of his time drinking and gambling. His reputation as a dangerous man did not abate, even long after the feud ended. To the contrary, he had killed several other men in various disputes.

Frank was having a great evening of poker, wining nearly every hand. After the game he collected his earnings, occupied a barstool and polished off a pint of bourbon. On his way out of the saloon, the weary Phillips barely noticed the silhouette of a man. This darkly dressed figure called out to him, as he untied his horse.

"Hey you're Frank Phillips ain't you?" asked the stranger.

The intoxicated man squinted to focus his eyes. "Yes sir, I'm him" he answered politely.

The man kept his distance Phillips. "You're the man, who brought in the Hatfield Bunch, ain't you?"

"That's right and what's your name young man?"

"Bill Bowen, but folks call me Slick. I've wanted to meet you for a long time." From the hitching post where Frank stood, he could barely see the person making conversation. His blurry eyes could discern the mere outline of a man standing under the shadowy awning of the corner bank building.

"Well, it's been a pleasure talking to you Slick but I need to get home to my wife." He climbed on his horse and was about to ride off when the young man again called out to him. His tone was unexplainably hostile. "Hey, where you going, I'm trying to talk to you."

Frank turned around on his horse, frowning at Bowen's rude remark. "Go home kid, I ain't looking for any trouble."

"I ain't looking for any trouble. I just want you give me a shooting lesson that's all. Come on and show me how good you are with that pistol old man," said Bowen.

Phillips paused for a moment, used his forehand to turn his horse and began to ride away.

"Don't ignore me!" yelled Bowen. He drew a concealed revolver from his long coat, firing at Frank's rear. He was hit in the middle of his lower back, causing him to somersault from his saddle.

The retired deputy felt a paralyzing pain in his back, so he couldn't move a muscle. He lay helplessly on hard cobblestone street, hazily looking up at the stars that occupied the night horizon. His thoughts were those of a man whose mind had drifted into a condition between fear and death.

Bill Bowen triumphantly walked the twenty yards over to where Phillips had fallen. He reveled in his act of treachery.

Frank looked up in a moment of lucidity. "Why kid, what did I ever do to you?" he asked.

"I wanted to be the one that shot the high and mighty Frank Phillips." With that Bowen nonchalantly pointed his pistol at Frank's head and killed him.

*****

Doc Ellis had good reason to be nervous. Inside the passenger car, he was notified that young Elias Hatfield was searching for him. A concerned porter had just overheard the young hothead say, "He was gonna kill the son-of-a-bitch who had his brother arrested."

Ellis was returning from a business trip that he had made to Charleston. The portly, whisker faced man removed a small caliber revolver from his suitcase. He examined the chamber even though he remembered loading it prior to packing his bag. His sweaty left hand tucked the pistol in his belt and walked to the rear of the Chesapeake and Ohio train.

The railroad depot was bustling with passengers exiting the train and the people who came to gather them. Doc Ellis stepped on to the rear deck of the last Pullman car, placing his shaking hands on the shiny brass handrail. He cautiously viewed the crowd, in an attempt to locate anyone who appeared suspicious.

Elias Hatfield was the eighteen year old son of the famous Devil Anse. Like other members of his family, his skill with firearms was exceptional. He had managed to conceal himself behind a stack of wooden freight containers. As the cargo movers began to load the crates on the waiting train, the young man stepped out from behind them. "This is for my brother Johnse," he shouted.
With steady aim, Elias fired three shots from his Colt forty-four, hitting Ellis twice in the upper torso. His large head catapulted backward, breaking the glass window of the rear door. His short frame slid down the door, leaving him dead on the platform.

For killing Humphrey "Doc" Ellis, Elias Hatfield was sentenced to three years in prison for the charge of second-degree murder. This was considerably more lenient than the sentence imposed on his older brother a year earlier.

In 1898, the late Mister Ellis had captured the unprepared Johnse Hatfield. He was the first man able to get one of Anderson Hatfield's sons across the Kentucky line. The long awaited trial was conducted in the sleepy town of Prestonburg. The accused man was charged with the 1882 murders of the McCoy brothers and the 1888 murders of Calvin and Alifair McCoy. The circuit judge hurried the trial along and sentenced the stunned man to life in Prison.

There was no appeal or escape from justice for the dandy whose behavior had helped to fan the flames of the bloody feud. He remained incarcerated at the Kentucky State Penitentiary for the next several years. The great commonwealth had not forgiven the Hatfields for acts of violence against the McCoy family. It was their intention to have Johnse rot in jail, thereby remitting payment for the crimes of his family. This was until fate intervened.

Conditions at the Kentucky State Penitentiary were reported to be deplorable. This included criticism about less than substandard food, inadequate medical care and excessive brutality. In response to this, Lieutenant Governor William Pryor Thorne decided he would tour the prison facility. As a public servant, one of his primary goals was prison reform. He genuinely desired make an honest assessment of situation, to determine whether there was any credence to the accusations.

"I think you'll find everything to be in order here at this institution sir," said Warden
Reese. The apprehensive man could barely keep up, as he escorted the quick stepping state Thorne through the recently cleaned up mess hall.

"Yes, well you'll know the outcome of my evaluation when you read my report," answered Thorne.

Wilbur Briggs sat at the crowded table at the prison mess hall. His large, muscular frame bulged inside of his black striped fatigues that fit him too tightly. Picking at his food, he sat pressed up against one of the fifteen other men that voraciously ate their meals. He eyes took sudden notice of the important state official who was walking across the scrubbed down dining room.

Briggs was an African American inmate who believed he was unjustly convicted of assaulting his landlord. Being a poor sharecropper, he did not have the means to secure competent legal representation. He had no appeal and was considered by officials to be another convict insisting on his innocence. Currently, in the second year of a ten-year sentence, he had nothing but time to contemplate his anger. He watched intently, as the Lieutenant Governor stood conversing with the prison warden. Wilbur was aware that a political bigwig was there to tour the prison facility.

The brawny inmate stood up, calmly walked over to the aisle then abruptly loped over to where the politician stood. The crazed inmate jerked the small man into a headlock, flinging him onto the floor. He straddled the terrified Thorne, throttling his neck in a glassy eyed state of maniacal anger. The horrorstricken warden called out for a guard, but he had momentarily left his post.

As the commotion ensued, Johnse Hatfield looked up from his bowl of watery tomato soup. Seeing that the warden's guest was in danger of losing his life, the slender mountain man reached into his pocket, retrieving a small penknife that he hastily unfolded. Jumping around the mess table, he ran at full speed plunging the small blade into Wilbur's beefy shoulder. "Are you crazy boy, get off this man," he shrieked in a shrill voice.

Briggs threw up his right fist, backhanding Hatfield, tossing him back onto the concrete floor. The hardheaded Johnse shook off the blow and quickly bounced to his feet. Sliding his left arm up underneath Wilbur's arm, he managed to cup his palm around the back of his neck. With his right hand he rapidly sliced his small blade across the big inmate's throat. At least seven times he repeatedly cut away at the front of his neck, while the berserk man continued to strangle the Lieutenant Governor.

As blood spewed out from Wilbur's gaping wounds, the once checkered floor was now a slippery vermillion pool. With his penknife, Johnse had managed to sever the jugular vein of the deranged convict. The cumulative affect of his multiple incisions finally stopped the large man, who collapsed onto the hard tile.

Johnse touched Wilbur's pulse to see if he was dead then helped the Lieutenant Governor stand on his wobbly legs. "Are you all right your Excellency?" He asked.

The trembling Thorne momentarily gasped for the air that he had been denied for ninety seconds. "Yes, I'm all right thanks to you sir," he said choking.

Within moments, a dozen overdue prison guards entered the mess hall, instantly collecting the other inmates.

Warden Reese, who had hidden under a table during the battle, scurried over to where Thorne and Hatfield were standing. Oh your Excellency, I'm so sorry. I hope you were not hurt" he said apologetically.

Thorne looked at the warden in disgust and pointed to body of Wilbur Briggs. "If I had waited for your men I'd be laying dead on the floor instead of that maniac. I'm here because of this man," he said patting his rescuer's wrist. "What's your name sir? He asked.

"Johnse Hatfield your Excellency."

The Lieutenant Governor placed his hand on Johnse's slender shoulder. "Well Hatfield, what would you say if I told you that you're gonna be leaving this place tomorrow."

"I'd say hallelujah."

Thorne quickly turned to the prison caretaker. "We're going to see to that first thing, right Warden Reese?"

"Yes sir, I'll draw up the necessary documents," Reese responded obediently.

The next day Johnse Hatfield walked out of prison, once again a free man.

■■■

CHAPTER SEVENTEEN: THE PAN AMERICAN EXPOSITION

"Why are you going to Buffalo father?" asked Joseph Kelly.

"I'm going to hear the President speak at the Pan American Exposition."

"The Pan American what father?"

Thomas Randolph Kelly stretched out his arms and tried to think of an easy explanation. "It's an exhibit of nations from around the Western Hemisphere," he replied.

"But what does that mean father?"

"It's like a big county fair, where all the neighboring countries from South America will display their latest advances in science, agriculture and export goods. Future business relationships will be developed with our country and these neighboring nations."

"But why father?"

"Why he asks" Thomas responded, smiling at his wife. "With each step we take toward progress and industrialization the world becomes a smaller place. We have reached a time when a person can travel by steamship anywhere they want in a matter of days. No too long ago, it took weeks to get any news from Europe. Now we can messages across the Atlantic Ocean in a matter of minutes.

The Kelly family sat at the dining room table, eating warm bowls of fresh steel cut oatmeal and raisin bread that Mrs. Kelly had prepared for them. Thomas sipped his Chase and Sanborn coffee while reading his morning paper. He was living the life that he had once dreamed about a dozen years earlier. He had married a former prostitute from Pikeville Kentucky and brought her back to his beloved New York.

Two years after they wed, the couple purchased a house in Brooklyn Heights. It was a modest three bedroom home, surrounded by a white picket fence. Debbie kept her promise and had been a good wife to Kelly. Their happy union had also produced two healthy children that Thomas adored. Their names were Joseph who was nine and Rose who was seven years old. Mrs. Kelly now directed all her attention to taking care of her loving husband and beloved children.

Kelly had become one of the Globe's most veteran reporters. He had shipped off to Cuba during the Spanish American War, writing dispatches about the brave but reckless heroics of Teddy Roosevelt. In 1900, during the Boxer Rebellion, he traveled to Beijing China, along with a relief column of American troops. During a skirmish with Chinese insurgents, the scrappy Irish reporter even took a razor sharp bayonet through his cheek. Now he was first in line to become editor and chief, as his boss was about to retire. His last assignment as a reporter was destined to be his most memorable.

"This bread is delicious honey, you've done it again" Kelly praised his wife.

"Flattery will get you anything your little Irish heart desires" Debbie replied.

"I desire to spend the weekend lying around with you and the kids. I don't want to do yard work, house repairs or anything when I get back from Buffalo."

Debbie poured her husband more coffee. "How long are you going for Tom?"

"Only two days. I'm going to cover McKinley's speech and have a little tour of the exhibits" he answered.

"I want to see the President too," Joseph chimed in suddenly.

"I do too," Rose added.

Thomas smiled at young daughter. "Sorry cutie but you're too young to go. He looked over at his son with raised eyebrows. "And don't you have school to attend young man?"

"Nope, it's Labor Day," Joseph answered triumphantly.

"Why not honey? I think it would be good for him to see how father makes a living. Besides, how many chances will he have to see the President of the United States?" Debbie asked, as she began to clear the breakfast dishes away from the table.

Kelly leaned over and rubbed his son's hair. "Well, I guess it's settled then. You're going with me to Buffalo."

"That's great father; where is Buffalo?

Thomas smiled at his wife and shook his head. "Are you sure he's our son?"

*****

After taking a twelve hour train ride with three stops, the Kelly's arrived in Buffalo on September 4, 1901. The two weary travelers ate an early supper and went to bed, attempting to rest at the noisy hotel. Though Thomas went out like a light, young Joseph couldn't sleep very well because he was excited about seeing the President.

The next morning, Thomas and his son walked the five blocks over to Lincoln Parkway, to the entrance of the Pan American Exposition. Joseph Kelly anxiously looked up to see a tremendous wooden beam that held an array of colorful flags from all the Latin American Countries. As the boy ran through the turnstile, he proudly noticed that the Stars and

Stripes flew above them all.

The Kelly's arrived early, at about ten o'clock in the morning. Before noon, they toured the multitude of exhibits from the neighboring countries, as well as visiting the Government, Horticultural and New York State buildings. Joseph marveled at the sight of electric lighting displays and threw a half-dozen Indian head pennies into the gushing majestic fountains.

Surrounding the exhibition promenade, were towering facades of Neo Renaissance buildings that were decorated with elongated spires and spectacular glass domes. These examples of artistic construction reflected the design styles of Stanford White and Henry Hobson Richardson, two of the most celebrated architects in America.

It was estimated that over one hundred thousand people were attending the exposition. The phenomenal turnout was in spite of the stifling, record hot temperature, which steadily rose as the day progressed. The vendors at the exhibition were not unprepared, as they briskly sold hand held, paper fans with name of the fair printed on them.

The Kelly's listened to the variety of marching brass ensembles, including the United States Marine Corps Bands. Joseph tapped his foot to stirring 4/4 meter renditions of "King Cotton" and "Stars and Stripes Forever." His eyes focused on the well-trained musicians who held the silver piccolos and golden trumpets. All the while, the clarion sounds of the counterpoint melodies filled the atmosphere. The music of John Phillip Sousa kept the pair adequately distracted while they awaited the arrival of President McKinley.

"Who are those soldiers father?" Joseph eagerly asked.

"I think they're from Brazil son, but I'm not sure. You saw all the flags out front, you tell me," Thomas responded.

The ten-year-old boy strained to look at the colors that one of the troops proudly carried. "I think they're from Costa Rica father."

The twenty-fifth president of the United States was scheduled to speak at noon and it was estimated that over fifty thousand awaited his appearance. He was not a minute late, ascending the flag draped speaker's platform at 12:02 in the afternoon. A line of perfectly dressed American Marines stood all along the front of the stage, serving as guards for the Chief Executive.

The Kelly's were lucky and managed to get a spot about thirty yards from the platform. Joseph thought McKinley was a tall, serious looking man, with a very square looking head. "He doesn't seem very happy father and why does he have a big hole on his chin?"

"He's about to make a speech son. He's not supposed to look

happy. And that hole's called a cleft son; a lot of men have them."

The President wore a black suit, with a white ruffled shirt that had a long, stiff collar. The popular and recently re-elected McKinley was greeted by a thunderous reception of cheers and applause. He momentarily waited for the hush that fell upon the sea of Americans who eagerly awaited his words of wisdom.

"President Milburn, Director General Buchanan, Commissioners, Ladies and Gentlemen, I am glad to once again be in the city of Buffalo and exchange greetings with her people, to whose generous hospitality I am not a stranger and with whose good will I have been repeatedly and signally honored," McKinley said in a resounding voice.

The citizens of Buffalo responded to his opening greeting with a loud cheer. "Expositions are the timekeepers of progress. They record the world's advancement" he told the crowd. The president also spoke of the need for the reciprocity of nations, relaxation of tariffs and the demand for exportation of American products. His speech was right in step with the theme of the exposition. It was a signal for the 20th century that the United States was emerging as a world power.

Thomas Kelly walked to the dispatch office that was located in the government building. He wired back a glowing review of McKinley's speech, which would be printed in the morning edition of the New York Globe. Joseph understood little of what the president had said. In spite of that he was fascinated by the pageantry of the occasion, speaking of little else for several hours.

That evening, Kelly and his son stayed to watch a display of electrical light illumination. It was said to rival the demonstration held at the Paris Exhibition a year earlier. The evening was closed by a spectacular presentation of fireworks, which was climaxed by a Niagara Falls display that spouted a shower of glimmering flames instead of water. Mister and Mrs. McKinley were delighted by the huge pyrotechnic likeness of the president's face, which featured the words "Welcome to McKinley, Chief of our Nation."

The following day, the president was scheduled to appear at an auditorium named "The Temple of Music." McKinley's intention was to allow the public an opportunity to shake hands with him. This was all Joseph needed to hear. He informed his father that they could not leave the exposition until he had met the Chief Executive. Thomas Kelly would not deprive his only boy of that experience.

The Kelly's waited in line for five hours, as McKinley was supposed to arrive at 4:00 PM. They stood along with thousands of others who also gathered in line, with hopes of greeting him. Thomas and Joseph arrived early and were only about one hundred and fifty people behind the front of the line. This advantage insured they would certainly be one of the lucky ones to shakes hands with the president.

The Temple of Music was a festive exhibit. It was a large pavilion enclosed on three sides, which was spacious enough to hold several hundred seated visitors, as well as accommodating a long line of standing admirers. During the previous day, an array of South American musicians performed at various intervals.

Joseph and his father wore straw hats to shade their faces from the blazing sun, standing patiently along side of the hall. To pass the long wait, the two struck up conversations with their neighbors in line. One of the men in line asked Joseph if he could name all the presidents up to Lincoln, which he did.

It was 3:58 P.M. on September 6, 1901, when the president's carriage arrived at The Temple of Music. He was escorted to the low platform, where he would stand for an hour to greet the public. The shallow scaffold was adorned with red, white and blue cloth, behind which was a backdrop, decorated with a sizable American flag. The hall was filled with the sound of chattering voices, as well as pipe organ music that blared at the rear of the building. Standing on the platform, along with the president, was two secret service agents. Their names were George Foster and Sam Ireland. The experienced agents they had previously guarded McKinley at several other public events.

"Bring in the people" McKinley instructed the gentlemen in charge of security. Under the direction of several armed Marines, the crowd was allowed to walk in slowly towards where the President was standing. In a single file line, with exposition guards observing the scores of citizenry, they anxiously ambled down the aisle.

It became exceedingly stuffy inside the hall that afternoon, as the canvass covered area was packed with far more people than was designed to accommodate. Many in line held on to their handkerchiefs. This didn't seem unusual to the secret service men. Everyone observed, was using them to dry their perspiring faces; everyone except a strangely somber man dressed in a poorly pressed blue suit.

To Joseph, the line seemed to travel with the speed of a garden snail. McKinley had been shaking hands for ten minutes when his security men futilely attempted to move things along. Thomas and his son were now only twenty people away from meeting the President. Near the front of the line, a short, thin man with unusually large hands was waiting. Thomas stared at him for a moment, noting that he had the blankest expression he had ever seen.

"It's an honor to meet you Mister President," said a tall farmer from Albany.

"Yes, thank you, nice to see you," McKinley replied, with a mechanical sincerity.

As people filed through, the guard at the front of the line continued to navigate them out past the scaffold. The narrow aisle, which stood in front of rows of chairs, was crammed too tightly with well wishers. This made it difficult for agent Foster to efficiently do his job. He lacked a clear field of vision to observe the over crowded passageway. When the small, Polish emigrant, reached the dais where President McKinley stood, Foster did not see the veiled thirty-two-caliber pistol he held in his sweating hand.

"Almost there son, don't forget to give the president a strong grip when you shake his hand," Kelly instructed.

"I won't father. This isn't something I get to do everyday," replied Joseph. The Kelly's now stood only steps away from the President of the United States. Thomas had met quite a few dignitaries in his life including the Prime Minister of England, but never a President.

It was eight minutes past four when McKinley reached out to shake the hand of the next person in line. The short man in the blue suit slapped the President's hand aside. He raised his handkerchief covered right hand and suddenly fired two gunshots. McKinley's eyes bulged and his pallor transformed from ruddy to ghostly white. The President reached down to touch his abdomen, felt blood on his shirt and at once realized that he had been shot. The stunned secret service agents supposed to protect him regained their wits. Agent Ireland tackled the attacker, who was also grabbed from behind, by several other agents.

"Don't let any harm come to him" is what Thomas overheard McKinley say to the secret service men who helped him o sit down in a chair. The would-be assassin was carried off surrounded by government agents and exposition security. Other quick thinking officers cleared all the other unnecessary pesonnel and spectators from the Temple of Music.

Kelly's journalistic instincts now took over. He had just seen President McKinley shot by some lunatic. He looked down at his son's face and noticed he was in a state of disbelief. The distraught child bowed his head while streaming tears dripped onto his yellow shirt. He slowly looked up into the watery eyes of father. "Why father…why did that man shoot the president?"

"I don't know son. It doesn't make any more sense to me than it does to you. I know you're terribly sad but I have a job to do now and you must help me do it."

"Why father? That man just shot the President. He just reached up and shot him.

"I know son, I was there too. But I need you to put on your brave little soldier's face and

go with me to the dispatch office. I need to wire the newspaper about what we just witnessed. You and I have just seen history made," Thomas explained.

*****

For six days, President McKinley fought valiantly for his life but died on September 13, 1901. On the week following his trip to the exposition, Joseph Kelly attended the first day of a new semester at school. The first assignment for the children was to talk about their summer vacations. His classmates sat on the edge of their seats when he told them he was only steps away from the President when he was shot by a madman.

Joseph Kelly would carry the memory of the McKinley assassination for the rest of his long life. "I hope I never have to see another President killed" he told his classmates. Unfortunately, he would live to see the murder of John Fitzgerald Kennedy in Dallas Texas some sixty-two years later.

Thomas Randolph Kelly went back to his new job, as Editor and Chief of the New York Globe. His account of the McKinley assassination garnered him nationwide acclaim as a pre-eminent journalist. In 1921, at age sixty-seven, the feisty writer would once again return to the Tug Valley. He bore witness to the great struggle of the United Mine Workers of America. His brilliant work helped expose the deplorable working conditions the miners endured as well as the despicably violent tactics of their employers. In 1923, he was awarded the Pulitzer Prize for journalism.

■ ■

CHAPTER EIGHTEEN: DEATH, THE DEVIL AND REDEMPTION

During the early part of the twentieth century, profound changes were occurring in the Tug Valley. Rich coal reserves in West Virginia and Kentucky were now being mined aggressively, which greatly affected the economic status of people who lived and conducted business in the neighboring states. Devil Anse was peacefully living life as a comfortable old timber merchant that enjoyed tending to his crops and livestock.

The sons of the famous feudist also assimilated themselves into the mainstream of society. When Cap completed his short stay in jail, he took up the study of law for sixth months. After he passed the West Virginia State bar, the reformed man opened his own legal practice. When business was slow, he took to the time honored practice of manufacturing mountain liquor.

After a quick responding Johnse was pardoned by Lieutenant Governor Thorne, he too walked the straight and narrow path. Shortly after his release, the former Hatfield Romeo procured gainful employment as a representative of the United States Steel and Coal Company. In his spare time he drank mountain liquor.

Two of Devil Anse's younger boys, Elias and Troy became entrepreneurs. Though not old enough to fight in the feud, they nonetheless established a notable reputation for themselves as expert marksman. The Hatfield men had always been celebrated for their remarkable shooting abilities. However, these tight knit brothers parlayed their skills into jobs as railroad detectives. In 1910, they invested their respective earnings in saloon that was located in the town of Boomer, West Virginia.

Carl Hanson was also a tavern owner, who operated his establishment in the nearby town of Cannelton. Since the liquor business in Logan County was fairly competitive, Hanson and the Hatfield boys negotiated a gentleman's agreement. There was a clear division of territory with an understanding that neither party would crossover into one another's area. Devil Anse raised his boys to be straight and they honored their part of the bargain. Carl Hanson had no such intention. He hired an Italian emigrant by the name of Octavo Gerome, who as salesman for their competitor didn't care if he sold liquor to Hatfield customers.

The Tavern belonging to M.J. Simms and his partners Troy and Elias was quiet on the afternoon of October 17, 1911. The electric fan slowly turned above the mahogany wood bar, providing little relief on this hot autumn day. A small swarm of flies mildly annoyed the proprietors, as well as the two rummies that occupied stools at the tavern.

"Did you talk to the Italian?" asked the burly Simms.

"Yes, we talked to him twice but it didn't do any good" replied the tall, slender Troy.

"We're gonna give that Dago bastard a warning he understands" added Elias Hatfield.

"Well, I suggest you boys make him understand. If we don't get Hanson and his greasy salesman off our backs we'll all be looking for jobs elsewhere," said Simms.

Troy grabbed his Smith and Wesson revolver, Elias reached for a sawed off Remington, twelve gauge loading both barrels with buckshot. They insisted that they didn't want any trouble with the Italian. Nevertheless, they did consider the possibility inflicting a beating on their rival if he didn't agree to stop soliciting their clients. Since the emigrant was known to carry a pistol, the brothers didn't want to be caught off guard.

Octavo lived in a small, dingy cabin, just off the main road between Boomer and Cannelton. The Hatfields walked the three miles towards his place, discussing other possible ways to stimulate business. Troy had the thought that one day they would own a fancy saloon in New Orleans or Savannah. When they arrived at the quiet bungalow, the former railroad detectives decided it was time to formulate a quick plan.

"Elias, I want you to go up to the front door, nice and slow; and I'll go around the back. But don't do anything until I get around back. We'll make sure that Dago don't sneak out the back and you be careful now boy" Troy said with a smile.

"Ain't I always" he replied, winking at his brother.

The two brothers split up, running around to opposite sides of the small cabin. Elias unbuttoned his long gray duster and tucked his shotgun inside by his right leg. Troy undid the strap on his oiled leather holster, pulled his revolver, spun the chamber, and then tucked it into his belt.

Octavo had a bad feeling in his gut as he attempted to eat his supper. He removed the pocket watch from his pinstripe vest and nervously looked at the time. Having previously been warned about encroaching on their territory by the Hatfield boys, the liquor salesman was jumpy but on the alert.

The Italian peered out a small opening in his window shade and observed that Elias Hatfield was approaching his front door. He ran to his back window, repeating the same procedure. He panicked when he saw Troy coming up to the rear of his place. Octavo retrieved his shotgun, quietly stepping over by his front window.

Elias went past the dirt walkway and took his first step on the wooden porch of small rectangular building. A terrific, loud blast exploded through the window, sending him reeling back onto the ground. The Italian had not waited to find out what the Hatfields wanted. In his mind, they had come for one reason only and that was to do him harm. Instead, he shot the first Hatfield intruder through the heart.

Troy heard the blast from behind the cabin and knew that his brother was caught by surprise. He quickly kicked in the back door of Octavo's place, but was shot by a second blast, as the fast reacting man whirled around and opened fire.

"You son-of-a-bitch" screamed Troy, as he was hit in the upper torso. He fell to his knees, putting all his strength and resolve into one last action.

Octavo froze with fear as he looked over at the wounded man, hoping he would keel over. He had now fired both barrels of his shotgun, which left him out of ammunition. It didn't seem possible that his young rival could have survived the first blast. Troy's legs wobbled for a moment but he stood up and steadied himself. Pointing his revolver, the mortally wounded man fired three carefully aimed shots before he collapsed to the floor.

Several hours later, when the two brothers had not returned the tavern, Simms realized there must have been trouble. He contacted the local sheriff, who rode his horse out to Octavo's place just before sunset. He was a friend of the Hatfield family, who was concerned about the fate of the young men. At the front steps of the cabin, he found Elias lying dead on his back. He stooped over to close the dead man's eyes. Sheriff Jim Todd hated to see his lifeless body with such a horrible blank stare on his face.

Unsure of the danger, the lawman slowly walked around to the back of the cabin and noticed the back door was swung wide open. He cautiously stepped inside the entrance, discovering Troy's body, which lay face down in a thick, bubbling bath of red gore. In a gesture in futility, he reached down to check the young man's lifeless pulse. "God almighty, what am I gonna tell their Pa?" he said out loud.

Sheriff Todd made one more grisly discovery before leaving the cabin. He found the body of Gerome Octavo, with a bullet in the groin, one in the center of his the forehead and one smack in the middle of his heart.

*****

Devil Anse managed to live through the most famous feud in

American history without losing one of his children. He had suffered the loss of a brother and a cousin, but he never had a child taken. When Death's Angel descended upon his doorstep, he was not prepared for the visit. Three days after the killings, the patriarch and his stunned family solemnly gathered at Island Creek, to bury the bodies of the two young kinsmen. After the ceremony, the old man went into seclusion for several days.

About a week after the loss of his sons, Devil Anse emerged from his cabin with an unexpected notion. The old man believed he had arrived at a fork in life's pathway. He needed a reason why he had to suffer the loss of his boys. He thought he had lived his seventy two years prepared for everything life could throw at him. Now for the first time, he had his doubts. He needed to understand if he was being punished for his sins. He sustained the belief that there was one man who could give him those answers.

William "Uncle Dyke" Garrett was a fire and brimstone Baptist Preacher, who had saved many a soul and was the most celebrated minister in all of Mingo County. It was mid afternoon, on the Sunday following the funeral of Troy and Elias. The reverend had performed two sermons and a baptism that morning and was now napping in the parlor of his home. He wasn't expecting any company to drop by, so he was a bit cross when his wife interrupted his rest.

"Will, there's someone here to see you," Mrs. Garrett said in a loud voice.

"Woman, who the devil is it?" he asked in an agitated tone.

"It is the Devil, its Anderson Hatfield."

"Oh, tell him I'll be right there" he instructed. Garrett put his trousers on and quickly came out to the porch to greet his guest. "My goodness, look who's here and on the Lord's day no less," he said jovially."

"How you doing Will, it's good to see you old rebel" responded Devil Anse. The two men had served together in the same regiment during the Civil War. Hatfield's forced smile gave way to a grim look. "I suppose you heard about Lias and Troy?"

"Yes, I'm sorry I missed the funeral, but I was invited to speak at a revival in Charleston last week" responded Garrett.

"Don't fret about it one bit old friend. I figured that you were probably off somewhere spreading the Gospel."

The preacher's face expressed his concern. "I think I know why you came today."

"I want to talk to an old friend, that's all. Sort a few things out in my mind. You know I've never relied on anybody but myself. For good or bad, I've always taken the bull by the horns. My family's been blessed but we had our share of troubles too, but I never lost any of my babies; it hurts Will."

Garrett saw something he never thought he would see in his lifetime. Tears were beginning to well up in the eyes of Anderson Hatfield. "I can't imagine how you feel. Having never lost one of my children leaves me without any measuring stick. But I'm sure you'll be able to sort it out."

"Will, for the first time in my life I'm not sure what I'm going to do. I've always been strong before, you know that nothing could stop me. Not a bear, a man or nothing else on God's green earth."

"Then what's stopping you now? You must realize that you will never get over the loss of your children. We all want to outlive our own seed. It's every man's worst horror to put sod on his sons or daughters."

"What am I going to do Will?" Devil Anse hung his head in his hands.

"You're going to have to learn to live with it. Somehow, you'll get past it but for now you'll learn to live with it."

Mrs. Garrett brought out a tray of lemonade for her husband and her guest. "Let's set a spell," Uncle Dyke said, motioning Devil Anse to sit on his porch. The two men leaned back on the huge redwood bench that decorated the front of the reverend's home. "How long have I known you old friend?"

"About fifty years I suspect."

"Fifty years, its hard to believe all that time has passed," Garrett said shaking his head. "Well I think I know you as well as any man," he added.

"I suspect you do" Devil Anse agreed, nodding his head.

The preacher drank his tart lemonade in almost one swallow, setting the glass down on the nearby tray. "I happy that you come to see me as a friend but I think I know the real reason you came." He looked his old comrade straight in the eyes. "I think you came here to get right with the Lord."

The tough old man mustered a slight grin of embarrassment at the discovery of his secret. "I know I've never been much for church going; but when you get to be our age, you start thinking about dying. My boys getting killed and in their prime, well that's something I just wasn't expecting. I suspect if there is a God, than he's been mighty good to me. I have a good family, plenty of acreage and a nice place to live."

"Of course there's a God. And he has been good to you, mighty good. I don't know another feller that's seen as many scrapes as you have and lived to tell about it," Garrett said enthusiastically.

Devil Anse felt good enough to laugh for a moment. "And you never will meet another feller that's done the things I've done or seen the things I've seen."

"You're blessed because the Lord never turned his back on you. You might have not remembered he was around for a while but he's always there. It's not too late for you Anderson Hatfield. You need to get right with the Almighty." The preacher pointed his finger at his friend's heart. "You need to be baptized, you and those boys of yours."

Devil Anse grinned at Garrett. "Do think the Lord has room up there for an old Rebel buzzard like me?"

"I told you once the Lord never turns his back on a soul. Not on you or anyone else who wants his grace" Garrett responded.

Hatfield shook his head. "You and me have been through a lot together haven't we? Remember? During the war we were together at Bull Run, Fair Oaks, Shiloh, Seven Days, Antietam and Fredericksburg; we've seen hard times. We've seen more men die in our lifetime then I'm sure either one of us care to remember. You've always been a friend to me and a good one. You know that I've always tried to live a good life. I never tried to cheat no one, except if you count one or two land grabs." The old man ran his fingers through his long gray beard. Pausing, he reflected on his thoughts for a few seconds. "Will, I once told a reporter feller that I belonged to the Devil's Church. I reckon what I meant was that the trees and mountains, the rivers and streams, they was my church. Now I reckon it's time to join a real church, your church Will. I reckon what I'm saying is that I want you to baptize me."

*****

Exactly a week later, a small congregation of parishioners was gathered at the waters of the Island Creek Tributary. It was a chilly Sunday morning and Uncle Dyke was filled with the spirit of the Lord. He had waited, hoping for many years that his old comrade would come to know the Father the way he did. That day had finally arrived and the preacher was about to baptize the most famous man in the county.

Will Garrett was dressed in a white and black robe with no shoes. As he escorted Devil Anse to the center of the stream, the preacher's long, silver hair blew back wildly in the cold wind. At his side were Hatfield's oldest sons Johnse and Cap, who had let their father talk them into being baptized. "A little saving will do you good," he assured them.

Before bowing in prayer, the preacher looked up towards the blue horizon and smiled at the assemblage. "We are gathered here today, before the eyes of the Lord our God and it is a good thing. Today, three of our friends will be forever linked to the one true God. He is the God of Abraham, the God of Jacob and the God of Moses, who led the children of Israel out of the land of bondage. The Lord our father will now join with us to lead these three men out of the chains of their earthly bondage.

Anderson, Johnson and William Hatfield, do you believe that, the Lord gave us his only begotten son; and that our lord Jesus Christ died on the cross to cleanse all of mankind of sin?" asked the preacher.

"Yes we do," the three shivering men answered together.

"Do you accept the Lord Jesus Christ as your personal savior?"

"Yes we do."

Garrett gently dunked each of the three men in the waters of Island Creek. "Then I baptize you in the name of the Father, the Son and the Holy Spirit."

That afternoon, there was a celebration at the Hatfield home. Devil Anse had his sons performed some renovations to his place, which included building a huge new porch and painting the exterior his house. For the purpose of making a dance floor, a makeshift wooden platform was constructed by a couple of local contractors. After the solemnity of the baptism, the guests were ready to celebrate.

A washboard player joined two fiddlers, a guitar player, a standup bass and banjo pickers provided an afternoon of homespun music. They musicians performed old Appalachian favorites including *The Virginia Reel*, *The Rose of Alabama* and *I'm a Good Old Rebel*, which was requested by the host and dedicated to his friend Will Garrett. The rectangular dance floor was filled with guests as the end of the afternoon approached. Cap, his wife Nancy and Johnse, who was accompanied by a new girlfriend named Annie, danced some of the fanciest two steps of the day.

For their last tune the band played "Amazing Grace, which was beautifully sung by twenty six year old Rosada Hatfield. A spectacular sky of brown, orange and yellow was the backdrop for the fine meal of Roast venison served on redwood picnic tables. For a family who only two weeks earlier had buried two of their own, this was a day of bittersweet fulfillment.

While they enjoyed their sunset dinner, Devil Anse chatted with his friend Will. "I feel better now. Thank you helping through this past week and for what you done today. I know me and my boys done the right thing, hitching up to the Lord's wagon. Seems like the best kind of insurance a man can get in this life. And if anyone needs his grace it's me."

Garrett smiled at his friend's previous remark. "I feel better too. When I die I don't want to be up in paradise without my old partner from the forty-fifth Virginia.

*****

The day after his baptism, Devil Anse wanted to clean the slate with regard to lingering legal charges against himself and his sons. He sent for his grandson Joe Glenn, who had followed in his stepfather's footsteps by becoming a lawyer. At age thirty, he was tall, handsome and quite affable and was making a good living in Mingo County.

As an attorney, Joe had established a reputation for being straightforward, with a desire to take on seemingly lost cases. He modeled himself after Labor Union and social change lawyer Clarence Darrow. Glenn had read about his celebrated career while studying law and admired his humanitarian efforts. This was a far cry from the rough edged boy who served time in reform school for killing a man when he was fourteen. He was now an eloquent, educated man, who conducted his fighting in a courtroom.

"We're all real proud of how you turned out Joe. Me, your grandmother and your father we're all real proud. And the way you represented them poor fellers against the Stony Mountain Coal Company, that was really something. Those bastards should all burn for what they done to them boys. That took guts even if you did lose," said Devil Anse.

The two men sat by the fireplace smoking cigars on a cool autumn evening. "Thank you grandpa, it's nice of you to say," Joe answered respectfully. "Daddy said you have something you would like me to take care of for you."

The old man walked around his grandson's chair and patted him on the shoulder. "Yes, I'd like you to go to Pikeville. I want you to see if you can make things right with the old charges against us. Go see Old Ranel's boy Jim McCoy, he's sheriff now. Tell him I want to make things right. Ask him if he can get all the old charges cleared off the books. And just to show him how sorry I am for the trouble between our families, I want you to give him a ten thousand dollar donation for his troubles," he instructed.

Joe's jaw nearly dropped when his grandfather told him the amount of money to hand over to Jim McCoy. "You did say ten thousand, didn't you?"

"You heard me right son. Tell Sheriff McCoy that I'm a Christian now and that's a little something from me to help heal old wounds. Now your father tells me you're the man for the job. He says your honest but could still sell shoes to a man with no feet."

Joe laughed at his grandfather's remark. "I think he said I could sell snow shoes to Eskimos."

Devil Anse began to chuckle. "Yes, I believe that was it. Now I want to you to spend the night and set out for Pikeville in the morning. Will you do this for me?"

"You know I will grandpa."

The following day Joe Glenn dropped by the office of the Commonwealth Attorney, to meet with Randolph McCoy's oldest son Jim. He was the same man who had once refused to bow before Joe's kindly old grandfather's Henry Rifle. This was the same James McCoy, who effectively testified against Wall Hatfield during his trial. The Sheriff of Pikeville was now in his early sixties, but remained formidable in his appearance.

"So you're Cap Hatfield's boy are you?" James asked the young attorney.

"Stepson, I'm his stepson by marriage," Joe answered respectfully.

The sheriff eyed the young man for few uncomfortable seconds. "Would you like some coffee? I just put on a fresh pot."

"No thanks."

The sheriff suddenly smiled at his guest. "You know I went to hell and back, trying to bring your stepfather and grandfather to task for what they done to my kin."

"You know I've heard the stories from my uncle Johnse," Joe said smiling back. "I heard tell that you didn't get off your horse one night for a certain man with whom we are both acquainted."

James Began to chuckle when reminded of his brief bout with Devil Anse. "I was young and full of hell. I was really angry about the whole feud business; but I've had a long time to mull things over in my mind." The sheriff poured himself a cup of coffee and stirred in some milk. "Unlike my own father, who still talks about the past, I've chosen to move on. He never let go of his ill will and it ate him up like a cancer," he paused, looking thoughtfully at Joe, "Well, I'm glad you decided to stop by and see me, though I can't imagine why."

Joe pulled a brown leather satchel up off the floor and removed an envelope, placing it on the desk in front of Jim McCoy. "I'll come directly to the point Mister McCoy. I'm representing Anderson Hatfield on a little matter of business. He would like to propose having any old criminal charges on the Commonwealth's books removed. Clean the slate so to speak." In professional manner, Joe spoke of his grandfather as if he were just another client. "Mr. Hatfield has been recently baptized and wishes to cleanse his soul and any legal issues that have lingered over the years. He wants things put to rest once and for all, between his family and your family." Joe glanced down at the desk. "Now, if you look inside that envelope, you'll find a check from him for ten thousand dollars. This is for you to cover any administration costs that you may incur while performing his request."

"Is that it son?"

"Yes sir that's it. So when can we take care of this little matter Sheriff?"

The old sheriff twirled his moustache, while calmly gathering his thoughts for a half a minute. "Sonny, I hate to disappoint you, but if you offered me ten times what you got on this table, I still wouldn't be able to do what you ask."

"Sorry to hear that sir," Joe replied.

"It's my blood kin you're speaking of. There are a lot of them in early graves on account of what happened between our families. No sir, I can speak of it no more. Now Mister Glenn, I respect you for coming here today and acting like a decent young man. I'll give your father credit for your good manners. Looks like he didn't do such a bad job raising you and just to show you there ain't no hard feelings between us, I'd like to take you to lunch."

Joe Glenn held in his disappointment, smiling politely in response to the sheriff. "Lunch sounds real good about now. It's a long ride back to Island Creek."

*****

Joe's grandfather managed to bounce back from the loss of his sons. He did so by relishing the time spent in the company of his surviving children and grandchildren. In the latter years of his life he did the things he had always done. He hunted bear, fished for trout in the stream that flowed past his property and continued selling timber and making moonshine. As a Christian man, he did all he could for his neighbors. The old rebel became even more renown for providing refuge for hundreds of travelers throughout the later years of his life. His legend, his generosity and his unflagging magnetism made him the most beloved man in the county.

Conversely, old Ranel McCoy was not living his golden years as one of God's happiest creatures. For the loss of his children at the hands of the Hatfields, he remained understandably bitter until the end of his life. He had been born during the early part of the nineteenth Century but managed to outlive his frail wife by several years. Poor Sarah had never quite recovered from her physical and emotional wounds.

In 1914 while staying in the home of his nephew, Randolph slipped and fell onto a cooking pit, which left him severely burned on over eighty percent of his aged body. A few months later he died from his injuries. At ninety years old and on his deathbed, he could still muster some well-chosen words about "Those damn Hatfields."

Randolph McCoy spent almost forty years focusing attention on his neighbors across the Tug River. He alone had wept an ocean of tears, which could have filled the Big Sandy River ten times over. The story of the New Years raid on his home had stirred national outrage, yet less than a dozen people attended the melancholic old man's funeral.

Devil Anse Hatfield died of pneumonia on January 7, 1921. He too, had lived to be a ripe old age. The day of his funeral there was no lack of attendance, as hundreds of people called on his family to pay their final respects. The old man's house was jammed packed with relations and guests who had come from all parts of the country to be with the immediate family.

William Garrett handled the funeral arrangements. He also carried out his old friend's last request. Several years earlier, Johnse and Cap had a falling out over a business deal gone awry. The once close pair was no longer speaking to one another. This had made their father unhappy but he had not been able to prevail upon them to reconcile while he was still alive. Garrett called out for the two oldest sons who now sat on opposite sides of the living room. "Johnson, William Anderson come here and see your Uncle Dyke."

The two brooding siblings obediently walked to the side of the old preacher, who stood strategically in the middle of the floor. "This bad blood between you two, it must end today, right here and right now," instructed Garrett.

Johnse and Cap stubbornly stared each other for an uncomfortable stretch, which caused some discomfort to their friends and family. "You lard heads listen to me, now I mean it! You're father wanted it that way. And I don't aim to see this day spoiled by you two acting like a couple of rotten kids. Now can't you boys finally grow up and act like men," admonished Garrett.

Johnse actually saw humor in the preacher yelling at two older men as if they were schoolboys. He was the first to crack, smiling sweetly at his brother. "You're getting fat," he told him.

Cap could no longer keep from smiling either. "Yeah, well you ain't so pretty anymore."
The still slender Johnse reached out his hand to shake and instead his larger brother pulled him close, hugging him tightly.

"I'm sorry little brother" said Johnse.

"Me too" responded Cap.

Garrett put his arms around both men. "Good, now as long as I live, I never want to hear another cross word said between you." The preacher turned to straighten Cap's necktie. "Now that we've settled things, let's go pay our last respects to your father." As friends and family exited the Hatfield home, there wasn't a dry eye on the face of any man, woman or child who had just witnessed what the preacher had accomplished.

Levicy was too sick to attend the funeral, which was conducted in the pouring rain. Before placing his body in the wagon for the trip to the cemetery, the sad old woman bid one last goodbye to her husband of more than sixty years. With the help of her sons Cap and Johnse, their mother stooped down to place a gentle kiss upon the dead man's lips.

People came by the thousands to attend funeral of Devil Anse, which was the largest in the history of the county. For several hours in the rain, family, friends and strangers filed past his open coffin to have one final look at the man before he was lowered into the earth. Although it was a dreary day, most people did not consider the ceremony to be a sad occasion. It was looked upon as more of celebration of a long, great life. Many of members of the McCoy family, former enemies of the old man, attended his burial.

About six months after the funeral, the Hatfields commissioned an Italian firm to carve a marble statue of their beloved patriarch. When the likeness was completed, it was transported to the family cemetery for a dedication. The entire clan, many of whom had contributed to the three thousand dollar price tag of the sculpture, attended its dedication. The fourteen-foot high monument can still be seen standing, near U.S. highway 119.

It has been said by some that the ghost of old Ranel McCoy haunts the Hatfield Graveyard. During his life, the unhappy man had once coveted what his neighbor had possessed. It was that same jealously over land holdings, timber and livestock that put many a soul into their graves. By that reasoning alone, could it not be possible that his wandering soul envies what Devil Anse has in death? After all, he has a tall, marble sculpture and Randolph doesn't.

About The Author

Phillip E. Hardy is staff writer for Sound the Sirens online magazine and also contributes artist evaluations to New Artist Radio. In addition to his record reviews for Robert Cray, Loretta Lynn, the Arcade Fire and the Scorpions, he recently contributed a review for the Academy Award nominated film "Capote". Phillip holds a Bachelor of Science in Business Management from the University of Phoenix and a Master of Management Degree from The University of Redlands.

Printed in Great Britain
by Amazon.co.uk, Ltd.,
Marston Gate.